"Merbeth's world building is fascinating—five human-settled planets, each distinct and littered with alien technology—but her multifaceted characters and their troubled relationships give this action-packed family drama its heart. A good read-alike for Lois McMaster Bujold's Miles Vorkosigan books, John Scalzi's *Collapsing Empire* (2017), and for those who want a grittier version of Becky Chambers' Wayfarers series." —*Booklist*

"This is an engaging start to a series that blends crime family drama with the sort of character-focused sci-fi that made Becky Chambers' Wayfarers series an award-winning favorite."
—*B&N Reads*

"It's everything you could ask for in a space opera."
—*Arcanist*

By Kristyn Merbeth

THE NOVA VITA PROTOCOL

Fortuna

Memoria

MEMORIA

The Nova Vita Protocol:
Book Two

KRISTYN MERBETH

orbitbooks.net

Cover design by Lisa Marie Pompilio
Cover art by Shutterstock
Cover copyright © 2020 by Hachette Book Group, Inc.
Author photograph by SunStreet Photo

Orbit
Hachette Book Group
1290 Avenue of the Americas
New York, NY 10104
orbitbooks.net

First Edition: December 2020

Orbit is an imprint of Hachette Book Group.
The Orbit name and logo are trademarks of Little, Brown Book Group Limited.

The publisher is not responsible for websites (or their content) that are not owned by the publisher.

The Hachette Speakers Bureau provides a wide range of authors for speaking events. To find out more, go to www.hachettespeakersbureau.com or call (866) 376-6591.

Library of Congress Cataloging-in-Publication Data
Names: Merbeth, K. S., author.
Title: Memoria / Kristyn Merbeth.
Description: First Edition. | New York, NY : Orbit, 2020. |
     Series: The Nova Vita protocol ; book 2
Identifiers: LCCN 2020014818 | ISBN 9780316454018 (trade paperback) |
     ISBN 9780316454032
Subjects: GSAFD: Science fiction
Classification: LCC PS3613.E67 M46 2020 | DDC 813/.6—dc23
LC record available at https://lccn.loc.gov/2020014818

ISBNs: 978-0-316-45401-8 (trade paperback), 978-0-316-45402-5 (ebook)

Printed in the United States of America

LSC-C

Printing 1, 2020

For my D&D crew, my second family

ACT ONE

CHAPTER ONE

Storm Approaching

Corvus

An ache in my scarred leg is the first warning of the storm to come. By the time I'm done hauling in the net with today's catch, the clouds have clustered thick and dark enough to blot out the red orb of Nova Vita. Anxiety twinges in my gut, but I force myself to take my time securing the fish and equipment. No matter what Nibiran superstitions have been floating around lately, it's likely nothing. There's no use sabotaging myself over bad weather. Yet as I race toward home, hoverboat wobbling in the wind, I'm chased by the same thought that's bubbled up again and again over the last couple of months.

Is this just a storm? Or a sign of something worse on the horizon?

Momma would have said that trouble always comes around eventually. General Altair would have told me to trust my instincts. Yet that caution wasn't enough to save either of them.

My worry deepens as Kitaya comes into sight. The streets are empty. The algae farms have shut down for the day, protective covers laid out over the watery fields. Platforms have lifted the buildings higher above ground level, and metal shutters have spread out to cover the dome-shaped structures. The island is on full lockdown. Normal or not, this storm will be a bad one. As the rain begins to fall, soft droplets swiftly accelerate into a heavy patter. With Lyre studying engineering at the university and the twins rarely reliable, I can only hope Scorpia is home to begin storm procedures on the houseboat, but I doubt it.

Despite my hurry to return to my family, I slow the hoverboat as I swing past the harbor, surprised to see two figures standing out on the docks. They're both wearing the simple, waterproof outfits of fisherfolk, but no fisherfolk would be lingering out here with a growing storm. One is crouched with his hands over his ears, and the other is gesturing wildly, though whatever she's shouting is swallowed by the wind.

"There's a storm lockdown," I call out to them, bringing my boat up alongside the pier. "You need to get out of here."

The woman turns to me. She braces her shoulders as if expecting hostility, her eyes wary in her brown face.

"We have nowhere to go," she says. She extends one hand in a half-realized gesture, and then yanks it back as if burned. "We're from...we live on Vil Hava."

I frown, trying to make sense of how two fisherfolk ended up stranded so far from home. A moment later, the hand gesture she was beginning to make clicks in my head. Once I know to look for them, it's easy to notice her stiff posture and the smooth skin at odds with her rough-spun clothing. I glance at the woman's wrist and find the telltale glow of a tattoo; then at the man, who is still covering his ears, unresponsive. The empty boat docked nearby completes the picture. They're Gaians. They must have wandered out this way from the refugee housing on Vil Hava to try their hand at fishing and panicked when the storm hit. They, like me, can't have missed the similarity to the deadly weather events that played a part in their planet's destruction. Drones have reported back that the situation has only grown worse there since the Gaians evacuated, and they have less than a month left until the deadline on their stay here.

Nibiru and Gaia have always had a fraught relationship, between their clashing views on the Primus aliens who first settled in this system, and the Nibiran-originated plague that swept through Gaia fifty years ago. The entire system was shocked when the Nibiran Council granted the Gaians a temporary stay on this planet. Of course, that was without my family giving the council the full truth of what had happened on Gaia, including the fact that it was President Leonis's use of alien technology that seems to have led to the planet's strange decline, and that she tried to hire my family to kill this planet's population so that her own people could move here permanently. We lied so that the Gaians wouldn't die for their leader's arrogance.

And it worked, to an extent. Leonis went to prison for wiping out the Titans, and we evaded the same fate despite our own involvement in that plot. And the Gaians have been safe here, for a time. But the Nibirans have always been superstitious, and certain parts of the population have been eager to claim that the Gaians must have brought this upon themselves somehow with their love for the Primus. They're not far off the mark—but still, most Gaians knew nothing of their president's scheme, and they don't deserve to suffer for it.

"There's a public storm shelter a few blocks in," I say, jerking my chin in that direction. "You can wait out the storm there."

"Are you sure they'll let us in?" the woman asks. "After the storm's already begun?"

Judging by how defensive she became when I first approached, I doubt that's the only reason she suspects they won't let her in. For the most part, Nibirans have been welcoming to the refugees—especially on Vil Hava, the planet's heart, where these two are from. But Kitaya is smaller, more isolated. And it's no secret that the circles of resentment have been growing lately, especially with the harsh weather riling up Nibiran superstition.

The hoverboat rocks beneath me, pummeled by the wind and rain. I should get home to my family, make sure the boat is docked and my siblings are home safe. I could take these Gaians there…but no. We have far too many secrets to invite strangers in. After a moment, I ease the boat into one of the dock's ports until I hear a click, shut it down, and step out. Once I press my thumb to the screen on the station, it locks there. "I'll walk you to the shelter," I say, and crouch down to extend a hand to the shaking man. "It's not safe here."

Once the Gaians are safely in the public shelter, I wave off the invitation to join them and make my way home on foot. The hoverboat will stay locked into the dock, assuming it survives the storm. I doubt I could steer it straight right now, with the winds throwing themselves against the island as though they mean to flatten it. And it's more important to take care of my family.

My family, who hasn't even closed the storm shutters yet. Our houseboat rocks wildly on the choppy waves, jerking at the end of the tether that secures it to the island, its windows fully exposed to the elements. I'm about to rush inside when I spot a familiar figure on the edge of the deck.

"Pol?" I slow as I approach. "What are you doing out here?"

He turns to me, one foot slipping in a way that makes my heart jump in fear. It's nearly impossible to save a man from drowning when the ocean's this rough, especially given his size. My little brother is thin after the Primus bio-weapon ravaged his body on Titan, but he still has a few inches on me in height.

He's also currently sporting a black eye, which at least partially answers my question, despite his silence.

"You and Drom get into another fight?" I ask, gently. He shrugs, mumbling something, and I step forward to touch his arm. "Let's talk about it inside, this storm is getting worse."

"Don't fuckin' baby me," he says, yanking away from me, but he stomps inside anyway.

The floor rolls with the unsettled ocean, and wind rattles the windows. Lyre is in the kitchen, standing on the tips of her toes and struggling to close a still-open window leaking rain into the house. I rush over to help her shut it.

"Why wasn't this done twenty minutes ago?" I ask, grimacing at the puddle of water on the floor. Lyre is soaked through and shivering, her curls flattened against her skull.

"I just got home from class," she says. "And Drom is looking for—" She cuts off as she sees Pol coming in behind me. "Oh, thank the stars." She raises her voice. "Drom, he's here!"

A few moments later, Pol's twin comes bounding up the stairs and slides to a stop in front of him.

"Damn it, Pol, I told you it was an accident..." She stops mid-complaint to catch her breath, and then bursts out, "Where the hell were you?"

He walks into the living room without a response. Drom follows him, looking frazzled.

"We need to lock down," I say, turning to Lyre.

She nods, her face troubled. "Scorpia isn't here yet."

I sigh. Of course she isn't. "Where is she? Visiting Orion again?" I ask, but Lyre only shakes her head, so I head out into the living room.

Pol is sprawled across the couch, staring up at the ceiling, his head lolling off the side and one leg up on the cushions in a way that looks distinctly uncomfortable. Drom sits at the opposite end of the couch, stewing silently.

"Do either of you know where Scorpia is?"

"Working," both twins answer at once, and then glower at one another as if offended at being copied.

"Doing what?" I ask, surprised that they both seem to know something I don't. Before either of them can answer, the door bangs open behind us. Scorpia stumbles in, dripping water.

"Where were you?" I ask.

"Wow, gee, thanks for the welcome home." Scorpia kicks off her wet boots. She flops over the back side of the couch, drawing a groan out of Pol as she falls right on top of him. "Sorry to disappoint you all with my presence!" She rubs her wet face on him while he grimaces and tries to push her off. After a few moments, he finally succeeds at dumping her onto the floor. She seems content to remain there.

I scrutinize her from across the room. It's obvious she doesn't plan on answering my question, but she doesn't look drunk, so I suppose I should be happy with that. I move to lock the door behind her, biting my tongue to hold back any scolding. At least she's here. We're all here, and we're all safe, and that's what's important.

After double-checking that everything is secure, I make my way to the couch as well. Pol stares up at the ceiling, his eyes wide. Drom feigns a yawn, as if she couldn't care less about the winds howling outside, but she scoots over to sit next to her twin, and he doesn't complain.

I take a seat on the opposite side of the couch, and Scorpia drags herself up from the floor and plops down beside me. She leans her shoulder against mine and gives me a tight-lipped smile. After another moment, Lyre squeezes her small frame into the tiny space left in the middle. My hip wedges hard against the side of the couch, irritating my leg. The couch is definitely not built to hold this many people, but nobody says a word about it. Around us, the houseboat lurches and shudders, fighting against the storm and the waves. I imagine us breaking loose from the island, floating alone in the middle of the vast ocean, sinking down to sit far beneath the waves.

"If you could go anywhere in the system right now, where would it be?" Scorpia asks, breaking the silence.

"Deva," both twins say simultaneously, and then grin at each other, their earlier irritation with one another apparently already fading. They don't look as strikingly similar as they used to, not when Pol is still a hollowed-out version of his old self, his skin pale and his eyes shadowed, but that smile is still the same.

"For the food," Pol says.

"For the parties," Drom counters.

"I would have to pick Deva as well," Lyre says, after giving it considerably more thought than our youngest siblings, though her birth-planet must be the obvious option. "It's not much of a choice, really, when it's that or Pax." She frowns down at her lap. "The system is a lot smaller than it used to be."

"I guess you're right," Scorpia says. "I would choose Pax, though." I suppose I shouldn't be surprised she would choose the only option that's illegal for our family, since it's the one place none of us were born. Still, I find it hard to believe that anyone would choose to go to that radiated desert. Catching my expression, Scorpia laughs and says, "What? It could be fun. Sounds like an adventure to me."

"I think I've had more than enough adventures for this lifetime," I say.

"Well, I haven't," Scorpia says. "I wanna go somewhere I've never been before. See something new. Be in a place where no one knows my name." She smiles, but it fades quickly as she lapses into an uncharacteristic silence. I study her face, about to ask her what's wrong, but she speaks up again just in time to interrupt the question. "What about you?"

"I don't know," I lie, while my mind goes right to Titan. I think of roaming the empty planet, the graveyard of my people. I think of kneeling in the snow and asking for their forgiveness for leaving them. For surviving them. I shake it off. It's a pointless, maudlin thought, and not the type of answer my siblings want to hear. None of them will understand, anyway. Each of us has our own birth-planet—Scorpia aside—but theirs have never been any kind of home to them. None of them have spent years trapped on the surface alone, like I did on Titan during the war. None of them have bled or killed for their planets. None of them have watched them fall apart in front of them. "Staying here wouldn't be so terrible," I say instead.

I'm surprised to realize that I mean it. After the tumult a few months ago, and the war before, this time on Nibiru has been a relief. Here, we can be safe. Accepted. We even have the approval of the council, which grants us more security than we've ever had before. We're no longer juggling dangerous jobs, and I no longer have to lead a life revolving around violence. In a place like this, we could build something for ourselves—something different than the lives Momma forced upon us from birth, and the roles that almost destroyed us. Given time, I believe even Scorpia could find happiness here, if she let herself. And I can let the past drift away, no longer forced to be a soldier or a criminal or anything more than...well. I'm not sure yet what I want to become, but for now, I'm content to have my family around me.

Moments after the words leave my mouth, thunder rumbles loudly enough to shake the entire room. The lights flicker, and Lyre lets out a nervous squeak, pressing farther down into the couch.

"You were saying?" Scorpia asks. Even she sounds strained, one hand gripping my arm.

"It'll pass," I say. She releases my arm and lets out a shaky breath. It reminds me just how much she hates feeling trapped in here. I put an arm around her shoulders and squeeze. "We're going to be fine."

We huddle together as the world rages outside.

Hours later, after the storm has receded and all of us have drifted off to our separate rooms, I toss and turn in my bed. The drumming of rain against the roof turns into distant gunfire; the wind once again howls like an angry god; and I am back on Titan. Back in the war, with a gun in my hands and my team at my back.

For a moment, it feels right. It feels almost peaceful. I'm back where I belong. But I sense the moment when it starts to change. The world distorts around me, the dream turning to a nightmare.

"Corvus?" Daniil says, and I turn to face him. "Don't leave me here," he whispers. I reach for him, but he dissolves into ash, and drifts away on the wind. Sverre is next, taking one lurching step toward me before he, too, falls, his accusing eyes never leaving me.

"Magda," I say. I look for her and am relieved to find her still there. Smiling, even. She steps forward, touching my face in a way I never let her touch me in reality, and leans forward to press her lips against mine. As she pulls back, black begins to ooze out from between her teeth and drip down her chin.

"Traitor," she says in a gurgling voice, a mouthful of black spilling out with the word, and then she takes out a knife and thrusts it toward my chest—

"Corvus."

I wake up with a start, and lash out. Only after my fist connects with warm flesh do I jolt back into consciousness, slowly grounding myself in reality. I'm not on Titan. I'm not in the war. I'm on Nibiru, at home, in bed—and it's my sister sitting on the edge of my mattress, one hand holding her jaw and the other extended to hold me back.

"Oof," Scorpia mutters under her breath. "*Ow.*"

Guilt crashes over me. "Oh, fuck. I'm sorry. I didn't mean— You know I would never—" I stop, unable to finish the thought. *I would never*...But I did. I might not have meant to, but I did.

She drops her defensive hand, works her jaw experimentally, and mutters, "S'fine."

"No, it's not." I want to reach out to her, but the sudden fear she'd push me away is too much to bear, so I sit back instead, clenching my hands in my lap. She gingerly presses her fingers to her cheek and jaw, testing the damage, before letting both hands drop to her sides.

"No harm done," she says, forcibly breezy. "Hey, at least you don't sleep with that knife under your pillow anymore, or this could've been a lot worse." She mimes stabbing herself in the neck, sticking her tongue out of one side of her mouth and rolling her eyes back.

"That's not something to joke about." I press my palms into my eyes, trying to ward off the burning behind them. "I told you not to startle me like that. You shouldn't have come in here."

"Yeah, well, you were crying out in your sleep again, and I wasn't gonna just sit on the other side of the wall and listen to it."

"You should have done exactly that," I snap, my voice coming out harsher than I intend. After a moment, Scorpia touches my arm and gently draws it away from my face. She studies my wet eyes, sighs, and pulls me toward her. I let myself rest my head on her shoulder, even though it makes my self-loathing spread like a stain across my mind. I'm pathetic. I know it. We both know it. "I'm sorry," I say again—this time both for hitting her and for forcing her to comfort me afterward, even though it should be the opposite. Sometimes it's hard to believe I was ever the one holding this family together. Now I can't even manage the problems in my own head.

"Hush," Scorpia says, resting one hand on my back. "You're fine. It's fine. It's over. Your brain just...hasn't caught up yet. But it will."

I wish I could believe her. These months have been peaceful. I thought that peace would be enough to keep the worst of my demons at bay—to chase away the nightmares, the parade of faces haunting me, the constant, scratching fear that something terrible is about to happen. I was wrong.

It's not always there. Sometimes I go hours, even days, without the past clawing its way up from the dark hole I've tried to hide it in. But then a child's firecracker will make me flinch and reach for a gun that isn't there, or I'll think I see a familiar face in a crowded restaurant and fight for the exit before I know what I'm doing. The world may be peaceful, but my mind is still at war. And I'm not sure whether it's my past or my common sense telling me that this peace can never last.

It's a frightening thought. Not for me—I've already begun to accept that there will never be true peace for someone like me—but for the innocent people of Nibiru and Gaia. For my siblings, who have been through enough already, and yet still haven't seen how horrible the world can be. I hope they never do, but I can't fight the feeling that they will. That they all will.

I can't fight the fear deep in my gut that tells me the worst is yet to come.

CHAPTER TWO

The Hero of Nibiru

Scorpia

When the morning comes, the sea is calm. Lyre and I run around opening the storm shutters while Corvus prepares breakfast. The tightness in my chest loosens at the sight of sea and sky and sun breaking through the clouds. It's still not the freedom of open space, but it's something.

Breakfast is simple Nibiran fare, thin slices of fish wrapped in strips of chewy, fresh algae. Most of us prefer it raw, but Lyre insists that hers be thoroughly cooked, and cuts it into small pieces before eating. The twins fight over the last drops of the last bottle of imported Devan hot sauce. Drom knocks over Lyre's coffee with one elbow, and she lets out a yelp as it splatters across her robe.

"Stars, not at the table," Lyre says, dabbing at her outfit with a napkin. "Scorpia—"

"Split it, assholes, or I'm not buying any more for you," I say, sipping my own coffee. "Seriously, please, give me an excuse. You know how expensive anything imported is getting?"

They grudgingly obey, and I finish my coffee before starting in on my own food. I'm getting real sick of fish and algae, but at least we're saving money, so I keep my mouth shut. Across the table, Corvus picks at his own food and tea, his eyes distant.

I can tell from the especially broody look on his face that he's still thinking about last night. I am too—hard not to when my face aches from it, though I think I did a decent enough job of covering up the bruise with makeup. If I'm lucky—

"Scorpia, what happened to your face?" Lyre asks.

But of course, nothing gets past Lyre. I swallow a sigh and slap on a smile instead. "Oh, this?" I reach up to touch my jaw, trying my hardest to avoid glancing at Corvus, though I can feel his eyes on me. "Well, uh, kind of embarrassing, actually." I rush to get the words out before he can speak up and ruin it, even though I'm not sure where I'm going with this yet. "I got up in the middle of the night to go take a piss, was too lazy to turn any of the lights on, and then...bam! Walked straight into the doorway." I lower my hand and push out an uncomfortable chuckle.

A moment of silence passes. Corvus and Lyre are still staring at me—him stricken, her verging on suspicious.

"You're an idiot," Drom says through a mouthful of fish, not even looking up from her plate. "Hear that, Pol? Someone nabbed your title of family idiot."

"Aw, shut up," he says, and shoves her arm, sending her next bite of food to the floor. As they erupt into squabbling again, I return to my food, glad that the spotlight seems to have left me.

Once the twins settle down, the morning returns to its calm quiet. It's rare to have a morning with all of us home together, and usually when we are, breakfast quickly dissolves into pure chaos. Typically Lyre is in a rush to go to school, or the twins are throwing punches instead of food, or Corvus is trying to implement some new household rule that will never stick. But not today. Today is the quiet after the storm, and I force myself to slow my eating and enjoy it.

"Remember how much Momma always hated raw fish?" Pol asks, and that peaceful quiet abruptly turns to a stony silence. I pause chewing my oversized bite of fish, as if afraid even that will be too loud in the suddenly silent room. Pol smiles down at his almost-empty plate, his expression wistful, completely oblivious to the way the rest of us have frozen mid-motion. "No matter how many times we came here, she always insisted we cook it first. Said it wasn't right."

I exchange a glance with Corvus, while Lyre stares down at her plate with a queasy expression, and Drom looks like she's barely restraining herself from forcibly making Pol shut his mouth. I swallow, and the mouthful feels dry and heavy as it slides down my throat.

"Yeah, I remember," I say, as Corvus shoots me a warning look. "She smacked it out of my mouth the first time she caught me eating it raw. You remember that?"

Pol's face reddens. "Maybe she was trying to protect you."

"Yeah, and maybe she was just being a bitch."

"Scorpia," Corvus says, "there's no need to be crass."

I roll my eyes, stuff the last bite of food into my mouth, and get up. "Whatever," I mumble through my half-chewed mouthful, and head for the door.

"You really sour everything, you know that?" Pol snaps at me as I walk by.

"Better than sugarcoating it."

"That's enough," Corvus says, even more sternly, which I didn't think was possible given his normal level of sternness. "This is not a subject for the breakfast table."

"Apparently it's not a subject for anytime," Pol says. He glares up at me. "Apparently all of you would rather just forget she ever fucking existed. You do realize she died *months* ago, right? Not a decade. Not even a year. Just a few months, and nobody wants to even mention her name."

Lyre and Drom are both staring down at their plates and clearly not intending to get involved, while Corvus looks accusingly at me, as if saying *fix this* with his disapproval. But what the hell does he expect me to do? I'm not going to sit here and listen to Pol talk about her like she was some wonderful part of our lives. Maybe she showed flashes of kindness to the rest of them, but never to me, and I'm not going to pretend otherwise.

"If the alternative is pretending she was someone she wasn't, then yeah, I'm perfectly happy to pretend she never existed in the first place," I say. "We're all better off without her, and that's the truth."

I was expecting Pol to explode at that, to keep arguing with me and let me pour out more of my frustration, but instead his dejected look makes shame burn in my chest. I swallow the rest of my words and shake my head.

"I'm going out," I say, avoiding meeting anyone's eyes. "Later."

Despite my words, Corvus follows me to the door. When I move to open it, he juts an arm out to stop me.

"He doesn't mean it," he says, glancing over his shoulder to make sure none of our other siblings overhear. "You know he doesn't really remember parts of it, and it's more fresh for him, so he's—"

"I know, I know." I bite the inside of my cheek, trying to stifle my frustration. "It's just hard to listen to."

"I understand." He lowers his arm, but before I can move, he asks, "Where are you going in such a rush?"

"I'm meeting Eri and Halon at the landing zone."

"Again? I didn't know they had access to Nibiru, and now they've been here twice in a month?"

"Well...I might've told customs they work for me. So, now they do have access."

His expression shifts from confusion to concern. "Scorpia..."

"What? It works out, they've got some off-world goods to

unload. They're worth a fortune here with how much trade has slowed down."

"Legal?"

"Mostly."

"Scorpia."

"Well, c'mon, someone's gotta make some credits around here." Though I intend it as a joke, a hint of bitterness creeps in, and Corvus's frown deepens. I've never confronted him about it, but we both know his daily "work" on that fishing boat isn't exactly raking in the riches for us. I don't intend to wait decades to save up enough credits for a new spacecraft. I *can't* wait decades. I'm already getting stir-crazy after a few months trapped here. I was born out among the stars, and I'm never going to belong anywhere else.

Luckily, I've got better things to do than fish. Corvus might be eager to forget about our roots and live some simple little Nibiran life, but I'm not. Lawful work has never been my strong suit. Nor has it ever proven to be particularly profitable.

"Just be careful," Corvus says, after a long pause. It takes all my willpower to avoid rolling my eyes. "There's been increased peace-keeper activity with the unease about the storms and the Gaians, and the council—"

"Has their eyes on us, yeah, yeah, I remember the first million times you've reminded me."

"I just don't want you to forget that our situation here is pre-carious," Corvus says. "We can't leave if something goes wrong."

"I know that better than anyone," I say. "But I know what I'm doing. Relax."

I head out the door before he can annoy me any further. Things have been pretty good between us in general since we've been on Nibiru; much better than the rocky times when he first returned to the family, at least. I'll never deny that I'm glad to have my brother back. And yet... he's still not the brother I remember, and I'm still dealing with that. Ever since we've arrived here, he seems content to sit around fishing all day. It's like he's completely forgotten who we're supposed to be, and where we belong. Our only home is out on a ship, not on this little boat on this simple planet. And someone needs to focus on getting us back out there.

Thinking about it makes my chest tighten again. I've never dealt well with being trapped on the surface, and this stay has been the longest since my childhood. Even then, when we spent years here on Nibiru until our little siblings were old enough to be useful on a ship, there was always the promise of *Fortuna* waiting for us out there. *Fortuna*, who was always my only real home. Now she's gone. I blew her up myself, shortly after she finally became mine, for the sake of saving Nibiru.

So, we're stuck here. The Nibirans have been grateful to us, and welcoming, but it's not enough. It's never gonna be enough.

I take a moment to pause, to focus on the open ocean and the sky and Nova Vita shining down on me. I tilt my head back and take a deep breath of fresh air, soothing the tension in my chest. At least I'm no longer closed in that cramped metal cage of a house that's never gonna feel like home. I'm outside. I'm not trapped.

Not any more than I was before the storm, at least.

I thought this part would get a little less nerve-racking after the first couple times, but here I am, sweaty-palmed and nervous again, especially since the customs worker keeps looking at me way too closely.

She types something on her keyboard, pauses to glance up at me. Types again; pauses again, squinting at my face. I fight back the urge to fidget and make my discomfort obvious.

"Something wrong?" I ask, leaning against the counter and forcing a smile.

"Oh, no. I was just thinking that you look familiar," the woman says.

My heart isn't necessarily racing, but it's definitely starting to jog at this point. The woman doesn't seem suspicious—yet—but any recognition in a situation like this is bad for me. "Well, I've been through here a few times to meet up with my employees," I say, resisting the urge to pull away and ruin the casual act. "And I have been told I have a particularly memorable face..."

"No, I don't think that's it," she says—a punch to both my ego and my hope that she'll let this go—and taps a finger thoughtfully against her chin. "I saw you...oh!" Her expression lights up. "You're Scorpia Kaiser!"

My heart stutters, and then begins to beat double-time. My smile fades despite my best efforts, and I weigh my options. Would it be better to run? No—she already knows my name. Deny it? No, no, she looks pretty damn sure. I'm stuck. "Er, yes?"

"Oh my stars," she says. "You're the hero of Nibiru!"

I blink at her as that sinks in, and my heart rate dips back toward normal. An incredulous laugh bubbles up in the back of my throat, but I stifle it. "Oh. Right. Yup. That's me."

Because as far as the Nibirans know, my family are just the people who stopped the *Red Baron* and the alien weapon they carried, and saved this planet from destruction. They don't know that I had previously cut a deal with Leonis to take the same damn job, for the sake of saving my brother. I may have changed my mind in the end, but that guilt is still heavy on my shoulders, making me want to cringe every time someone calls me a *hero*. If things had gone just a little bit differently, my family and I would be locked up beneath the waves just like Captain Murdock and the *Red Baron*'s crew—including poor Orion, my old friend who turned to our side in the end yet was still imprisoned with the rest.

But I force a smile, and the woman lets out a sound like a teakettle releasing steam, beaming at me. If this were anywhere other than the customs office, I might try to swing this in my favor, maybe try a little bit of flirting. But it's impossible to ignore the fact that we *are* in a customs office, and having anyone get familiar with my face and name here is bound to be very, very bad for me. Still, there's no tactful way to extract myself from this situation, so I maintain a grin as the woman insists on taking a picture with me, her face squished against mine, and hope she doesn't notice how sweaty my palms are.

I shake them out as I walk down the dock to the landing zone. As the adrenaline fades, looking around this place fills me with such an intense longing that it almost stops me in my tracks. This place overflows with memories. I remember stepping from *Fortuna*'s ramp onto the landing dock a hundred times over, filling my lungs with that first breath of Nibiran air that always tasted so fresh and clean. I remember waiting here as a kid, watching the sky and waiting for *Fortuna*, grinning so hard my face hurt when I saw Momma walk down the ramp.

And now, the dock is empty but for one familiar ship. Despite the ache in my chest, I smile at the sight of Eri and Halon stepping out onto the docks, and wave with enthusiasm I don't have to force. After that first, obligatory conversation in which I had to explain to our two old allies that I lied to them previously and my mother is dead, rather than retired—that was awkward—it's always been pleasant to meet with these two. Even after my lies, they've surprised me with their kindness…and their business proposition, which I was eager to snap up.

I wrap Halon in a hug and kiss him on both cheeks before giving Eri the more reserved, Paxian handshake he prefers, grinning widely all the while.

"It's good to see you two again!"

"Glad to see you, too," Eri says. "For a while there, we weren't sure we were gonna make it. There's been some talk I'm not too fond of."

My smile fades. I haven't heard any talk. Frustratingly, I've hardly heard about anything going on outside of this planet at all. "What kind of talk?" I ask, but then wave a hand as they hesitate. "Ah, right, we can get to that over lunch."

"Actually," Halon says, "I'm afraid we don't have time for that today."

"What? Really?" Disappointment hits me harder than it should. Even more than the fact they're old allies and new business partners, I always look forward to seeing Eri and Halon because they're a reminder that a wider system still exists out there, and other worlds are waiting for me. I feel so damn isolated here. With both the *Red Baron* and *Fortuna*—may she rest in peace—out of commission, the already-small world of interplanetary trading has shrunk even more. And since Nibiru's main trade was with Gaia and Titan, the only places with much use for its algae exports, that's slowed to barely a trickle. It's hard to even get news from the outside, let alone good company. "I mean, I get that you're busy. It's just that we always have lunch, and..."

"We're sorry to miss it as well." Eri reaches out and squeezes my arm. "But I'm afraid it's only getting trickier out there." He looks at his husband again, sighs, and leans forward, lowering his voice. "It's Deva and Pax."

"Still arguing over Titan?" It makes me queasy to think about how quickly both of the wealthier planets went after Titan's resources, but I guess I shouldn't be surprised.

"A few days ago, all of Deva's scouting drones went dark," Eri says. "We just got word that Deva retaliated by seizing a Paxian mining vessel on its way there."

"Oh. Fuck." My belly goes cold. Even when they mentioned bad news, I didn't think it would be *that* bad. "When you say mining vessel..."

"There were Paxians on board," Eri says, confirming my fears.

"Now imprisoned on Deva until they get reparations for the drones, which Pax is refusing to take responsibility for. So..." He reaches over to take his husband's hand. Both of their expressions are grave. "Well, we're not sure what's going to happen now."

My stomach drops. As bad as this news is for the entire system—and it's pretty damn bad—it's even worse news for the two of them. Their marriage has allowed them to travel between their two home-planets safely even with border laws so tight, but if war breaks out, I'm not sure what will happen to them. That must be why they're in such a rush to get off Nibiru. If they land one day and find out that laws have changed, one or both of them could be in danger. Will they have to choose one planet to remain on? Or will they be forced apart either way?

Selfish though it may be, I also can't help but think about what this will mean for me and my family. I've been clinging to the hope that we'll be able to acquire a ship and get off this planet soon... but what will that matter if the rest of the system is at war by the time we make it out there? What if we're really trapped here, after all?

I wrench my thoughts away from there and try to focus on the two in front of me again. "I'm sorry," I say. "If there's any way I can help..."

"Appreciate it, darlin'. We'll figure it out. Maybe this will blow over and we'll be back before you know it, but if not... well, we interplanetary businesspeople are a resourceful bunch, right?" Eri smiles at me, and then points a thumb back to the ship. "Anyway, we've got some presents for you."

Eri and Halon leave me with a heavy heart and even heavier cargo. Customs gives the crates a thorough-enough search that my pulse spikes, but they finish the inspection without any trouble. The lady I spoke with earlier even gives me a luggage cart to help haul it out, along with a wink, but I'm definitely not in the mood for flirting now.

I drop the majority of my haul back at the houseboat before heading out again. Normally I wouldn't risk trying to sell wares that were just delivered today, but the news from outside has me itching to get something done. With trouble brewing both on and off Nibiru, the best thing my family can do is keep our options open, and for that we need a ship more than ever. I may be the only one who's space-born, but it's obvious none of us really belong here, no matter what Corvus wants to believe. When things get bad, outsiders like us will be the first ones in danger. And if there's a war brewing between Pax and Deva, I have to speed up my timetable. We need to get out of here...and I need to find a way to get Orion out of Ca Sineh and bring him with us. I made a promise to him, and I intend to keep it. I don't have a concrete plan yet, so I need to work on the next best thing: making as much money as possible. Credits mean options.

Luckily for me, the bars are always packed after a storm. This seaside bar attracts mostly fisherfolk and algae farmers—not that anywhere on Kitaya gets much of anything else. Some of the patrons lost their equipment or aren't ready to brave the still-choppy waves yet, while others, I suspect, are eager to drown their nerves after a too-close brush with a natural disaster. Or perhaps a not-so-natural disaster, if the rumors are to be believed.

I'm no superstitious Nibiran, but even I'm not sure what to think. We know that the situation on Gaia began when President Leonis unknowingly unleashed an alien weapon disguised as an agricultural tool, but we still don't understand *why*. Maybe it is possible that the Gaians brought something to Nibiru. Nobody knows.

But right now, I need to focus on the situation at hand. The crowd works well for me, even though the room stinks of salt and fish. I sidle up to the bar and order myself a beer. I probably shouldn't be drinking, and especially not drinking in public where word can get back to my siblings, but I'll look suspicious if I order nothing…and beer *barely* counts as alcohol. Drink in hand, I take a sip and search the bar for an opening.

I eventually home in on a woman sitting alone. She's broad-shouldered, with a hooked nose and ample tattoos covering her right arm. The hand wrapped around her beer glass is large and callused. I grab my drink and slide into the seat beside her. She takes a moment to glance at me, but when she does, she looks me over in a way that is far from unwelcoming. It gives me a desperately needed boost of self-esteem, and I don't have to force a smile.

Still—like every time I've tried to get someone into bed over the last few months—there's a weird dip in my gut like I'm doing something wrong. No matter how hard I try, I can't seem to forget the fact that there's only one person I want right now. But she's made it clear she's not interested, so I push Shey's face out of my mind and focus on the woman in front of me.

"Aren't you that lady who helped save the planet?" she asks, and my self-esteem wilts again. Damn it. If that's the only reason she was looking at me, I might be out of luck.

"I sure am," I say. No choice but to lean into it at this point. "And you…" I scrutinize her face. "*You* look like the sort of woman who doesn't shy away from a risk." For an unsettling moment, my words send me down a half-forgotten path of memory, to similar words I spoke to General Ives on Titan, trying to sell a world-ending weapon to an already-doomed planet—but I wrench myself away with a jolt. Stars, it's been a while since I thought about that. The woman in front of me leans closer.

"That what you fancy yourself, *hero*?" she asks, grinning. "A risk?"

I grin back, and lean in to whisper conspiratorially.

"Truth be told, I'm more of a risk than a hero, most days."

"That so?" She casts another appraising look over me. I don't shy away. "You don't seem so dangerous."

"Well, I've been told I'm full of surprises," I say. "More than usual, today, actually."

As her eyebrows rise, I reach into my left sleeve with my right hand, palm the packet hidden there, and let it show just long enough for her to glimpse it before pocketing it again. Her eyebrows lift farther, and she leans back slightly, glancing around to check if anyone is paying attention to us.

"Is that what I think it is?" she asks, voice lower than before.

"If you're thinking it's the purest Sanita you've ever laid eyes on, then yeah."

The woman's eyes go round. "I thought the supply was cut off? Heard it's impossible to get your hands on any."

"Close, but not quite."

"Then it's gotta be expensive as all hell."

"Prices have gone up, yes, but so has potency. Fewer dealers mean only the best survive." I tap my chest and smile. "Trust me, it's well worth the price."

"Hm." The woman is eyeing me with interest, but still leaning back. I haven't won her over yet. "Not sure I can afford a habit like that."

"Oh, did I not mention it's totally nonaddictive? One of the many perks. Save it for a rainy day, if you will." Only after the words are out of my mouth do I realize they probably hit a nerve. Her eyes shadow, as her mind no doubt follows the trail to the recent storms. Rather than backpedaling, I decide to plunge forward. "I mean, literally! Say you're out in the open sea when one of those storms hit. Some of this for you and your crew will keep you all clearheaded and efficient. Might just save your life. Soldiers on Titan use—" Shit. Another sore subject. But nothing to do other than keep going. "Used to smoke some before battle, keep their heads clear."

I'm so busy trying to save my sales pitch that I barely notice the whispers stirring the bar until my client starts to get distracted. I glance over my shoulder, unsure what the quiet clamor is about. After a few seconds, a coherent string of words finally reaches me: "—*councillor outside*—"

"Oh," I say. "Shit—"

By the time I turn back around, my would-be client has already disappeared, likely heading for the back door. I should do the same, but a sudden hush falling lets me know I'm already too late.

Of all the shitty timing...but I shouldn't worry too much. Surely it isn't *that* rare for a councillor to make an appearance, even at a place like this. It can't have anything to do with me. Soothed by that thought, I pick up my beer and take a long swig. As long as I pretend everything is normal, resist the urge to glance over and risk being recognized by the councillor, I should be able to avoid any unwanted attention and—

"Scorpia Kaiser?"

I choke on my beer at the sound of an alarmingly familiar voice close behind me. Still coughing, beer splattered down the front of my shirt, I throw on a grin and turn. My heartbeat rises even more as I face Councillor Oshiro. The youngest member of Nibiru's council is dressed in a traditional blue robe, dark hair loose around their shoulders.

They smile thinly. "Ah, so it is you. I heard a rumor that the 'hero of Nibiru' was out and about."

I wipe a hand across my mouth to rub away some beer foam, and clear my throat.

"Well, I try to keep a low profile, but you know how people can be," I say, waving a hand breezily and trying not to wince as I feel

27

the Sanita shift in my sleeve pocket. "I'm sure you get the same celebrity treatment, no? The people do love their councillors!"

Oshiro glances pointedly around the bar. They *are* a popular councillor, especially so after the prominent part they played in the Interplanetary Council a few months ago and Leonis's subsequent arrest, but... not so much in places like this. I didn't exactly choose the classiest bar to sell drugs in. All of the other patrons are carefully avoiding looking too hard at either the councillor or the bodyguards waiting at the door. Rather than dig my hole any deeper, I down the rest of my beer in one big gulp to avoid having to speak.

After letting the silence drag out in what I suspect is an intentionally uncomfortable manner, they say, "Though I'm terribly sorry to bother you when you're so... busy"—they glance at my beer again before continuing—"I'm here to request a favor."

"Favor? From me?" I point a finger at my chest.

"You are the 'hero of Nibiru,' after all."

I suppress a grimace. I'd really like to turn them down, especially when I have no idea what I'll be getting myself into, but I can't think of a polite way to get out of here. Even prying for more information could damage my reputation and relationship with the council. Oshiro is one of the few who seems to genuinely like us—or at least Corvus, who they've met up with a couple times over the past months. And given how prone my family is to getting ourselves in trouble, we can't afford to get on the council's bad side. We already had to call in a favor once to bail Drom out of jail. We owe them.

Plus, if anyone can help us get off this planet, it's the council. It can't hurt to earn some points with them.

"Well, sure," I say. "You know me. Always happy to help."

"Wonderful." The councillor heads for the door without another glance back at me. I stay where I am for a second, rolling

my eyes skyward and wishing there was a way for me to slip out
the back entrance and go home, before pushing myself to my feet
and following.

"So," I begin as we stroll down the streets, passing various market stalls. I try to sound casual and ignore the fact I have drugs
tucked into my sleeve. "What can I do for you, Councillor?"

"As I'm sure you're already aware, this weekend is the official
inauguration of the new Gaian president."

I nod. I've heard something about a new president being voted
in to replace Leonis; her entire cabinet was purged after the truth
about Titan came to light. Or the half-truth, at least, since my
own family's involvement was buried. I can't be bothered to feel
too bad about that. Momma was the one who made the deal with
Leonis and sold an alien weapon to General Altair. The rest of us
were just along for the ride at that point, trapped under her cruel
thumb. None of us were aware that the weapon she sold them
would wipe out the entire planet. Even Momma may have just
been an unknowing pawn of Leonis. We still don't know exactly
how much she knew, and we never will.

I haven't heard anything about this newcomer, but she *has* to be
better than the woman who massacred the Titans and conspired
to do the same to Nibiru.

"While this is a cause of celebration for most Gaians," Oshiro
continues, "and we were happy to grant them permission for an
event to commemorate it on Vil Hava, we have had some growing
concerns over the last few weeks. Especially given her...rather
unorthodox beliefs."

"Beliefs?"

"She belongs to the Church of First Divinity," Oshiro says, not
quite managing to purge the disdain from their tone. "Primus
worshippers."

"Ouch, yeah, that's probably going to get a few panties in a twist," I say, wincing at the thought of what a commotion it would cause. Pretty poor timing, given the recent storms and unrest over the upcoming decision about the Gaians' future. Everyone in the system—crazy alien-loving Gaians aside—has the good sense to be wary about the extinct aliens who first settled on these planets, but the Nibirans have always had the strongest distrust of all, banning alien tech in its entirety. "So, uh, you're canceling the thing, right?"

"We cannot. Not only would it upset the Gaians, but it would send a message to those who already do not approve of their presence. I'm sure you've heard of the recent troubles."

"Yeah." After my high hopes for the Gaians and Nibirans getting along, it's been disheartening to watch the anti-refugee sentiments crop up. As much as I think the Gaians deserve to be knocked down a few pegs, I never would've wanted this. They still deserve a home. "So…" I'm still not sure why Oshiro is approaching me about this. What could I possibly do to help? "Sounds rough."

"We are hoping to make the occasion slightly less polarizing by having a few speakers who are not associated with the Gaian government. I'll be giving a speech, along with a few others, but we all think it may be helpful to have someone less…well… official."

They glance over at me, stopping there, and my brow furrows. Once it sinks in, I stop walking. Oshiro halts a few paces later, and turns to frown at me.

"What, *me*?"

"You are widely hailed as a hero, by both the Gaians and Nibirans," they say, eyebrows lifting at my confusion. "You and your family helped initiate our peace agreement and stopped a ship that would have killed us all."

"I mean, yeah, sure, I played a part," I say, shrugging in an attempt to downplay it. "But that's...I'm not..." I wrestle with both my words and my thoughts, trying to get a grasp of why I'm so immediately and vehemently opposed to the idea. Me, speaking at a political celebration? Me, expected to help soothe relations between the Gaians and Nibirans? I guess I can understand why they would come to me. And yet... "I can't."

"If it's a matter of funds, I'm sure we can afford to pay you a small speaker's fee."

"How much?" I ask, automatically, and then shake my head. "No, no, never mind, doesn't matter. I just...wait, is Ambassador Leonis going to be there?"

"I believe she—"

"Wait, wait, don't answer that, either," I say quickly, waving a hand to silence them again. The councillor levels an unimpressed look at me, and I clear my throat. I need to stop getting distracted. I know there can only be one answer to this, no matter the payment or my personal feelings. "With all due respect, Councillor, politics really aren't my thing. And especially given the state of things lately, I feel like my presence would help no one."

And especially not me or my family. I've seen exactly where getting involved in these things can lead. I've seen my family torn apart, forced to risk our lives again and again for the sake of the greater good. I'm proud of what we did. I'd do it again. But when we chose to do that, it was because we were the only ones who could. Frankly, I'm still shocked that we survived. But now? Surely there are more capable people to take the reins. Especially when my family is still nursing our wounds and finding ourselves...and doing our damnedest to find a way out of here.

Plus: All those risks we took, all these people calling us heroes, and where did it get us? Stranded and nearly broke on this planet, unable to do anything to help Pol with...whatever it is he's going through. Entangling ourselves any further in this complicated political situation is only going to hold us down. I may be desperate for credits, but not this desperate.

"I see." Councillor Oshiro's tone is mild, but I detect a new iciness in their tight expression, and suppress a wince. "Well. If you've made up your mind, I will not bother to try to convince you otherwise. But please know that you and your family are still invited to attend the event, if you so please."

"We're honored," I say, knowing full well I have no intention of going anywhere near it.

"And, on the off-chance that you change your mind, you know how to contact me."

"Sure." I turn to go.

"One more thing, Scorpia?"

"Hm?"

"Take your business elsewhere in the future. You're not above the law, even if you are the 'hero of Nibiru.'"

I suppress a wince. Damn. I thought I got away with it.

"Not sure what you're talking about, Councillor," I say, after a moment of uncomfortable silence. "I am, of course, an upstanding citizen. But, uh, if I hear about anyone doing anything unsavory here, I'll tell them to keep their business off this island in the future."

Oshiro stares at me for a moment longer, and finally nods in a way that feels like a dismissal. I turn away and rush toward home.

"Shit, shit, shit," I mutter as I go. Bad news, all around, and I suspect it's only going to get worse from here. We need to figure out a way to get off this planet, and fast.

CHAPTER THREE

Fortune's Wheel

Corvus

When I return for the day, I usually have a quiet home to myself for a few hours before the others trickle in. I'm surprised to hear voices coming from inside when I dock the hoverboat. All of my siblings are home, from the sound of it. I hurry my steps, assuming that something must be wrong, but stop when I reach the doorway and see them gathered around the table.

Scorpia is seated with a strange array of items spread across the surface in front of her: fresh produce and freeze-dried fruit, spices and wine, and more. The majority of it must be from Deva, and all of it has been virtually impossible to find on Nibiru over the last few months, considering how little trade has been coming in. Our younger siblings are all crowded around Scorpia, eagerly waiting—except for Drom, who immediately reaches out to grab a bottle of Devan fireberry sauce from the pile.

"You're welcome," Scorpia says, and hands a packet of freeze-dried jerky over to Lyre. "This is for you."

"Real Paxian jerky?" Lyre's eyes go wide.

"I don't understand how you can eat that creepy cow meat," Drom says, a moment before squeezing hot sauce directly onto her tongue.

"Paxian cattle are a scientific marvel," Lyre says defensively, clutching the jerky to her chest. "...And also quite delicious."

"Gross."

"You *must* be aware that what you're doing at this very moment is abhorrent to most people, yes?"

"Pol, here you go, bud." Scorpia hands over a handful of small plastic tubes, which he squints at. "Nutrient paste, extra protein. Supposed to help you gain weight."

Pol breaks into a broad grin and leans down to hug her.

"Thanks," he says. "And did you get any—"

"Corvus!" Scorpia interrupts, finally looking up to see me standing in the doorway. She and Pol exchange a glance before he pulls back and tears open one of the pods of paste with his teeth. He wanders into the living room, Drom close behind, and Lyre heads downstairs, presumably to hide her snacks somewhere the twins can't find them.

Scorpia grins at me. "Hey. Got you something, too." She grabs a jar off the table and tosses it to me. "High-grade Sanita paste."

"What?" I scrutinize the small jar and its contents. Ten percent pure Sanita. That's close to military-grade painkillers on Titan. "That's..."

"It's legal here. I checked."

"It must be worth a fortune." I look up from the jar to her grin. The gesture is touching, but it's the type of gift that's too grand for me to be entirely comfortable with. I have nothing to give in return, and it's so far above the snacks she gave our younger siblings that I can't help but feel guilty receiving it. "Are you sure?"

"Yeah. No prob. Should help with your leg."

An uncomfortable thought crawls up from the back of my

mind: Could this be a distraction? A bribe? Is this her way of trying to prevent me asking into the rest of whatever she got from Eri and Halon, after I mentioned my concerns earlier? But the pleased look on her face makes me feel terrible for even thinking it, so I pocket the jar. "Thank you. I appreciate it."

I look over the rest of what she's set on the table again. None of it seems illegal, but none of it seems particularly profitable, either, which again rouses my suspicions.

"Eridanus and Halon really went out of their way to stop by Nibiru and drop...this?" I ask, picking up a bag of meat-flavored chips and dropping it again.

"Those are tasty, don't knock 'em till you try 'em," Scorpia says. "And is it so hard to believe that they wanted to stop by because they, y'know, care about us? Why are you always so *suspicious*?" I only stare at her, and she rolls her eyes. "Okay, fine, they also gave me some comms and other stuff to sell. These are mostly just gifts for everyone." She returns my pointed stare. "Gifts. Because they care. Because they're *nice*."

"'Other stuff'?" I question, and she groans. "I'm just trying to make sure they're not using you. If you get caught with anything illegal, you're the one who will end up with the consequences, not them."

"Nobody's using anybody. It's a mutually beneficial arrangement, and it's also my business that I am perfectly capable of handling on my own, thanks very much." Before I can respond, she continues, "By the way, I had an interesting run-in with Councillor Oshiro today."

It's an obvious subject change, but much as I want to continue discussing the issue at hand, it's clear she doesn't intend to say more. "Iri? About what?"

"Oh, is it *Iri* now?" Scorpia asks, breaking into a grin.

I shake my head. "What did they want?"

"They asked us to attend the inauguration of the new Gaian president. Guess it's gonna be some kind of fancy political shindig."

She laughs. "They even asked me to make a speech. Can you believe it?"

"Ah." I can believe it, especially since the councillor already approached me. But Scorpia is the one more suited to speeches, and the face people know as a hero, which I don't envy her for. I knew it would grate on her that the council came to me first, so I asked Iri to approach her directly. It didn't sound like a terrible idea to me, so I'm not so sure why Scorpia is eager to make a joke of it, aside from the fact that she makes a joke of everything. I lean against the wall. "What did you say?"

"You kidding? Even if I liked listening to boring political speeches for hours, and even if this new Gaian president wasn't an alien-loving weirdo, and even if it wasn't obviously going to blow up in everyone's faces—" She pauses, considering. "Well, then I might go for the free food. But, no. It's a terrible idea."

"It's a chance to further cultivate our relationship with the council."

Scorpia gives me an incredulous look. "Did you miss the whole part about it inevitably turning into a shitfest? Why are you—" Her expression shifts. "Oh. They already told you, didn't they? Tell me you didn't say yes."

"I told them to ask you instead. But I'm not sure why you're so eager to decline. They're politicians, it's not like anyone's going to start throwing punches over a disagreement."

"Well, there was that one time—"

"This isn't Deva."

Scorpia lets out a frustrated sound, running a hand through her hair. "I mean, come on. Even putting that whole mess to the side, do we really want to get more involved in political bullshit? Look where it landed us last time."

I hold out my hands to gesture to the houseboat around us. "It didn't end so badly."

"It could've gone a lot worse. We got lucky."

"Maybe you're right. But you're the one who's so eager to get off the planet. Do you think the best way to get there is selling off-world snacks?"

Scorpia stares at me. Then she lets out a loud groan, resting her elbows on the table and putting her face in her hands. "Stars damn it. Why do you always have to make so much sense?"

"Someone in this family has to." I cross the room and take a seat beside her. "This could be a good opportunity for us. The more favors we do for the Nibiran Council, the more likely they are to do one for us."

" 'Cause saving their whole planet wasn't enough?" she grumbles into her hands. After a moment, she raises her head, looking over at me. "You really want to do this?"

"I think it's a good idea. Especially if it keeps us in Ir— Councillor Oshiro's good graces. They've been kind to us."

Scorpia scrutinizes my face, sighs, and shrugs. "Fine," she says. "But I'm not making a speech."

"Fair enough."

"And…since we're compromising and all, I want one more thing."

I wasn't aware we were bargaining, but I suppose I should have expected Scorpia to try to wring some advantage out of this. "All right," I say, warily. "What is it?"

Two hours later, all five of us are standing outside of a tattoo parlor in the seedier part of Kitaya.

"You sure this is a good idea?" I ask, staring up at the flickering neon sign in apprehension.

Scorpia bumps her shoulder against mine and grins. "Aw, come on, you already agreed. You can't back out now."

"I guess you'll never let me live it down if I do."

"Nope," Drom says, stepping up from behind me. I glance over at her, and then Pol and Lyre, who are both hanging back and watching my reaction. I suppress a sigh. I've been pushing back on this idea since Scorpia first brought it up a month ago, and I'm still not entirely sure how I managed to get roped into it in exchange for my own perfectly reasonable request. But it's hard to say no now, when the others have already agreed.

"Fine," I say, grudgingly. "As long as Lyre is still up for it."

Lyre steps forward, smiles at me, and moves past us to reach for the handle. "Of course I am. Didn't Scorpia tell you the design was my idea?"

Inside, the shop employees stare at us with obvious trepidation as we crowd into the lobby. There's barely enough space for all of us in the tiny shop. Lyre takes out her comm and gives the closest person a small smile.

"Hi. I made an appointment a couple weeks ago? We're the Kaisers."

"A couple weeks ago?" I murmur, glancing at Scorpia, who only grins. "You were going to harass me into this either way, weren't you?"

"Yup," she says, completely unashamed.

The man relaxes. "Ah, of course," he says. "My, you're all…quite a bit bigger in person." He eyes the twins as he says it. Drom shoots him a sharp grin, while Pol doesn't seem to notice, his eyes glazed over and wandering the room. The man looks back at Lyre. "Well. We can get started right away, then."

By the time we emerge, it's late enough that the streets are nearly empty. While my siblings eagerly compare their completed tattoos, I stare down at my own in silence. I chose to get it on my forearm, just under my war-brand. Two reminders of the past: a mark that made me a soldier, and now a mark of my family—the wheel of fortune. The idea to get a matching tattoo in memory of *Fortuna* was Scorpia's idea, but the design of the simple, black-and-white wheel is all Lyre's, a symbol pulled from myth and undeniably appropriate. It makes my heart ache a little.

"Turned out pretty good," Scorpia says, pulling my attention to her. She sidles over next to me and holds her arm against mine, placing our two matching, mirrored images side by side. "Not such a bad idea after all?"

I smile, some of that ache in my chest fading away. "It certainly wasn't the worst you've ever had."

"Seriously, though, how long is this gonna hurt for?" She winces down at her arm. "It stings like hell."

"Don't know what you're complaining about," Drom says. "Ours are way bigger, and you don't see us whining about it."

Pol turns his bare back to us to demonstrate. The twins' design is the same as ours, but theirs stretch from between their shoulder blades down to the smalls of their back. When he turns back, he's grinning, all signs of his earlier shakiness gone.

"It's really not as painful as I expected," Lyre says. Her own tattoo is smaller than the rest of ours, placed on the back of her neck, where it will only be visible if her long curls are pinned up like they are now. She hasn't spoken much about her reasoning, but I have my suspicions. Tattoos are widely accepted here on Nibiru, but less so on her birth-planet, Deva, in the professional world. Lyre doesn't talk much about what she plans on doing for the future, but if I know my little sister at all, then I know those plans must exist—and that she would never set the bar for herself lower than the stars.

The stars that Scorpia is staring up at now, a longing look in her eyes. I reach out to touch her hand, and she turns to me, her lips twisting into a wistful half smile.

"We'll get there," I say. "The system's not going anywhere. It'll still be there, waiting for us."

"I…" she starts, and then stops, shaking her head. "Yeah. I know."

But for now, I'm just happy for the feeling of ground beneath my feet and my siblings around me.

CHAPTER FOUR

Political Bullshit

Scorpia

Remind me why you're so set on going to this thing again?" I call out to Corvus as I finish putting on my outfit. This custom-tailored, express-ordered suit feels and looks damn good, if I do say so myself, but that's little reassurance for my anxiety over the event tonight. "It's gonna be a shitfest. Total shitfest."

"Maybe we'll be surprised," Corvus says from the other room. "Are you ready yet? We're going to be late."

"Yeah, yeah, one minute." I finish messing with my hair, give myself a final once-over, and head out into the living room to meet him.

Corvus is waiting on the couch, his hair and beard freshly trimmed, wearing a pale gray formal Nibiran robe that arrived a few days ago, which I suspect was a gift from Oshiro. It would have been a nice gesture, with its high-quality fabric and tailored cut, if not for the sleeve being tied off halfway down his forearm to leave his Titan war-brand on full display. The whole outfit is clearly designed to show him off as a Titan survivor, which rubs me the wrong way, though Corvus doesn't seem bothered by it.

"Is that what you're wearing?" Corvus asks, his eyebrows shooting up.

I look down at myself and frown. "Yes? Why?"

"Well, it's very…" He fumbles for words for a moment. "Devan?"

"It's a suit. I look good in suits." I double-check in the mirror just to be sure, and grin at the reflection that greets me. "In fact, I look damn *great* in suits."

Admittedly, the metallic silver fabric and plunging neckline are probably better suited to a high-end Devan club than a presidential inauguration…but to be fair, nobody specified a dress code.

"You do realize this is a political event, and a primarily Nibiran one at that? It won't be anything too garish."

"Well, I'm bored of robes." I brush my hair out of my face, eye my reflection one last time, and turn to face him again. "And you're the one who was going on and on about the 'dangerous political climate.' All the better if the style comes off Devan. That way I'm not taking any sides fashion-wise, yeah?"

Corvus sighs. "Don't pretend this is anything more than you trying to get a certain someone's attention."

"Can't imagine who you mean." I force a grin and brush past him out the door. "Come on, let's get this over with."

My anxiety heightens as we draw closer to the event. Vil Hava is swarming with peacekeepers today, and the building we're headed toward—a wide, disk-like structure on a raised platform, with a huge staircase leading up to its doors—is on full lockdown. They're clearly anticipating trouble, which again makes me question why the hell we're here. I'm throbbing with nervous energy as we wait in the line to get past security.

"I just don't get it," I say, for probably the dozenth time. "The Gaians already have plenty of issues. Now they appoint a stars-damned Primus worshipper? They have to know it's going to piss the Nibirans off."

"Please keep your voice down," Corvus murmurs, eyeing a small group of what I suspect to be Gaian lawmakers ahead of us in line. "The Gaians are afraid," he adds, once he seems sure we haven't gained their attention. "They need something to believe in. Khatri provides that."

"What, her belief in alien fucking?"

I drop my voice to a near-whisper, but Corvus winces anyway, looking both ahead and behind this time to make sure we've still evaded attention.

"Scorpia, stop," he says sternly—but I only wait, knowing he won't be able to resist the bait. He doesn't disappoint me. "And it's not that they want to . . . they *worship* them. In fact, I'm almost one hundred percent certain that what you're suggesting would be blasphemy."

I lean closer to him and whisper conspiratorially, "I bet you ten thousand credits that Khatri would fuck an alien if she had the chance."

"You don't have ten thousand credits. And I'm not going to bet on the sexual fantasies of the new Gaian president."

"Maybe I'll find her tonight and ask."

"Do. Not. Do. That."

"I'm just saying, you should place your bets now—"

"Hello, Officer," Corvus says loudly as he steps forward in line, effectively cutting me off. "Corvus and Scorpia Kaiser. We were invited by Councillor Oshiro."

I suppress a laugh as I pull out my comm. But my amusement fades into anxiety again, a spike of old fear hitting me as I show the officer my documents. "Honored" guest of Nibiru or not, I'm still an off-worlder, and it's hard to let go of that familiar dread that I'm going to be rejected for it. But the officer merely looks over our documents, checks our names against the guest list, and waves us past. I let out a relieved breath as we walk onward.

Vil Hava is called the Isle of Flowers for a reason, but the grounds surrounding this building have a particularly dazzling spread of deep red blooms, covering everything but a winding stone walkway. A soft breeze rustles the petals, making the field ripple like an ocean of red around us as we approach the steps.

After the huge staircase—which leaves Corvus a bit winded, though I pretend not to notice—a pair of security guards once again check our names and documents before ushering us past. I'm not sure what to expect inside, since this building, unlike the vast majority on Nibiru, has few windows.

Nibirans are never the type to go over-the-top, even with the fanciest of functions . . . so I suspect the Gaians had a heavy hand in planning this particular extravaganza. Corvus and I both stop on the threshold, looking around the room. When our eyes meet again, his expression is vaguely dismayed, while I can barely hold back laughter.

"Nothing too garish, you said?"

"I . . . cannot believe they authorized this."

If whoever planned this party was aiming to show off as much Gaian tech as possible while still maintaining an air of sophistication, then I suppose they succeeded. The building is luxurious in a way that makes me want to break something. There's a glittering chandelier that's floating midair, with bubble-like orbs of light cascading out around it to illuminate the entire room. Everything is made of plush fabric or real wood, no hint of the utilitarian metal that most buildings are made of. With no natural light leaking in, the room is dyed a warm, rich shade of yellow, only heightening my feeling that we've stepped into some alien world. There are opulent tables full of food lining the walls, well-dressed servants with trays of crystal glasses filled with bubbling drinks of various colors. The whole event looks like something from Deva.

The venue is full of a mixture of Nibiran and Gaian attendees. Even after months of coexisting on this planet, it's a simple thing to tell the two apart—the rarer Gaians stick out like sore thumbs with their rigid postures and starched-as-ever fashion. Most still wear their characteristic gloves as well, though at an event like this, most of them are made of lace or thin silk, more decorative than practical. Even so, I'm surprised that more didn't decide to shirk them for this. There's been a whole lot of buzz lately about certain Nibirans finding the gloves offensive, both as a reminder that Gaians still dwell on the past plague, when they first came into fashion, and for the implication that the people they come into contact with must be dirty in some way.

As the thought strikes me, I sidle up to Corvus, who seems deeply uncomfortable already.

"Think the new president is gonna come out with or without the gloves?"

Corvus glances around before responding. "Without, if she's smart. It would be a peace-making gesture."

"Not so sure she's the peace-making type."

"She could surprise us."

"Wanna make a bet on it?"

Corvus shoots me a thin-lipped look of disapproval that, for a disorienting moment, reminds me of Momma. "Not the time or the place. Please, could you stop with the bets and make an effort for one night?"

I try to shake the moment off, though my stomach still curdles uncomfortably, and force a smile. "Yeah, yeah. Never a time or place for fun with you."

I nudge him playfully with one shoulder to take off any sting the words might have, and continue onward, leaving him to mingle and have some oh-so-serious political conversations I would probably spoil with my presence. He makes his way straight over to Iri Oshiro, who pulls him into a conversation with a gloved Gaian man.

I'm more interested in the food table. Most of it is standard Nibiran fare—fish, fish, and more fish, served raw and grilled and curried and in all manner of ways—but they've included a few Gaian dishes as well. That must be mostly for diplomacy's sake, since I'm not sure even Gaians prefer their strange assortments of pickled vegetables and rehydrated fruit and heavily salted meats. It's all carefully arranged to look pretty, but I know from experience that it looks a lot better than it tastes.

I grab a skewer of charred fish glistening with a sweet glaze and gnaw at it while I survey the rest of the party. A number of people turn away immediately, trying to pretend they weren't staring at me.

Most of the looks are more curious than hostile, but the attention still makes my skin prickle, even though it was what I was aiming for with this outfit. No matter how much I groaned about coming to this event, I know it's a great opportunity to mix with the upper echelons of Nibiran and Gaian societies. I could be making some powerful friends right about now—or better yet, making some sales. These kinds of business connections are exactly what my family needs. It's going to take ages to make enough credits to buy our way off-planet at this rate, and as Eri and Halon made me realize, we're running out of time. If the council won't help us, maybe someone else will. One conversation here could change things for us.

And yet, now that I'm here, surrounded by these glitzy decorations and important people, the thought of walking up to someone and trying to start a conversation fills me with absolute dread. My suit, which I was so damn proud of, suddenly feels gaudy and cheap—just another sign that I don't belong in this place. I don't even belong on this damn planet, but this event only highlights the feeling, my awareness of it a constant throb in the back of my head. I can't fight off the feeling, not even when I see Corvus casually conversing with Oshiro and another councillor in one corner of the room. Corvus can fit in wherever he goes. But I've always been on the outside. Here is no different.

Then the crowd parts, and my brain short-circuits as I spot a familiar face all the way across the room. Shey Leonis is dressed in a gown of rippling cobalt fabric, high in the neck and stiff in the shoulders like Gaians favor, but loose and floor-sweeping in the Nibiran way. Her hair is coiled in a complicated-looking updo, and her hands are bare, and damn, I almost forgot how gorgeous she is.

I freeze. Half the reason I agreed to come to this stupid thing was to get a chance to talk to Shey, but my courage has officially fled. For a moment I entertain the thought of crossing the room, taking her hand, saying something that will make her throw back her head and laugh in the way she only laughed when I was funny enough to make her forget propriety.

Then she glances up, and her eyes meet mine. She's far enough away that I can't tell whether they widen at the sight of me, or if she stops talking out of shock or a natural lull in the conversation, but I have my hopes. Her gaze lingers on me for a moment, another moment, a third—and then she turns away, and resumes her conversation, and doesn't look back.

I stare at her a second longer before wrenching myself away with a quiet curse. I'm not sure what I expected. The two of us talking like old times, even though she's made it obvious she doesn't want me around anymore? Last time we met, she made it clear she was saying goodbye. Choosing her people over me. As if I ever stood a chance with someone like her, anyway—she's the daughter of an ex-president, an ambassador, a Primus scientist, and I'm...what? Not even a smuggler anymore. Just a lowly drug dealer. A petty criminal.

Did I think this stupid suit would make me belong in her world any more than I did before? I'm not sure what the hell I'm doing at this party. Not even Shey wants me here. Everybody knows I don't belong. Me and my family should be locked up under the ocean right now just like Orion and his crew, not attending some ridiculous political party, and sooner or later someone is going to realize it.

Suddenly it feels like there are too many eyes on me, too many bodies pressing in. My heartbeat is a drum in my ears; my suit is stiflingly hot, tight enough to restrict my lungs. I push my way through the crowd as politely as I can manage with panic welling up in my chest.

"Oh, Scorpia Kaiser," one man says, bowing to me as I try to pass him. "The hero of Nibiru herself. I've been waiting for an opportunity to thank you for all that you've—"

"Not right now," I snap, half-breathless, and push through.

I fight my way to an open space in the back of the room, and a hint of a cool breeze leads me to one of the building's few windows. Elbows resting on the sill, I lean out and suck in air that tastes like salt and rain. I focus on the cool breeze on my face and the distant crash of waves against the shore. I could really use a fucking drink right now, but the fresh air will have to do. After a few gulps of it, my heartbeat slows.

But once the sound of my heart fades from my ears, it's replaced with a new noise—something I can't place at first. Almost like the rumble of an approaching storm, but not quite. I frown, leaning farther out the window, and as the wind shifts, I hear it: voices. Lots of them. Chanting something.

A moment later, I finally get a glimpse at what's coming: a winding line of people trampling through the field of flowers, wielding scowls and signs. Across the nearest one is a message scrawled in bold letters: GAIANS, GO HOME.

Shit.

CHAPTER FIVE

Outsiders

Corvus

Despite Scorpia's worries about the event—which echoed my own, though of course she's always much more outspoken about these things—the inauguration seems to be going smoothly. Councillor Acharya makes a speech that goes over well with the crowd, drawing applause from both Nibiran and Gaian attendees.

"Well, that's an encouraging start," Councillor Oshiro says beside me.

"Were you worried?" I ask, glancing sideways at them.

They raise a glass of champagne to their lips. "Officially, I can't comment on that," they say, smiling around the rim of the glass.

As a perceptible change in atmosphere ripples throughout the room, I turn my attention back to the stage. Ambassador Shey Leonis is making her way to the mic. Though the event and the potential unrest in the crowd must be daunting, she shows no hint of hesitance as she stands on the stage, her bare hands folded neatly behind her and her chin high.

But I'm sure the one thing the crowd notices most is her striking resemblance to her mother. As she steps up to the microphone, a murmur swirls throughout the crowd. I find myself holding my breath, but after a moment Shey begins to speak, unruffled.

"Hello, people of Gaia, and gracious citizens of Nibiru, who have been our hosts and neighbors for these past three months," she begins, sweeping her eyes over the crowd. Only a faint tightness at the corners of her eyes and mouth show any hint she's bothered by the whispers.

Having Shey speak is a bold move. Though the Nibirans loved her at first, as soon as news about her mother being held responsible for Titan broke, her political status became controversial at best. I'm surprised the Gaians haven't replaced her yet—but then again, with the current upheaval, perhaps they don't have the time to deal with yet another political maneuver. They've only just managed to agree on a new president.

I barely pay attention to her speech, instead focusing on the reactions of the crowd. Even the Gaians look uncomfortable, many of them murmuring among themselves. A few pointedly turn their backs to the stage and focus their attention on food or drink instead. I look for my sister but can't find her in the crowd. I'm surprised she'd miss a chance to ogle Shey, but perhaps it turned out to be too painful for her. After everything we went through together, I don't believe the two have spoken since the first arrival of the Gaians on this planet.

Shey's speech gets polite applause from the Gaians and mostly silence from the Nibirans beyond. Oshiro winces beside me, and we exchange a sympathetic glance. It's hard for me not to feel bad for Shey. She's done her best to be a good ambassador, and the agreement between Nibiru and Gaia wouldn't have been possible in the first place without her. She betrayed her mother, snuck onto our ship, and pled for her people in front of their longtime enemies in order to save the Gaians. But she'll never be able to stand on a stage again without the crowd seeing the shadow of the ex-president on her features. Any hopes she had for a career in politics have been thoroughly destroyed now. Shey must know that as well, but she still manages to smile as she departs the stage, composed as ever.

"Well, I suppose that means it's my turn," Oshiro says with a flicker of a nervous grin. "Wish me luck."

"You have nothing to worry about," I say. The words aren't empty. Despite Oshiro's youth, relative newness to the position, and the fact that they represent one of the smallest islands on Nibiru, their popularity has grown exponentially over the last few months.

I was grateful to Oshiro for helping put Leonis away in Ca Sineh, and I've grown to consider them an ally. Perhaps even a friend. I give them a small, respectful bow as they depart, and they incline their head gratefully before taking the stage.

Just as they begin to speak, Scorpia pushes through the crowd to my side.

"We need to get out of here," she murmurs in my ear. I frown, turning away from the stage to face her.

"I know this isn't your type of event, but it's only just begun. The president hasn't even—"

"This isn't about *me*. There's a mob headed right for us, and I don't wanna be around when they get here."

Concern flashes through me—but I push it aside. She's likely being dramatic, as she's always inclined to be. "I'm sure security is more than capable of handling them." I turn back to the stage, intending to catch at least part of Oshiro's speech, and hoping they didn't glance out at the crowd and spot me completely disengaged.

Scorpia lets out a frustrated hiss through her teeth, digging her fingers into my arm. "You didn't see this mob."

"Just wait a few minutes."

"Lastly," Oshiro is saying, "I would like to thank two people who may not have political significance but are hailed as heroes of our planet nonetheless."

"I'm serious," Scorpia says in my ear, "we gotta go—"

"Though not Nibiran by birth or blood, during our time in need, they did not hesitate to risk their lives for the sake of ours. They put aside their personal needs for the sake of the greater good, and as a result, our beautiful planet still stands."

"Scorpia, stop," I mutter, trying to pull away from her.

"Friends and allies, please put your hands together for Corvus and Scorpia Kaiser."

Scorpia and I both freeze as one of the hovering lights shifts to just above us, placing us in a spotlight. Scorpia pries her fingers off my arm while I do my best to smile for the crowd and their polite applause.

"This is the fucking worst," Scorpia says through gritted teeth. I resist the urge to glare at her with the eyes of the crowd on us, and give a small, Nibiran-style bow. After a moment, she grudgingly does the same.

"And next, I would like to welcome to the stage Gaia's new president: Chandra Khatri."

Oshiro's final announcement brings thunderous applause from the Gaians in the room and a lukewarm smattering from the Nibirans. Scorpia gives me a warning glance, but I shake my head. Even if Scorpia is right to be worried, we can't walk away as Khatri takes the stage without it being seen as a brash political statement, especially not right after Oshiro brought the room's attention down on us. Even Scorpia seems to recognize that. She folds her arms stiffly over her chest, but holds her place, eyes on the stage.

Chandra Khatri takes the spotlight with a serene smile, either oblivious or impervious to the divided reception to her presence. She's a tall woman in her early sixties, with long, black hair tied back in a winding braid. While some Gaians have adopted a more

Nibiran style of clothing since coming to the planet, her outfit today is a distinct homage to her home-planet's favored style: white gloves stark against her deep olive skin, black-and-white dress laced tightly up to her neck, squared-off shoulders giving her a distinguished silhouette. Around her neck hangs a symbol of her more controversial side: a black piece of Primus material in the shape of a tentacle. I barely suppress a groan. The accessory is not going to do her any favors with her dissenters—strictly speaking, I'm not even sure it's legal here—but I suppose she doesn't care about that.

"My people," Khatri says, spreading her hands out toward the crowd. "In these difficult times, I am so honored, so humbled, that I am the one you have chosen to lead us toward Gaia's future. And no matter where we are, no matter where we go, Gaia will always have a future. Our world may be unreachable, our cities leveled, but we carry our history with us. We are a living legacy, and so long as we are here, Gaia can never truly die." She pauses, looking out over the crowd. "I know the wounds of the past are not easy to heal, and that your trust will not be easy to win. We have been lied to and betrayed in the worst possible way by a leader we once trusted. We have been uprooted from our home and placed in a strange land. With pain behind us and uncertainty ahead—"

Khatri pauses as the sound of shouting comes from outside, turning nearly every head in the room in the direction of the doors. A few of the security guards make their way toward the entrance. The muffled sound doesn't die down, and the crowd stirs uncomfortably. But after a moment, Khatri continues:

"With pain behind us and uncertainty ahead, it's more important than ever that we choose hope—"

The front doors open, and a wave of noise from outside drowns out the rest of Khatri's words. Someone hastily closes it again, leaving the room in silence for a few moments before worried murmurs begin to swirl around the room. Scorpia gives me an

I-told-you-so expression as all of the building's security move in a synchronized manner toward the doors.

Khatri tries to continue her speech, but a moment later she's surrounded by her personal guard. After a brief argument, she acquiesces and allows them to escort her backstage. Oshiro and the rest of the councillors are all being whisked away with brisk efficiency as well. Within a few minutes, all of the high-level politicians have disappeared from the room, leaving the rest of us to fend for ourselves.

"Well, this went about as well as expected," Scorpia murmurs, and tugs on my arm. "Lucky for us, I already scoped out the back exit. Follow me."

We sneak around the side of the building, and against my better judgment, I agree to Scorpia's plan to "get a better look" before we go. The crowd forming around the entrance to the building has taken up a straightforward chant of "*Gaians, go home.*" Many sport signs or banners scrawled with similar sentiments, along with crossed-out depictions of black Primus statues or crude depictions of Khatri. Disgust coils in my belly, and I have to turn away before it turns to anger and encourages me to do something I regret. I pull around the side of the building and press myself against it.

I'm shocked to see how many of them are here. There are hundreds of protestors spread across the building's steps and grounds, crushing the flowers beneath their heels. I thought the Gaian hatred on Nibiru was a niche sentiment, especially on Vil Hava, where the bulk of the refugees live, but the size of this crowd says otherwise. With their numbers, the security guards are barely able to prevent them from swelling into the building.

"What the fuck," Scorpia mutters, peering out at the crowd from around the corner of the building before retreating back to join me. "Are they serious right now?"

"Seems so."

"I don't understand," she says, shaking her head in disbelief. "I mean, I'm fully aware that Gaians can be a pain in the ass, but *jeez*. What do they want them to do, go back to a planet where storms are literally ripping cities apart? Don't they realize that's as good as killing them?"

"They don't care. They just want them gone." I shrug, releasing a sigh. "We knew this wasn't going to be easy. It's going to take a lot more than a few months to mend the rifts between the planets."

"I just thought things would change when they met face-to-face," Scorpia says. "I thought *they* could change."

"Some won't. Some will. But most of them are going to need more time."

"Time the Gaians don't have."

"I know."

We lapse into silence, and I listen to the seething hatred of the crowd until it makes my chest burn. Despite my words to Scorpia, I have to admit that I expected better than this as well. It's one thing to hate someone you've never met, but another entirely to look another human being in the face and decide that they don't deserve to live. Part of me wants to do something...but how can I fight this? How can we step up when we're outsiders ourselves?

By the time we arrive home, sweat soaks my clothing, and my leg feels ready to collapse, giving me a more pronounced limp and growing frustration. Every time I think I've accepted the hindrance of my old injuries, a time like this comes along to remind me that my body will never be the same as it was before. I'm supposed to be the warrior of the family, the one to keep the others safe, but as we reach the houseboat Scorpia has to help me up onto the deck.

I head inside and collapse onto the couch, grimacing as I stretch my leg out and let it come to a rest on the coffee table. The house is silent; our younger siblings must either be out or sleeping downstairs.

Scorpia grabs me a glass of water, setting it on the table beside the couch with a heavy thud, and then sinks into an armchair and glares at me.

I'm exhausted, but I suppose we might as well get this over with. "Spit it out."

"I told you it was a bad idea. We never should have gone there. And we should have left the second I told you."

"I know. You're right."

"But you always just—what?" She stops, frowning. "Oh. Thought it would take more than that to get you to agree," she says, and then goes silent, seemingly at a loss about how to continue now that we're not having the argument she was anticipating.

"The rational part of me knew it was a terrible idea all along. We don't belong at a place like that. But..." I shrug, unsure how to explain myself. "I still...wanted to try. Or at least pretend. For a little while."

Scorpia's face softens. "Yeah. I get it. Feels good not to be outsiders for once."

"But it can't last."

"It never does," she agrees. "People always look out for their own first. But that's why we've got each other."

In the quiet, I think of Momma, and the phrase she told us a million times: *Blood comes first.* Maybe she was right after all.

CHAPTER SIX

The Job

Scorpia

Corvus and I agree that everyone should stay home for a couple days while the fallout from the riot dies down. News updates inform us that it wasn't as bad as it could have been. There were no casualties—some injuries, but mostly minor. Unfortunately, though, the incident has only made the anti-Gaian protestors more bold and outspoken. Corvus stays glued to the television for updates, his face a mask of consternation, while I try to keep busy with other things.

Such as worrying about the stash of drugs sitting in my room, which is starting to feel like a bigger problem now that I know at least one councillor is aware of my dealings. Thinking about that makes me feel a bit nauseous. In any other situation, I would be finding a new place to hide it until I'm sure I've shaken off any suspicion, but unfortunately the given tumult means going out now would only draw more attention to myself. So, I have little to do other than sit in my room and chew my fingernails down to stubs. As soon as this blows over, I need to find a way to relieve myself of this product, and quickly.

On the third day after the riot, the doorbell rings.

"You expecting company?" I call out to my siblings.

Corvus murmurs a negative, and Lyre shakes her head. The twins are down in their rooms, but I can't imagine they would have anyone to invite over. Frowning, I head to check the security cameras. My stomach sinks at the sight of familiar council robes. It's Oshiro, long hair pulled back in a ponytail.

I rush over to the door, which Corvus is headed toward without any apparent concern.

"Don't answer that."

"What?" His brow furrows. "Why?"

"It's Councillor Oshiro."

Corvus still looks confused. "So what's the problem?"

"The problem is…" I scramble for a convincing lie. "Listen… it's…" Really, I don't know why I'm bothering to try to hide this from Corvus. He always finds everything out eventually. "It's Sanita."

"Oshiro isn't going to care about a little Sanita."

"It's… uh… more than 'a little' Sanita. And Oshiro… may be aware of its existence."

Corvus's expression grows stormier. "You've been dealing."

"I mean, like I said, someone in this family's got to make some credits."

"You could have at least told me."

"Well, what did you think I meant by 'off-world goods'?"

Corvus sighs, raising one hand to massage his temples. I gnaw on my lip, folding both arms over my chest and waiting for him to make a judgment call. After a moment, he lowers his hand.

"I'm not going to ignore them," he says. "After what happened at the inauguration, this could be important. But I'll make sure they don't come inside. Stay out of this, and we'll discuss it later."

"Fine," I agree, and scoot to hide on the other side of the door, just out of Oshiro's sight while still close enough to overhear the conversation. Corvus looks like he wants to argue, but after a moment he shuts his mouth, shakes his head, and opens the door.

"Councillor," he greets, inclining his torso in a small bow. "To what do we owe the honor?"

I bite my nails.

"Oh, please. As I've told you, there's no need to be so formal. Iri is fine." Even through my worry, it occurs to me how different Oshiro sounds when speaking to Corvus, and I have to resist the urge to roll my eyes. But of course, he's everyone's favorite. "I do apologize for the unannounced visit," Oshiro continues. "May I come in?"

I shake my head vehemently enough that Corvus must see it out of the corner of his eye. He clears his throat, hedging for a moment.

"That depends. Do you have a warrant?" he asks. I wince. I would've gone with something a bit more subtle, but Corvus has always been a terrible liar.

"You mistake me. Nobody is in any kind of trouble. In fact..." A long pause. "I am here on behalf of the council to ask...well. A very large favor."

Now that piques my interest. I hadn't expected the council to come to us for any more favors after the way the inauguration went. What else could they possibly want from us? Corvus clears his throat and glances around, his eyes snagging on me for a moment, and I hold up a hand and rub my fingers together. A big favor from the council could mean big money.

Corvus turns back to Oshiro.

"A favor? Or a job?"

"I'm afraid I can't discuss specifics without a bit more privacy. If now isn't a good time, perhaps we can schedule a meeting?"

While they talk, I run through possibilities in my mind. The council…a favor…as a thought occurs to me, all other concerns flee my head.

"That might be—" Corvus is saying, when I push forward and stick my head around the door.

"Hang on," I say. Oshiro blinks at me, but doesn't comment on my sudden appearance. "This favor. Does it possibly involve going off-planet?"

Corvus looks at me sharply, but I keep my eyes on the councillor.

"Please," they say, "may I come in and sit down?"

But they tilt their head in a barely discernable *yes*.

A few minutes later, the three of us sit at the table in the middle of our messy kitchen. The sink is overflowing with dirty dishes, and there's an awful smell drifting out of the too-full trash, but Oshiro doesn't seem to pay it any mind. Corvus gets us mugs of sweet mint tea, a Nibiran staple and generally polite gesture. My leg bounces. I can barely contain my excitement until Corvus sits down.

"So," I say, once we're all finally seated. "What's this favor, Iri?"

"Oshiro, please," the councillor corrects me. I resist the urge to wince—or to glare at Corvus, who seems to be trying very hard to suppress a smile. The councillor takes a long sip of tea and leans back in their chair. "As I'm sure you've noticed, we are in a rather precarious situation at the moment. The Gaians' stay on our planet is nearly up, and there is still no plan for what to do with them next. Gaia remains uninhabitable, and while Titan is as safe as it ever was…" They pause, hesitating, eyes flicking toward Corvus. "It is...not an ideal option, as you can imagine. The Gaians are not used to such a climate and have almost nothing to help them adapt."

"I've heard many died in the early days on Titan," Corvus says, after an uncomfortable moment. "The remainder survived only by violence against the less fortunate. I wouldn't wish that fate on the Gaians, or anyone."

"Neither would I, but some on the council disagree," Oshiro says.

"Having the Gaians here isn't so terrible, is it?" I ask. "I mean... aside from the riot and the...it's *mostly* fine, right? Do you really need to kick them out when the time is up?"

"I, personally, do not believe that we do," Oshiro says. "But the council is divided. As it stands now, Vil Hava is overcrowded, our food supply is strained, and our economy is struggling with the loss of exports to Gaia and Titan. The Gaians are eager to work, but unqualified for the hard labor jobs that are available to them, so many of them are, to be frank, a burden. It could take years for them to learn a trade that's useful here. Years longer to plan and build a new island for them to make their home on." Oshiro sighs, curling long fingers around their teacup. "But these are problems we anticipated. The more pressing concern at the moment is... well, you've witnessed the weather yourselves."

"Nibirans are so damn superstitious," I say, waving a hand. "It's just weather. Nibiru's had storms before."

"Likely so. It's not entirely unusual. But our people are concerned. And it is true that we still do not know the full extent of what happened on Gaia or why. As far as we know, it could be possible that the Gaians brought the danger of their home with them, somehow. Leonis has been less than forthcoming, and it is hard for us to argue against superstition when we lack facts."

"So what can we do about it?"

Oshiro smiles at my eagerness. Corvus looks less enthusiastic, his arms folded and his face guarded, but he nods for the councillor to continue.

"One of the scientists who worked with Leonis on the bioweapon came forward," Oshiro says. Corvus and I exchange a glance; this is news that hasn't been made available to the public. "They do not know much but were able to point us in the direction of the tunnels beneath the surface of Levian. There is a Primus research facility underground, where we have reason to believe there may be proof of what happened on Gaia. But sending an official investigation not only would require us to jump through some rather complicated political hoops, but we fear it also could cause panic here. So...we were hoping to ask you to investigate in our stead, and report your findings back to us."

"You have a ship for us?" The words tumble out of me. I can't hold back my excitement. I'm almost ready to agree right off the bat, but Corvus holds up a hand before Oshiro can answer. I deflate a little.

"Last we heard, Gaia was dangerous enough that it required a rapid evacuation, and has been getting worse," he says. "What makes you think it's safe for us to visit now?"

"I won't deny it will be dangerous," Oshiro says. "Most of the drones we've sent have been lost. The ones that have managed to report back have not brought good news. The storms continue, with no sign of stopping."

"Well, I can fly a lot better than some dumbass drones," I say, thumping a fist on the table. Corvus gestures for calm again, but I roll my eyes at him. This is the chance we've been waiting for. Maybe our only chance to get the hell off this planet.

"We need to think carefully about this," he says. "It's not just your life at stake. Unless you plan on leaving the others behind."

"Of course not," I say, but then bite my lip as his words sink in and dampen my mood. He's right, of course. He usually is, loath as I am to admit it. If I agree to this, I'll be agreeing for my entire family, and placing all of us in whatever danger this plan will bring. I turn to Oshiro. "Is it possible for us to land safely?"

"It won't be easy, but we would not be sending you if we believed it wasn't possible," Oshiro says. "Drones have confirmed that the tunnels I spoke of are still intact, and more sheltered from the storms than the surface. Once you are there, you should be safe. The difficult part will be arriving and leaving."

"We can do that," I say, and look at Corvus. "I can do it." His expression is still doubtful. I reach over and touch his arm. "We may just be the only people in the system who can pull it off," I say, very gravely. He always falls for that heroic shit.

But now he grimaces and pulls away. "Don't try to pull that on me."

My overly serious expression cracks, but I don't let up. "Oh, come on, Corvus. At least think about it. This is a chance to get off-planet! And..." I pause, glancing at Oshiro. "Actually, could we have a couple minutes alone to talk?"

"Certainly." They stand up and move to the living room, leaving us.

I scrutinize my brother, trying to get a sense of what he's thinking. "What gives?" I ask, after a few seconds. "I thought we were waiting for a chance to get off-planet. It's not like we've ever been big fans of staying in one place for long. Especially when the situation here is so heated. It'd be nice to have options."

Corvus leans back, his eyes dropping to the table. I stay quiet and let him think. Surely he has to realize how volatile Nibiru is right now. Whether the council decides to let the Gaians stay or go, there will be dissent. Maybe the violent kind. And even aside from that, our family has never belonged here. We've never truly belonged anywhere at all except for a ship. And while we've been accepted here more than anywhere else, only Drom and Pol are citizens here. If things get ugly, the rest of us might get lumped in with the Gaians as outsiders.

"This isn't my decision to make," Corvus says. "Or yours. We need to discuss it with the entire family. We've been building a life here, and you can't expect everyone to drop it and leave. Lyre has her education, and Drom has friends on the island, and..."

"And Pol needs a doctor," I say. "A real doctor, not some superstitious Nibiran who's gonna freak out the moment we mention an alien weapon." He's still dealing with lingering side effects of the Primus bio-weapon and his time in cryosleep, and we've been keeping the fact he was infected with an alien disease to ourselves. But the moment we get a ship, we've got all sorts of options. It's not like the Nibirans are going to be able to drag us back here once they let us free. We could go straight to Deva, or Pax, and if we had funds from a mission like this to pay for a doctor...

"You're right." After a moment's further consideration, he says, "You have my support, as long as the others agree."

I grin. "Good. But keep up the reluctant act, maybe we can squeeze some extra payment out of them." I raise my voice, saying, "Oshiro, come on back!"

The councillor returns to the room, looking not exactly pleased about the informal summons, and takes a seat again. "Yes?"

"I'm still working on my brother, but he raised a good point. We are getting paid for this, right?"

"Of course. You will be rewarded handsomely by the council. And the ship will be yours to keep once the mission is through."

All thoughts of dragging out further payment flee my head. Even better if we don't have to steal the ship. I'm eager to say yes already, but I try to rein myself in, think about this. "One more question."

"Of course. Anything." Oshiro's words come out surprisingly eager. I pause, considering. I wonder what the council's plan is if we say no. Do they have a backup option? How much can we wring out of them if we go forward with this?

"You said you've got a ship for us? Something that doesn't scream 'official Nibiran vessel' if we happen to be spotted by curious drones from our planetary neighbors?"

"As a matter of fact, we do. We've spent the last month piecing it back together," Oshiro says with a small smile.

"Surely you don't mean—" Corvus starts.

"You fixed the *Red Baron*?" I burst out before he can finish the sentence. Corvus gestures for me to lower my voice, with a pointed glance down to where the rest of our siblings might be listening, but I can't contain myself.

"Yes. We seized it as government property after the crash, but we're willing to relinquish it to you if you're willing to do this for us."

"*Baron*'s nowhere near as pretty as *Fortuna*, but it'll do," I say. "Though we'll have to come up with a better name..."

"We don't know the ship," Corvus says, but it's getting harder for his dour input to dampen my excitement. This is a damn good opportunity, and Corvus has to recognize that. "We'll have to assess its condition before we fly the craft into a hostile environment."

"Okay, but if the *Red Baron*'s our ship—*potentially*—you should know there's one other problem," I say, unable to stop smiling despite my words. Time to see just how far the council is willing to go for this.

"Yes?" Oshiro asks.

"I've been in the *Red Baron*'s cockpit before. It's a complicated machine. I'm gonna need a copilot."

Corvus looks at me, his forehead creased. I watch his face clear and then darken as the realization hits him. "You know that's not an option," he says. "Be realistic."

"Where else do you expect to find a decent pilot on Nibiru?" I ask. "The councillor made it pretty clear we can't have anyone government-affiliated, and this planet isn't exactly rife with ships, so-o..."

"I'm open to suggestions," Oshiro says uncertainly. Corvus grits his teeth and looks down.

"Orion Murdock," I say. "He knows the ship, and he's *almost* as good as me behind the wheel."

"And he's locked up in Ca Sineh for his involvement in a plot to wipe out the entirety of Nibiru," Corvus butts in, shaking his head. "Scorpia. That's too much to ask and you know it."

Or is it? If we're really the council's only option, they might just get a lot more flexible about this. Oshiro especially has seemed sympathetic to my pleas to release Orion in the past, and voted to allow it, though the other councillors shut the motion down. I look at them, trying to read their expression.

"Ah." Oshiro looks down at the table, folding their hands in front of them. "That pilot."

"He shouldn't be locked up in the first place," I say. "He helped us. He's not going to be a threat to anybody. And he's good at what he does." I look at Corvus, silently begging for him to back me up.

Corvus meets my gaze. I know he agrees that Orion doesn't deserve to be locked up in Ca Sineh...but I also know he's not personally fond of him. Nor is anyone else in my family. Not only was Orion part of the crew of pirates that plagued our family for years, and the son of the captain who was Momma's personal enemy, but he and I spent years lying to both of our crews about the nature of our relationship.

"*If* we decide to take this job, which we haven't yet," Corvus says, and gives me a meaningful look, "we will need a second pilot."

Not exactly the ringing endorsement I was hoping for, but it'll have to be enough.

"I cannot help with the release of a criminal of his status," Oshiro says. "Not on my own. And even if I could convince the rest of the council, it would take too much time. You'll barely make it back in time for the Gaians' deadline as it is." They hesitate. "There's nothing that can be done . . . officially."

My heart—which started sinking as they began to speak—surges back up again.

"And nonofficially?" I ask, leaning forward.

"First you have to promise me that you'll do no harm to the prison guards or peacekeepers."

"We prom—"

"We can't promise that," Corvus says before I can finish. I frown at him. "But I will personally swear to you that there will be no harm beyond what's absolutely necessary, and no casualties." He hesitates, and then adds, "We'll bring only nonlethal weapons. No guns."

I want to argue, but I bite it back. This is a hard sell and we both know it. I guess I should be thankful that Corvus is willing to go along with the idea at all.

Oshiro looks up at the ceiling rather than at either of us, lips pursing as though they're deciding whether or not they really want to say whatever's on their mind.

"Have you ever considered," they begin, "what would happen to the prisoners in the event Ca Sineh flooded?"

After our conversation is done, I jump at the opportunity to escort Oshiro out, hoping it will give me a chance to slip out the door behind them, but Corvus trails after us and hovers just over my shoulder as we bid each other goodbye. He turns to face me and leans back against the closed door, studying me in silence that only feels heavier the longer it goes on. Stars damn, he really has gotten good at that striking look of disapproval. I bite the inside of my cheek and stare down at the floor, willing myself not to speak up and make it worse.

But of course, I'm the one who breaks first.

"Why are you looking at me like that?" I shift my weight from foot to foot. "What were you expecting?"

"Maybe a little warning that you were keeping a stash of illegal drugs in our house?"

I throw my hands up.

"I told you I had a job! What did you think I was doing?"

"You told me it was *mostly legal*."

"I mean... it's dried stuff, not living plants, so it's not *incredibly* illegal."

Corvus pinches the bridge of his nose between two fingers and shakes his head. "I didn't realize Eridanus and Halon stooped to transporting drugs."

"Stooped to? We used to transport drugs!" I say. "And, well, arms dealing hasn't been exactly booming since..."

"Since Titan."

"Yeah." I drop my eyes, fighting back a burst of shame. I've been avoiding mentioning the planet as much as I can, because every time it comes up, he gets that *look* again. "So they're branching out." I clear my throat and shrug. "They offered to bring me on board at one point, but... they don't have enough room for all of us."

"If you're so desperate to get off-planet, maybe you should've gone."

I blink in shock, my head snapping up to him again. "And leave you all? No. You don't mean that."

"You know I would never *want* you to leave," he says, his voice softening. "But it's clear you're unhappy here. I don't blame you, but I can't watch you bring us all down with your recklessness. The rest of us are building lives here. *Normal* lives."

"What? I..." I'm so taken aback that it takes a moment for words to come. "This is who we are. Who we've always been. We're criminals. Smugglers." I roll my eyes. "One little good deed and suddenly everyone thinks we're knights in shining fucking armor."

"We saved the system. It's not just one little good deed. People aren't going to forget that, especially not here, and neither should we." He shakes his head. "You can't be some drug dealer lurking in the shadows anymore. Your actions are going to have consequences for all of us. You need to think about that."

"I think about it every stars-damned day! You think I'm doing this just for me? You think I turned down that chance to get off this stupid planet for *me*?" I take a step forward, glaring at him. "Things might be good for us right now, and you might be happy playing at being a fisherman, but Nibiru isn't always gonna be safe for us. Nowhere is. Maybe the situation here blows up in everyone's faces, maybe they find out we lied to them about the *Red Baron*, maybe Leonis tells everyone we were involved in what happened to Titan...I don't know what it'll be, but I know something is gonna catch up with us eventually. We can't hide here."

"So we run?"

"Or we fight. Either way, we need a ship. We need options. We need to be *together* on this." My words come out almost pleading. I don't understand how he doesn't get this. He knows this isn't the life for us.

Corvus sighs, a long, defeated sound. Then he steps forward and reaches out to clasp my hand.

"Okay," he says. "Together. Always."

*　　*　　*

Later that night, I gather everyone at the kitchen table to tell them the news. Even after Corvus's dour response, I expect my younger siblings to be excited, but instead my announcement is met with blank stares.

"Leaving Nibiru?" Pol asks, after a moment of silence. "Forever?"

"Not forever. We'll just go back to mainly living on a ship. Traveling around again."

The twins exchange a look I can't decipher. Lyre purses her lips.

"So back to smuggling? When we only have access to Nibiru and Deva, and Nibiru's economy is in its current state? That seems inadvisable," she says.

Her lack of enthusiasm is disheartening, but luckily, I've already considered this argument. "You're thinking too small," I say. "Even if we can't turn a decent profit on Nibiru for a while, if Gaia is really accessible, we can scavenge for tech left behind there. Ship materials out of Titan while it's in a legal gray zone. Partner with Eri and Halon to get access to Pax. We've got options."

"Fair points. But what about my studies? Are you expecting me to up and leave without finishing my degree?"

I thought attending the university was just something to keep Lyre busy while we were stuck here, but from the look on her face now, I'm guessing I miscalculated. "I mean...an education here is worthless on the other planets. Surely you'd rather get a degree on Deva, right? You still want to settle there eventually, don't you?"

Lyre lets out a small laugh. "Do you have any idea how much that would cost? It's free here, and would open more doors for us on Nibiru. On an accelerated track, I can finish in two years."

Before I can answer, Drom chimes in, "This job sounds boring anyway. Can't you do it yourself and swing back for us after?"

"Not like there's gonna be anyone to fight," Pol agrees.

"I..." Words fail me as fear squeezes my chest. Shit, I wasn't expecting this. Not at all. And the idea of splitting the family up fills me with cold terror. I always feared we would separate in a moment of catastrophe, but maybe it's the times of peace I should've been afraid of. The allure of a normal life that's possible for everyone except for me. I look at Corvus for support, but his expression is thoughtful, and he says nothing. In a moment of panic, I turn to Lyre and say, "I'll pay for your degree on Deva."

"Deal," she says, so eagerly that I realize I probably have no clue what I just agreed to.

"Are we bribing each other now?" Corvus finally speaks up, tone heavy with disapproval.

"What do we get?" Drom asks.

I try not to grimace. Corvus is probably right—this is a bad idea—but it's too late to turn back now. "What do you want?"

After considering for a moment, she says, "The deed to the houseboat."

That's...surprisingly reasonable for Drom, and easily doable. "Okay. Done. Pol?"

"A Primus gun."

"Ugh. Fine." The things give me the creeps and will be a pain in the ass to find, but at least it's probably less expensive than what I've promised the others.

"Oh, shit, that's a good idea," Drom says. "Too late to change my answer?"

"If she's changing, *I* want the houseboat," Pol says.

"Then I'm not changing."

"You already said—"

"You two can work it out among yourselves," I say, loudly, before they can spiral into a full-on argument. "Everybody happy?" One by one, my siblings nod their heads...except for Corvus, who says nothing.

Not even that can ruin my mood now. I break into a broad grin. "Great. Now let's start planning a jailbreak."

CHAPTER SEVEN

The Jailbreak

Corvus

I sit at the wheel of our stolen hoverboat while Scorpia paces behind me. Both of us wear masks that conceal our faces; two local heroes can't be seen springing a prison break, after all. The island is quiet at this time of night, though the faint sound of music drifts to us over the ocean. Whether it's coming from land or sea, it's hard to tell.

I'm tense sitting out here, vulnerable, in the waves. This would be easier if Nibiru's skies darkened at night like the Earth-imitating light cycles of spaceships do, but this planet, like all of them, is locked with one side forever facing red Nova Vita. The sun beats down on us, and even though we've done nothing wrong yet, it feels like someone will realize our plan at any moment. But we need to be in position for when Scorpia's contact hacks through Ca Sineh's security and triggers a flood evacuation.

"Damn, it feels nice to get back to some good ol' fashioned criminal activity together," Scorpia says. She stops pacing to lean against the back of my seat, looking out at the prison with me.

Only the wide disk of the upper part of the building is visible. The cells and the rest of the prison are deep below the surface. "It's been too long, don't you think?"

"Not really." I was content with life as it was. Not that I expect her to understand that. The twins would be having a lot more fun with this than I would, but they're off with Lyre, preparing for the trip. We told them we needed them there, stocking up on food and other supplies, but in reality Scorpia and I agreed we wanted to keep them out of this in case it goes wrong. Oshiro was very clear that they won't be able to help us if we're caught.

"You're no fun," Scorpia says.

"I prefer legal entertainment."

"That's an oxymoron," she says. "Unless we're talking about Deva. Why couldn't we have gotten stranded on Deva? At least things would be interesting there."

"If this were Deva, your pirate friend would have been executed," I say. "And likely us as well."

Before she can respond, a siren's wail cuts through the quiet night. I straighten up in my seat, eyes locked on the flat disk of the prison ahead. Was the alarm meant to go off? Does that mean the plan is working, or that it's already gone awry?

Scorpia's comm rings. She picks it up, listens, and hangs up again. "Go," she says.

I take off toward the prison. Scorpia, clinging to the back of my chair, lets out an excited whoop barely audible above the rush of wind.

Ahead of us, an egg-shaped pod breaches the surface and bobs on the waves. I've never seen the cells of Ca Sineh before—they seem impossibly small to house a human being—but the way Scorpia leans forward to squint at the numbers on the side means it must be one. As Oshiro explained to us, when the prison thinks it's flooding, it detaches each individual cell and sends them up to the surface for an emergency evacuation. They'll float there until someone arrives to let the prisoners out.

"Not him," she shouts. "We're looking for cell 435."

All around us, more oval cells are bursting up through the water, released from the prison below. I swing the boat in a wide arc around the main building, letting Scorpia inspect the cells one by one. My nerves heighten with each rejected pod. It's only a matter of time until the peacekeepers arrive, and I'd been hoping to avoid any fighting.

Scorpia lets out a triumphant shout, slapping a hand against my shoulder hard enough to sting.

"There! That's him!" She points out a cell floating to our right. I turn sharply enough that she barely keeps her grip on the chair.

As soon as we pull up to hover alongside the cell, I stop the boat and stand.

"Hold us here," I say, and jump over the gap to the cell. It rocks beneath me, and I nearly lose my footing as my bad leg slips across the wet surface.

The cell doors, automatically sealed during an evacuation and only opened with two guards' thumbprints, present a second challenge to breaking prisoners out. But this is one we were already equipped for. My Primus knife has been locked up in my room ever since we came to Nibiru, because of both its dubious legality on this planet and all the bad memories associated with it. Taking it out now feels like I'm dangerously close to opening the floodgates on those memories, but the immediacy of the situation at hand is enough to keep them at bay.

I jam the blade into the crevices of the door and saw my way through. It's an agonizingly slow process. Whatever the Nibirans used to build these doors, it must be incredibly strong to resist a Primus blade like this. Soon sweat trickles down the back of my neck, and the muscles in my arms ache. I wipe my brow and gauge the situation around me, but we're not in immediate danger yet. After a few more minutes of struggling and a final heave, I pull the door open enough for a body to squeeze through.

"Orion," I call out above the wind. "It's the Kaisers."

Orion edges forward so I can see him, squinting up at me in disbelief and raising one arm to ward off the sunlight. He's thinner than I remember, his tan skin bleached a few shades paler. I'm surprised how quickly imprisonment must have affected him; it's only been a few months since I saw him during our fight aboard the *Red Baron*. I've never been inside Ca Sineh, but everyone has heard the stories. I used to think they were exaggerated. Life in prison sounds so clean compared to Deva's public executions and Titan's brutal sense of justice. But watching the way Orion stares up at the sunlight like he never thought he'd see it again, I'm less certain.

Even aside from the change in his appearance, the sight of him is jolting in a way I didn't expect. He's another reminder of a piece of my past I'd rather leave behind. A piece that is floating in another one of these cells, where he belongs.

Nobody but me knows the truth that Captain Murdock revealed during our final battle to save Nibiru three months ago: that before they were rivals, he and Momma were romantically involved, and that I'm his biological son. Momma never wanted me to know, and I wish I had never found out. I considered telling my siblings but ultimately decided to keep it to myself.

As far as I know, Orion isn't aware of any of this, either. Murdock picked him up from the streets of Deva, so there's no shared blood between us, nor any relationship akin to siblings, but there's still a strange connection. Having him around may mean digging up a truth I'd rather leave buried.

After a moment's hesitation, I sheathe my knife and extend a hand to Orion to help him up. He sways slightly as I let go, staring down at the water and then up at the sky.

"Wind," he mutters hoarsely. "Forgot about wind."

The moment he's safely over the edge of the boat, Scorpia abandons the wheel and pulls him into a tight hug. I turn away to let them have their moment, scanning the surrounding waters for any signs of the peacekeepers. A few boats approach on the horizon, but we should be long gone by the time they arrive. Relief swells in my chest. It seems I'll be able to get through this without hurting anyone after all.

"What did I tell you?" Scorpia asks. "I got you out. Now where's Izra? What's her cell number?"

My attention snaps back to them as Orion mumbles out a number, still distracted by the wind ruffling his hair. He stares out at the world like he can hardly believe that it's real.

"That's not part of the plan," I say. The already-risky plan that involves bringing a pirate on board. I'm not letting some unstable deserter on our ship.

"It is now."

"The councillor is already putting themself on the line for this. If we lose their trust—"

"What about Izra's trust?" Scorpia's voice lashes like a whip. She helps Orion into a seat and turns to glare at me. "The council doesn't need us. Izra does. No one else is gonna save a criminal like her. And she helped us out, same as Orion. We can't leave her here." She pauses. "Even if she is a terrifying woman with a gun for an arm."

"And then we do what with her?" I ask. "We can't leave her on Nibiru. She'll have nowhere to go."

Scorpia pauses, and then says, "Well, half of our muscle is out of commission."

I turn to the peacekeepers' boats, close enough now that I

can make out the officers standing at the helm with their stun-sticks in hand. My muscles tense in preparation even as my heart sinks. It's been a long time since I had to fight, and my promise to Oshiro weighs heavily on me. A promise still means something to me, even if it doesn't for my sister. But I've argued enough with Scorpia to know I'm not going to get anywhere with this.

"Fine." I jerk my chin at the wheel. "You drive. We're going to have company soon."

There are too many damn cells to check, and we were lucky to find Orion before the peacekeepers arrived. That luck doesn't strike a second time. Boats pull up on either side of us as we search for Izra, and I check to make sure that my face mask is secure and the tattoos on my arm are covered.

"Get down," I tell Orion. He flattens himself against the floor of the boat without being told twice, and I grab the baton hidden under one of the seats. At a flick of a switch, it comes to life, electricity dancing up and down the plastic length of the weapon. It's peacekeeper-issue, meant to stun rather than kill. I'm not sure how Scorpia managed to get her hands on it—they're not legal for citizens, let alone noncitizens—but I'm grateful to have a weapon that won't require me to take a life. We might be breaking the law here, but I'm not going to kill peacekeepers trying to do their job. I'm not that person anymore.

I thought it would be hard to hurt people again. But my muscles are all too eager to remember a soldier's stance.

When the first peacekeeper steps onto the side of our boat, I lunge forward without a moment's thought, lashing out with the baton. His muscles seize, and he falls over the side with a mighty splash. Part of me fills with an old and deeply ingrained satisfaction; another part of me worries. I didn't consider what would happen if they fell, paralyzed, into the water. Will he survive the fall?

No time to look back and check—two more are already making the leap over to our craft. I've barely dealt with them when another two come from the other side, rushing toward Scorpia while I'm distracted. I tackle one to the deck, sending both of us sliding across the slippery surface. The other is on Scorpia. The entire craft jerks to the left as she loses control of the vehicle, nearly sending me and the man I'm entangled with off the edge of the boat.

I grab one of the seats to prevent myself from falling, and the peacekeeper clings to my leg. The boat is still listing heavily to one side, and I struggle to hang on, the weight of the man dragging at me. I kick at him once, twice—and finally dislodge him with a boot to the face.

Near the wheel, Scorpia is still grappling with the last of the officers. As I get to my feet, she shoves him off. He stumbles across the wet deck. I lurch forward, my own footing unsteady. Before I can reach him, Orion juts a leg out from his hiding place, kicking the officer's feet out from under him and sending him toppling over the edge. He and Scorpia share a smile before she retakes the wheel and gets us back on course.

The ocean around us is strewn with floating cells and peacekeepers treading water—and beyond, even more peacekeeper boats are approaching. Many more. I curse and make my way to the front of the boat, leaning down to shout in Scorpia's ear. "We're running out of time."

"Just a little longer," she shouts back, her gaze never leaving the water ahead. "We can do this."

Ca Sineh is a small prison, but it still seems like an impossible number of cells in the water around us. I grit my teeth and keep my mouth shut as Scorpia winds through the mess surrounding the prison, even as the peacekeepers draw closer and closer. Finally, we find the one we're looking for. I jump over to the cell, this time employing Scorpia's help while Orion keeps the boat steady.

The moment we pry the door open, Izra lunges for us, a makeshift shiv gripped in her hand. Scorpia yelps and scrambles back, nearly toppling into the water.

"Well if that's how you're gonna be, maybe we won't rescue you!" she shouts down at Izra, while I only glare at the woman. Orion seems rightfully ruffled by his experience in the underwater prison, but Izra looks the same as always: all lean rage, her one good eye narrowed in fury, the other a mess of scar tissue. I thought I could stomach this, but the black rectangle on her pale wrist, covering the war-brand like the one I wear, makes me sick. *Deserter*, a voice in the back of my mind whispers. *Traitor*. It shouldn't matter anymore. But still the feeling is there, simmering in the back of my mind. Still my gut says we can't trust her.

Izra's scowl doesn't fade as she recognizes us, though she does let her weapon clatter to the floor.

"Come on," Scorpia yells, jumping over to the boat. "They're closing in on us, let's go!"

After a moment, I hold out a hand. Izra takes it, and I pull her up. I drop her hand like it's burned me the moment her footing is sure, but she pays me no notice, already jumping off onto the boat. Only once we're both on do I realize her left arm—the one with the built-in Primus weapon—is locked up in some kind of metal mechanism. The arm hangs down at her side, and she moves awkwardly, hefting the weight.

Orion jumps up to hug her as she gets close; she tolerates his embrace for a couple of seconds before she shoves him off and takes a seat.

I glance back at the peacekeepers' boats as Scorpia takes off toward land. This little hoverboat will outrun them with ease, but it doesn't make much of a difference. I move over to my sister and bend down to speak in her ear.

"You know how easy this will be to trace back to us," I say. "Orion disappearing from the prison would be one thing, but both of them—"

"I know, I know," Scorpia says. She's grinning despite my words, clearly pleased with how this operation has gone. "It's all right, Corvus. By the time they come looking for us, we'll be off-planet and way out of their reach."

"You do realize we'll have to come back after the mission is done?" And by going off the plan and betraying Oshiro's trust, we may have lost one of our only allies here.

Scorpia shrugs. My words don't even put a dent in her smile.

"We'll see about that," she says. "As far as I can tell, there's no reason not to just beam the information back to the council and head wherever we want, right?" She sits up straighter, grin widening. "A trip to Deva sounds pretty nice."

As the words sink in, I realize how very foolish I am. Maybe she was right in our last conversation—I've forgotten who we are. Who she is, always saying one thing and meaning another. It's possible Scorpia never planned to come back to Nibiru from the very start. Now that she has a ship, she can do whatever she wants.

I take a seat on the edge of the boat. The two pirates are sitting on the other side, talking in lowered voices with their heads close together. All of this for them...I can only hope Scorpia isn't a fool to trust them.

I sigh and look out at the open ocean, wondering if this will be the last time I see it.

CHAPTER EIGHT

The Crew Assembled

Scorpia

The jailbreak went about as smoothly as we could've hoped for, but it's only a matter of time before the authorities figure out which prisoners are missing and make the connection to a certain loudmouthed off-worlder who was very outspoken about their release. We need to get off-planet before that happens. We ditch the hoverboat and race straight to our new ship.

The Nibirans have popped out all the dents and washed off years of dirt and rust and stars-know-what else was clinging to the hull, so the *Red Baron* looks practically brand-new. The ship is still ugly as hell, a bulky old cargo ship long past its expiration date, but at least it's clean, and—fingers crossed—functional.

And, most importantly, it's all mine.

I have about five seconds to savor the sight before I spot the twins and Lyre arguing at the base of the cargo ramp. They should be ready and waiting on board, but instead, both of the twins have their bags at their feet on the dock.

"What the hell is going on?" I ask as I approach. "We gotta go now."

They all turn to look at me. Lyre is hiding her anxiety behind a thin veneer of irritation, Drom has her jaw set, and Pol is caught somewhere between his twin's expression and guilt.

Drom's the first one to speak up. "We're not coming."

"What do you mean, not coming?"

"I believe the concept is self-explanatory," Lyre says, a waver in her tone betraying all the worry she's trying to hide. "And since she's not coming, of course Pol isn't, either."

Of course the stars-damned twins have to pull something like this now. I blow out a frustrated breath and look back at Corvus, but he's busy glaring at the two ex-pirates who are hovering nearby.

"You two need to get on the ship in case the authorities show up," I say, jerking my head at Orion and Izra. "Lyre, Corvus, go with them and make sure everything's locked down for launch. I'll handle this."

Lyre looks like she wants to argue, but Corvus takes her arm and leads her into the cargo bay, and the two ex-pirates follow close behind, leaving me with the twins. I fold my arms over my chest and look from Drom's stubborn expression to Pol's half-guilty one. "So who's gonna tell me what's going on? We already talked this over and made our deals. You agreed."

"That was before you decided to spring a jailbreak," Drom says. "The council never agreed to this, did they? You're not planning on coming back to Nibiru."

"They . . . they didn't *not* agree," I say, unable to bring myself to lie outright.

"I should've known. You're always full of shit. Pol and I are staying here."

A surge of that old fear rushes over me again. They want to

leave, like I always knew they would. "Like hell you are," I say. "You belong with us."

"Some of us have a life, Scorpia," she says to me, hands clenching at her sides. "If that prissy-ass Gaian had even an ounce of interest in you, you wouldn't be in a rush to leave, either."

I push down a spark of hurt. "Yes. I would. Because the family comes first."

"Oh, are you spewing Momma quotes now, too?" she asks, and barks out a laugh. "Guess I shouldn't be surprised. You're just as bad as her sometimes."

Silence falls like a guillotine. We've barely mentioned Momma—or the loss of her—in the last few months, and never like this, as a weapon against each other. We all just nurse our own quiet pain, the same way we always have. After a few moments of staring at Drom, struggling to come up with something to say, the whirlwind of emotions inside me gradually condenses into a cold anger. How dare she compare me to Momma after everything I've done for us? How can she possibly think that? I'm nothing like her.

"You know what? Fine. Stay, if you want. Figure out how to take care of yourself. And figure out how to take care of Pol, too." I jab a finger at Pol, too angry to care that he already looks mortified after Drom's words. "We still don't know what the bioweapon and the cryosleep and the Gaians did to him. For all we know, he's just gonna get more sick. I hope you're ready to accept responsibility for whatever happens to him."

Guilt hits me the second I shut my mouth. I know it's not fair to use Pol against her, especially not when he's standing right there. I know I'm only lashing out because I'm scared. But I can't bring myself to take any of it back when it might be the only thing that convinces them to stay with us.

After a moment, Drom bends down, grabs her pack, and heads

up the ramp into the cargo bay. Pol does the same, with one last look back at me that makes the guilty pit in my stomach grow to twice the size.

Before I can follow, Corvus emerges from the ship, gun in his hand. "Someone's coming our way," he says, nodding toward the island.

I turn and see that he's right. A lone figure is rushing down the dock toward us. I doubt one person could do much to stop us right now...but they also have no reason to be here except for us. We're the only spaceship docked here.

"Could it be Oshiro?" I ask, squinting down the dock at whoever it is.

"Doesn't look tall enough," Corvus says.

"Then..." I stop because as the figure draws closer, I suddenly recognize them. That ramrod-straight posture. Those long dark waves of hair. I know exactly who it is. "Shey," I say, her name barely a breath.

"What is she doing here?" Corvus asks, his tone openly accusatory.

"I don't know any more than you do." Shey clearly had no interest in speaking to me at the inauguration party. Why would she be here now? Stars, *why* now, when we're about to rush off-planet and I have no time to spare for her?

But I'm also not going to leave this planet—maybe for the last time—without knowing why she came. Corvus looks at me, awaiting an explanation, but I only gesture for him to get back. "Let me talk to her."

"We need to go, Scorpia. The peacekeepers could arrive any minute."

"I know, I know. Just...give me a minute."

He shakes his head, but retreats into the ship, leaving me alone to meet her. She comes to a stop a few paces in front of me, breathing hard, her hair in disarray. She's wearing formal robes and has a small bag slung over one shoulder.

For a few moments, we only stare at each other.

"Shey," I say, finally. A surge of complex emotions tangles up my thoughts and stills my tongue. I don't know how to feel, coming face-to-face with someone I had tried to resolve myself to never talking to again. Now, here she is in front of me, and all of a sudden it's like that ache in my chest never went away. For the first time in months, something I want is within my grasp, and then she has to show up just in time to taunt my heart with her presence.

Unless she's here for something else entirely. Such as the two highly wanted criminals currently on board my new ship. Does the council already have suspicions? Would they have stooped so low as to send Shey to stall us, knowing my weakness for her?

"Er, sorry," I say, and clear my throat. My heart is pounding, but I need to act normal. Which, for me, means... "Ambassador Leonis," I say in an exaggeratedly formal tone, with an equally over-the-top bow. "What an honor... no, a pleasure... no, dare I say a *privilege*, to be blessed by your presence."

Shey lets out a soft huff of a laugh as I straighten back up. She smiles up at me in a way that, even now, makes me melt a little.

"Glad to see you haven't changed a bit," she says. "Though my own status has. I'm no longer an ambassador, I'm afraid, so you'll have to find another excuse for your theatrics."

"Huh?" I drop the ridiculous act instantly, my brow furrowing. "What do you mean?"

"Haven't you seen the news?" Seeing my look of confusion, she continues, "In light of the debacle at her inauguration, Gaia's new president has decided to relieve me from my office due to my 'controversial' family ties. With the current state of things, I can't say I disagree with the decision."

"Well, damn," I mutter, unsure what else to say.

"I wasn't terribly qualified for the position anyway."

"I doubt whatever stuffy old person they replaced you with is going to do a better job."

She smiles, but it's tinged with sadness.

"So, my brief political career has ground to a halt, and there aren't many opportunities for Primus research on this planet," she says. As she pauses, my heart stutters while I try to figure out what she's going to say next. What does this mean for her, for me? Why is she here? Is she no longer so concerned about our "different walks of life," as she put it, now that she's no longer in the public eye? Then, she says, "I'd likely go insane with too much free time, so I was glad to hear from your sister."

Another pause while I try—and fail—to make sense of that. "My . . . sister?"

Shey's brow furrows.

"Didn't she tell you that she asked me to come here?"

"No. What . . . wait, which sister are we even talking about?" I ask, growing more confused by the second and trying to fight off the bitter disappointment creeping up on me.

Right on cue, I hear footsteps on the ramp behind me.

"Oh, good. You made it," Lyre says, coming to a stop at my side.

I should've guessed. Not even Drom would be callous enough to spring Shey on me without any warning whatsoever, but Lyre is exactly that cold when she wants to be.

"What is this about?" I ask, as she steps closer and exchanges a formal Gaian greeting with Shey, both arms crossed in an X over their chests. "A little warning would have been nice, you know," I mutter more quietly.

"Well, I wanted to make sure you were sober for this," Lyre says, making no effort to drop the volume of her tone. My cheeks heat.

"What the hell is that supposed to mean?"

She ignores me, turning instead to Shey, who is starting to look rather bewildered.

"Thank you for coming," Lyre says. She makes a small, one-handed Gaian gesture I recognize as a signal of respect. "And I was sorry to hear about you being removed from your position. You were an adept ambassador in a most difficult time."

"I appreciate it." Shey gestures something back that I don't recognize. I grit my teeth. Gaian manners always grate on me, but it's especially annoying now, when I'm caught in the middle and no one is giving me any clarity.

"Okay, okay, can we cut the Gaian niceties and get to an explanation of what the hell is going on?" I snap. "We're supposed to be rushing off-planet right about now, Lyre, so what is she doing here?"

Shey wears the same affronted face I've seen her make dozens of times at my harsh off-worlder manners, but Lyre merely gazes up at me.

"Well, we were about to set off on a dangerous trip to Gaia without out a single Gaian to help us navigate the planet," she explains, with all the patience of explaining something complicated to a small child. "It seemed ill-advised to me. And, seeing as there isn't exactly an overabundance of Gaians that we can trust on a covert mission, and Shey has been recently relieved of her other duties, I figured she would make a great fit."

"Wait, wait, wait." I can see the logic in what she's saying, and yet... "You invited her on our mission? Without even running it by me?"

"Well," Lyre says, "you invited two pirates, so I didn't believe we were being particularly picky about who we're bringing along."

"Pirates?" Shey asks, aghast. "Is that some sort of joke?"

Both of them are making me want to rip my hair out right

now. I'd really love to give Lyre an earful, and have more than a few minutes to talk to Shey without committing to spending weeks with her on an off-planet mission, but we don't have time for any of it.

Corvus emerges from the cargo bay. "Scorpia," he says, "we need to go. Now." A moment later, his eyes find the luggage Shey brought, and he looks at me with fresh suspicion.

Regardless of the glare, I'm happy to see him right now. "One sec," I say to Shey, holding up a finger, and race up the ramp. I grab Corvus by the arm and pull him to the side, glancing over my shoulder at Shey one more time before focusing on him. "Lyre invited Shey to come along," I say. "What do you think?" I know what I think already, but I'm not sure whether or not I can trust my feelings when it comes to Shey. Plus, being in charge of my family is a daunting-enough task. Now, with the addition of a couple of ex-pirates and potentially an ex-ambassador, things are getting awfully complicated.

At least I can rely on Corvus to be straightforward. His frown has become almost reassuring in its familiarity. He lets out a world-weary sigh, and says, "I think this is a mess already."

"That's kind of a given, with our family."

"But I think Lyre is right," he says. "Shey would make a good addition to the crew. She knows Gaia, she knows the Primus. I trust her."

I blink at him, taken aback for a moment. Corvus had some serious issues last time Shey was on board, and spent the whole time believing she was some kind of Gaian double agent, so it's especially relieving to hear that he trusts her now. And if I'm being honest, it's also a relief to hear that this is *actually* a good idea, rather than just seeming like it because of my own bias. Despite everything that's happened between us, I can't deny I was eager to invite Shey on board the moment the opportunity presented itself.

I've missed her, even though she's been determined to ignore my existence.

"But the real question is whether or not you can handle her being around," Corvus says, as if reading my thoughts. I scoff at him, flapping a hand.

"What? Come on. I'm not some heartbroken teenager. I can be an adult about this." He looks doubtful. "I can! It's not…" I start to say it's *not a big deal*, but my tongue trips over the words. Corvus will know they're a lie straightaway. I clear my throat, rubbing the back of my neck with one hand. "I can push my feelings aside for one mission. I mean, you know I want this more than anybody. It's our chance to get a ship. To be able to go off-planet again. I'm not gonna let anything screw that up, and I wouldn't be inviting Shey if I thought it was going to be an issue."

After a moment, Corvus nods. "All right," he says. "But is she aware you're not planning on coming back to Nibiru?"

"Well…" I hadn't considered that. "We can figure that out once we get there."

Instead of arguing, he merely says, "You're the captain."

I realize, with a jolt, how long it's been since I heard that title. How long it's been since I had a ship to let me claim it. Hearing it now, a grin spreads across my face. Despite all of these complications arising, this still feels right. It feels like what I'm supposed to be doing. What I was born to do. This ship will never be *Fortuna*, but it's still a big step toward the future I want.

"Damn right I am," I say. "Now, one last thing before we go…"

Since there are no peacekeepers coming for us yet, and we'll be off-planet in a few minutes even if they show up now, I insist on gathering everyone on the dock for a few minutes before we take off. Everyone grumbles about it, especially Corvus, but at the end of the day I *am* the captain. So they obediently gather at the base of the ramp and watch as I pull out a can of red spray paint and step up to my new ship with a grin.

"This thing may be irredeemably hideous, but we can at least give her a new name." I spray the letters blocky and bold while the rest of the crew watches. Once it's done, I wipe my hands on my jumpsuit, step back, and admire the work.

"It's crooked," Lyre says.

"Shut up. It's perfect."

"Really crooked," Pol agrees. "But I like the name."

I roll my eyes, and take my first steps onto *Memoria*. Once I'm just inside the cargo bay, I pause, looking back at my make-shift crew and wondering if I should say something. They wait on the dock in uncomfortable silence, nobody quite sure what to make of the others now that they're all gathered together for the first time. I can't say I blame them. I'm probably the only one who would vouch for every person here on the mission...yet now my nerves are getting the best of me. We've got my family of crimi-nals and all of our various baggage, two pirates freshly liberated from prison, and a former Gaian ambassador. How the hell is this group supposed to get through a mission without killing one another? How am *I* supposed to find a way to lead them? I barely managed to keep my own siblings together last time we were all on a ship.

I try to think of something inspirational to say to break the silence, but Drom beats me to it.

"We seriously bringing two of Scorpia's exes along on a job?" she asks.

My cheeks burn. *Shit.* I was really hoping to approach that in a more delicate way. Now my mouth hangs open as I struggle to find words to make this any less awkward.

Orion and Shey, wearing matching, perplexed expressions, both look at Izra. She's too busy rolling her eye in annoyance to notice at first. The moment she does, her face hardens in a deeply disgusted scowl.

"Never in a million years," she says.

After a further moment of confusion, their gazes find each other instead. Orion's eyebrows shoot up.

"Wow," he says, genuinely impressed.

Shey, considerably less so, looks over at me and says, "Well, I can assure everyone that I am here for professional reasons, and professional reasons only."

I clear my throat, trying to pretend that doesn't sting. "Yeah, yeah, we're all professionals here. Glad we got that out of the way. So, now there's no need to bring that up, uh, ever again." Drom grins at my glare. Shey is staring down at her feet now, and Orion is still looking at her. "And we need to get going. Come on, Orion. Everyone else, strap in for launch."

I stride off without another word. After a moment, Orion's footsteps follow.

Before now, I didn't think about how strange it would be to walk on board the ship of our longtime enemies. Not so long ago, we fought a bloody battle here to save the planet we're now leaving. Corvus was nearly killed by Orion's adopted father, and Izra skewered me through the shoulder with that horrible alien weapon of hers before she turned to our side. The scar gives a throb of old pain at the memory, and even though she's tentatively an ally now, I have to admit I'm glad that her gun arm is locked up in metal casing.

Anyway, it's not their ship anymore. It's mine, and unlike the complicated circumstances that left me with *Fortuna*, there's no question about ownership this time. No trouble inherited from Momma to make me feel like I have to follow in her footsteps. Maybe it's good that we don't have to live on a ship haunted by her ghost.

Even though this craft is even older than *Fortuna* was, it feels less lived-in; the hallways seem cold and hard and impersonal, and the place stinks of whatever chemicals the Nibirans used to clean it. The closed doorways we pass remind me how little I know about the layout of this ship. I'll have to take my time exploring later. For now, I make my way straight to the cockpit.

As I step in I can't help but relive my last time in this room: watching my beloved *Fortuna* self-destruct, clutching Corvus's hand as we careened toward a crash-landing on Nibiru. But then I shake it off, force myself to look at the cockpit with fresh eyes, and let myself be dazzled by it. This cockpit is a pilot's dream, wide open and comfortable, with an expansive dashboard far beyond what my old ship was equipped with. I sink into the cushiony lining of the main pilot's chair, sigh with contentment, and spin in a couple circles to take it all in. This is a far cry from my old seat, with all its sweat and whiskey stains, and the cramped space I used to call home. *Fortuna*, forgive me, but this is clearly an upgrade.

Orion takes the copilot's seat and grins at the look on my face. "Not too shabby, huh?"

"Can't complain." I trail my fingertips lovingly over the dashboard before opening up the diagnostics, and I'm pleased to see the hologram flicker up showing red, red, red. All systems go. I spin the image of the ship, shut it off, and move through the launch procedures. Feeling Orion's eyes on me, I ask, "How's the copilot chair?"

"Haven't sat here since I was first learning the ropes," he says with a laugh. "But it feels great. Feels like freedom."

I grin at him, pleased that he doesn't sound miffed about the demotion to copilot. "Looks like the Nibirans did a good job of piecing the ship back together. I thought she was scrap metal for sure."

"At least the damn algae-eaters did something right." Though he says the words breezily, there's an edge to his tone now, a flicker of anger across his face. For some reason my first instinct is to leap to the Nibirans' defense—they've done a lot for me and my family, after all—but I stifle it. Orion has the right to be angry after what they did to him. Being locked up in Ca Sineh is one of the worst fates I can imagine.

"Hey," I say softly, reaching out to touch his hand where it grips his armrest. "You're out now. And you're never going back there. I'm gonna take care of you, like I promised I would."

He nods, silent, in a way that seems to end the conversation. But when I try to pull my hand back, he takes it in his own.

"Thank you," he says. "For rescuing me."

"Of course." I smile, but feel a flicker of uncertainty as I note the way he's looking at me. What would Shey think if she saw this moment? I shouldn't care. She's the one who left me. And yet...some part of me does care. Cares, and hopes that Orion isn't expecting us to fall in bed together again. At least not until I figure out this tangled situation. I squeeze his hand and pull away. "You're my friend. I wouldn't leave you behind."

If it offends him that I'm clearly pulling back, he doesn't show it. Instead, he just grins and says, "And the best pilot you know. Can't forget that."

"Second best," I shoot back, relief lightening my shoulders, and run my hands across the dashboard in front of me. Damn, it feels good to be behind the wheel again, even before we've lifted off. I already feel more at home than I ever did on the houseboat. That gnawing restlessness has settled into a certainty that I'm where I'm supposed to be. "All right, here we go," I murmur, and check the indicators to confirm everyone is safely strapped in before starting launch procedures. A grin stretches across my face as I hear the rumble of the engine come to life. This ship isn't *Fortuna*—no ship will ever be *Fortuna*—but she feels close. Painfully, wonderfully close.

And this is it. My family's chance for a fresh start, together. A new ship that, if we're lucky, will one day feel like a new home. And now I don't have to try to be Momma's daughter, or the hero Nibiru thinks I am, or anyone else. I've got a whole system of possible futures to explore, and all the freedom I could ever ask for.

The moment we launch, my heart soars up, up, among the stars.

Once we're safely out in open space, I leave Orion to watch the cockpit so I can wander my new ship. I'm not sure yet if it will ever be what *Fortuna* was to me, but for now, I'm just grateful to have a place to call my own—and a way off-planet, of course. I was really getting tired of all the sea and storms and fish for every meal.

Though, despite my excitement over gaining a ship, I still can't shake the eeriness of wandering these halls and thinking of the old fights here. Just being here gets my heart pumping. I find the spot where Izra shot me during our last fight, another where she shot Drom, a hallway Captain Murdock once dragged a half-conscious and bleeding Corvus down to throw him at Momma's feet. Bad memories of bad fights, places I swear I can almost see the years-old bloodstains.

But none of that is the ship's fault, and we've got time to make new memories. I trail my fingers along the metal corridors, wander the huge mess hall and the kitchen, glance down the corridor with the crew's quarters. There's also a whole second floor belowdecks, where Lyre is already hard at work acquainting herself with the engine. I shudder a little as I step into the empty cargo bay and see the door to the medical area on the opposite wall, and retreat before my brain can pull up the image of Corvus with the bio-weapon flasks and a grenade in his hand.

There's also plenty our old ship didn't have: a leisure room with a television screen, a gym complete with weight training equipment and sparring supplies. There's even a full armory, its walls lined with personal lockers, though the Nibirans must have cleaned out all of the pirates' old weaponry and replaced it with body armor and survival supplies we're likely meant to use on Gaia.

That gives me pause. Right. The job. I backtrack to the engine room and poke my head in again. "Hey, Lyre." She turns to me, arms folded over her chest, clearly annoyed at a second interruption. "The Nibirans sent over a document full of information for when we get to Gaia. Might be redundant now that Shey's here, but I'm going to send it to you to look over."

"What, is it too long for you to read? Not enough pictures?"

"Oof, so snappy! Have some respect for your captain!" I clutch my chest in mock hurt. "I thought you would be interested in reading it, you love that shit." And, yes, my attention span started to short-circuit after skimming the first few paragraphs, but I'm not *completely* lying.

"And it never crossed your mind that I might be busy figuring out a new engine before a risky landing?"

I hold up my hands in surrender. "Fine, fine, I'll send it to Corvus instead. You focus on the engine."

But as soon as I turn to go, she says, "I suppose you might as well send it to both of us, in case I find some downtime."

I grin. So predictable. "Sure thing," I say, heading out to continue admiring the ship. *My* ship.

That sparks another thought, and I race back up the stairs and across the ship. I pass the twins, who are squabbling over rooms while Corvus wearily supervises, and head to the door at the very end of the hall. The only one with a metal plate declaring its title: CAPTAIN'S QUARTERS.

I hit the pressure pad to open the door, and gasp before I even step inside. I got a glimpse of the other rooms on this ship on my way here. They're all utilitarian little boxes with bunks built into the walls and tiny toilet stalls—not even showers, since it seems the pirates used a communal one downstairs. They're more spacious than the cramped quarters we had back on *Fortuna*, but not by much.

This, on the other hand, is one of the nicest rooms I've ever seen in my life. It has a walk-in closet, a personal bathroom with a whole damn *tub*, soft lighting I can adjust by touching a screen on the wall. The room even has a personal viewing window out to the openness of space, right beside the ridiculously huge bed. I throw myself onto the mattress, relaxing with my face buried in a pile of pillows for a few moments before I prop myself up to look out the window. I finally get a hint of the feeling I've been hunting for.

I'm home.

CHAPTER NINE

Old Wounds

Corvus

Scorpia insists on gathering everyone in the mess hall for our first dinner on the new ship. When she asks me to cook, I'm eager for an excuse to disappear into the kitchen. Surely there's no way having everyone crammed in the mess hall doesn't end with chaos, and not the good kind. The room itself is huge, but I'm not sure any space would be large enough to properly accommodate our disparate collection of crew members with their various oversized personalities. Scorpia doesn't ask me to bet on anything unsavory for once, but if she did, I might just put some credits down on an imminent fistfight.

Yet, when I emerge from the kitchen an hour later to announce that the vegetarian curry is finished, I'm surprised to find everyone talking among themselves without any apparent issues. I pause to soak it in: Shey and Lyre having a quiet but lively conversation at one corner of the table, Orion and Scorpia swapping bad jokes and laughing themselves breathless at the other, Drom comparing muscles with a less-than-enthusiastic Izra while Pol looks on with obvious jealousy.

Some of the tension in my shoulders eases. Maybe this won't be a disaster after all. Scorpia does have a way of bringing people together. I'm reluctant to interrupt the various conversations, but after a few moments I clear my throat and call out, "Dinner's ready."

That, predictably, leads to a mad rush into the kitchen. The twins lead the charge, with the ex-pirates close behind, while the rest trickle in at a more reasonable pace.

Orion gasps dramatically at the huge pot still bubbling on the stove, and leans against Izra with a hand pressed to his forehead, pretending to swoon. "Oh my stars, I've been eating prison food for too long," he says. "Corvus, I could kiss you right now."

"I would prefer if you didn't," I say, which sends him and Scorpia into another bout of laughter.

"I'm just very grateful it's not fish," Lyre murmurs quietly to Shey behind me.

We serve ourselves portions of curry and rice on the metal trays I found in the ship's cabinets and gather around the table again. I sit between Shey and Lyre, but move aside to let them continue their conversation about Primus theory and its ties to Gaian history, since it quickly loses me. On the other end of the table, Orion regales the twins with a story about robbing a ship of Devan businesspeople while they listen with rapt attention. Izra occasionally jumps in to contradict him or add gory details, also to the twins' delight.

Scorpia is nodding along and pretending to listen to his story, while very clearly stealing glances across the table at Shey instead. The moment she finally looks away to ask Orion a question, Shey glances over at her, and then quickly turns back to Lyre before Scorpia notices.

I shake my head, content to sit quietly and eat my food. If nothing else, it's going to be an interesting trip.

Despite that pleasant first dinner, my mood sours over the next couple of days. I didn't realize how accustomed I had grown to solitude until it's been forcibly taken from me. *Memoria* is bigger than *Fortuna* was, but not nearly big enough to avoid that same cramped feeling of being stuck in an enclosed space with the same group of people, day in and day out. There are enough problems within our family that it would be awkward if it were only us, but the addition of Shey and the two pirates makes matters even more complicated.

Scorpia doesn't understand why I dislike them as much as I do. She assumes it's a matter of their previous profession, or long-term rivalry with our family—as though either of those reasons isn't enough to warrant a healthy amount of distrust toward them. But it's not just that, though I'm willing to let my sister believe it is. Both of them are walking reminders of parts of myself I'd prefer to leave behind. Izra, the last Titan other than myself, and a traitor to our dead people. Orion, who likely doesn't even know of the unfortunate tie that binds us in the form of Captain Murdock—his adopted father and my biological one.

I've spent these last few months trying to free myself of my past, but it feels as though both of them chain me to it now. How am I supposed to move forward when they make it impossible to forget?

At least it's easy enough to avoid Orion, because he is glued to Scorpia's side, and both of them seem to be constantly talking in a way that makes me wonder if either one ever pauses to actually listen to what the other is saying. The rest of the crew seems to be still struggling to adjust to ship life like I am, but the two of them fill all the empty spaces with their presence and laughter. I wonder if Scorpia has noticed Shey eyeing them whenever they're in the same area, or the way she's decided to hole herself up in her room.

But that's not my problem. Instead I task myself with keeping an eye on the other pirate. The deserter. Izra only appears for meals, otherwise she's locked up in her room—the one right next to the captain's quarters, which she was fierce about reclaiming even though it's completely identical to all the rest. Her weaponized arm is still locked up. I'm glad Scorpia doesn't trust her enough to ask me to cut that open, at least.

It doesn't take Izra long to notice my scrutiny of her. At breakfast, she meets my stare with an unabashed one of her own, walks over, and slams her tray of food down on the table opposite me.

"Do we have a problem?" she asks.

I take a bite of food. "That's up to you."

"Is it? 'Cause it seems to me that you've already made up your mind."

Her eye shifts to the brand on my wrist—proudly displayed, unlike the one on hers that's been covered up with a tattoo. She must have had it done off-planet at some point; no one on Titan would ever agree to do such a thing. Clearly following my train of thought, she lifts her own wrist and grins at me. Even with a smile on her face she's all sharp edges, feral and dangerous enough to make me wish I was carrying a weapon.

"I mean, maybe I'd consider apologizing for all the times I tried to kill you and your family over the years, but I'm guessing that's not the real issue here, is it?" she asks. "It's this." When I neglect to answer, she lets her arm fall to the table, and her smile drops as suddenly as if a switch was turned off. "You know the war's over, yeah? Surprise: Everyone lost."

I should walk away, now, before this escalates. But her words hook under my skin and tug at the anger simmering beneath, pulling it up toward the surface.

"It's not about the war."

Izra coughs out a harsh sound. I can't tell if it's meant to be a laugh. "You remember the same planet I do? It's always about the fucking war."

I hold her gaze steadily, keep my tone smooth and cold. "It's about you being a coward and a traitor," I say.

The last vestiges of anything resembling humor drain from Izra's expression. She leans forward, bracing her elbows on the table, her eye burning into me. "Guess it's a testament to Titan brainwashing that it sticks even after they're all dead."

"I'm not brainwashed. I'm—" I pause, words failing me. What am I? Loyal, when I left the war as soon as I had the chance to? Patriotic, when I never wanted to fight in the first place? I was never a true Titan, not in their eyes or my own. Doubt strikes me for a moment, but I push it aside. Whatever I was or am, I'm still more Titan than she is. I did my duty to my planet, paid my dues in sweat and blood and three years I will never have back. No matter how things turned out, that will always be my truth, and the Titans will always be my people. "Respectful," I say finally. "At the very least, the Titans deserve that."

"Do they?" she asks, her eyes still holding mine in a challenge. Her lips twist. "You're so eager to defend them. *You*, an off-worlder."

"I'm not—"

"I was born and raised on Titan," she continues, speaking over me. I grit my teeth and fall silent. "I loved it there. I loved my mothers and my father, my siblings, my comrades-in-arms. I watched them fall one by one to the war, and learned to hate the enemy. Then my sergeant told me to burn down an enemy village with all the civilians still trapped inside, and I realized we weren't a single bit better." Her voice doesn't rise as she continues, her tone flat and harsh. She searches my face. "Does that seem noble to you, *Sergeant* Kaiser? Tell me, are you proud of the things you did in the war?"

A small, shameful part of me sees the point she's making. I saw the ugly side of the war myself. But what war isn't ugly? And the war was necessary. There were lies and propaganda, but would anything have been better if everyone knew the awful truth?

"I saw the flaws on Titan as well, and I tried to make a difference," I say. "You could have done the same. But instead you turned your back on your world and ran. Left behind people who I'm sure loved and trusted you." I think back on my team on Titan—think of Daniil's bright smile, Sverre's steadfast loyalty, Magda's playful teasing—and my heart feels heavy. It was hard enough for me to leave them behind even after finishing my three years, and that was with a duty to my family pulling me away. To abandon them for nothing more than to save my own skin? I never could have done it. And no matter how Izra justifies it, it will never be less of a blemish to her character that she did.

"You know what I think?" Izra asks, her lips curled in a contemptuous sneer. "I think you hate me because I know you. Probably better than anyone else on this entire ship."

I give her a cold look. "You know nothing about me."

"Don't I?" she asks. "I'm guessing you sanitized your war stories for your precious little siblings, if you told them anything at all. Maybe you've even managed to convince yourself that serving in the war was some noble thing, something to be *proud* of." She spits the word, leaning closer to my face—close enough that she could bite me if she wanted to. "But I know the truth. I know that nothing about a war is anything to be proud of." I want to jerk away, to cut her off before she continues, but something glues me in my seat. I can't look away from her eye, narrowed and furious, and the scar tissue that remains of the missing one. The truth of the war is written in that scar, just like it's written in my own.

"I never said I was proud of anything," I say, "but at least I didn't turn my back on my people."

Her smile stretches, cold and ruthless.

"My people," she repeats. "My people, who took me from the wreckage of my village, and turned my hate into a weapon, and then sent me out to destroy places just like my home. And I was always so careful to leave no survivors, because I knew that they would grow up to be just like me." Her hand darts out, grabbing my chin, and I narrowly stop myself from taking a swing at her in response. Instead I grab her wrist. Her thumb runs along the length of my scar. "They had me torture enemy soldiers for days. Threaten to murder their families if they didn't speak. And then they had me go through with it. Burn civilians in their beds. Would you have stayed, if they told you to do those things? Would you have finished your years of service and walked away with your head held high?" She scrutinizes my face and then releases me, shoving my head back and stepping away, her wrist slipping free from my grip. "You know what? I think you would have. Maybe you did. Maybe that's why you hate me most of all. Because I was the one brave enough to run from it."

I realize only when she's done talking that my breath is coming in short, hot bursts, adrenaline flooding my body in anticipation of a fight. This rage—this pent-up violence—used to be normal for me, but not anymore. Not in a long time. And she's brought it out in me again. *Damn* her.

"Nothing you can say is going to convince me you're anything more than a coward," I say, struggling to keep my voice level. "Now get the fuck away from me."

Izra lets out a low chuckle that makes me half-certain there's no way this conversation can end without blood being drawn. But after another moment, she grabs her food and heads for the door. She pauses just in the doorway and glances back at me. "I know exactly what I am," she says, "and I have no reason to convince anyone of anything. But it's obvious that's not the case for you, soldier boy."

I wander the decks in an attempt to cool off, avoiding the sound of Orion's voice and Scorpia's answering laughter booming down the hall. It feels like I can't go anywhere on this ship without hearing them, but I know that going back to my bunk will only mean stewing in the silence, so instead I try to lose myself in the metal hallways and constant rumble of the engine and find some semblance of privacy.

My feet take me belowdecks. I pass by the engine room and see Lyre poring over the machinery inside; she pauses to give me a small wave before I go forward. There's a supply closet bigger than my quarters back on *Fortuna*, a breaker room, a communal shower that is uncomfortably reminiscent of the ones we always used on Titan, and more. Gradually, I lose my anger in the thrill of exploration.

At the end of the hallway, I find the twins occupying a smaller room outfitted with rubbery mats rather than metal floors. Of course this would be the room they gravitate toward. There are weights and other training devices here, too, but the twins have shoved them aside in favor of punching each other in the middle of the room. At least they're both wearing training gear to soften the hits, which is honestly the most surprising part about the entire situation. Neither of them pays me any mind as they circle one another. I take a seat against the wall and watch.

Drom is barely winded. Pol is panting, wobbly on his feet, face red and his lip split open; but he doesn't look like he intends on backing down anytime soon. He takes a step forward, broadcasting his clumsy next swing loud and clear. Drom dodges, and hits him in the chest hard enough to drop him to one knee. I grimace, but swallow the urge to interfere as he rises again, spitting to the side and gesturing for her to come at him again.

This time, she knocks him flat on his back. He lies there, winded, while she looks down at him and brushes off her sparring gloves.

"Too slow," she says flatly. "Maybe you need someone more on your level? Should I get Scorpia down here?" She taps her gloved fist against her chin, pretending to ponder. "Lyre, maybe? Think you could handle her? I'm not so sure."

"Fuck you," Pol wheezes out, and struggles to his feet once again.

His next punch clips her jaw, but she hits him back much harder, sending him to the floor again. He lets out a pained, breathless sound that reminds me of the one he made during our fight on Titan. I grimace, fighting the memory and the guilt.

I watch him hit the mat twice more without managing to land a single solid hit on her. The third time, I can't take it anymore.

"That's enough," I tell them. I thought sparring might be good for them, but it's obvious after only a couple of minutes that this is going nowhere. Pol's not learning anything from this, just getting shoved around. And with the way Drom is goading him, he's liable to get himself hurt worse than he already is. Drom turns and glares at me while Pol struggles up to one knee, his chest rising and falling rapidly, his face flushed.

"He'll tell me when he's had enough," Drom says.

"No, he won't," I say. We both know how stubborn he can be. Such as now, when he finally struggles to his feet and levels a glare at me.

"Stay out of this," he spits at me, swaying on his feet, still struggling to catch his breath. "Come on, Drom. Let's go."

She takes a step toward him, raising her gloves again, her face a stony mask.

"I said that's enough," I say, louder this time. Pol ignores me, still focused on Drom, but she glances over her shoulder at me and hesitates as I stand up.

Pol swings. His fist hits her right in the sternum, and she stumbles back, coughing and red-faced, and falls to one knee.

"*Hey,*" I shout, heading toward them. "Back up—"

Before I can reach them, Drom goes for Pol's legs, and they both go down in a shouting tangle of limbs. Drom pins him down and punches him in the face, a hit that would've broken his nose if not for the padded gloves. He rips off his own gloves and grabs her by the hair, yanking her head to the mat.

I finally reach them, and haul Drom off him, taking an elbow to the stomach for my trouble. Pol scrambles to his feet and lunges for her again, but I drop her and grab him instead, shoving him backward. Face twisted in frustration, he kicks me in my bad leg, and it crumples. I hit the mat on one knee with a grunt of pain. Both twins immediately, guiltily back off.

I stay on one knee, breathing hard, and slowly rise to my feet, trying to reclaim some sense of dignity. My leg throbs, but the humiliation is worse. I should have been able to handle them— *especially* Pol. I look back and forth between the twins, who both avoid my eyes.

"He started it," Drom says sullenly, before I can say anything. "With a cheap hit."

"Fighting clean doesn't win you anything," Pol says.

"Don't you fucking quote Momma at me right now—"

"Stop it," I say through gritted teeth, and am surprised when they do. I take a deep breath and try to control my anger. "Drom, go to your room," I say. "Pol, stay here, I want to talk to you."

Drom gives me an incredulous look. "You trying to *ground* me?" she asks, rising to her feet, and lets out a dry laugh. "You're not in charge of me."

But at least she leaves. Pol sinks to a seat on the map, arms wrapped around his knees, chest still heaving. I ease myself onto the mat beside him and sit, cross-legged, listening to the air wheeze in his lungs.

"I'm sorry," he murmurs, when I remain silent. "I forgot about your leg."

"That's all right," I say. The embarrassment still stings, but I can't muster up any anger over it. He didn't mean to hurt me. He shouldn't have even been able to. "I'm more concerned about you. You need to stop pushing yourself like this. It's only going to slow down your recovery."

"How long is it going to take for me to get better?" he asks. Now that the anger's drained out of him, he looks suddenly vulnerable, his shoulders slumped and his lower lip wobbling. It's hard to believe he was throwing punches just a few minutes ago. Then again, he's always been like that—bursting with emotions, only knowing how to express them through violence. No wonder he's having such a hard time containing them now, when his body is still so weak.

"You know I don't have a good answer for that," I say softly, wishing I did. Wishing I knew anything that could make him feel better. "You just need to take some time to rest."

"I've been resting on Nibiru," he says. "It didn't help. Now we're back on a ship, doing something important for once, and you want me to keep sitting around? Everyone else is here for a reason. They've got their jobs, and they're good at them. And I'm just...useless."

"Don't say that. Your job right now is getting better. That's the best thing you can do."

"Well I'm shit at that, too." He lets out a strained laugh, running his hands through his buzzed-short hair. "Fighting's the only thing I was ever good at. Now I've got nothing. I'm deadweight."

He glances at me, his expression souring. "You wouldn't get it," he says, standing up. "You've always been good at everything."

Hearing those words from his mouth ignites a deep ache in my chest—but I can't seem to find the words to comfort him. I can only watch as he limps out of the room, looking utterly miserable.

CHAPTER TEN

Bad Ideas

Scorpia

Orion and I are the only ones in the mess hall, both stretched across benches on opposite sides of one of the many tables, and I'm trying to stop laughing long enough for him to finish telling me his story.

"So there I was, stranded in Zi Vi's red-light district without any pants," he says, and I'm overcome with laughter again. He cuts off, unable to contain his own snickering—but stops as someone else enters the room. I sit up and watch Corvus approach us.

Every time Corvus looks at Orion, there's this flash of something intense in his eyes before he suppresses it. I can't imagine he would look at someone like that just for being an ex-pirate, even though that's what all his complaints center around. He doesn't even look at Izra like that, and she's a crazy deserter with a gun for an arm. But whatever it is he has a problem about, Corvus hasn't been forthcoming, and knowing him it'll take at least a week of brooding until he is, so all I can do is wait for him to come out with it.

"Scorpia," he says, completely ignoring Orion, who is suddenly very interested in his mug of tea. "The twins have been fighting again."

"Shit. Was it a bad one? Anything broken?"

"Just some scrapes and bruises."

"Oh." I relax. Sounds like business as usual for them, then. "Okay, good."

"*Good?*" Corvus questions, his eyebrows rising. "Aren't you going to do something about it?"

"I mean…" I shrug, not sure what he's getting at. "You already broke it up, right? What is there left to do?"

Corvus stares at me for a second. He cuts a look at Orion, and back to me, then says, stiffly, "Let's talk in private."

Before I can answer, he stalks out into the hallway. I heave a sigh, direct a dramatic eye roll at Orion, and get up. "Sorry. I'll be right back."

"Good luck," Orion says, with a mock-solemn salute.

I find Corvus waiting in the hallway, leaning against one wall with his arms folded across his chest. He looks like he would very much like to say something but is trying to hold back.

"C'mon, out with it."

"You're spending a lot of time with him," he says, glancing at the door behind me.

"With my friend who's been locked up in prison for three months? Yeah, of course I am." Noting his skeptical look, I insist, "We're *friends*. And even if we weren't, I don't believe my sex life is any of your business."

"That's not what I'm saying. Why do these conversations always…" He stops, grimacing. "You're the captain, Scorpia. You need to consider the consequences of your actions. And others' actions as well."

"I don't understand what you think I should do here. Not socialize with anyone? Throw the twins in a brig for a little scrap?"

"I'm expecting you to act like a captain. You can't show favoritism like this, or tolerate fighting on your ship. What if it was Izra picking a fight with someone? Or someone going after Lyre, or Shey?"

"But it wasn't. It was just the twins."

"I'm saying it's easier to establish a line now rather than trying to draw one after the fact," he says. "Look, as I've said before, it's different now that it's not just our family on board—"

I groan, throwing my hands up. "Oh, here we go."

"You wanted this responsibility, Scorpia. You brought us all along for this. Now you need to step up and start taking it seriously. You have a real crew, and they need a real leader. It isn't a mantle you can choose to take off whenever you feel like it."

"You think I don't know that?" I ask. "You think I don't feel the pressure?" It's laughable to hear him call this a "real" crew, when we both know it's actually just a jumble of people with debatable ties to one another. Shey is only here because of the job, as she's made clear from the fact she spends all of her time in her bunk. Orion and Izra are only here because they don't have any better options, and half of my family didn't even *want* to come. Corvus seems to think the secret to keeping everyone together is to keep a tight rein on things, but to me, it seems like that will only drive them all away, especially when we've all been burned by too-strict leaders in the past. "Look, I get it, all right? And I'm doing my best here to keep everyone happy. But I'm not just gonna throw away who I am. I'm never gonna be Captain Murdock, or..." I cut myself off, shaking my head.

"Or Momma?" Corvus prompts. "You can say her name, you know. We can talk about it. We don't have to all pretend she never existed."

I let out a sharp laugh, turning my face away from him. He can be so condescending sometimes, and I don't think he even realizes it.

"Sure, we can talk about it, as long as I don't say anything remotely hypocritical, right? Then all of a sudden it's *crass* and *disrespectful to the dead*, as if she deserves—" I huff. "No, you know what? This is not about me, so stop pretending it is. The only reason you're so intent on me changing how I run my ship is that we have 'outsiders.'" I accompany the words with dramatic finger quotations to make sure the full force of my sarcasm comes through. "If anyone hasn't dealt with Momma being gone, it's you. 'Cause you're acting—"

Just like her. Remembering Drom saying similar words to me and how deeply they cut, I force myself to stop. I thought being on a ship would help bring my family together again . . . guess I forgot how much Corvus can make me want to bang my head against a wall. I don't want to fight, but he makes it difficult sometimes. "Okay," I say, after a few moments. "Okay. Here's an idea. How about I'll go talk to the twins about what happened, and you stay here and make nice with Orion?"

Corvus's face twists into that strange, unreadable look it always does when Orion comes up. He's silent for a few moments, and then says, "I fail to see how they're equivalent."

"Well, I'm the captain, and that's my call. You say you want to keep the crew together, so here we go. We'll both put in an effort." I put a hand on his back and push him toward the mess hall, which he grudgingly allows. "Go on. Talk to him about whatever you've been sulking about ever since we got on board."

Part of me is afraid to leave Corvus and Orion alone after there's already been one fistfight on the ship today. But he's going through with his part of our bargain, so that means it's my turn. Pol's room is empty, so I go to Drom's next door, taking a moment to gather myself before I knock.

"What do you want?" Drom calls out from within, which I take as permission to enter.

She's doing push-ups on the floor, with enough sweat on her brow that it's clear she's been doing them for a while. I sit on the edge of her bed and wait for her to finish. After a few minutes, she sits back on her heels, panting, and looks over at me.

"What?"

"I heard you and Pol were fighting."

Drom rolls her eyes. She stands up, grabs a towel off a hook on her closet, and wipes her forehead. "He was fighting. I was trying not to break him."

"That's not what Corvus said."

She grimaces. "Fucking Corvus. He thinks he's helping, but I swear, all he does is make everything worse."

I choose not to comment on that, and instead pat the bed beside me. She joins me, still scowling. "I know it must be hard to be cooped up on a ship again," I say. "For both you and Pol." She says nothing, so I prompt, "Seems like you two have been fighting a lot lately. I mean, more than usual."

"Yeah." Drom wipes sweaty hair out of her face, her scowl relaxing into something less closed-off. "I just...don't know how to deal with him anymore. He says he wants me to treat him the same as always, but he can't take it the way he used to, so it just ends up with him feeling worse and worse until he fuckin' explodes." She sighs. "It always used to be easy between us, you know? If we had an issue, we'd fight it out, and be better in the morning. But now he can't fight, so he *stews* instead, like he's Corvus or something, and..." She trails off, looking sheepish as she seems to realize how much she's pouring out right now.

I'm not sure what to say, other than, "We knew there would be side effects."

"Well I didn't think he'd be a completely different person!" Drom bursts out. "It's like I barely know him anymore."

I'm quiet for a long moment, wrestling with my thoughts. I

wish I could disagree with her. I still see flashes of my baby brother—those tumultuous emotions interspersed by moments of startling sweetness—but none of us can deny that he's changed. And guilt eats at me as I realize for the first time how hard this must've been on Drom. No wonder she wanted to stay on Nibiru, where at least there were distractions, and she didn't have to face her changed twin all day every day.

"You know, I felt the same way when Corvus came back."

She glowers at me. "It's not the same."

"You don't think so? You don't see how different he is, even now?" I lean forward, lowering my voice. "Corvus and I grew up together. We did everything together. Now, you know he still hasn't talked to me about those years on Titan? At *all*? It's like this huge piece of him I'll never know, and I'm just supposed to be okay with that."

She's silent for a long moment, but finally, she glances up at me and asks, "So how do you deal with it?"

"Very well on some days. Not so good on others," I say, automatically falling back on a joke, but as she scowls at me I hold up my hands. "No, no, I mean…" I trail off, hesitating. It's a good question, really. How *do* I deal with it? We've patched up a lot of the holes in our relationship, but that doesn't mean it's what it was before. Not even close. And it still hurts sometimes, thinking about that, and about the person he was before. I still miss that version of Corvus, sometimes. I'm sure he misses the old version of me, too. "I guess… I guess I've just accepted it," I say with a small shrug. "I gave up on trying to get back the version of him from before—the version *I* want— and accepted that the person he is now is who he had to become to get here. And I've chosen to love that person, too, and not hold it against him." I glance at her, flushing. I'm not used to talking to anyone like this, let alone Drom. I'm surprised she didn't cut me off to tell me to stop being dramatic already. "Does that make any sense?"

"No," she says, and grimaces down at the floor. "It's a shit answer. Doesn't help at all. You're supposed to tell me how to fix it, not tell me *not* to fix it."

"I mean, it's a shit situation," I say. "So sometimes shit answers are all you have." I study her face, and then add, "And sometimes things can't be fixed. Not really. Sometimes the best thing you can do is accept something and move on."

"Like Momma?" she asks, looking up at me. I freeze for a moment, startled by the question, and force down an urge to make a stupid joke or avoid answering.

"Yes, like Momma," I say. "Losing Momma...and all of the things that she did to us before, all of the ways she hurt us... that's not something that can ever be fixed. But we *can* decide to move on."

"Pol doesn't want to move on," she says. "He's mad that the rest of us have started to. He wants to talk about her all the damn time. And he gets mad anytime anyone says something bad about her. Says we need to respect her memory, even though she was..." She trails off, her mouth twisting to the side.

"She was awful," I finish for her. "It's okay to say it, no matter what Pol thinks. She really was, Drom. She hurt all of us a lot. Pol included, even if he hasn't realized it yet."

"But she loved us, too," she says, though it comes out almost like a question, the last word trembling on her lips.

It's easy to forget how young she is sometimes, and how very unqualified I am for conversations like these. I bite my own lip, considering the words and wrestling with my response. "Yes, I think she did," I say. "But really, that just makes it worse."

I head back to the mess hall, intending to investigate whether or not my younger siblings decided to stock up on any alcohol for the trip—one glass to celebrate our new ship can't hurt, surely—but instead, I walk into the kitchen to find Shey making herself a pot of tea. We both stop and stare at one another for an uncomfortable moment. Shey's spent most of her time shut in her room thus far, and even at occasions like our first dinner together as a crew, she seems to be avoiding me. I've been doing my best to accept that. She made it clear she's not interested in being around me long before this, and I'm not going to continue to chase after her when my attention is unwanted.

But instead of taking her tea and disappearing again, she holds up a mug and asks, "Would you like some?"

We end up sitting across from each other in an otherwise-empty mess hall. Every clink of a teacup seems to echo in the room. I sip my tea and try not to grimace at the bitter taste. It must be Gaian; no one else would subject themselves to drinking something so objectively terrible. But Shey, of course, sips it with what appears to be enjoyment.

"I've been meaning to talk to you," she says, looking up at me. "It's been a long while since we've had a chance to speak alone, hasn't it?"

"Yeah, I guess so," I say, lightly, as though I'm not thinking about us pressed together on the beach precisely two months and twenty days ago, and it hasn't crossed my mind at least once a day ever since. "What do you want to talk about?"

"About..." She hesitates, toying with the handle of her mug. "I know things between us have always been complicated. And I would prefer for them not to be."

That could mean so many things that I have no idea how to interpret it. I struggle with my words before finally asking, "Meaning what, exactly?"

She hesitates, and then folds her hands on the table, looking at me steadily. "I don't want you to think that I sought you out because of any lingering feelings. I am here as a professional, and I have no issues with keeping our relationship strictly that."

I should've expected this. I got the basic message loud and clear long before this conversation. And yet, hearing it now still gives me a bitter taste in the back of my mouth that has nothing to do with this disgusting Gaian tea. I try to subdue my messy feelings before speaking. "I understand," I say. "I'm not going to do anything to make you uncomfortable while you're on my ship, Shey. You don't have to stay in your room avoiding me."

She looks down into her tea and bites her lip in that way that always drives me crazy. "I know it's unfair of me to feel this way," she says, softly, color creeping into her cheeks, "but even though I tell myself it's illogical, it is hard for me to see that you've moved on."

I freeze, cup of tea halfway to my mouth. "Moved on? What are you...?"

I cut off abruptly as Orion walks into the mess hall. He waves at us before continuing into the kitchen to rummage through the cabinets. I turn back to Shey, but she's already gathering up her things, her vulnerable expression now completely shut off.

"Good night," she says, and leaves before I can stop her.

I stay where I am for a moment, blinking and trying to process that. I just can't catch a break today—it's hard conversations all the time.

I need a drink.

When I enter the kitchen, I find Orion has beat me to it. He turns to me, bottle of wine in hand.

"Conversation with Corvus was that rough, huh?" I ask, trying to force some levity.

He pours himself a very large glass. "Do I have you to thank for whatever that was?"

"Thought it would be good for you two to hash out any issues."

"Well, he said he had to tell me something, sat there silently for a very uncomfortable amount of time, and then said 'never mind' and left."

I burst out laughing as Orion takes a long sip of his drink. "That is…even worse than I expected," I say once I finish, wiping tears out of my eyes. "I'm sorry. If it helps, my conversation with Drom was also deeply uncomfortable." I gesture toward the bottle he's still holding. "So I'll take some of that."

Orion hesitates. "I thought you quit?"

Damn whichever of my siblings decided to mention that. "It's wine, not whiskey. One glass isn't going to do any harm." I step forward, touching his arm. "C'mon."

He glances from the bottle to my hand on his arm, shrugs, and pours a second glass. "Just one," he says, putting the bottle away and handing the second—much smaller—glass to me. "That's it. And don't tell Corvus, since I suspect he's looking for a good reason to toss me out the air lock."

"Promise," I say, and sip my wine. Intense sweetness hits the back of my tongue, followed by a heavily spiced aftertaste and a lingering burning sensation. I cough. "Oof, really? Fireberry?"

"I'm still Devan at heart, after all," he says with a laugh.

I lean against the counter beside him, taking another hesitant sip as we lapse into silence. This weird intermingling of sweet and spicy has never been my favorite, especially since I know from experience that drinking too much can lead to vomiting up what feels like pure fire, but I'll take what I can get.

"It's strange being back here without the rest of the crew," Orion says after a few moments, looking down at his glass. "I guess it must be strange for you, too."

"Definitely," I say. "I keep walking around corners and expecting someone to shoot at me. But…those captain's quarters are well worth any weirdness."

"Is that so? I've never been allowed in there."

"What? Never?" I'm surprised—I would've thought Orion, of all people, might've been allowed in. Murdock was his father, after all. Then again, I guess I was never allowed into Momma's room on *Fortuna*, either. The realization fills me with a sudden, fierce desire to make things right in some way, and prove I'm not like them. I grab Orion's wrist and pull him toward the door. "Well, come take a look!"

It isn't until we're in the hallway leading to my quarters that I realize how it must look for me to be dragging Orion back to my room, both of us with drinks in hand. But the doors are all closed, and there's no one here to witness us step into the room together. And even if there was—so what? I'm the captain, and I can do what I want, even if the thought of Shey in particular seeing us together makes my stomach feel squirmy. But she's the one who broke things off and said we should keep it professional. I shouldn't care.

Either way, the look on Orion's face as he steps into the room is well worth my discomfort on the way here. I shut the door behind us while he stares around, openmouthed.

"That bastard," he says, "had us sleeping in boxes while he—" He cuts off, gesturing at the bed and looking at me. "May I?"

I bow dramatically, sweeping a hand out toward the bed. "Be my guest."

Orion sets down his wineglass and throws himself on the bed, burying himself in a mountain of pillows and sheets. His reaction is so similar to mine that it sends me into a fit of laughter—but as he rolls onto his back and looks over at me from the bed, my reaction very quickly shifts away from amusement and toward something I really shouldn't be feeling right now. I look from his body, lean muscle all stretched out over my rumpled sheets, to the familiar planes of his face—those angular cheekbones and pretty hazel eyes, the half smile teasing at one corner of his lips.

Bad idea, I tell myself. Even though I think Corvus's view is too uptight, I have to admit he's probably right that I shouldn't fall into bed with any of my crewmates... especially so in the first few days of the trip, and *especially* with Shey on board as well. As much fun as Orion and I have had in the past, my feelings for Shey are much deeper, and much more complicated. I clear my throat, looking around the room for a distraction. It doesn't take long for my eyes to snag on something.

"You know what I haven't had a chance to try yet?" I move over to the bathroom, grin, and turn on the water for the tub.

A few minutes later, as we're both stripping down to our underwear, it strikes me that this was likely not the best distraction when I'm trying not to think about how attractive Orion is... but at least it successfully shifted the mood away from how he was looking at me before. We're both giddy and playful now, laughing as we struggle to get our clothes off without spilling our drinks, pushing each other out of the way to be the first one in. I use my captain card and jump in first, with him close behind.

The tub is—amazingly—big enough for us both to fit comfortably. I stretch my feet out across his lap, and he absently rubs my calf with one hand, raising his drink to his mouth with the other. My own glass is nearly empty, and between the alcohol and the warm water, I'm feeling pleasantly hazy.

"I guess if things had gone differently, this room would've been mine one day," Orion says, looking out over the captain's quarters.

Now that's an extremely effective way to kill my buzz. I take a swig of my wine, resisting the urge to down it like a shot. Instead of responding, I scrutinize him, trying to gauge what he's feeling—but instead my eyes are drawn down to a scar I hadn't noticed before, an ugly, jagged thing cutting across his left side. Something inside me twists. "That's new."

"Oh," he says, following my eyes. "Yeah." He hesitates. I'm already thinking of a way to change topics when he continues,

"Turns out that even criminals aren't exactly fond of people who almost destroyed an entire planet's population. I had to learn quickly which guards hated us enough to look the other way when things got bad in Ca Sineh."

"Shit," I say, softly. "I'm sorry."

"To be honest, that wasn't the worst of it." He pauses, looking down into the water between us. "Some days I even wished for trouble. Because it was better than the monotony. *That* was the worst thing. Just...endless days blurring into each other, sitting in that tiny cell, thinking that was what the rest of my life was going to look like." He swallows hard. "Thinking about never seeing the sun again. Never biting into another fresh sunfruit, or drinking fireberry wine, or..." He trails off and takes another sip of his drink, rolling it around his mouth before swallowing. "I'm not sure how much more I would've been able to take."

Just imagining being trapped in a place like Ca Sineh fills me with a deep sense of dread. I remember the panic that gripped me when I spent just one night in a low-tech jail on Gaia. That was bad enough, but to be caged indefinitely, deep beneath the ocean, without even the comfort of fresh air and sunlight on your skin... and to think Nibiru's treatment of prisoners is considered more humane than some other planets. I know I'd rather die a good death than end up in Ca Sineh. "That's horrible. No one deserves to live like that," I say softly. After a moment's consideration, I add, "Well, maybe Leonis does."

Orion laughs, but his expression quickly darkens again. "I'm grateful you came for me and Izra. But when I think about the rest of my crew still trapped there...or my dad, I..." His voice breaks, and he stops, pressing the back of one hand to his mouth. "Sorry," he says, clearing his throat. "This must seem ridiculous to you. I know I shouldn't miss him, after everything he did. It's his fault we all ended up in Ca Sineh. But...he's still my father.

121

He rescued me from the streets on Deva. Gave me a life on the ship."

I'm not sure what to say to him. If anyone in this system does deserve Ca Sineh, Captain Murdock is probably on the list, for trying to wipe out an entire planet for his own self-gain. I think both of us know that. But at the same time, I understand. His feelings toward his father must be as complex as mine toward Momma, no matter what terrible people they both were. "It's not ridiculous. I get it. I, um…" I hesitate. Maybe it's his honesty, or the wine, or the fact that this is the first time I'm talking about it with someone other than my family, but an uncomfortable truth spills out of me. "I miss Momma, too, sometimes. Even after everything. Like you said, she was all I had for a while. My other options were a lot worse."

It's humiliating to admit it aloud, after everything she did to me and my family and all the times I've snapped at Pol over bringing her up. But somehow it feels easier to tell Orion than talk to my siblings about it.

He nods, and says, "And I imagine she was the same as my dad. Not so terrible all of the time."

"Which made it all the more terrible when they were."

"They really were alike in some strange ways. Not that I ever would've dared say it to either of their faces."

"Maybe that's why we make such good friends," I say. "Well, that and the fact that we're both ridiculously good-looking, of course." He laughs, and I raise my glass. "Cheers to shitty parents?"

"And to being ridiculously good-looking," Orion agrees, clinking his glass against mine.

I finish my drink, and sit with the empty glass in hand. The ache to refill it makes me glad the bottle isn't here to tempt me.

"I'm not gonna be like them," I say, eager both to move the conversation in a lighter direction and to distract myself. "I'm gonna be better."

Orion grins. "I believe it."

"With me in charge and you as my copilot, we can take on the whole system," I declare, buoyed by the way he's looking at me. "I promise, we're gonna get *so* rich, and have a great time doing it. It'll be..." I trail off, embarrassment worming through my optimism as I realize I might be getting a bit ahead of myself. We haven't really talked about what Orion plans to do now. He might expect me to drop him off on Deva the second we're done with this job. "I mean, if you want to stay, that is."

"You rescued me from the system's most infamous prison, and now you're offering me riches *and* an easier job? Pretty hard to say no." He laughs, but then his expression shifts, becoming more serious. "I'm not going anywhere."

The words ignite something warm in my chest. It's almost embarrassing how good it makes me feel to hear that, and to have someone look at me with such open admiration. My family might be here because they're my blood—and, okay, because of some light bribery in a couple cases—and Shey for "professional reasons" and Izra because she can't legally be anywhere else in the system, but Orion is choosing this. Choosing me.

After a few quiet moments, Orion plucks the glass out of my hand and sets it aside. I had almost forgotten I was still holding it, and that part of me is still craving more wine.

"Such a gentleman," I tease, and he leans over me, suddenly very close. I let out a slightly uncomfortable laugh. "Or not."
Bad idea, I scold myself again—but I find myself automatically responding to him anyway, my face tilting forward so our noses brush, my hips aligning to his so it's all too obvious that only a couple layers of wet fabric separate our bodies.

"Probably not," he murmurs, his breath sweet and spiced like the wine we've been drinking.

I should turn away, stop this before it goes further. But I can't deny that part of me is aching for this: the closeness, the chance to forget—if only briefly—how complicated everything outside this room is. So I don't pull back, and he leans closer.

If I can't have Shey, I think—and that quickly aborted thought finally jolts me out of my haze.

"This is a bad idea," I blurt out just before he can kiss me, and he immediately pulls back.

He stays close, though, studying my face from a few inches away. "I remember you saying that the first time," he says. "Right before you—"

"Oh, I remember," I say quickly, with a small laugh. I don't need the reminder when I'm already wrestling with my self-control. "But I'm your captain now. I can't go around hooking up in supply closets." I clear my throat. "Or bathtubs, as the case may be."

"Why not?" he asks—but he's easing up further, sitting back on his heels, water dripping from his shoulders. "Who's going to stop you?"

"I mean, it just seems irresponsible."

"So you're being responsible now?" He arches a brow. "Dark times indeed."

"Oh, shut up."

"Two days captaining this ship and you've already lost all sense of fun. Truly, a tragedy."

"Shut *up*. I am plenty of fun even when I'm not taking my clothes off."

I splash him, and he laughs, splashing me back. It quickly escalates into an all-out water war, and I slide closer and attempt to wrestle him under the water, and then—and then suddenly I'm on his lap and my arms are around his neck and we're kissing, his tongue sliding against mine and his skin hot against me. Our past trysts have always been rushed, breathless fumbles, fed by the fear of getting caught, and I fall back into that habit now, quickly moving to discard what little is left of his clothing.

But he grabs my hand and pulls back. "Wait," he says, breathing hard. "Didn't we just talk about how this isn't a good idea?"

"I know," I say—but *knowing* and *wanting* are proving to be two separate things entirely. I'm flushed and frustrated and confused, and I want this, and what the hell is the point of being captain if I don't get anything that I want? Surely this is just some harmless fun anyway. It always has been, with us. "And we also talked about our childhood trauma before that, so this whole thing has been very, very weird, but I want—I want—"

I lean forward again, but he shakes his head, and I pull back.

"Do you want me," he asks, uncharacteristically serious, "or do you just want a distraction?"

I blink at him, and try to search for an answer, but one doesn't readily come. "I..."

"It's important," he says. Then he takes my hand and kisses it, gently, which somehow makes me blush more than anything else did. "I don't want this to be something you regret in the morning."

I stare at him. Before I can say anything, there's a knock at the door. We both turn toward it, and then exchange a glance.

"Just ignore it?" Orion suggests. I'm inclined to agree, given that this conversation feels far from over, but a second, louder knock makes me stand and climb out of the tub. Whoever is here, they're not going to accept silence as an answer, and if they keep that up, they're going to wake the whole damn ship. I wrap myself hastily in a towel before going to answer it.

Izra stands outside, her eye narrowed in a glare.

"Do you need something?" I ask, leaning against the doorway to obscure her view of Orion behind me.

"These walls are really fucking thin," she says. "And I am trying to sleep." She points to the room beside mine—the one that shares a wall right next to the bathtub. "Right. On the other side. Of that wall."

"Oh," I say. "Sorry, I didn't realize—"

"Hearing your inane conversation was annoying enough, but if I have to listen to the two of you fuck in a bathtub, I am going to throw myself out the air lock and take both of you with me."

I wince at her volume, glancing up and down the hallway in the worry that one of the other doors will open. "Okay, okay," I say, gesturing for her to keep it down. "I got it. Message received."

"Better be," she snarls, and storms back over to her room.

I pause, taking another guilty glance around before retreating into my own quarters. Orion is climbing out of the tub now, shaking water out of his hair, wet boxers low on his hips and clinging to his skin in a way that makes me avert my eyes to focus on doing what I have to do.

"Shit," I sigh, running a hand through my hair. "Guess it's officially time to call it a night, then. Um..." I fumble with my words. "Thanks. You're probably right. This is not a good idea. Us, I mean."

I'm surprised to see his face fall, just a little, despite the fact that he's the one who was clearheaded enough to stop this before it went too far...but a moment later, he shrugs and gives me a small smile.

"Well, we make good friends," he says, bending down to retrieve his clothes.

"We definitely do," I say with a laugh. Once he's dressed, I give him a gentle push toward the door. "Now go on before the crew starts to gossip."

"Understood, Captain," he says with a wink.

As the door shuts behind him, I sink onto the edge of my bed, wiping wet hair out of my face. Sitting in this grand room all alone feels surprisingly disappointing. All this time I wanted to be a captain, to have my own ship and my own crew. I thought it would grant me the freedom I've been craving. Instead, it seems I have to give up what I want to keep it.

Stars damn it. This shit can never be easy, can it? I lay back on my too-big bed, blow out a sigh, and wonder how I'm going to get through this trip without getting laid.

CHAPTER ELEVEN

The Ruins of Levian

Corvus

The mood on the ship changes as we approach Gaia and the reality of the situation sets in. No one is sure what to expect when we reach the planet. Shey, Lyre, and I gather in the leisure room to pore over the document the council gave us. With Shey here to help with the Primus tunnels, and Lyre taking notes on how to use the Nibirans' equipment to test the air, soil, and water for hints about the nature of the climate shift, I focus on how we'll endure the severe weather conditions on the surface. The council has equipped us with suits for our protection, Gaian-made and sturdy enough to withstand a hurricane.

"Where did the council say they found all of this?" Shey asks, flipping through the pages about the Primus tunnels with her eyebrows drawn together in thought.

"One of the scientists who worked with your mother came forward," I say.

"This is highly classified information. I didn't even have the clearance for most of this. It's...I know it's hard for you to understand, but with the way my people view the Primus, giving this up is more than treasonous. It's practically blasphemy."

"Perhaps they reconsidered their priorities after what your mother did."

"Or maybe they realized that a life sentence in Ca Sineh is a very long time," Lyre says.

"I suppose," Shey says, but her expression remains troubled.

No amount of preparation can make us ready to enter Gaia's atmosphere. I recall a variety of difficult landings throughout my life, especially on Titan, where the storms were a constant, howling threat determined to keep us from landing on the surface. I thought this landing would be along the same lines, the ship pummeled by winds and rain.

I may not have been conscious for the crash onto Nibiru a few months ago, but this is closer to what I imagine that must have been like. I'm not sure if it's the conditions or the ship, but whatever the cause, the craft lurches and dips, groans and shudders, jerking this way and that. It sounds like it's going to fall to pieces at any moment. Once, there's a distinct screech of metal that sounds like a part may have ripped free. I shut my eyes and brace myself in my chair.

If nothing else, I'm reassured by the thought that we're in Scorpia's hands. I would trust no one else to get us there safely.

The landing seems to take hours. But finally, the ship thuds onto solid ground. My head jerks forward, and a curse hisses out around my mouth-guard. I spit the gooey paste into one palm and take a few long moments to regain my bearings. My head spins. Outside, I can still distantly hear howling winds and the patter of rain against metal. We aren't safe, but at least we survived the landing.

I unstrap myself and head out to the cargo bay. Halfway there, I hear the screaming.

My footsteps increase to a run, and I burst into Pol's room. My brother is still strapped into his chair, writhing in the restraints, his face a mask of agony. Drom stands next to him, her hands held half up, like she wants to touch him but isn't sure if she should.

"What happened?" I bark, pushing past her to let Pol out of the chair. He slumps against me, shuddering.

"I—I don't know!" Drom says, her hands still up, her eyes wide. "He started about five minutes ago. I couldn't get to him when we were landing, I didn't know what to do—"

"Make it stop," Pol says. He rips free of my grasp and stumbles away, pressing both hands to the sides of his head. His fingers press into his skull so hard it must hurt. His eyes roll wildly. "Somebody make it stop."

"Make what stop?" I reach for him again, but he pulls away with a groan, pressing his back to the wall. "Talk to us. I can't help if you won't tell us what's wrong."

"The noise, that noise . . . my head, it's going to explode. Please."

I stare at him for a moment longer, and then turn to Drom, who is watching Pol with a tormented look on her face. "I'm going to get something to sedate him. You keep an eye on him until I get back." I take off to the medical bay, scramble in the drawers until I find a sedative and a needle. By the time I get back to the twins, Pol is curled up in the corner with his head in his hands, his breath coming in panicked bursts. Drom crouches beside him, a hand on his shoulder.

"Okay, Pol, this is going to help you," I say, slowly approaching. He looks up at me—eyes wide and frantic—and jerks back as he sees the needle in my hand.

"No, no, no—no needles!" he says, and then grips his head again, letting out a low moan of pain.

I pause. My heart aches at having to force this on him, adding more trauma where he already has plenty, but we don't have a choice. "Drom, hold him."

She grits her teeth and grabs his arms, holding him against her. "Calm down. It's going to be okay."

As I draw close, Pol thrashes against her, struggling to break free, but he's in no shape to fight against her. One of his flailing fists hits her in the side of the face. For a moment she looks so furious I'm afraid she'll retaliate, but instead she only shifts her grip and holds him tighter. I lower myself to the floor, and between the two of us, we manage to hold him still enough for me to get the needle into his arm. He gasps.

"No, no, make it stop," he mumbles, and his eyes flutter shut, body going limp. I stay where I am for a moment, making sure he gets the full dose, before pulling back. Drom holds on to her twin, her arms tight around him, and glares at me as if this is somehow my fault.

"What the hell was that?" she asks. "He's never done that before."

"Trust me, if I had any idea, I would tell you."

She sucks in a shuddery breath, turning her face away. I give her some time before saying, gently, "Let's get him onto the bed."

We lift him between us—a feat that was once difficult even with our strengths combined, but now it hardly takes any effort at all—and carefully place him on his bunk. Drom lifts his head to put a pillow beneath it and sits at the edge of the mattress. I take a seat beside her.

"It's just going to keep getting worse, isn't it?" she asks, her eyes on the floor.

"We don't know that."

"But it's obvious. He just gets worse and worse all the time, and we have no idea how to help him, do we?"

After a moment's hesitation, I determine there's nothing helpful

I can say that isn't a lie. Instead of speaking, I put an arm around her shoulders. She doesn't lean into me, but she doesn't pull away, either, and chews her lip with her eyes still on the floor.

A few minutes later, Scorpia comes in to find us like that.

"What's with all the noise?" Scorpia asks, before her eyes land on Pol. "Oh, shit. Is he okay?"

"He's sedated," I say. "We're not sure what happened."

"He was yelling something about a noise," Drom says, hunched over her twin like she means to protect him from the world.

Scorpia crosses her arms over her chest, frowning thoughtfully as she looks down on him. "He's said something about Gaia being 'loud' before," she says. "I didn't know what he meant, but...maybe it's something to do with the storms? Some kind of reaction?"

"He's never freaked out like this during the storms on Nibiru," Drom says.

"Well, I think the best thing we can do for him is get off this planet as soon as possible," I say, and stand, making my way to the door. "So let's do our job. What's the plan, Scorpia? Are you going to stay with the ship?"

"Why would I do that?" she asks, following me out to leave the twins in peace.

I glance at her, eyebrows rising. "Because we might need an emergency liftoff, and you despise the Primus?"

"Okay, true, but...I'm also the captain, and I'm not missing the whole damn mission. Orion can keep the ship ready in case of emergency. Me, you, and Shey will head into the tunnels while the rest stay here."

That stops me in my tracks. She bumps right into me and stumbles back a step, muttering a curse. "So you're leaving the pirates with the ship?" I ask, lacing my voice with disapproval.

"I'm leaving our *crew* with the ship, you judgmental ass." She glowers at me. "Seriously, you need to get over it at some point. Or you can stay here to keep an eye on them, if you want. But I'm going. I'm the captain. And like you said, that means stepping up."

As much as it annoys me to have my own words used against me, I can't come up with any counterargument that isn't incredibly hypocritical. I'm not sure which idea is worse—leaving the pirates with full reign over the ship, or leaving Shey and Scorpia alone for an important mission. I'm not sure what's going on between them—it's been all awkward glances and avoiding being in the same room together since the start of this trip—but it's clear that it's something complicated. Finally, I say, "I guess it's fine, as long as Drom and Lyre are keeping an eye on them."

"Already handled," Scorpia says, surprising me. "Lyre's not happy about being left behind, but she's gonna have to deal with it. I told her to take samples near the ship for today. Now let's get this over with."

Shey meets us in the armory to prepare. While *Fortuna* had only its dingy little supply closet near the ramp, *Memoria* has an impressive, fully sized room with lockers lining the walls. Some still have old nameplates attached: Captain Murdock, Izra, and Orion, among other names I don't recognize. The twins have already carved their names into a pair of side-by-side metal doors to claim their own. I open an unlabeled one to find it stocked up with supplies the Nibirans have provided: body armor, weaponry, canteens, compasses. In the back hang the suits for weathering the surface, made of puffy orange material.

I show the others how to pull it on, and the button to press on the neck so that the suit tightens to conform to our respective sizes. We each attach a survival backpack that hooks up with a water-dispensing straw inside the helmet, and I point out how to deploy emergency flares and grappling hooks. The fingertips of each glove can be used for both lights and painting a neon-green substance used to mark one's path.

"Good shit," Scorpia proclaims, using the latter feature to paint her name over Captain Murdock's old locker nameplate. "Think the council's gonna let us keep these? Maybe we can pretend we lost them on Gaia…"

"Perhaps we should focus on the mission first," Shey says, but she smiles nonetheless, and writes her name neatly on the locker beside Scorpia's.

The moment I step out onto Gaia's surface, wind slams into us, as if trying to force me back onto the ship. My suit's heavy boots keep my feet glued to the ramp, but the sight of Levian—or what's left of it—is what really holds me in place.

The once-gleaming capital city has been almost completely leveled, its buildings reduced to mounds of scrap metal. More than a storm, it's as though some giant, malevolent hand has crushed the city beneath its palm. A faceless black Primus statue towers above the wreckage. I've never had Scorpia's aversion to the alien technology, but it looks menacing even to me. It's the last thing left standing in the wake of this destruction—but not even the Primus could survive whatever happened in the system during their time. Are we watching humanity dive headfirst toward the same fate? Were these statues left behind as a warning?

I'm struck with a deep, pervasive sense of foreboding…and an unexpected ache in my chest for the planet that was my childhood home. I haven't set foot here since before my service on Titan. Now, I'll never lay eyes on the shining, structured city of Levian again. Never see the school I went to as a child, the paved streets I raced through with Scorpia, the elegant cafés of the Turill district or the glamorous Itsennen clubs part of me always wished I could afford. My feelings toward Gaia have always been mixed, but there were parts of the planet that I loved. Aspects of its culture that I was once desperate to be a part of. When I was a child growing up here, I wanted nothing more than to be accepted by its proud people, to be welcomed as one of their own rather than viewed as an impolite outsider.

A wave of guilt follows the sense of loss. Somehow the nostalgia feels like a betrayal of Titan—my birthplace, my second home, destroyed by the leader of the very planet I now mourn. I am not sure if seeing Gaia laid bare, storm-ravaged and void of life much like Titan, should feel more like justice than another thing to grieve. But I can't help but feel that I've lost yet another home. *Fortuna*, Titan, Gaia. All gone. Nearly every place in the system that has held meaning for me has been destroyed over the span of a couple of months. Now, I'm left adrift in a system in turmoil. Nibiru was the last safe place, but after what we did there, that may be gone now, too. For a moment, I let myself close my eyes and soak in the grief.

"Oh, damn," Scorpia says over the comms, her footsteps coming to a stop beside me. She lets out a low whistle. "Didn't think it would be this bad."

I open my eyes to look at her. Surely her feelings must be as complicated as my own, given her messy past with this planet. She looks over the ruins of the city, and then her eyes focus on the alien statue and narrow.

"Well, serves this shithole planet right," she says finally, and directs a raised middle finger toward the statue, shining a light out of her fingertip for extra effect. She continues forward without hesitation. I sigh and shake off my lingering nostalgia before following her.

"Don't go too far ahead," I call out, stepping over a piece of scrap metal that was once a building or vehicle. "If there are tunnels beneath us, the ground could be unstable now."

Scorpia waves a hand in acknowledgment and continues on ahead, picking through the rubble. I glance back at Shey, who is standing on the edge of the ramp, her hands clutched to her chest. She looks out at the remains of Levian—her hometown, I realize—and takes a deep breath before coming after us.

As she meets my eyes, she hesitates, and then presses two fingers from each hand together in a Gaian gesture of mourning—a motion usually reserved for the funerals of loved ones, only appropriate if used toward someone who also knew the dead and shares in your grief. It's small and subtle enough that I know it must be meant only for me. After a brief pause, I return the gesture, holding it long enough that I'm certain she's seen it, and then drop my hands and follow after Scorpia. We don't have time to spare on mourning. It seems we never do, these days.

CHAPTER TWELVE

Buried Secrets

Scorpia

S hey leads us through the ruins of Levian with her usual rigid poise. Even aside from the clunky suits and the storm beating down on us, I can only imagine how painful it must be to walk through the destroyed remnants of what was once her home. It's surprisingly hard even for me. I never had any love for this place—in fact, I remember decrying it as the "worst city in the system" on at least a few occasions—but I still had memories here. Mostly bad, but not all.

This is the place where Corvus and I grew up. It's the place that, in many ways, made me the person I am today. It's also the place where I met Shey—Shey, who walks ahead of us with her back straight, slowly sweeping her eyes over what was once a collection of buildings and roads, a thriving center of her home-world. But she remains silent and dry-eyed, shoulders stiff beneath her skin-tight suit, her pace never slowing.

Part of me wants to reach for her, try to support her in some way, but she walks far enough ahead of us that she never gives me a chance. I guess maybe this is the sort of thing that someone has to shoulder for themselves, anyway. Maybe her pain would only be tarnished by my own stained memories of this place.

The storm rages on, and the terrain only grows worse as we approach the city and the howling winds are joined by torrential rainfall. The slick rubble makes every step a chore. But my suit does its job, keeping me dry and warm and sure-footed. When the rain gets heavy enough that it becomes hard to see, I activate my heads-up display to mark the others ahead of me.

When the markers stop moving, I know what must be coming up, but my heart still races as the Primus statue looms out of the rain. It's disconcerting to see it and remember the last time I was here, our hovercraft parked right at its feet and my siblings laughing at my discomfort. Now, it's the only thing that stands untouched by the destruction, while the city around it lies in ruins. As if the damn thing wasn't creepy enough before.

Shey moves around to the back of the statue. I follow, and watch as she bends down and presses her fingers to its base, moving aside a small panel I wouldn't have known to look for and revealing a screen within. She enters a password, and then presses her thumb to the screen, and a click comes from somewhere nearby. When I glance over my shoulder, I see a patch on the ground where the dirt has crumbled, revealing the outline of what must be a hidden hatch.

"So that's why the Gaians were so anal about not letting anyone near the statues," I say.

"Well, there's also the matter of great historical significance." Shey doesn't turn to look at me, but I imagine I hear a smile in her voice. "But, yes, mostly it was to protect government secrets."

"You really didn't look at the council's documents for this mission at all," Corvus says, his voice deeply disapproving.

"Are you surprised?" Shey asks, in a way that makes me think maybe I should reevaluate that smile I thought I heard before. "Could you help me with this, Corvus?"

While the two of them move to open the hatch, I circle around to the front of the statue again. I stare up at it, willing myself not to look away even as my chest constricts and goose bumps break out all over my body. I've always been terrified of these things... just like I've always feared the rest of Gaia. I tried to convince myself that it was hatred I felt, but I know in truth that it was always fear. Fear that I didn't belong, that I'd never belong, that I didn't deserve to belong.

Now, the people of Gaia are indebted to me and my family, and the only thing that remains of their world are these ugly-ass alien statues. And I'm a stars-damned hero.

So why does it still hurt to see this place? a small voice in the back of my head asks. *And why are you still just as scared as before?*

I grit my teeth and, in an attempt to defy the fear forming a cold pit in my stomach, reach out to touch the statue. Even with a glove between me and the alien material, my fingers shake as they draw close, and something deep inside me writhes with discomfort. But if I can do this—if I can prove to myself that it's nothing more than a cold, dead relic—maybe I can finally shake this crawling dread that fills me every time I see the damn things. But the moment my gloved hand touches the statue, I gasp and jerk back, stumbling away several steps, my eyes going wide.

"Holy shit," I breathe.

"What?" Shey asks, frowning over at me. I look at her, and then quickly back at the statue, afraid to take my eyes off of it.

"It's... it's *warm*," I say. My stomach is still roiling at the memory of the feeling penetrating the glove—not an intense heat, but the warmth of a living thing. That battles with my earlier memories of the statues, like my first encounter with one, where I bumped a knee against it and felt the cold of it shock me all the way to my bones. "Did you . . . do something over there? Activate it?"

"What? No." Shey's brow furrows. "That's not possible."

"Well . . ." I gesture wordlessly at the statue. Corvus is approaching now, too, drawn by the commotion. He stops at my side, and we both watch as Shey once again draws near to the statue. She tentatively reaches out to place her hand on the surface. As soon as she makes contact, she gasps and recoils, clasping the glove to her chest.

"Impossible," she whispers, and her shoulders start to shake.

For a moment I feel a strange sense of satisfaction at seeing her, a Gaian, *finally* show a reasonable fear of an alien relic. But that triumph withers as she reaches out again, this time placing both hands on the statue. When she turns to us, I see it isn't fear that's making her tremble. Her expression is joyous. Reverent.

"It's a miracle," she says.

I stare at her for a moment, and then glance over at Corvus, who is staring up at the statue with an undeniable hint of the same awe on his face.

"Oh, for fuck's sake," I say. "Let's get this over with so we can get the hell out of this place."

My determination to move forward doesn't last long. The hatch Shey has revealed opens into a dark, damp-looking tunnel. Once we climb down the ladder, it extends out ahead in near-total darkness, sloping gently downward. I was expecting something more fortified and high-tech in nature, but this thing is earthy and incredibly unreliable looking. I'm surprised it survived when the rest of the city fell.

"Are we sure these tunnels are safe?" I ask, eyeing the low overhang. "I mean, with the storms and all, couldn't it be unstable down here?"

"These tunnels were made by the Primus," Shey says, stepping forward without a moment's hesitation. She glances over her shoulder at me. "Which means they've existed for thousands of years. I highly doubt they're going to choose this moment to suddenly lose stability."

"I don't know," I say, still hanging back. Despite what she's saying, all of my instincts are screaming that going into that tunnel means death. The nearness of that Primus statue and its inexplicable warmth already has my nerves all riled up, and the thought of setting foot in a tunnel hidden beneath it makes me so anxious I want to gag. "The universe seems to have some kind of weird grudge against me and my family, so honestly, it wouldn't surprise me." I force a laugh.

Shey rolls her eyes in a slow, deliberate motion, and then turns and begins to walk.

"Fine then, I'll handle this on my own," she says without turning around.

Even Corvus is looking at the tunnel with a worried expression, his frown lines used to their full effect, and he normally has no issue dealing with the Primus like I do. But after a moment, he follows her, and I grudgingly trudge along behind them. Once I shut the latch behind me, the tunnel is pitch-black, forcing each of us to light up the fingertips of our gloves. The light shifts eerily as we progress, and I try not to think of the weight of the earth above us or the darkness of the tunnel ahead.

We don't travel long before hitting a set of doors of glossy Gaian steel. Shey slips off a glove to try her fingerprint on the biometric scanner, but the screen flashes green in denial. "My clearance isn't high enough. I assume you have something for this?"

Corvus bends down and removes a device from his pack. As he attaches it to the scanner and it begins to do its work, Shey removes her helmet and unzips her suit. Corvus and I do the same.

The air down here is musty and damp, and the storm is a distant roar above. We grab our packs, and I double-check that mine still holds my flashlight and other survival supplies. My comm already has no signal, as we expected.

"It should be safe beyond this point," Shey says. "It's a secure research facility. I've seen some of it before, though never unaccompanied."

"On a scale of one to Primus statues, how creepy should I expect it to get down here?" I ask, but she doesn't dignify the question with a response.

The tunnel widens as we continue farther downward, the ceiling pulling away. As I start to get the unnerving impression that we're entering a widening mouth, we reach a second set of doors, and my feet come to a stop.

It's immediately clear these doors are not of human origin. An intricate pattern of swirls much like tentacles stretch across their length, made of black Primus material. The rest of the door is glistening and gray, and when Shey steps forward and presses both bare palms against the door, her hands sink in a few inches. I cover my mouth to hide my disgust.

A light pulses beneath her hands, and crawls upward, filling into a spiral pattern that swirls all the way up to the ceiling. For a moment, the pale blue light is nearly blinding; and then the doors release a strange, shuddering sound—like a person letting out a long, low-pitched sigh—and begin to fold outward, revealing the dark tunnel beyond. The air that the inner tunnel breathes out is moist, and warm.

I try to keep my mouth shut, but a strangled sound of anxiety escapes me nonetheless. When Shey and Corvus turn to look at me, I say, weakly, "Yuck."

"If it bothers you too much, turn back," Corvus says.

I grimace. More than anything, I want to do as he suggests...

but what kind of captain would I be if I turned away from a challenge? And furthermore, what would Shey think of me? No. I'm not walking away now. I've made it this far, and it's time to face my fears. I stride forward, passing by the two of them as they watch me.

"Let's just get a move on," I say, and press onward with them close behind. I pause as I hear the sound of the doors shutting behind us, turning to watch as the light from above cuts off completely. I shiver in the darkness, but before I can grab my flashlight a faint glow appears. The tunnel walls are coming to life, lit by a type of moss I've never seen before. It grows along the walls in swirling patterns reminiscent of the Primus doors, lighting the area in dim shades of blue and violet. The light, so very different than either the familiar glow of Nova Vita or the soothing yellow tones of a ship, makes me uneasy.

As we continue, ever downward, the lights grow along the walls, following our progress and keeping our area of the tunnel well-lit. When I glance back, I see that they've faded behind us.

"What is this?" I draw near to the wall to get a closer look at the glowing moss, though I resist the urge to reach out and touch it. "Some kind of abstract art deal?"

"We're not sure," Shey says. "It was here when we found it."

I jerk back from the wall with a grimace. I should've known it was alien shit. At least I didn't touch the stuff. Now I imagine the Primus sliding through this tunnel on their creepy inhuman feet, marking these swirls with their tentacle arms.

"Just wait until we get deeper," Shey says, her voice echoing off the walls. Now that I pay attention to it, I hear every footfall in the tunnel, even the soft sound of our breathing. We're so very far from the surface that there's no outside noise to interfere, though I imagine a storm is still raging overhead. Shey turns to smile at me. Maybe it's just the odd lighting, but the expression seems suspiciously reassuring, like the way a doctor would look at a child before giving them a needle to the arm. "Trust me, you've never seen the Primus like this," she says.

No matter how excited Shey sounds, there's no way I can listen to that sentence with anything but dread.

The deeper we get, the harder it becomes to walk. At first, I think it's only because of my growing exhaustion—but I soon realize it's more than that. The floor is getting muddier, sucking at my boots like it wants to hold them in place. The air, too, is becoming more humid. I wipe sweat off my forehead and look around at the others to see if they're having as much trouble as I am. Shey seems relatively unbothered, though Corvus's limp has grown more pronounced.

"Why the hell is it so *wet* in here?" I ask, unable to take it any longer.

"Well, evidence says that the Primus were probably amphibious," Shey says, pausing to wipe her forehead with one sleeve, which gives me a good excuse to pause and catch my breath. "It's likely why they never settled on Pax."

"Wait, seriously? They lived in the water?"

"We believe they were born from eggs placed in the water, and traveled between land and water later in life." I wrinkle my nose, but she continues before I can comment. "Don't say it's disgusting. There's absolutely nothing wrong with that."

"I'm just thinking about how slimy they must have been," I say, and give an exaggerated shudder to display my displeasure.

"You are truly unbelievable," Shey says. "You do realize we owe life as we know it to the Primus? These planets are only inhabitable for us because they were here first to terraform them."

I think about that for a moment, and then say, "Doesn't mean they weren't gross as hell."

She sighs and continues onward.

After what feels like hours but is likely only about thirty minutes of traveling, the path opens into a wider, darker room. As I step through the entrance, I click on my light, sweeping it around the darkness. The walls glisten as it crosses over them.

"You couldn't have installed some lights down here?" I ask, swinging the beam toward Shey, who raises an arm to shield her eyes.

"There's no need," she says. "You'll see soon."

"I really, really don't like when you say cryptic shit like that."

I also don't like how suspiciously wet and huge this room is. When I point the light upward, the beam doesn't even touch the ceiling. We must have traveled deeper than I thought.

"The tunnels go much farther, but if this is what I think it is, I believe we may be able to find the information we're looking for here," Shey says.

"Here?" This is just an empty cavern. I was expecting computers and fancy machines ready to spit out the data and files we're looking for. "With the . . . what, the rocks?"

Shey lets out a surprisingly loud laugh that ricochets around the room. As soon as it escapes her lips she puts a hand to her mouth, as if surprised, but when she lowers it she's still smiling. "Not quite."

We follow her over to the center of the room, where a small spire of rock juts out of the ground. At least, it appears to be rock at first glance, but as we get closer it soon becomes clear that it's actually black Primus material, shaped like a thin stalagmite. When Shey presses a hand to the top, it begins to emanate a faint blue glow and a rumbling sound. A moment later, she removes the top and reveals a dark, wet-looking interior.

"Is that—" I start, and Shey plunges her hand in. She presses her fingers against what must be a gooey, pliable substance.

"Ugh. How do you even—" I cut off and gag as she puts her

hand farther into the thing with a wet squish, slapping a hand over my mouth as bile rises in the back of my throat. "Urgh," I murmur through my fingers. "Disgusting. Is that as slimy as it looks? Or even slimier?"

"Not helpful, Scorpia," Corvus says, though I can't help but notice that even he looks a little green in the face over the alien tech.

"Hush, I need to concentrate," Shey says. She takes a deep breath. Then she goes completely, eerily still. Her face goes slack. Her eyes roll back in her head. She stays on her feet, unmoving, her eyes almost totally white.

"What," I say, flatly, staring at her in dumbfounded horror, and then at Corvus. "What just... is that... is this normal? Or should we be scared?"

"I'm not sure," he says, taking a hesitant step toward her. "...Shey?"

A moment later, she blinks, and her eyes return to normal. "There we are," she says, in a completely mild tone, hand still submerged in the alien whatever-it-is, like she didn't just go full exorcism-face a few seconds ago.

"What the *fuck*," I say, and the room begins to change around us.

CHAPTER THIRTEEN

Lost History

Corvus

Light spreads across the floor, stemming from the device Shey is using and creeping in blue-and-violet swirls like the ones we saw on the walls on our way here. As they reach the sides of the cavern, they continue moving, becoming more brilliant as they climb higher. It soon becomes clear that the walls of this place are not stone, but something thin and membrane-like, with lights pulsing behind. As it spreads, the light twists into shapes that I recognize as alien runes, though about half of them are the same bright-green symbol. I can assume the color, shockingly opposite our red sun and so rare in nature, meant the same to the Primus as it does to us: an error, or a warning.

Scorpia—who retreated to the very edge of the room the moment the floor started lighting up—stares at the area around us with silent, intense suspicion of everything that's happening.

"Incredible," I murmur. "What is this place?"

"We believe it's their equivalent of a computer database," Shey says. As she turns to survey the room, the runes shift like rippling water. She breaks into a wide smile. "I've never had access to one so expansive. This is...wow. I can only imagine what a wealth of information it could provide."

As pleased as she looks, I can't help but be disheartened. "How will we find what we're looking for?"

"Considering we don't *know* what we're looking for? I'm not sure. Trial and error until something stands out, I suppose."

"That could take ages," Scorpia says, speaking up for the first time since the room transformed into an alien database. She stands with her arms folded stiffly across her chest, and seems to be trying very hard not to look afraid.

"We could also travel deeper into the tunnels," Shey says. "Though I believe the next major point of interest is a couple of hours farther."

Scorpia shudders. "No, here is good. Do your thing."

"As you say, Captain."

Hours slither past, as Scorpia paces and I sit on the floor and watch Shey painstakingly search through the database, occasionally pausing to check the Nibiran document I forwarded to her on our trip here. Most of what she does with the alien device seems to produce no result at all, or a flicker of another toxic-green symbol. The few that do seem to work only show expanses of more unreadable alien runes. It's clear there is a wealth of information here, but none of it is understandable to us.

"This thing broken, or what?" Scorpia asks after what must be the hundredth attempt. Shey doesn't answer, her brow furrowed in concentration.

"It's very old," I say, keeping my voice quiet so I won't distract her. "And built for a different species. It's going to take time."

Just as I finish, the room changes around us once again. The runes on the walls dim, the floor glows brighter, and a hologram begins to unfold in the middle of the room.

My breath catches as it rises. Even Scorpia is silent with awe as the image of a Primus statue forms. It towers above us, roughly the same size as the physical ones. But green runes surround the statue—most of them the same one, repeated over and over again in strokes of neon color. It's frustrating to look at it. Someone was trying to convey a message here—something important, possibly dangerous—but it's been lost.

Still, there's a nagging, half-realized thought scratching at the corner of my mind. The statues that are now warm, the warnings on this image... I walk in a slow circle around the hologram, my eyes skimming over the green symbols.

As much as this feels like an important discovery, Shey is unable to produce anything more than this image. After further hours studying it from every angle possible, she switches back over to where she was before, and the hologram dissipates.

"I don't know if the Nibirans realized how complicated this would be," I say to Scorpia, keeping my voice low. "They said a scientist pointed them toward these tunnels, but it could take weeks to peruse this room, let alone go farther."

"And if we don't head back within the next couple days, we'll miss the deadline for the vote about the Gaians," Scorpia murmurs back. "But maybe we should call it a day for now." She raises her voice and says, for Shey's benefit, "I think that's enough for today."

"Now?" Shey asks. "We've barely started."

"It's late," I say. "And the others have no way of contacting us while we're down here."

"No point in wearing ourselves out the first day here," Scorpia says, when Shey looks ready to argue more. "We'll come back in the morning with clear heads."

Shey doesn't look happy about it, but she keeps her mouth shut and nods nonetheless. Together, we begin the trek to the surface.

*   *   *

The walk back is much longer uphill through the muddy tunnels, and the storm has only worsened outside. By the time we make it back to the ship, we're all exhausted. I pause only to check on Pol, who is now sleeping soundly with Drom at his side, and eat a quick freeze-dried meal before falling into bed.

Winds assault the ship all night. Despite my fatigue, I barely sleep, and in the morning I have to drag myself out of bed to prepare breakfast. I put together a generous spread, knowing the work that lies ahead of us today.

Pol and Lyre are the first to shuffle in, both bleary-eyed. She picks dried fruit and nuts out of her porridge. He busies himself creating a multilayered salted-fish-and-protein-paste sandwich between flat disks of algae bread.

"Looks like you're feeling better," I say, fighting back a twinge of nausea as he dips the creation into his coffee before taking a massive bite. He makes a noncommittal sound through the mouthful of food.

"Please close your mouth when you chew," Lyre says, wrinkling her nose.

He swallows thickly, turns, and belches in her face.

"You. Are. *Disgusting.*"

Others trickle in one by one. Shey looks exhausted, Izra as unbothered as usual. Drom sits next to Pol, and Orion beside Izra.

Scorpia is the last to wander in, yawning and pouring herself some coffee before taking a seat next to me. She makes her way through three cups and half a bowl of porridge before she stands and clears her throat.

"All right, everyone," she says. "The good news is that the tunnels beneath Levian seem safe. The bad news is that it looks like this job is going to take a bit longer than the Nibirans anticipated. Shey and I are going to return to the room we found yesterday, and, Lyre, I'd like you to come with us and see if you notice any-thing we missed. Corvus, I want you to take a second team to scavenge for any tech we can find to sell. You choose who to bring, but Orion should stay with the ship, along with someone else, in case we need an emergency liftoff. Our comms will be cut off in the tunnels, so I don't want anyone alone, just in case."

I glance around, weighing my options. Regardless of what Scor-pia thinks, splitting up the pirates seems like an obvious choice. But I'm not eager to be alone with the deserter. "I'll take Izra," I say. She doesn't even look up from her breakfast. "And Drom."

Pol chokes on his mouthful of food, coughs, and looks up. "What about me?"

"You were bedridden yesterday."

"And I'm not today."

I should have thought of this before deciding to bring Drom. But, guilty as I feel, we can't risk it. I look at Scorpia for help.

"Pol, buddy, you scared us all yesterday," she says. "Sorry, but you need to take a day off. Maybe tomorrow." He scowls down at the table, but doesn't complain, so she continues, "Okay, well, hurry up and eat, everybody. Clock's ticking. We need to leave by tomorrow night if we want to make it back to Nibiru before the Gaians' deadline is up."

CHAPTER FOURTEEN

Alien Civilization

Scorpia

Lyre is uncharacteristically chatty from the moment we enter the Primus tunnels, eager to discuss everything she sees with Shey. As the two of them walk side by side and discuss alien theory, I lag behind.

"Just wait until you see this alien computer shit," I say, trying to avoid ending up a third wheel. "I think it's creepy as hell, but you're gonna love it, Lyre."

"I'm sure I will," she says, without glancing back. "I read about it in the file the Nibirans gave us. You know, the one you made me read on the way over, only to decide to leave me behind yesterday?"

Shit. "I wanted to make sure it was safe down here."

"If anywhere is unsafe, it's the surface," Shey says. "Yet you had no qualms about sending a team there to rifle through the ruins of my hometown." She glances over her shoulder, eyes narrowed in disapproval. "You could have had them search for further leads in the tunnels."

Double shit. "If you two can't figure out what we need to find, I doubt anyone else is gonna be much help."

"Which is why you should have brought me yesterday," Lyre says.

I roll my eyes up to the ceiling. "Okay. I'm just going to shut my mouth now."

After a few moments of silence, the two of them resume their easy chatter, and I drag my feet along and stare forlornly at the back of Shey's head. The only reason I wanted to come into these tunnels again today is that I wanted another shot at closing the distance between us, but it looks like I'm not going to get a chance.

Down in the database room, Shey shows my sister the image of the statue we discovered yesterday, and after they spend some time scrutinizing it, they set their minds on figuring out the menu. Using her comm, Lyre sketches out a branching diagram, filling in notes and symbols as Shey moves through the alien runes.

Their conversation loses me shortly after that, and I resort to playing solo card games on my comm. The hours ooze by with agonizing slowness.

"Well, now that we've ruled those options out," Lyre says, while I yawn, wondering if anyone will notice if I take a nap, "let's try this one?"

My yawn cuts off in a gasp as the room begins to change. This shift is even more dramatic than when the image of the statue formed. I rise to my feet and stare as a hologram spreads out to fill the room, wall-to-wall and ceiling-to-floor.

When it finishes, five huge orbs hang in the room, forming a neat line down the middle. Parts of the image are glitched out, fuzzed over with green static, but they're still clearly recognizable as the five planets of our system. The farthest from me, Pax, is pale green. The rest glow a dim red: rainy and overgrown Deva, the endless ocean of Nibiru, the beautiful Gaia we stand on now, and Titan.

My throat constricts as I stare at the planet that my family helped destroy. The planet where Momma died along with everyone else because of the deal she made with Leonis. Even though I had no direct part in it, guilt still gnaws at me.

Lyre moves through the room toward me. At first I think she might be feeling some of the same guilt I am, but her expression is full of nothing but wonder as she gazes around at the hologram. "This is incredible," she says, and reaches out to touch Titan. The moment she does, the room shifts again, and I let out a startled exclamation. Titan grows to fill the huge cavern as the hologram zooms in. Lyre, looking delighted, moves in closer to the surface.

A surface startlingly different than the planet I remember. It's icy and mountainous, yes, but there are also plants sprouting out of the snow—pale red vines crawling over the valley walls, velvety black flowers sprouting between cracks in the rocky hillside.

"I've never seen anything like that on Titan," I say—but then again, I never had any reason to venture far from Drev Dravaask on my visits. If Corvus was here, he might be able to tell us more...Lyre, on the other hand, has her eyes elsewhere. She lets out a gasp as she spots something on the horizon of the image, and quickly moves the hologram toward it. Gradually, she zooms in on what must be an alien city.

"Guess the Primus were hardier than us squishy humans, if they were living on the surface," I murmur, fighting off a wave of revulsion as I stare at the strange alien structures. They're all so bulbous and fleshy and *wet*. The city looks like a cluster of fish eggs. Which reminds me: "But if they were amphibious and needed liquid water, shouldn't that have been impossible for them?"

"They had a great deal of technology we don't understand," Lyre says.

"There also may have been different subspecies of the Primus on different planets," Shey says, but the words are absentminded; her face is flushed with excitement, her eyes bright as she looks out at the hologram. "But this is *incredible*. These images must be from when the Primus still lived! Oh, this is—We have to see Gaia!"

She and Lyre can hardly contain their excitement as they work their way through navigating back to the full spread of planets and then zooming in on Gaia. I retreat to the side of the room and sit down again, still dwelling on what we saw of Titan, but those thoughts are banished as Shey and Lyre find what they're looking for.

Gaia's surface is absolutely covered with a sprawl of alien civilization—impossibly tall spires like jagged teeth, rounded structures that look like sacks of fluid on the verge of bursting, twisting tubes that look like fat intestines. All of it glistens wetly, with long strings of something webby and mucus-like stretching across much of it.

"Fascinating," Lyre murmurs, pressing a hand to her mouth as she stares up at the image.

"Wow," Shey says, her eyes shining in the light. "All of this... and these tunnels are all that remain." She wipes her eyes with her free hand, the other still deep in the Primus device. "Such a shame."

I look back and forth between them, disbelieving. "You two are kidding, right?" I jab a finger at the hologram. "That is repulsive. It looks like it's covered in *snot*. And, holy shit, it's no wonder you Gaians couldn't grow anything on this planet if the aliens covered the entire surface with this bullshit."

"You are undeniably biased," Lyre says, "but I suppose you do

have a point. If the Primus cities are anything like human indus-
try, building a civilization like this may have wrung the planets of
resources. Just as we did to Earth."

But Shey shakes her head stubbornly. "Their technology
was mostly organic in nature, so there's no reason to believe it
would be as resource-intensive as ours. Some Primus weaponry
even seems to be made out of bone-like materials. They weren't
wasteful."

I stare at her. "They made *weapons* out of *bones*," I say slowly,
"and you find that *impressive*."

She ignores me, zooming in further on one of the cities. As the
image closes in on the squishy wetness of one of the buildings,
I gag and turn away, unable to take any more. No matter what
these two think, that Primus city is nothing short of disgusting.
By the time I turn back, Shey and Lyre are eagerly exploring the
other planets.

I take a seat against the wall and watch as they travel through
them one by one, starting with Pax. There's little to see there but
desert, as the aliens never settled there. Deva looks much the same
as the world we know, though the alien cities cut through wider
swathes of the jungle than even Zi Vi does, and there's no sign of
the plants impinging on their communities as they do on ours.
Nibiru looks similar as well, our man-made islands replaced with
shimmering disks that float above the water, with long, thin spires
hanging down toward the waves. Even I can admit the sights are
fascinating—albeit gut-churning—but none of it comes close
to Gaia, and our two Primus enthusiasts soon cycle back to that
hologram, and pass hours discussing and exploring the alien cities. I lose track of the conversation and am content to zone out. If
anyone's gonna figure out what the hell is going on here, I doubt
it's going to be me. Just wrapping my mind around all of this alien
shit is starting to give me a headache.

Despite their much greater enthusiasm for the topic, I can tell the long hours are getting to Shey and Lyre as well. The conversation gradually draws to a lull, and Lyre sits beside me, gazing up at the hologram without commentary.

"There's an incredible wealth of information here," Shey says. "I could spend the rest of my life analyzing this."

"But does it have the information we're looking for?" I ask.

"I don't know…but this started with a Primus weapon, and my intuition tells me the secret is linked to them. I'm just not sure how." Shey bites her lip, slowly retracting her hand from the alien control panel. The holograms fade away, the planets receding, reducing the room to the dim cave we first entered. "And it can't be a coincidence that the statues are suddenly warm. Perhaps it's in response to something…"

"There's also the image you found in this database," Lyre says. "And the fact that the storms on Gaia tend to form above the statues."

"I feel like we have all of the pieces, but I'm not quite sure how they fit together." Shey sighs, and nods to me. "I think I've seen enough for today. I'd like to take notes on everything we've seen and compare it to my own research before returning tomorrow."

Her expression falters after she says the words, no doubt processing the reality of them. Tomorrow. Our last day here, if we stick to the Nibirans' schedule—and given the tension on the planet right now, I doubt they'll be happy to wait for us. We need to find something to give them before things get any worse for the Gaians.

But Shey doesn't need any reminders of that. I throw on a smile as I stand up, and pause to squeeze her shoulder as I head for the door. "It feels like we made a breakthrough," I say—and immediately lose my confidence as she glances at my hand on her shoulder, her expression unreadable. I cough and pull it back, running my fingers through my own hair instead. "Uh…good job. Both of you."

Stars, why is this so awkward? Before she can respond and embarrass me further, I head for the door and begin the trek up to the ship.

Everyone's spirits seem down at dinner. Corvus and his team spent all day in the ruins of Levian, but found little more than some cracked comms and a couple hovercrafts to haul back. Pol isn't feeling well again, and sleeps right through the meal. Shey retreats to her room with her food, continuing to pore over her notes the same way she has ever since we got back. Lyre claims she's going to look over the Nibiran document again, but she can barely keep her eyes open after the long day.

At night the ship creaks and rattles, and I toss and turn in my too-large bed, my mind stuck down in those tunnels beneath the city. My thoughts flash to Shey's hands against the huge black doors, the alien runes filling the cavern, the warmth of the Primus statue beneath my palm, the image in the cavern surrounded by urgent and unreadable messages. There's something here… something important. I'm sure of it. But it hangs frustratingly out of reach.

I hope it doesn't evade us for long. The Gaians need us to find an answer soon—and I don't like being here. This planet isn't safe anymore, and as winds throw themselves against the ship, I can't help but think of them like fingers trying to scrape us off of Gaia's surface. But as soon as I think of the image, my mind changes the fingers to the slithering tentacles of the Primus, and a huge statue leaning over *Memoria*, metal creaking as it wraps itself around the ship—

"Ugh." I shake the thought off and sit up, tossing the covers aside. My nerves have been a mess after being in those tunnels.

Unable to stay still any longer, I head to the kitchen to grab a glass of water. Or maybe a glass of something else—just enough to sleep soundly, I tell myself. It's not like anyone will notice. The metal floor is cold beneath my feet, the darkened ship quiet around me. It's soothing to see nothing amiss in the ship's corridors.

But it seems I'm not the only one awake. Light leaks out beneath one of the doorways: Shey's room, if I'm not mistaken. All other thoughts, even ones of whiskey, flee my head. I hesitate outside, reaching for the door and stopping myself twice before I finally work up the courage to rap my knuckles against it.

The door slides open a few moments later, and Shey peers up at me, dressed in a silky robe and slippers with her hair tied up. Behind her, a speaker plays one of those Gaian songs that blends a steady synth beat with nature sounds, shifting from birdsong to the rush of a waterfall to a soft hiss of wind.

"I'm sorry. Is the music too loud?" she asks.

"Oh, no. Just saw that your light was on. Wanted to make sure everything was okay." It's distracting to see her so comfortable like this. Her robe shows quite a bit more of her skin than I'm used to seeing. It feels like I've stumbled upon a private moment, though she doesn't seem at all self-conscious about looking this way in front of me. Maybe things like that really are far from her mind now.

I clear my throat and shift my eyes to the room behind her. The bed is neat and unslept-in, and the floor is covered with an array of papers and screens.

She follows my gaze and flushes slightly. "I couldn't sleep," she says. "Tomorrow's our last day here, and I feel like we're nowhere close to an answer."

Guilt nips me. Of course, I should have known that all the worry I'm carrying over this mission is amplified tenfold in her. I search for something to say that won't feel like empty promises.

But it's difficult—I've seen a lot of things on a lot of different worlds but never come up against a problem that felt so far out of my expertise.

"Well, you should get some sleep," I say, eventually. "We'll need that brain of yours at its best to figure this out. And I'm sure you've looked over your files a hundred times already." I pause, considering. "Maybe I should bring them over to Lyre's room. She can read them in the morning, see if she catches anything you missed."

She blinks up at me. "Why, Scorpia," she says, lips curving into a small smile, "are you captain-ing me right now?"

I lean against the doorway, grinning despite myself. "I might be."

"Well, don't think I don't notice what you're doing...but really, it's not a bad idea." She goes to gather her papers into a neat stack, and I avert my eyes as she bends down and her robe shifts to reveal a distracting amount of leg. I recover by the time she hands the papers over. There's an uncomfortable pause as we both look at one another, both waiting for the other to say something.

"Well," I say, finally. "Good night, then."

"Scorpia?" she says, just as I'm about to turn away. "What happens if we don't find an answer in time? If the Nibirans vote before we figure out the truth about what happened here? With the uncertainty about Gaia looming, and the superstition among the Nibirans, I'm afraid..." She trails off, hesitating, and then says again, more finally, "I'm afraid."

I pause, wrestling with my words. The truth is I have no idea, but I can't say that when she's looking at me like this, searching for some thread of hope to hold on to. "If we don't find an answer fast enough," I say, forcing a smile, "then I'll bullshit them to get us more time. No problem."

Relief crosses her face, but suspicion chases close behind. "You really think you could convince them?"

"Clearly you've forgotten that you're speaking to a master bullshitter," I say. "I'll just send them a message like…" I shift the papers to one hand and cup the other over my mouth, imitating the sound of hissing static. "Vital information discovered on Gaia…*dire importance* that you wait for us…signal…breaking up…" I stop, drop my hand, and shrug. "Something like that."

Shey presses a hand to her mouth, her eyes crinkling. "Very convincing."

"Maybe I'll make Corvus do it. That ultra-serious tone of his could really sell it."

She smothers a laugh in her palm and then lowers her hands to her sides. "Well, it's good to know you've got a plan."

"Of course I do. What kind of captain do you take me for?"

It's nice to see a smile on her face as she says good night. But as the door shuts between us, mine melts off my face. I look down at the papers in my arms—covered in words and images, Primus runes and pictures of the statues, all sorts of things I can't even begin to understand.

I really hope we can pull this off.

CHAPTER FIFTEEN

Dangerous Truths

Corvus

Another storm breaks on our final day on Gaia, this one the worst yet. I doubt anyone gets much sleep with the wind making the ship shudder and groan like a living thing.

I make breakfast and watch Scorpia through the doorway as she winds her way through the assembled, haggard-looking crew. She moves with no sense of urgency, pausing to exchange casual greetings and give cheerful encouragement to various people. But as she makes her way into the kitchen, she leans back against the counter, and one of her legs starts to jump, heel tapping against the floor.

"Everything okay?" I ask.

"Yeah. No. I don't know." She glances at the doorway and lowers her voice. "We spent all day in those tunnels yesterday, but I feel like we're nowhere close to an answer. If we can't figure it out today..."

"I know," I say. "What can I do? Should we bring a second team into the tunnels?"

"I don't know if I want anyone other than Shey messing with the alien shit. But I could use you down there today. We found this hologram of the planets, and it's..." She pauses for a moment, brow furrowing. "It's hard to explain. I'd like you to take a look at it. There's something off with Titan, but I don't know the planet well enough to put my finger on it."

I shut off the stove and add the last touches of seasonings to the eggs while I consider that. A hologram of Titan. She's asking me to face my dead planet again. But judging from the hesitant way she's looking at me now, she knows it's not an easy thing to ask of me. The fact that she's asking anyway means she must think it's important. "All right," I say. "If that's what you need from me, I'll come with you."

Between the worsening weather and the fact that Pol is holed up in his room complaining of a headache again, Scorpia decides that the rest of our crew should stay on the ship while I accompany her and Shey into the tunnels. It's a struggle just to get there, and Shey looks on the verge of tears when we finally arrive, no doubt thinking of the transformation of her home-world and the fate of her people depending on us. It's heavy on my mind, too.

Even after days of exploration, stepping into the Primus tunnels still feels like trespassing on ground we were never meant to tread. I would take the storms above over this quiet strangeness any day, but my sister needs me here, so I follow her as I promised I would. We return to the same chamber as we did on the first day. I'm not sure whether to take that as a sign that the room is promising, or merely that our progress has been so slow we haven't been able to move forward.

Shey seems exhausted, but she navigates the system with confidence now, following the alien runes until the room shifts even more dramatically than it did for the image of the statue on the first day. A new hologram begins to unfold—and unfold, and unfold, filling the entire width of the room with the five planets of our system. The deserts of Pax, the jungles of Deva, the unbroken stretch of water on Nibiru, Earth-like Gaia before the storms ravaged it, and...

Shey and Scorpia are silent as I approach Titan, my icy birth-planet. Seeing it now is a reminder of everything I've lost, and everything we're fighting for now. I stand in front of the huge world, and stretch out a hand to touch it.

The other four planets disappear as Titan expands to fill the space, the hologram zooming in on the ice planet. I have to step back to get a clear picture of it. It's a closer look at Titan now, an aerial view—but not the Titan that I knew. The view is close enough to see the spread of cities across its surface, strange architecture that I recognize at first glance to be alien. The curved edges and bulbous shapes are all too reminiscent of what the aliens left behind. But even beyond the sprawl of alien cities, the image is strange.

Scorpia steps up beside me, glancing at my face in what I assume is an effort to gauge my mood. I stay focused on the hologram, touching the image again to zoom in further. "I thought something was off, but I haven't seen much of Titan outside Drev Dravaask," Scorpia says.

"It's..." I reach into the hologram, zooming in further and further, until finally it's a close-up of a single valley. A valley covered in the familiar ice and rocks that have always coated my home-planet, along with an expanse of beautiful, black flowers. Above stretches a red sky, completely unmarred by storm clouds. "It's nothing like Titan," I say, still staring. "Nothing like this grew on Titan while I was there. Nothing but frostroot grew naturally, and even that only underground. The climate was too harsh, the surface too cold." My brow furrows as I consider. "Are the other planets different as well?"

"Not that I noticed," Scorpia says. "Aside from, well, the alien shit."

"Show me."

"I'm warning you, it's real gross," Scorpia warns me, as Shey obliges. She flicks through the other planets, showing me the vast alien civilizations spread across all of the worlds but Pax. Gaia is the most striking of all, clearly the crown jewel of the Primus and the heart of their civilization. Even among the twisting, organic-looking structures, the Primus statues tower above it all, given a wide berth despite how crowded Gaia's surface is. There isn't even a fence like the Gaians constructed when they settled here; the statues are left alone. Almost as though they're something to be feared rather than something to be protected. I think back to the hologram of the statue, the bright-green symbols screaming warnings even across the language barrier, and something stirs in the back of my mind.

"Go back to Titan," I say. Shey obliges, and I zoom in again on the valley, the Primus city built on the surface of the planet. I search until I find what I'm looking for: a Primus statue.

"They had them there, too," I say, stepping back. "They must be buried beneath the ice now." I glance at Shey. "You said the storms here tended to form just above the statues, correct?" She nods, and I look back at the image. "The storms here...their suddenness and severity, the way radar couldn't predict them like normal storms...storms on Titan were the same. They're one of the main reasons we could never build on the surface. The Primus could never have built those structures in a climate like that. So something must have changed. Just like it did here."

I look at Shey, who stares back wordlessly, her lips pressed together as if she's afraid of what will come out if she lets it free.

"The storms always felt unnatural," I continue. "What if they were? What if the awful weather was never a natural feature of Titan?" The storms were a terrible thing, vicious and consuming, like a concentrated effort by the planet to rid itself of us. Just like the adverse conditions bombarding Gaia. "What if what's happening on Gaia happened on Titan first, in the early days?"

Shey's eyes are wide and frightened.

"When my mother tested the bio-weapon on Titan, she thought it proved that it didn't have any adverse effects on the planet," she says slowly. "But if whatever we triggered on Gaia had already happened there, maybe it didn't prove anything. Maybe any use of the Primus's technology sets off...something. Some kind of reaction." Her brow furrows. "But why would that be? The Primus lived here for centuries. They terraformed the worlds to suit their species."

Something about that stirs a thought in the back of my mind again, but I still can't quite grab ahold of it. I frown out at the holographic planets, considering.

"Maybe the planets went to war with each other," I say. "Maybe they devised weapons that would deliberately undo their terraforming. Make the worlds uninhabitable for their enemies."

"But why would they do such a thing? If the bio-weapon used on Titan is any indication, the Primus already had the technology to cause wide destruction without harming the planet. Why would they deliberately destroy other worlds, rather than taking them to use for themselves? It makes little sense, strategically."

"True. So, if we assume they wouldn't deliberately destroy other planets...that it was an unintended side effect..." I think aloud. There's something still digging at the back of my thoughts, wanting to be heard but not quite reaching the surface. I remember Shey saying something to us when she first snuck aboard our ship to tell us about what happened to Gaia—something about the planet itself trying to get rid of them. I remember it mirroring the way I felt about Titan, the storms that always seemed like they were trying to rip us free. Like the world itself wanted to buck our control. Almost like...

Something finally snaps into place.

"They terraformed these worlds," I say. "Made them suitable for life. What if that wasn't all they did? What if they built in a sort of..." I gesture toward the planets, toward the red glow around four of them. "Defense mechanism? Intended to ward off threats?"

There's a moment of silence as that sinks in.

"So when President Leonis used that alien tech in the Gaian fields, ruined their own soil, they would've triggered it," Scorpia says, turning to look at the holographic image of the planet. I look past it to Titan, thinking of those black flowers, flowers my people never knew existed. A truth long-buried beneath ice and war.

"I'm thinking Gaia's not the only one," I say, my voice coming out hoarse. "People always say Titan's war started shortly after it was settled. Years before they had real contact with the other planets. If they had only seen this, if they had known what the war had done to their planet, then..." Grief chokes me. Maybe it's foolish and idealistic of me to think a conflict as long and pervasive as the Titan civil war could've been stopped by the sight of some flowers, but part of me clings to that idea so tightly that it makes my heart ache. I wish I could show them. I wish they had lived long enough to see this.

Silence falls again. But after a few long moments, Scorpia says, "Leonis had to know about this."

"I was never privy to information that classified, but I agree. Someone had to know," Shey says. "After my mother's use of the Primus technology backfired and our planet began to fail, they must have put this together just like we did."

"And that's why she was so desperate for a new planet that she gave Momma the bio-weapon," Scorpia says.

"Desperate enough that she orchestrated the massacre of the Titans to test it out," I say. Not only did she kill my people, but she knew about the alien technology that ruined their planet, and refused to share it.

The old anger is as bitter as I remember. I have to turn away from the hologram to fight it down before it becomes the pulsing rage that once consumed me. Scorpia steps to my side, resting a hand on my shoulder. "We made her pay for it," she says, and I nod to her. It doesn't erase the pain, but it does make it easier to manage.

"To test it out," Shey says, rolling my previous words out thoughtfully. While I dwell on the past, it's clear from the look on her face that her thoughts are racing ahead. "To make sure the weapon wouldn't damage the planet before she used it on Nibiru. That was important enough to her that she risked the exposure of her plan with the assault against Titan. As though…" Her expression clears, her mind evidently racing to a conclusion faster than her words can keep up. She turns back to the hologram, concentrating, and the room shifts as she zooms in on Nibiru.

"Uh, Shey," Scorpia says. "Care to share with the rest of us?"

"Be quiet for a minute. Corvus, will you zoom in on one of their cities?"

Brow furrowed, I hold my questions for now and turn back around to do as she says, bringing up the image of one of the disklike alien cities. I move in closer, and closer, and then stop as I see what I believe she was searching for: a Primus statue.

"I never knew they had those creepy things on Nibiru," Scorpia says.

"They must be buried in the ocean now." I think of these alien structures crumbling, the statues falling down, sinking deep beneath the waves to rest on the ocean floor. They wouldn't show up on our radars; Primus technology never does. The Nibirans may not even be aware of their existence. Foreboding fills me as I think of the image in this cavern covered in warning-green symbols, and the warmth of the statue above us now.

"As I thought," Shey says softly. "... Let's look at Deva."

Cold dread fills me as I follow her train of thought. The Primus terraformed all of these planets—with the exception of Pax. I already know what we're going to find before Shey zooms in on Deva, and once again finds a statue, sitting with a ring of bare ground around it that even the jungle doesn't dare to touch.

"All of the planets have them," I say. "Buried beneath the ice on Titan, within the ocean on Nibiru, the jungle on Deva..." I shake my head. All this time, we never realized. "They're everywhere. And if what you're saying is true, then..."

"Then all of the planets except Pax have a defense system like the ones that destroyed Gaia and Titan," Scorpia finishes, and we share a horrified look.

"So what happened here could happen everywhere."

I look out at the holographic planets, the sprawls of thriving alien civilizations that are now dead and empty ruins. All of these years, humanity has always wondered what could have possibly happened to the Primus, a species that seemed so much more advanced than our own.

"I think it already did, once," I say, and a heavy silence settles over the room.

"Perhaps this isn't such a terrible thing," Shey says finally to break it, her voice full of fragile hope. "It could encourage peace among the planets, knowing that war would almost certainly ensure mutual destruction. I don't think anyone will be eager to shrink the size of our system even further."

I exchange a glance with Scorpia behind Shey's back. Judging from my sister's expression, her thoughts have followed the same trail mine did, straight down the path opposite of Shey's idealism.

"It could also do the reverse," I say grimly. "It gives the planets the knowledge of just how vulnerable they all are. And how easy it would be to kill off their enemies without ever setting foot on the surface. We don't know exactly what it takes to trigger one of these defense systems. It's possible that all it would take is one unexpected missile launch."

"And Pax would *really* be sitting pretty," Scorpia says. "They'd be the only ones immune."

Shey looks back and forth between us, aghast. "You can't really think that. The Primus must have installed these systems to prevent war. Humanity could heed their example, and..." She trails off, seeming to realize what she's saying anew in light of what we've discovered. This must be immensely difficult for her. Not only is she trying to process the news that her mother rendered her home-planet uninhabitable, but now she also has to reframe her entire view of the aliens she's spent her life studying. This must come doubly as a shock, so I'm not surprised that she seems at a loss for words now, her expression pained.

"And look how well that worked out," I say, as gently as I can manage, and shake my head. "Frankly, I'm not surprised. You've never seen what a war can do to people. Even the best of them are capable of more horrible things than they could imagine."

She looks at me, shaking her head, and says, "I mean no offense, Corvus, but...not everyone is like the Titans."

I fight back the instinctive surge of anger at her words, and force myself to speak calmly. "Yes, they are," I say. "And I truly hope that they're never put in a situation that forces them to realize that."

CHAPTER SIXTEEN

Dead Worlds and Hard Decisions

Scorpia

The trek through the tunnels feels even longer on the way back, impossibly slow with the information we just learned weighing on my shoulders. Everyone is silent, the tunnel quiet but for the sound of ragged breathing. My heartbeat drums in my ears as my thoughts return again and again to those holographic planets, the statues, the long-buried truth of the Primus civilization and how very close humanity has come to meeting the same fate. And we haven't escaped that fate yet. Given the current state of the system, humanity is still toeing the brink of no return, and we all know it.

Once we pass through the set of Primus doors, I call our small group to a halt, the first words anyone has spoken since we left the room. Corvus and Shey gather around, both looking at me like they hope I have an answer to an impossible question.

"So," I say. "Gaia is a dead world." Given that humanity was able to settle here after the Primus royally screwed themselves over, we know it won't last forever, but we have no idea how long it could take. "Aside from Pax, the rest could follow. The Primus were stupid slimy assholes who wiped themselves out with their own technology. And we're some of the only people in the system who know." I fold my arms over my chest and tap a foot on the ground. "This is some heavy shit. We need to figure out how to handle this information."

"We have to tell Nibiru," Corvus says.

"Do we?" I ask. "The place was already a mess when we left. With this information, I'm guessing the Gaians can kiss goodbye any possibility of being allowed to stay there. And if Nibiru has this information but the rest of the planets don't, we're handing them a dangerous amount of power."

Even Corvus, for all his talk of loyalty, goes silent at that.

"You have so little faith in people?" Shey asks.

"People? Nah. I like to think I give most people an honest chance," I say with a shrug. "But *governments*? Fuck no, I don't trust them. And that has proven, time and time again, to be a good call." I look back and forth between Corvus and Shey. "Look: Nibiru's not in any imminent danger. I don't see the issue in waiting until the planet's a little more stable to break this news to the council. Frankly, at this point, I'm more concerned about what this information means for Deva if they go to war with Pax, but there's not much we can do about that. So right now, I think the best thing we can do is step back. Stay out of it. Get our business back up and running so that we'll have options if shit does hit the fan."

Corvus considers this for such a long time that I worry he's prepping an argument. But in the end, he nods. "I agree."

I look at Shey, who seems more hesitant, but she eventually nods as well. "As long as there is no imminent threat, I will abide by your decision."

"Okay, good." I smile. That was a lot easier than expected. "So then..."

"There is one more issue," Corvus says. "This information is valuable. And dangerous. And the more people that learn it, the more likely it is that someone will spread it. I suggest we keep this to ourselves."

I shift uncomfortably. "You're suggesting hiding it from our own crew."

"It will put our younger siblings in danger."

"And you don't trust Izra and Orion with it."

Corvus sighs. "No," he admits. "I don't. I barely trust myself with it, if we're being honest. If we're captured, threatened with lifelong imprisonment or worse—if our siblings are threatened—" He cuts off, shaking his head. "Anyone will break under the right circumstances. And we're not sure how long the pirates will stay with us. They're not bound to us in any way. Would you truly be willing to let them leave knowing they have information that could bring the entire system down?"

As I think, Corvus watches me silently, and Shey stares down at her feet, hands clasped in front of her.

What he says is logical, that it's probably in everyone's best interests, but I still don't like it. I already feel sick at the thought of hiding this secret from everyone. I thought that we were done with hiding shit like this after the whole issue with Leonis, but now it feels like we're right back where we started. "Stars damn, I really hate this. But okay. We'll keep it among ourselves, for now."

Shey wraps her arms around herself and shivers. "I understand," she says. "Now, can we get out of this tunnel? It's making me feel rather ill after what we just learned."

"Told you this place was creepy from the start," I say, and set off toward the surface.

173

*   *   *

Once we reach the mouth of the tunnel, the weather is the calmest it's been since our arrival. We pick our way across the wreckage of Levian and back to the ship. The ramp is open, and the twins are sitting just inside the cargo bay, looking out at us as we approach. They're probably irritated about being ordered to stay behind, but at least they didn't venture out.

Once we're inside, we strip off our surface equipment, and Shey heads directly up the stairs without a word. I pause next to Pol, reaching down to touch his shoulder. "You feeling better?"

"No," he says flatly, without looking up. I frown, looking at Drom—who only shrugs—and then back at Pol, whose eyes are fixed on something in the distance. I turn to follow his gaze. The back of my neck prickles with warning as I realize he's staring directly at the Primus statue.

Corvus crouches down beside our brother. "Do you...know something, Pol?"

"I'm just tired of the noise," he says, his eyes unmoving. "Can we go?"

I exchange a glance with Corvus. As much as I want to unpack what the hell he means by that, he's probably right—our first priority needs to be getting off this planet. Then we can figure the rest out.

"Absolutely, bud. We're getting out of here as soon as humanly possible. Where is everyone else?"

"Dunno about gun-arm lady," Drom says. "But I think Lyre is with Orion." And then she waggles her eyebrows in a way that I don't like at all.

"...What? No, she isn't. You're screwing with me."

"She totally is."

"Yeah, okay, hilarious." I shake my head. "Everyone go get ready for launch. Corvus, handle the ramp."

I head up the stairs before anyone can respond—especially Corvus, who I'd prefer to keep as far from this situation as possible, assuming Drom really isn't screwing with me. The rest of the ship is quiet and empty, but as I approach the cockpit, the sound of voices reaches me: Lyre's soft and mild words, and Orion's bright laughter. I pause where I am, fighting a strange feeling in the pit of my stomach that I have no right to feel. But after a moment, I shake my head and press forward, clearing my throat loudly to announce my presence. Just in case.

Lyre is sitting in my chair, and Orion is in his usual copilot seat. She's gripping the wheel, and one of his hands is on top of hers, showing the proper positioning. She smiles at him in a way I rarely see her smile at anyone. As I walk in, they both turn to me, and he quickly draws the hand back. She folds her hands in her lap, smile disappearing.

"What's going on?" After the day I've had, the words come out harsher than I intend. The two of them exchange a look like they've been caught doing something wrong.

"Your sister was interested in a crash course on piloting," Orion says after a moment. "She's a fast learner." He nudges her, and her lips curl again, like she doesn't want to smile but can't quite stop the expression. "Looks like I've got some competition for the copilot position."

I'm not in the mood to give more than a wan smile in response. When Lyre sees the look on my face, her smile tips downward.

"What happened?" she asks, immediately all seriousness. "Did you find something?"

"Yes. We got what we came for." I jerk my head at the door. "Go get ready for launch."

"What—"

"Now, before another storm hits."

Lyre frowns at me but obediently gets to her feet and heads out. I take my chair, tapping my fingers on the armrests for a moment before I begin prep for launch. Orion follows my lead, sneaking sideways glances at me.

"That bad, huh?" he ventures eventually, with a nervous flicker of a smile.

I swallow hard. Now that we're out of those tunnels, it's really setting in how very huge this information is. The mystery of the Primus has haunted humanity for generations. Though I guess that's not entirely accurate, if at least a handful of Gaians were sitting on this information the entire time. A long line of Gaian presidents must've known at least a couple pieces of the puzzle. I should be surprised by the cruelty of keeping something like that from the rest of the system while places like Titan suffered, but then again, it is the Gaians.

But now we have the information, too. And I guess we're hiding it just like they did. It sounded logical when Corvus explained it, but now I feel a flicker of doubt, realizing we're no different than the xenophobic assholes who kept this secret for so long. Still, he did have a point—this information is so monumental that it will paint a target on the back of whoever knows it. I need to think hard before I drop that responsibility on anyone else I care about.

"Yeah," I say quietly. "That bad." I sit up straighter, placing my hands on the wheel. "But let's just worry about getting out of here right now."

"Sure thing, Captain."

Once I've confirmed everyone's ready to go, we launch in silence. Though I know our problems will follow us no matter where in the system we go, it still feels good to leave Gaia behind, with all of its storms and its aliens and its secrets. At least out here, I feel like I'm in control of what happens next.

I take a deep breath as we leave the planet's atmosphere, relief flowing through me as I look out into the openness of space.

"Scorpia," Orion says, his voice tightly wound with concern. "There's a—"

The whole ship shudders as something slams into us.

CHAPTER SEVENTEEN

Under Attack

Corvus

've just unclipped from my launch chair when the entire ship lurches hard enough to knock me off my feet. My grunt of pain is swallowed by the wail of the alarm. I get upright as soon as I can, grabbing my chair for support, and take off toward the cockpit.

"What the hell was that?" I ask, my eyes darting over the screens. I don't glean much from the flashing lights and warnings. But even to my untrained eye, it's obvious that something has damaged the ship. Both Scorpia's and Orion's faces show pure panic.

"Trying to figure that out right now," Scorpia says, her hands flying over the controls, sweat beading on her forehead. "We've been hit, by, um..." She throws up her hands, letting out a hiss of frustration. "Fuck if I know. Radar still isn't picking up shit. It couldn't have been debris, so..."

"So we're under attack," I say.

"Looks like it," Orion says when Scorpia doesn't answer. "They must be cloaked."

"Who could be attacking us out here?" It doesn't make any sense. There's nothing in this area of the system but two dead planets.

"I don't know. Scrappers?" Scorpia says. "I've been broadcasting loud and clear that we're from Nibiru and don't mean any harm, but—"

The ship shakes from another hit, and I barely stay on my feet this time.

"With cloaking technology and weaponry? No. Those aren't scavengers." I stare at the radar as I think. The only other, more horrible, possibility is that this is either Deva or Pax, making it an act of war. But why? Do they suspect what we learned on Gaia? Are they trying to keep it from getting out?

Another shot rocks the ship. I stumble and grab on to the back of Scorpia's chair for support.

"Does it really matter?" Orion snaps. "They're about to rip us apart!"

"Okay, okay." Scorpia taps at her computer. "Looks like the shot came from here, so we have some idea of where they are, but we still can't see anything. No telling how big they are or how advanced the ship is." She leans back, chewing her thumbnail. "We have to assume that if they have tech like this, they're faster than us, so no use running. I don't suppose your dad was hiding any illegal ship weaponry?"

Orion shakes his head. "Just the grappling hooks."

"Guess we work with what we've got, then."

After a moment's pause, Orion says, "You've got to be kidding me."

"Well, if you see any other options, speak up right fuckin' now."

"Are you talking about dragging the armed, cloaked ship of unknown origin *closer* to us?" I ask, staring at Scorpia with the same disbelieving look that Orion is giving her.

"Well, we can't outrun them in this ungainly piece of shit, so seeing as our other option is to sit here and get slowly ripped apart, yeah," Scorpia says. "We can pull them in and fight in close quarters." But then she glances between me and Orion, her confidence cracking. "Right?"

I swallow hard. When she puts it like that, I suppose we don't have a choice at all. "I'll get everyone armed and ready for combat."

She turns to Orion and begins discussing the best way to latch on to a target we can't see. I hover for a moment longer, some part of me holding out hope that another solution will present itself. But it doesn't, and so I quash that hope and head out to the middle deck. Most of the others are in the hallway or peering out of doorways, summoned by the alarm but not sure how to proceed. I slap the button on the wall to shut off the noise and glance up and down the hall. Making an announcement like this seems like it should be Scorpia's job, but I suppose since we need her at the wheel, it falls to me. I clear my throat.

"Our ship is under attack by an unknown vessel," I say. My voice comes out loud and steady, devoid of emotion—the voice, I realize with a jolt, I used when I slipped into sergeant mode on Titan. A voice I hoped I would never have to use again. Maybe I wouldn't have, if we had stayed on Nibiru—but it's too late for that now. I steel myself and continue. "As we can't outrun them and have no ship weaponry of our own, our only option is to latch on to them and force close-quarters combat. Everyone head to the armory, gear up, and meet me down in the cargo bay."

One by one, the heads sticking out of doorways bob in acknowledgment. Drom and Pol look as ready for a fight as ever, Lyre is grim, and Izra's expression is unreadable, but at least she nods her agreement while meeting my eyes. Shey is the only one who hesitates.

"Everyone?" she asks, her voice faint.

"We'll keep you in the back, but we need every weapon we can get right now," I say. She must be still reeling from what we learned on Gaia, and part of me wants to apologize—on my own behalf for asking this, on Lyre's for bringing her on board, on Scorpia's for dragging her into this whole mess in the first place—but I swallow it down. We have no idea what we're up against, and one additional gun on our side could make the difference between life and death for all of us.

After a moment, Shey takes a deep breath, dips her chin, and steps out of her room. I'm sure she's never seen a single moment of combat in her life, but she seems prepared to face it, as she faces everything. I spin on my heel and head for the armory before I can change my mind.

Soon after we reach the cargo bay, I hear the telltale heavy thunks of our grappling hooks deploying. I hold my breath, waiting, and...

And nothing, until the ship rocks with another impact. I brace myself against the wall to keep my footing, and grit my teeth. We missed.

I stay silent, but Izra curses, no doubt making the same realization. The others cast worried glances at me. "Focus on the fight ahead. The ship can handle a few shots." I hope it's true. *Memoria* is a tough ship, but I'm not sure how much it can take.

After our pilots reel the grappling hooks back in, and we take another hit, we launch once more. I close my eyes this time, hoping the others don't see my expression—and *Memoria* jerks as they make impact. A few moments later, there's a grinding whine as we begin to reel the enemy ship toward us. Scorpia's plan is working thus far, for better or for worse.

"So how many are we up against?" Drom asks, suiting up in

full combat gear. We're lucky the armory was still stocked with body armor, and we brought our own weapons in case of trouble.

Another hit shakes the ship as we pull the enemy in, and I brace myself until the shaking passes. "We don't have a full count," I say after a beat, hoping I can avoid betraying exactly how little information we have on the enemy—which is to say, none at all.

"Sure, but we can hazard a guess from the size of their ship, yeah?" Izra butts in. I glance at her for a moment before returning my attention to my own armor. She's already wearing hers, and looks like she was born for it, but I can't seem to get the straps right. It takes me a moment to realize it's because my hands are shaking. I clench my hands into fists to hide it, and look around to see if anyone noticed. Mostly everyone is too busy preparing for battle, but Izra is watching me like a hawk. I meet her stare with a glower.

"Their ship is cloaked," I say, loath to let the information slip through my teeth but not seeing a way to avoid it. "We're not sure what we're up against yet."

Shey's hands, fumbling with the clasps of her armor, go still. Her head whips up toward me. "Cloaked? That technology is rare, is it not?"

"It's..." Again, I can't see a way around telling the unfortunate truth. I wish Scorpia was here instead of me. The man I once was, the Titan soldier, would have been equipped to deal with this, but I'm not that man anymore, and this crew is far from a group of Titan-trained soldiers at my command. "It's not unheard of, but...yes. We have to assume we're dealing with a well-equipped and high-tech adversary."

"So we have literally no clue who or what or how many we're up against?" Drom asks for clarification. I force myself to meet her eyes.

"We have no choice but to fight," I say, in lieu of directly answering her questions. Her face goes pale, but she sets her jaw, nodding once before finishing suiting up. She leans over to whisper something in Pol's ear, and squeezes one of his shoulders. He shakes her off with a scowl and bounces on the balls of his feet, jittery with apprehension.

Everyone else in the cargo bay is silent. Izra begins to pace back and forth in front of the ramp, like a predatory cat, while Lyre stays in the back of the room near the twins. Shey still hasn't managed to finish donning her armor, so I head over to help her. She looks up and meets my eyes, her hands going still as I take over.

"I'm afraid I'm not well-versed in combat rhetoric, so please tell me plainly: Is this as bad as it seems?" she asks, her voice a low enough whisper that no one else can hear it. I swallow a lump in my throat and force my hands to keep moving.

"Yes," I say. "We won't know exactly how bad until we come face-to-face with them." I meet her eyes, making sure she understands. "We can try to surrender, but it isn't a coincidence that we ran into someone out here. And if this ship was any less durable, those shots would have killed us already."

Shey pushes her shoulders back. Seeing her fully geared up in combat armor, I can almost believe she's prepared for a fight, but the fear in her face betrays her. Still, she asks, "How can I be the most useful?"

"Stay out of the line of fire and try not to shoot anyone on our side. Have you ever used a blaster before?"

She huffs, looking offended. "I'm not *that* useless. I've been through self-defense training."

"Good. Time to put it to use." I walk toward the ramp and turn to address the entire room. "We're pulling them in now. Once they're caught, we'll use an adjustable bridge to cross into their ship as carefully as we can." I pause, looking around. "They have the advantage here, especially since we know so little about the ship. But we have to find our way to their systems, damage them enough that they won't be able to chase after us. The second that's done, we retreat." I focus on Izra. "Our goal isn't to win this fight. It's to get away. If they seem willing to negotiate, we'll do that rather than fight. Understand?"

"Sir, yes, sir," Izra says with a lazy grin. I grimace. That will have to be good enough. At least everyone else looks appropriately serious as we set up the bridge to board their ship. Now that they're flush against our own vessel, they've stopped firing and gone silent; preparing to be boarded, no doubt.

Izra shows us where to find the device they used to hack their way through the security of other ships' doors, and Lyre sets it up.

"We're just about in," she says after a couple of minutes, and I nod to her, taking my position alongside the door so I can take point. Izra takes position just behind me, Drom on the other side with Pol next to her, while Lyre and Shey retreat to the back as I instructed them earlier. I pause to check that everyone is ready— weapons held up, eyes on the door. Once I'm satisfied, I take a breath and hit the button to open it. I step forward, ready to board the enemy ship—and a body slams into me.

Caught off guard, I lose my footing, and my bad leg gives out. I tumble backward, slamming hard into the metal floor with the assailant on top of me. The enemy is covered head to toe in matte black armor, their face concealed by a helmet with a darkly tinted visor. The barrel of their weapon, a heavily advanced-looking laser rifle, points directly into my face. But though I brace for a blow, the enemy stares down at me and doesn't fire.

I struggle to free myself from their weight, but I'm pinned to the floor and helpless. Out of the corner of my eye, I see the twins race forward to help—but before they can reach me, another armored enemy emerges from the ship and intercepts them. A third follows close behind, and races past my shocked crew and up the stairs. Izra and Shey peel off after them.

No others follow. Only three of them—but with this kind of tech and heavy armor, I'm not sure we can handle three. Yet the one who has me pinned still hasn't made a move. Maybe there's another way. Nobody has fired the first shot yet, my own side hesitating with me at the enemy's mercy, their side's reasoning too opaque for me to guess at. But perhaps they're not eager for a fight after all.

"My name is Corvus Kaiser," I say, struggling to speak with the weight pressing down on my chest. "This ship is in the employment of the Nibiran Council. We don't mean you any harm."

There's a muffled sound of speech, too quiet for me to discern, from within the helmet. But apparently the words aren't meant for me, because one of the other armored persons turns suddenly and sharply away from the twins to stare directly at me. Even with their face concealed, I imagine eyes boring into me—but a moment later, Pol slams into them and sends them both tumbling to the floor, with Drom joining the tussle a moment later.

"*No,*" I shout. "Wait, we can still—"

The helmeted enemy whirls their rifle around and slams the butt of it into my face. Pain blossoms from my cheekbone, and stars dance in my vision.

"Wait," I gasp again, and someone behind me opens fire, peppering the person holding me down with shots that ping uselessly against their armor. They turn their attention on another target and lift their weight off of me just slightly—giving me enough room to grab my knife from its sheath on my leg. "We don't want to fight," I shout, giving them one last chance to reconsider as my fingers close around the hilt. Once I do this, there will be no turning back.

As I hesitate, the person opens fire on someone behind me, and

I hear a cry of pain. I grit my teeth, pull out the knife, and stab it as hard as I can into the enemy's side. It cleaves through their armor and the skin beneath, and once I yank it out, blood gushes up from the tear and spills onto the floor. They reel back, and I grab the barrel of their gun with my free hand—gritting my teeth at the searing heat from having just been fired—and shove it upward as they shoot again, sending it pinging uselessly against the ceiling. I rip the gun from their hands and struggle to my feet. They step back, and press a hand to the tear in their suit; when they remove it, a gooey black substance surges up to seal the wound, and hardens into the same material as the rest of their armor.

Damn. Whoever we're up against, they have technology the likes of which I've never seen before. I open fire on them with their own weapon, but the shots do nothing. They advance on me while I continue firing, and as I toss the useless weapon aside and grab my knife again, they swing an armored fist into my gut that sends me sprawling, winded, to the floor.

Before I can recover, the assailant picks up their gun, grabs my leg, and drags me.

I'm so dazed—and shocked that they aren't putting a shot through my head to end it—that I don't realize what's happening as the world slides by around me. By the time I catch on, they've dragged me to the entrance of the adjustable bridge. I curse and grab the corner of *Memoria*'s door, clinging with all my strength. They may not be trying to kill me now, but I'm sure whatever fate awaits me on that ship is no better.

"I need backup!" I shout. For a terrible moment, it seems like everyone is too wrapped up in their own frenetic battles to heed me, and my stomach lurches as my fingers begin to slip.

Then Pol is at my side, peppering the armored stranger with laser-fire. They drop their gun and raise an arm to defend their visor, and give me a vicious tug with their other hand—but a moment later, they're forced to release me as Pol throws himself at them.

They grapple while I struggle to my feet. I lunge forward, knife in hand, as they grab Pol and slam his head into the metal wall. I jab the knife deep. It cuts through the hard shell of their armor, finally doing some damage—but they turn and slam an armored fist into my chest, sending me stumbling backward. I hit the wall and fall with a breathless, choked sound as the air is forced from my lungs.

The armored stranger—my knife still protruding from their back—kicks Pol in the side as he tries to rise, and I scramble up again and lunge at them. I slam my fist into the visor, again and again. My knuckles split. Blood splatters across the tinted visor. They hit me hard in the ribs, but I muster up another punch that smears blood across the material. They finally manage to knock me to the floor.

For all my efforts, I didn't put so much as a crack in the visor—but judging from the way they swipe at it, I obscured their vision with my blood. They sit up, and after a brief hesitation, reach to press a hidden pressure pad just beneath their ear. The helmet clicks off, and clatters to the metal floor.

Shock freezes me in place. For a moment, all I can do is stare, my mind wiped blank.

Impossible.

Yet here he is.

I take a small, shallow breath, and then another, before I manage to speak. "Daniil?"

Daniil Naran, once the best soldier under my command, stares at me. His face doesn't hold the same utter shock that mine must wear, but he still looks nearly as overwhelmed as I feel. His lips part slightly as if he means to say something, but then his expression hardens, that indecipherable emotion firming into rage. He steps forward and kicks me, hard, in the chest.

Pain shoots through me as I skid back, my chest feeling crushed beneath the armor. I gasp for air and sit up, but can't bring myself to reach for the weapon that clattered to the floor beside me. I rise onto one knee, staring up at the hard mask that Daniil's familiar face has become.

"Wait," I say, the word coming out barely a breath from my air-starved lungs. Daniil advances on me, but I raise my hands in the air rather than trying to fight or flee. "Please, how are you alive? Are there others?"

Daniil stares down at me with a contemptuous twist to his mouth. I stay very still, keeping my eyes on him. There's still a fight raging on in the cargo bay behind us, but it feels as though we're the only two people in the world.

"Magda and Sverre are dead," he says, crushing my delicate hope with a pitiless and flat voice. "They're all dead, because of what you and your family did. *Traitor.*"

"No," I say, staring up at him in horror. "No, you don't understand. I had nothing to do with what happened."

"Don't lie to me," he says. "Altair told us everything. Your mother, the deal—*everything.*" He grabs me by the throat and drags me to my feet. "Altair sent the others out to try to stop it, before we knew what was happening. Sverre, Magda, all of them, all sent out to fight an invincible enemy, not knowing they were doomed the moment they stepped outside. He sent everyone. Everyone but me." I try to speak, but his armored hand tightens on my throat and cuts the words off. "Because you told me to stay in Fort Sketa, and I listened. Because I trusted you. You were supposed to come back for me!"

I claw at his hand with both of mine, struggling to get enough room to breathe. If I can just talk to him, I can fix this.

Over Daniil's shoulder, I see Pol dragging himself to his feet, blood trickling down the side of his face. Before I can gasp out a warning or a command to stop, Pol jumps at him. He tears the knife from his back with a spray of blood. Daniil cries out in pain, drops me, and whirls to face him, gun swinging up to aim directly at Pol's face.

Time slows. I see anger twist Daniil's face, Pol's shoulders set in a refusal to back off, blood glistening on the blade of my Primus knife gripped tightly in his hand. I'm still on the ground, weaponless. There's no way for me to intercept them in time. No way that a shot from Daniil at this range would be anything short of lethal. My mind seems to freeze—but instinct kicks in.

"Stand *down*, Naran!" I shout, my voice hoarse.

Daniil falters, just long enough for someone to fire from behind me and clip his ear. He curses and retreats back toward his own ship, pressing one hand to the wound and sending off a burst of laser-fire meant more to suppress than to damage. Pol lurches forward as if to follow, but I launch myself at his legs and take him down, ignoring his protests.

"Katrin, it's done," Daniil shouts. "Retreat!"

I pin Pol down while he struggles and curses, and hold one hand out toward Daniil—a plea? A surrender?—and he stares at me, and doesn't fire. A moment later, another armored soldier bounds past us to join him on the other side, and skids to a stop, assuming a defensive posture in front of Daniil.

I stay where I am, hand still raised. Our eyes meet one last time before he hits the pressure pad, and metal seals us off on two opposite sides.

Something in my mind feels broken in the aftermath of the fight. I stare at the sealed cargo door, trying to process what just happened and what it means, but my brain can't seem to move past the image of Daniil looking down at me, hatred burning in his eyes.

"I could have taken him," Pol says, dragging me back to the present. He yanks out of my grip and struggles to his feet, glaring at me. His face is a mess, blood dripping down his chin, and his eyes are bloodshot.

Something clicks into place as I climb to my feet as well. "You're on Sanita again," I say, and a low fire ignites in my chest. "Damn it, Pol, not only did you risk yourself, but you sabotaged me. I was trying to talk to him."

"Why the hell would you talk to someone who was trying to kill us?" he asks. A moment later, his expression shifts. "You called him by name. I heard it. You knew him."

"I—" I cut myself off. I don't want to explain this, not now, not like this, not when I'm still processing what happened. And not when my own crew needs tending to. I turn to survey the damage. Drom and Lyre are in the back of the room, the latter fussing over a wound on Drom's arm; both look scuffed up, but not badly injured. Izra and Shey aren't here, nor are Orion and Scorpia, who were meant to join us in the fight. I frown, and my mind returns to Daniil's words again: *It's done.* And the one armored soldier who never returned to their ship.

"Lyre, take the twins to the medical bay and do what you can," I say, grabbing my knife from the floor before heading toward the stairs. "I'll check on the others."

The hallways are quiet and empty, with no sign of which way the enemy must have gone. I make my way through the ship, pausing at every doorway and corner to listen in case someone is lying in wait. But I encounter nothing but silence until I reach the hallway leading to the cockpit.

There I find the missing enemy soldier. The Titan woman— she's young, no older than the twins—lies on her back, green eyes glassy and unseeing, her throat slit. Her helmet lies a few feet away... along with a bloody, detached ear. My gaze moves from the severed body part to Izra sitting against the wall. Once I see the blood smeared around her mouth and the knife clutched in her hand, it's easy to piece together a basic idea of what happened.

"Those were Titan soldiers," I say. I'm sure she's made that realization herself, but I feel the need to say it aloud.

Izra nods, her face expressionless. "I know the armor. Special ops."

"How... how is this possible? How are any of them alive?"

"Don't know." She gets to her feet and looks down at the young woman's body. After a moment, she spits a wad of pinkish saliva onto her face. "Hopefully not many of them." She smiles at me with blood on her teeth. "Seeing as we're both traitors and all."

I shake my head. I'm not sure how I even began to think she might understand how I feel. Unable to muster up a response, I move past her and into the cockpit. Orion and Scorpia are at their posts and look mostly unharmed—unlike the dashboard.

"What happened here?" I ask, gesturing toward the exposed and torn wires. It looks like someone shoved their fist inside and ripped out as much as possible, but only in this one section.

"They seemed to have a serious vendetta against our communications system," Scorpia says, keeping her attention on her controls rather than looking at me. Orion is similarly plugged in, his eyes roaming the array of screens in front of him. "She went straight for it. Was gonna follow it up by shooting both of us when Izra and Shey showed up."

That must have been what Daniil meant by *it's done*. I file the information away for later. "And where is Shey?"

"Oh, she, uh..." Scorpia tears her eyes off the screen to look around. "She was doing great right until she got a front-row seat to Izra biting that lady's ear off. Must've run off afterward. I should check on her, but..." She returns her attention to the controls, trailing off.

"She'll be fine. Everyone's fine." I reach forward and squeeze her shoulder. "Do what you have to do."

She breathes out a sigh of relief. "Okay. I'm just making sure we don't have any other cloaked surprises headed our way. Everything good on your end, Orion?"

"I think we're in the clear, but I'll keep looking."

"Good. Good." She glances up at me. "So, uh...did we kick their asses, or what?"

"Well, we fought them off, but we only killed this one. The other two escaped."

Scorpia goes silent.

Orion rips his attention away from his screens to give me an incredulous look. "I'm sorry," he says. "Did you just say there were only three of them? Against our entire crew? And we only managed to kill *one*?"

"Yes."

He stares at me for a moment longer, shakes his head, and returns to his duties.

"Stars above," Scorpia mutters. "That's insane. Who the hell were they, with that kind of tech? Devans? Paxians?"

I take a deep breath, wrestling with the answer. "You should call a meeting as soon as you're sure we're in the clear," I say. "Everyone needs to hear this."

CHAPTER EIGHTEEN

Honesty

Scorpia

I look out over my crew as they gather in the mess hall, taking stock of the damage. Based off the one enemy I saw, we're lucky to have escaped without any serious injuries. Everyone is thoroughly scuffed up and rattled, but all in one piece, and Corvus must have patched up the worst of it while I was ensuring we're not being trailed by anyone.

We're still waiting on Corvus to finish cleaning up the med bay and join us, so I shake off my lingering nerves, put on a brave face, and turn to my captain duties. I move around the room, checking in with everyone—gently ruffling Lyre's hair, squeezing the twins' shoulders, staying very far away from Izra when she shoots me a death glare the moment I start to approach. I instead take a seat next to Shey, who still looks shaken a few hours after the fight.

"Are you okay?" I ask. "I heard you witnessed Izra in action, which is... a pretty rough induction into battle."

Shey turns faintly green in the face at the reminder. She steals a nervous glance in Izra's direction before looking at me.

"She's terrifying," she confides quietly. "It was all terrifying. I believe I may have nearly shot your brother on accident, and was almost shot myself, and..." She stops, looking up at me. "You go through situations like this all the time, I suppose."

"Well, I wouldn't say all the time, but it..." I trail off as she reaches up and pushes the neck of my jumpsuit to one side, exposing the puckered scar where one of Izra's spears once pierced my shoulder. I swallow hard as she brushes her fingertips across it, frozen, as if afraid a sudden motion will startle her away. Her eyes hover on the scar before flickering up to meet mine again.

"You are so brave," she says, pulling her hand back. "I don't know how you do it."

I hurriedly adjust my jumpsuit to cover the scar again, feeling weirdly exposed. My face flushes. "I mean, sure, maybe a little bit, as long as there's no creepy alien shit involved," I joke weakly, but her eyes remain serious.

"And you rescued Izra even after she did that to you," she says. "I don't think I could ever forgive someone for something like that."

My mouth feels dry. I clear my throat. "I guess when you screw up as often as I do, you learn to be pretty forgiving."

"You are...truly fascinating, Scorpia Kaiser."

As much as I want to sink into this moment and let myself believe it's only the two of us in this room right now, the feeling of being watched makes that impossible. I glance around, finding first Drom, who gives me a suggestive eyebrow waggle, and then Orion, who quickly looks away.

I'm saved from trying to find a polite way to excuse myself from the situation when Corvus enters the room. I spring to my feet right away, moving around to the front of the room to join him. He looks utterly exhausted, and doesn't seem to be aware of the blood splattered across the front of his jumpsuit.

"We could all use some rest," I tell him, quietly. "We could meet up in the morning instead."

"No. I need to do this now."

He gestures for me to take a seat, and so I do, crossing one leg over the opposite knee. Corvus turns to survey the rest of the room and raises his voice to address us all. "Let me be frank," he says. "Those weren't Devans, or Paxians. Those were Titan soldiers."

Izra is the only one who doesn't look utterly shocked at the news. My own mouth drops open. I know Corvus would never claim such a thing unless he was certain it was true...but how? We were on Titan when the bio-weapon was released. We saw the aftermath. The Interplanetary Council confirmed the lack of survivors with their drones.

My mind snaps back to what Eri and Halon told me. Devan drones being shot down, Pax denying responsibility. If the Titans really had cloaking technology...if they've just been hiding out there this whole time...

"Does this mean Momma could still be alive?" Pol asks, shattering my train of thought. I turn to stare at him, realizing with an odd, sinking feeling that the thought hadn't even occurred to me, and then at Corvus. The rest of the room is silent.

He shakes his head, and I feel a guilty spark of relief. "No," he says, with far more patience than I think I would have managed. "Based on what the Titan soldier I spoke to said, the survivors were in Fort Sketa when the weapon dropped. Far from where the destruction began, and likely where they were keeping the ships. Momma was with the team that dropped the bio-weapon on Vin, in Isolationist territory. There's no way she made it out."

"But do we know that for sure?" Pol asks, his face still hopeful in a way that feels like a knife to my chest. "The Titans could have lied. She could have—"

"She's dead, Pol," I snap, unable to contain myself. "And we have more important shit to worry about. Just stop. She's dead and gone."

Pol turns to look at me—face crumpling, eyes starting to brim—and then stands and rushes out of the room. Drom looks as though she's about to follow him for a moment, but then she shakes her head and turns back to us instead.

Shit. I'm gonna have to fix that at some point, but for now, we have bigger issues than our family drama. I turn back to Corvus. "So what the hell are the Titans doing with ships like that?"

His expression twists into guilt. "They were building a fleet. General Altair had plans to leave the planet and find a new world to settle. But I never imagined those plans were this far along."

"You sure about that?" Izra asks, abruptly butting in. "You were real eager to preach about Titan loyalty to me when we all thought they were dead. Now we're supposed to believe you wouldn't try to cover for them if you knew they were still alive?"

Corvus's look is stricken. "I would never lie about that."

"Enough," I tell Izra. "I trust my brother. But..." I lean back. "If what you're saying is true, then they have a whole fleet cloaked out there, not just a few stray ships."

"We can assume the survivors reported back to the main fleet," Corvus says. "Even if that was just a scouting ship ahead of the rest, the fact that they're out near Gaia means they're moving away from Titan, toward the rest of the system."

My shoulders slump as I finally realize something. "And they went straight for our communications system," I say. "To make sure we couldn't tell anyone what we know."

"Which means they have something planned," Izra says, "and it's not to fuck off and look for some mythical new planet." She looks straight at Corvus. "They're going to do what Titans do best. They're going to start a war."

"We don't know that," Corvus says. "If this is Altair's fleet, and he's still in charge, he won't be eager to start another conflict."

"Right," Izra says. "So the Titans are sneaking across the system in a cloaked fleet, right at the moment when Deva and Pax are at each other's throats, Nibiru is overburdened by refugees, and the Gaians are vulnerable, with no nefarious plans whatsoever."

A heavy silence settles over the room; not even Corvus has an argument.

"It's hard to deny when you put it like that," Lyre says, with an apologetic glance at Corvus. "But even if some Titans survived, we know they suffered heavy losses from the bio-weapon. Drones have confirmed that much. What could they hope to gain from attacking another planet?"

"Revenge," I say. "They'll go after the Gaians."

"Altair wouldn't endanger his last surviving people for that," Corvus says. "But...he did tell me he wanted a better home for his people than Titan. With the rest of the system in turmoil, and Nibiru unprepared..."

"Nibiru would be the best target regardless," Lyre says. "If Titan is wounded, they'd have no chance against Pax or Deva. But Nibiru?"

"He could try to pull the same shit as Leonis," I say. "You really think he would do that?"

Corvus folds his arms over his chest and stares down at the table, conflict written all over his face. "He may believe he has no other choice."

"And we have no way of warning Nibiru what's coming," I say. Corvus looks up at me, and our eyes meet in a shared moment of horrified realization. We agreed to keep the information about the defense systems to ourselves unless there was imminent danger, but I don't think any of us imagined exactly how imminent that could be.

And even aside from the fact that the Titans have superior training, and technology, and the element of surprise, Nibiru will have no idea that a single attack could be all it takes to destroy their entire planet.

I slump down in my chair. If I didn't have so many eyes on me right now, I would succumb fully to panic, but I manage to stave it off for their sakes. Still, my mind is empty of any suggestions to fix this.

"Of course there's a way of warning them," Shey speaks up. She clasps her hands in front of her, the anxiety clear on her face, but her voice stays steady. "We go there and warn them directly. It's the only way."

"No way in hell am I going back to Nibiru," Orion says. He looks straight at me instead of Shey. "You promised me. I'm not getting thrown in Ca Sineh again."

Before I can respond, Shey says, "This is a *little* more important than just you."

"Is it? Really? We'll arrive in time to give the Nibirans maybe a couple days of warning. What is that going to do?" Orion looks around at everyone now, holding his hands out. "And then we'll be trapped with the rest of them. We won't be able to fight past the Titan fleet. We barely managed to survive a scrap with *three* of them on a scouting vessel."

"He's right," I say. "If we go to Nibiru, we have to accept the very likely possibility that we won't be able to leave before a potential war breaks out."

"If we go?" Orion asks, his brow furrowing. "Don't tell me you're entertaining the thought of going there."

"I'm entertaining all options right now. It's a shitty situation." One of my legs jumps, a nervous tic I can't suppress right now. "It's not just a matter of warning Nibiru about the Titans. We also have to deliver the information we gained on Gaia. It's vital."

"So vital that you've neglected to share it with us, of course," Izra drawls from her corner.

Guilt churns my stomach, but I keep my mouth shut.

"Well, whatever this oh-so-secret-and-vital information is, we can transmit it to the Nibirans from Deva, where it's safe," Orion says. "It'll only take another week to get there."

I glance at Corvus, who looks on silently, his lips pressed into a firm line. Normally, Orion's suggestion would be a reasonable one. But he doesn't understand how dire this situation is, or how disastrous it could be if we leaked the info to the Devans as well. "We need a secure line for this information. And a week might be too long," I say. "We're talking a lot of lives at stake. And there's no guarantee going back to Nibiru means going back to Ca Sineh, Orion. I'm sure the council will have better things to worry about than looking for a couple of escaped prisoners."

"I'm not willing to take that chance."

"For the record, I'm not, either," Izra says. She's still in a pose of complete relaxation, boots kicked up on the table. "No point in getting ourselves killed for the Nibirans."

"Why am I not surprised that it's the two of you arguing for this?" Corvus mutters darkly.

"Okay, everybody relax," I say, as both ex-pirates turn their glares on my brother. Drom steps up to his side, folding her arms over her chest. "We're just talking things out right now. Everyone deserves a chance to speak their mind."

"My people are at risk," Shey says, looking at me pleadingly. It's damn hard to keep a clear head when she's making those eyes at me. "I need to return to them. Please."

"There is one other option," Orion says. "The ship's got a couple emergency pods. We could drop her off on Nibiru and continue on to Deva."

"With the Titans right on our heels?" Izra asks. "Those things are slow as hell. They'll get blown out of the sky."

"I'll risk it," Shey says, without hesitation. "If there's a chance it'll get me there—"

"I'm going to Nibiru, too," Drom says abruptly. "If there's a war, I'm going to fight in it."

"You absolutely will not," Corvus says.

The conversation dissolves into petty squabbles—Corvus and Drom, Orion and Shey, none of them listening to me as I try to get everyone to shut up. Only Lyre is paying any attention to me at all, her face drawn and worried and a little hurt, as she's no doubt realized I haven't told her about what we learned on Gaia, either. Izra watches it all with a smirk on her face.

"Okay, everybody shut the fuck up," I yell, and successfully startle them all into silence. Everyone's attention shifts to me. I take a breath, trying to gather my thoughts. "Thanks, everyone, for your opinions, but this is my ship and the decision is mine." I sweep my eyes over them, and am pleased to see nobody disagreeing. Yet.

Again, insecurity bites at me—how am I supposed to expect them to follow me when, no matter what choice I make, I'll be disappointing some of them?—but I push it aside. The best I can do is compromise, and try to avoid a solution that ends with half the crew hating me.

"We took this mission for the Nibirans," I say, speaking slowly and carefully. "Given what we know now, we can't just turn our backs on the people who employed us, and sheltered many of us." Shey is nodding, which encourages me; Izra lets out a derisive chuckle, which I choose to ignore. "But that doesn't mean planting ourselves in the middle of a war, either. That's a little above and beyond our duty to the council." Especially not when the very planet we land on may be in danger. "So..." I drum my fingers on the table, thinking. "We'll go to Nibiru. Make a quick stop there, give the information to the council, and then head to Deva. I know it'll be risky, but I think if we're fast enough we can beat the Titan fleet. With me and Orion in the cockpit, I know we can pull it off."

There's a long pause after I speak.

"That's more than just risky," Corvus says, and my heart sinks at the look on his face. "There's no guarantee it will be possible. You'll be putting us all in danger trying to make it to Deva from there."

"And what if the Nibirans drag us all off to Ca Sineh the moment we arrive?" Orion demands. "Or, hell, seize the whole ship?"

Damn it. Now, instead of half the crew hating me, *everyone* is looking at me like I'm an absolute idiot. But if I back down now, it will only make me look indecisive. I know the plan is risky, but any other option will mean ignoring someone's legitimate concerns. "To reiterate," I say, speaking above the clamor of voices in the room, "I am the captain. And that is my decision."

I try to sound strong, but as I look over the faces in the room, I see nothing but doubt.

Once it's clear the conversation is over, I'm eager to leave the room. But I barely make it out to the hallway before Orion hurries up to my side.

"Can we talk?" he asks, when I slow but don't stop entirely. "Privately?"

"I think I've said everything I need to say," I tell him. More than anything, I just want to be alone right now, away from all this pressure. My head is reeling from everything that's happened in the last couple days. But Orion pulls ahead of me and forces me to stop.

"Scorpia," he says, softly, eyes darting behind me where the others are exiting the room now. Corvus glances over at us and pauses, but I wave him away. "You know what's going to happen if we go back to Nibiru. You told me you'd take care of me."

"I've made my decision," I say—but my resolve cracks as I see the look of genuine fear on his face. I reach out and touch his arm, trying to soothe him. "I'll figure something out."

"You don't understand," he says. "You don't know what it was like in that place. I can't go back there."

"You won't," I say, even knowing there's no way I can guarantee it. "Listen, we...we have leverage, okay? I can't tell you right now, but what we learned on Gaia is huge."

"And yet you can't tell me anything about it," he says. I fumble for words, and he pulls back, shaking his head.

"I promise it's going to be okay," I say, desperate to make him believe me.

"You always were a good liar," he says.

He turns and walks away before I can say another word.

Later, I'm alone in my room when a knock comes at the door. I'm tempted to climb into bed and pretend I'm already asleep. I don't want to face whoever is on the other side of that door, whether it's Corvus coming to berate my stupidity, or Orion asking once again for me to reconsider, or Lyre passive-aggressively prying into what we learned on Gaia. The decisions I've been making lately have been hard enough without everyone trying to guilt me for them.

But after the visitor knocks again, I groan and walk to the door. Finding Shey on the other side surprises me—she is possibly the one person I didn't consider that I might find waiting here.

She looks up at me, her hair still damp from a recent shower, wearing a loose silk robe that makes my imagination wander even after the exhausting day I've had. "May I come in?"

As if I have a choice. I invite her in and shut the door behind her while she takes a seat on the edge of my bed, looking around the luxurious room. I sit a few feet away from her, waiting for her to speak.

"I know that many people on this ship are displeased with you right now, so I suppose I just wanted to tell you that I believe you're doing the right thing," she says. "And I don't say that only because I agree with your decision." She pauses, looking up at me. "I meant everything that I said to you earlier. I think that you're very brave, and you make an incredible captain, and you inspire change in everyone around you. You see something in people that no one else does. You helped me find a part of myself I'm not sure I would have been able to discover on my own. And I…" She pauses again, color rising in her cheeks. I resist the urge to jump in, though part of me is screaming for her to get to whatever the point of this is and stop leaving me in agonizing suspense. "You're different now," she says, finally, brushing a curl out of her face. "Or perhaps I am. Likely both. Um." She shakes her head and lets out a nervous laugh. I've never seen her so flustered. "I am doing the absolute worst job of explaining myself. But what I'd really like to say to you is that, after we go to Nibiru, if you choose to leave and go elsewhere—I would be honored if you would accept me as a part of your crew. I would like to come with you, if you'll have me."

Once—even just a couple days ago—it would have meant everything to me to hear these words from her. But now, all I feel is a deep weariness. I feel like I'm already shouldering so much, and now she drops this on me? Is she flirting, or screwing with me, or just stating facts? Is she just looking for a ticket off-planet, or does she want to be with me? I'm tired of dancing around these issues and talking in circles. I'm *tired*. Why did I have to fall for a Gaian woman?

"Why?"

She blinks at my bluntness. "Why…what?"

"Why do you want to stay with me? Why are you on my ship in the first place? Why are you in my room in the middle of the night?"

"That's what I'm trying to explain to you right now."

"But you're not. You're not explaining anything." It's hard to stop once I start unloading everything that's been on my mind. "You kissed me on that beach and then ignored my existence for months. Then you came into my life again but insisted our relationship is strictly professional. Now you're sitting on my bed telling me all this, looking at me like that? Asking me to let you stay even though you've been holding me at arm's length the entire time you're here?" I let out a frustrated sigh, and she only stares at me, looking taken aback. I guess this isn't the response she was expecting, but I need to say this. "Of course you can stay on my ship, Shey. Especially if there's danger on Nibiru. I was preparing to dump my pride and beg you to come with us if that was what it took. But you know how I feel about you—how I've always felt about you—and if you're going to stay here, I need you to be honest with me about what you want, because I'm tired of trying to figure it out myself." I look at her, half pleading. "No matter what the answer is, it doesn't change anything. You will always have a place here. If you really want this to be strictly professional, I can live with that. But I can't live without any answer at all."

Shey stares at me. Swallows hard. Then she slides closer, reaches out, and gently takes my hand. "You have always frightened me, Scorpia," she says, and I brace myself for a rejection, since that seems like a particularly awful way to start any other sort of response. But she continues, "Because even when I first met you, when I made one of the most terrible mistakes of my life in thinking you were nothing more than a credit-hungry smuggler... and even later, when I knew my association with you could ruin my political aspirations and everything I have worked so hard for... and even now, when I have to watch you every day with someone else, and know that I asked for this and have no right to feel jealous... ever since the moment we met, I have always wanted you."

"Oh," I say quietly. I don't know what to say—don't know how to put words to all the fear and hope intertwined inside me right now, making my heart race—so I lace my fingers with hers instead. And then, belatedly, awkwardly, I say, "What about when I was wearing that really nice suit at the inauguration?"

Shey sighs. "Yes, then too, you insufferable woman."

"Knew it," I mutter. My heart is really pounding now, making it hard not to deflect with more joking around, but I try to suppress the urge. "Uh...Orion and I are just friends, by the way. Already cut that off."

"Oh," she says.

"Yeah. So." I clear my throat. "...I mean, we could keep doing this thing where we pretend we're not into each other, it *is* kind of fun in its own way, but..."

She leans forward and kisses me, cutting off the rest of whatever babble was coming out of my mouth, and it quiets the million anxieties crowded in my mind. I take her gently by the waist and pull her closer, kissing her more deeply. With her in my arms, everything outside of this room feels very far away.

To my surprise she immediately straddles my lap, sitting up so she can look down at me, her robe slipping down one shoulder in a way that makes my mouth go dry. I tilt my head up to kiss her again. I kiss her lips, the curve of her neck, the revealed shoulder. The sweet smell of her hair, the softness of her skin, the way the silk bunches under my hands and the robe slides up to reveal more of her thighs—all of it drives me wild in a way that makes me wonder how I ever thought I wanted anyone else. I don't think I've felt this way about anyone before, and it's making my heart beat too fast and giving me an urge to blurt out a thousand stupid little things I like about her just to release some of the pressure in my chest.

But for once, I manage to keep my mouth shut. Instead I

undo the tie on her robe and let my body do the talking—my lips against her neck, my hand sliding between her thighs. And after the first time she moans my name, I press her into the bed and kiss down her stomach and spend hours learning new ways to make her do it again, and again, and again.

CHAPTER NINETEEN

Loyalty

Corvus

Titans attach little sentiment to corpses, and this woman would doubtlessly be proud of dying in battle for her cause. Still, it feels disrespectful to dump her body in a cryosleep chamber, especially when Drom drops her upper half like a sack of garbage. I grimace and finish the job of arranging the corpse myself while she stands back and scowls. Personally, I would rather send the body out the air lock so I no longer have to look at it, but Lyre was concerned the Nibirans won't believe that the Titans have returned, so Scorpia agreed to prepare just in case.

"I saw the way you acted toward that Titan," Drom says. "He never should have walked out of here alive. He almost killed Pol."

I straighten up, wiping sweat off my forehead. "Well, Pol is fine. And it's not that simple."

"It should be." Drom squares herself up in the doorway so I can't move past her. "It better be, next time. If the Titans are really coming to start a war on Nibiru, you're going to have to pick a side."

She says it as if it hasn't been weighing on my mind already. As if I've been able to think about anything other than that possibility ever since I discovered that the Titans still live. I should have been able to celebrate their survival, not fear for the consequences of it. I should have been able to clasp Daniil against me like I did when we said goodbye on Titan, not see hatred twist his face into something unrecognizable while he called me a traitor.

"Get out of my way."

"Here, let me help you out. One side sheltered you, the other side wants you dead. One welcomed the Gaians onto their planet, the other is coming to start a war. Pretty easy, isn't it?"

"The Titans are only in this situation because of what our family did," I say, frustration lending my tone a sharp edge. "And the Nibirans only embrace us because they don't know we nearly did it to them as well."

Drom's certainty flickers. "That's..."

"As I said. Not that simple. Now *move*."

She finally steps aside. I head straight to my room, grateful for the click of the door shutting me off from the rest of the ship, and sink down with my back against the metal.

As much as I hate to admit it, she is right. If there is a war, I will have to pick a side eventually. But how am I supposed to do that, when the Titans hate my family because they falsely believe we're traitors, and the Nibirans love us because of the lie that we're heroes?

If this turns into war, it will be between Titan, the planet I was born on, went to war on, the planet me and my family helped destroy; Gaia, where I spent my childhood and gained my education; and Nibiru, where I spent my teenage years and helped raise my siblings, and the planet that took me and my family in as their own.

How am I supposed to choose when all sides are my people?

*   *   *

I thought the trip to Gaia was tense, but it was nothing compared to the days following Scorpia's announcement. Hardly anyone speaks to one another. Most of the crew stays in their own rooms—with the glaring exception of Shey, who spends her nights in the captain's quarters. As much as I want to be happy for my sister, that gives me a flicker of worry. Relations between the crew are already strained after her decision, and she should be trying to soothe tensions right now, not spending all of her time with one of the few people on board who seems to agree with her decision.

But she's made it clear that I don't get a say in her love life, so I respect that, and instead try to relieve some of her duties in the cockpit when I can, keeping an eye on the indicators when she's otherwise preoccupied.

We have no idea what those Titan ships are capable of, or whether or not they'll catch up to us before Nibiru. Luckily, there are no signs of trouble from outside the ship…but it's certainly brewing inside. Nobody says or does anything particularly alarming, but I can *feel* it. I've felt it before on *Fortuna*, when Momma would descend into icy silence when she was angry with us; the air would be thick with it, making us all tiptoe and whisper around the ship, waiting for the inevitable blowup.

The pirates seem to be at the center of it. Izra is more bristly than usual, snapping at the twins when they ask her for more stories, glaring at me like she's itching for a fight, retreating to her room with her meals. Orion sulks around the ship looking jilted, and progressively more agitated as we approach Nibiru. His eyes grow more bloodshot and shadowed every day.

I remain on high alert, waiting for them to try something, for someone to erupt from the pressure, but we approach Nibiru without issue. I'm surprised to find that we're one day out from the planet.

At breakfast, I wait for the rest of the crew to dig into their meals before pulling Scorpia aside. "So what's our plan when we arrive on Nibiru?"

"We get in, we break the bad news to the council, and we get out," Scorpia says with a shrug.

I suppress a frustrated sigh. "You have to face the possibility it might not be that easy. What are we going to do if we end up trapped on Nibiru when the Titans arrive?"

"We won't."

"You can't know that," I say, frustration growing. "You must know—"

"Look," Scorpia says, cutting me off. Her voice drops, tone shifting to a more serious one. "I'm not an idiot, okay? I know it might happen. But I just...can't think about that possibility right now. We have to go to Nibiru and warn them. That much is clear. After that...we're just gonna have to deal with whatever comes next. Even if that means—"

Before she can go on, her voice is drowned out by the sound of an alarm. Green lights flare in the room, and the speakers blare. Not the same alarm as when we were hit before, but an odd and pulsing noise. I step out into the mess hall, where a sense of panic is already growing among the others.

"No," Scorpia says, following me. "That can't be the Titans, can it? Did they catch up with us? Orion, what does—" She turns, and stops. "...Orion?"

I whirl around, stomach dropping as my eyes confirm what I already suspected. He's gone. Izra is still leaning against the wall beside the doorway, inspecting her nails as though they're far more interesting than everything else happening.

"The cockpit," I say, heading for the door. "He could be taking us off course."

"Nah," Izra says as I brush past her, giving me a disinterested glance. I pause. "That's the alarm for the emergency escape pod."

"*Shit*," Scorpia says, and sprints past me and down the hall. I follow as fast as I can, cursing the limp that has only grown more pronounced after our skirmish with the Titans.

It's clear from the moment I arrive that we're both too late. Scorpia bangs her fists against the sealed metal doors out of sheer frustration.

"No, no, no," she says, pressing her forehead to the metal. "How could he? Why? He'll never outrun the Titans and make it to Deva! We talked about this!"

I step up to the window and frown, watching the escape pod grow smaller and smaller. But it's not headed in the direction of Deva, nor in the direction of Nibiru. It takes me a few moments to realize what it must mean. "I don't think he's trying to."

"What?" Scorpia pulls away from the door and turns to me, wiping her eyes with one shaky hand. "What are you talking about?"

"I think he's doing something far more stupid than that," I say. "I think he's going toward the Titan fleet."

Scorpia sends away everyone but me and Izra. We sit across the table from the ex-pirate, who regards us with an expression verging on bored.

"Yes?" she asks, after a full minute of silence from Scorpia. I glance at my sister, also wondering what the holdup is. Scorpia's eyes are dry at this point, but she just stares down at the table, looking utterly lost.

It seems it's my turn to step up, then.

"You knew Orion was going to do this," I say, looking steadily at Izra.

She meets my gaze without hesitation. I expect her to deny it, or at least skirt around the question, but instead she only says, "Yep."

"So you let him leave? To go to the Titans?" Anger slowly grows in my chest. Izra always seems to know exactly how to get a rise out of me. "You know they'll get what they want from him and kill him."

"I told him as much," she says, and shrugs. "Told him there was no way in hell I was going there to be tortured to death. He made it clear he'd rather face that possibility than go back to Ca Sineh."

Beside me, Scorpia puts her face into her hands. I hold Izra's gaze, trying to keep her attention focused on me rather than on my sister, who is clearly headed toward a breakdown.

"We could have found a way to protect him," I say. "We could have at least discussed it—"

"We did discuss it. None of you listened," Izra says, her tone sharpening now, that veneer of indifference cracking. "So he made a decision. And he deserved to make that choice for himself, even if I thought it was a fucking stupid one."

After she leaves, Scorpia and I sit in silence. She still has her head in her hands, and I'm trying to find the best way to speak to her delicately. In the end, I settle for being straightforward.

"Does he know about what we found on Gaia?"

Scorpia raises her head and looks at me dully. "That's what you're worried about right now?"

"Scorpia, if that information gets into Titan hands, it could—"

"They're going to kill him," she says. "And it's my fault."

"It's not your fault. Izra said it herself, he made his own choice." I lean forward, touching her arm. "But I need to know how much information he has. We have to assume everything he knows will be passed on to the Titans." *One way or another*, I think, remembering what I know of Titan interrogations. Even though Orion and I never saw precisely eye to eye, I remember his easy laughter and feel sorry for him.

Scorpia shakes her head. "I didn't tell him. And that's the

whole fucking problem. Orion…" She pauses, pressing a hand to her eyes for a few seconds before lowering it and continuing. "He knew I was hiding something. If I had just trusted him—if I had made it clear why it was so important to go to Nibiru, told him about the defense systems, then—then maybe he wouldn't have done this."

"If he was willing to betray you, he would have done it at some point."

"No," she says. "That's not true. Trust goes both ways. He never would have taken a risk like this if he had more faith in me." Her eyes well up again, her breathing getting shakier. "I hid things from him, chose Shey over him, ignored him when he tried to tell me how scared he was…this is my fault. I failed him."

I reach out for her, to comfort her, but she pulls away and stands up. "I need a drink," she says, and storms out of the room before I can stop her.

CHAPTER TWENTY

The Choice

Scorpia

I rifle through the kitchen cabinets, ignoring Corvus's eyes watching me from the doorway.

"Please don't do this," he says.

"Fuck off." I move on to the drawers and storage beneath the sink. Kneeling on the kitchen floor, desperately searching for something to numb the pain, I'm well aware that I look pathetic. I feel pathetic, too. It's been a long time since I felt so thoroughly pitiful, and I hoped I would never be here again, but I guess it always comes to this.

Except I can't seem to find a single stars-damned drop of alcohol on this ship. I don't understand. It was here before. I've seen the twins drinking beer, and Orion and I shared that bottle of fireberry wine—

Just thinking of him, even for a second, hurts so badly that I gasp a little, and press my hands to my eyes to ward off tears. Because I can't think of him without imagining what the Titans are going to do to him, and that it's all my fault for letting him down.

"Scorpia," Corvus says. He takes a cautious step forward, but when I whip around to glare at him, he stops. "You need to decide if we're still going to Nibiru. If Orion tells the Titans we're heading there, they will target us. There's no way we'll be able to leave again once we arrive."

Even in my current state, I know that he's right. But every time I try to think too hard about the future, fear pulses through me and makes my thoughts grind to a halt. I can't seem to think of a future that isn't terrible, and I'm tired of being responsible for decisions.

"It doesn't matter where we go," I say, hollowly. "If the Titans are starting a war, it's not gonna end with Nibiru. They're not gonna stop. Pax and Deva are already at each other's throats, so it's all..." I throw up my hands. "It's all gone to shit. We're not gonna be able to do anything about it."

"The information we have from Gaia could stop all of this," Corvus says.

"Yeah. Maybe. Or it could make it a million times worse."

"That doesn't mean we should do nothing."

"You know what?" I look at him, and hate myself a little when I see the spark of hope on his face, but I continue anyway. "If you're so smart, Corvus, why don't you figure it out? You're in charge now. Congrats."

I turn and begin rummaging through the drawers again. I'm halfway through my second search when I realize what must have happened. Someone must have come and taken everything while we were talking to Izra. Not Corvus, who was with me the whole time, which means...

"Lyre!" I yell, and storm past Corvus toward her room. He trails behind me, still silent. "What the hell did you do with the booze?"

I bang against the door until my knuckles feel bruised, but

she doesn't open it. Eventually I give up and press my forehead against the metal.

"Scorpia…" Corvus takes a step forward, but I hold out a hand to stop him.

"Don't fucking come near me," I snap at him, my voice rising. "This is all—" *All your fault*, I want to say, but I know that's not true. It's mine. It's all mine. I wipe the back of my hand across my eyes impatiently. "I'm a sham. I'm a fucking sham, all right, and you all never should have put me in charge." I suck in a quaking breath. "We're all walking around like we're fucking heroes when we're the ones who did this. We're the ones who destroyed the Titans. We're the ones who hid the truth from Nibiru. Now all our lies are catching up to us, and…and it's exactly what we deserve. What *I* deserve."

Corvus is looking at me with a horribly sad expression. I can't bring myself to meet his eyes.

"That's not true," he says, quietly. "And keep your voice down. You don't want everyone to hear this."

"I don't give a single fuck. I don't want this anymore. I don't know why I ever did. I'm tired of everyone expecting me to be anything other than what I am."

Despite the words, when I imagine one of the twins or Shey peeking out of the doorways to witness this, it feels like something has grabbed my chest and squeezed. Even through the growing haze in my brain, I know he's right. I shouldn't make them witness this. I can't bear to let the twins see me like this after everything they've been through. Drom especially. I still remember that conversation about her imitating me in vivid detail, and I don't want her to realize I'm backsliding now and feel the need to do the same herself. And Shey…Shey would never look at me the same way again.

As much as I want to fall apart, I can't let myself crumble in front of my family. Not now. That isn't who I am anymore, and they need me to be a version of myself who isn't an utter mess. I have to keep my shit together—at least until my family is safe. I need to shove everything I'm feeling down where it can't get in my way.

"Fine," I say, stepping back from Lyre's door. "If you're going to keep looking at me like that, I'd rather be alone anyway."

After a rough landing with Lyre as my copilot, I rush down to the cargo bay to meet up with the others. Corvus and Shey are ready to join me on the surface, and Lyre and the twins hover anxiously in the back of the cargo space, watching us. Izra must be in her room.

"I still think you should bring me," Lyre says. "I really think we—"

"No. You keep the ship ready to go. This is just a quick in and out, and then we're off to Deva and away from this mess," I say, stepping up to the ramp. I don't miss the quick look exchanged by Corvus and Lyre. I know they doubt whether or not my plan will be viable, but I can't let that bother me. Right now the only thing holding me together is the belief that we'll be able to make it out of here before things get ugly. I have to keep believing I haven't both lost Orion and trapped the rest of the crew on a war-torn planet.

"These council assholes better be ready to see us ASAP," I say as I hit the button to open the bay door. As it slides open, I step out onto the ramp—and halt as I find it surrounded by a dozen peacekeepers. "What the hell is this?"

"Welcome back to Nibiru, Captain Kaiser. We've been sent by the council to escort you directly to meet with them," one of the peacekeepers at the front says, with a respectful bow to me. "I must insist you come with us immediately."

No amount of polite phrasing and bowing would prevent the spike of fear in my chest. I know this isn't Gaia, and these aren't the brutal law-enforcers I spent so much of my life afraid of, and that we're lawfully employed by the council, but I still don't like this. Especially not when we staged a jailbreak last time we were here, and we still have two—no, one wanted convict waiting on our ship. Judging from the way Corvus steps up to my side and eyes the peacekeepers, he's of the same opinion.

"Mind if I ask what the rush is?" I ask, taking a small step forward. "Not usually the council's style to send such a . . . robust escort."

The officer bows again. "Everything will be explained to you at the Council Hall, but I'm afraid time is of the essence."

Shit. I don't like this. I don't like it at all. I'd like nothing more than to run back onto the ship and take off, and the Nibirans probably wouldn't be fast enough to stop us . . . but we're here for a reason, and coming here was always risky. Whatever this is about, we still have to do what we came here to do. The entire planet is at stake.

But my family might be as well. I wave Lyre over, and when she leans in close at my gesture, I whisper into her ear, "If you don't hear from us in an hour, take off without us."

Her head jerks back. "What? Scorpia—"

"You've got this." I squeeze her shoulder before turning and heading down the ramp. Corvus is right on my heels, and Shey comes close behind. My heart is thudding in my chest, but at least I know that no matter what happens, Lyre will take care of the twins. She'll do what's necessary.

My unease grows as the escorts rush us toward the center of the island without even a proper customs inspection. By the time we arrive at the Council Hall, my heart is in my throat. Entering a completely silent room full of councillors does little to ease my nerves. Neither does the fact that the guards immediately close and lock the door behind us, sealing us in a room brimming with tense silence.

Shey presses close to my side, taking my hand in hers. Corvus keeps his eyes on the guards behind us, his shoulders squared and his jaw set. I look over the seated council members, trying to find a friendly face or a hint of what's happening among them, but not even Oshiro will meet my eyes. They look down at their folded hands, rubbing one thumb nervously across the opposite hand. At the end of the row is a new face: Gaia's freshly appointed president Khatri, seated in a metal chair below the raised dais that the rest of the councillors are seated at. It must grate on her Gaian pride, but she remains the perfect picture of poise, her gloved hands folded in her lap.

Tension thickens the air in the room, making it feel hard to breathe. Stars, after everything it took to get here, including likely paying with Orion's life, I hope I didn't make a grave mistake deciding to come back.

"Well," I say, trying to sound as lighthearted as I can manage. "Not exactly the warm welcome I was expecting. Someone want to tell us what exactly is going on here? Last I checked, we took a risky job as a favor to you."

After another tense moment, Heikki, the eldest of the council and usual spokesperson, finally clears her throat and speaks. "To be frank, after days of no response to our messages, we weren't sure if we should expect to see you again," she says, leveling a steely gaze on me. "And a transmission we received last night raised further questions."

My mouth goes dry. "What transmission? From who?"

Heikki hesitates, and then says, "From the survivors of Titan."

Shit. Shit. So much for warning the Nibirans about the approaching Titan fleet…and judging by the way the council is eyeing us right now, I have a sinking feeling that we're about to regret not telling them the full truth about what happened on Titan.

"Show us," Corvus says from beside me. I can't bear to turn and see the look on his face; the pained hoarseness of his voice tells me enough about how he's feeling right now.

When Heikki hesitates, Oshiro speaks up. "They deserve to see it." They look up only briefly before dropping their eyes again.

After nods from a few other members from the council, Heikki pulls up a screen from her desk. She presses a button, and I raise a hand to my mouth as the familiar face of General Kel Altair appears.

CHAPTER TWENTY-ONE

Decisions and Consequences

Corvus

I n all the time I knew General Altair back on Titan, I never once saw the man with a single hair out of place. He always seemed like a permanent rock among the tumult of war, impossible to ruffle, impossible to read. The latter is still true, but the man looks years older than the last time I saw him. He is gray and ragged, harrowed and tired. But his Interplanetist uniform is still sharp and pristine as ever, and his eyes are still the eyes of a warrior.

"I am General Kel Altair, the leader of what remains of Titan," he says, those cold eyes boring into the camera. It feels like he's looking right at me. Judging me and finding me guilty. "Three months ago, an atrocious and cowardly assault was made on my planet. You thought us wiped out, and most of us were." He shuts his eyes for a moment, as if the pain is too much to bear, before looking into the camera again. "But some of us survived. We waited, and we bided our time, and now we are here to collect the justice that you owe us."

Scorpia's hand squeezes my arm, but I can't bring myself to tear my own gaze away from the message. My heart is a hammer against the inside of my ribs, threatening to break free. Again the feelings from before surge up: the aching hope I hadn't dared to let myself feel, and an overwhelming wave of terror. Titan justice only means one thing.

"The Gaians are the ones responsible for this attack. They declared war on us, and it is war we will bring them," Altair continues. "Nibiru: Our fight is not with you. If you do not wish to become a part of this, we have three demands. First, that you grant us the temporary usage of the island Aluris. Secondly, that you no longer harbor and protect the Gaians. And lastly, we demand the immediate surrender of ex-president Talulah Leonis, and all of her accomplices in the attack on our planet, including Scorpia Kaiser, Corvus Kaiser, and the rest of their traitorous family."

Scorpia sucks in a small gasp beside me. I manage to contain my own emotions, but my heart sinks down, down, downward.

"If you refuse to surrender these war criminals, we will have no choice but to launch a full assault against your planet and destroy anyone who stands in our way. That includes any other planets who decide to become involved." He pauses to let that threat linger. "You have twelve hours to respond. We will see you soon."

Is that what Altair and Daniil truly believe of me? That I'm a war criminal? That I betrayed them in the worst possible way? I've spent these last few months defending the Titans, arguing for retribution, and now...now they're back, and consider me no better than the woman I fought so hard to imprison.

That shouldn't be what I'm focused on right now, not when so much else hangs in the balance, not when the council is staring at us and waiting for an explanation. Yet I think of the cold hatred in Altair's voice when he said my name, spoke it alongside the likes of Leonis, and my chest aches. I have to find a way to make this right. They have to know that I didn't betray them. That none of us knew what Momma and Leonis had planned for Titan. The rest of us were just unknowing pawns.

"This is bullshit," Scorpia says, and the fear in her voice finally yanks my attention fully back to the tense council room and our current situation. "Are you really gonna believe his word over ours? After everything we've done for you?"

I can see from Scorpia's face that she's on the verge of panicking, so I step forward, placing myself between her and council.

"It is true that our mother was involved in the destruction of Titan, but my siblings and I had no knowledge of the deal that took place. Whatever Altair believes—" I pause, swallowing. "That's the truth. We had no hand in what happened on Titan. We barely made it out alive ourselves, and our mother paid for her involvement with her death."

"Say what you like, but you must understand how this looks to us," Govender says, fixing me with a flinty look. I don't like to hear her speak against us; she's a quieter member of the council, but when she does talk, others listen. "First, there is the matter of the escape of two prisoners from Ca Sineh on the very day you leave the planet—"

"We've already discussed this," Oshiro says, immediately. "The breakout has already been traced back to a group of Gaian extremists not linked to the Kaisers."

"Prisoners who, I may add, were linked to the attempted release of a Primus biological weapon on this planet," Govender continues, as if the other councillor hadn't spoken. "Now, we have a general of Titan accusing the Kaisers of being involved in a similar attack on his planet. Surely no one can deny that this looks suspicious."

"I have always argued that we place too much faith in these outsiders," Heikki says. "We've been pinging their ship for days with no response, and now they show up half a day after this transmission? This is too much to be a coincidence. And if handing them over to the Titans along with Leonis could prevent a war—"

Oshiro stands up, pale cheeks splotching red. "Don't you even dare to suggest such a thing, Heikki. It's low even for you. The Kaisers saved our planet from destruction."

Oshiro's defense of my family does little to reassure me. Two councillors have spoken against us now. And Heikki, while generally cautious and conservative, is usually not the type to suggest such drastic action. If she's saying this, others are thinking it. We need to take charge of the conversation, but Scorpia isn't speaking up. I have a sinking feeling that she's teetering on a dangerous brink right now; Orion's abandonment already hit her hard, and she's always feared the council turning on us like this.

"What we have to tell you today may very well save you again," I say, stepping forward. I give a grateful nod to Oshiro, who sinks back into their seat without turning their glare away from an affronted-looking Heikki. "We could argue all day about what happened on Titan, but far more relevant to both the question of our loyalty and the current situation are the results of our recent mission to Gaia on your behalf."

That silences the room. I continue, "You gave us a ship. We could have gone anywhere in the system. But we chose to complete the job you asked of us, and then chose to return despite knowing we may end up trapped here. We encountered a Titan ship days ago. We have the body of one of their soldiers to prove it. They destroyed our communications system, preventing us from reaching you. We returned even knowing about the approaching Titan fleet, because the information we found is important enough to warrant the risk. So, before you judge us, you need to hear it."

I launch into my explanation of our discoveries: the information hidden beneath Gaia, the holograms of the planets, the warm statues and our evidence for what we've begun to call the Planetary Defense Systems. The council is silent as I speak, though I notice a few of them glance in the direction of President Khatri, who remains stoic and silent with her eyes studying my face. I try to keep my own eyes on Councillor Oshiro, the most familiar face on the council and the one I have the most hope will advocate for what's right.

As I finish, Oshiro presses a hand to their mouth and lowers their head. All is silent for a few moments as the council processes the information.

"So what you're telling us," Councillor Acharya, who always wears his emotions openly on his face, says, "is that if the Titans come here, we have no chance of victory. Even if we fight them off, our own planet will turn against us."

"That's not—" I begin, but it's too late; it seems that was the cue for the council to panic. Several people begin to talk at once now. Govender accuses Khatri of knowing about this all along, while she earnestly swears she had no idea; Heikki and Oshiro are arguing once again; Acharya has started to cry.

At a loss, I look over at Scorpia, who catches my eye and starts to back toward the door. It's clear she wants to take advantage of the chaos and sneak out while we can, but I shake my head. If we walk away now, we will look guiltier than ever. More importantly, we can't take the chance of them thinking we were lying about the defense systems. I have to know that they're taking this threat seriously.

Heikki stands, gesturing for quiet, and the others obey. "For now, we must assume that the Kaisers are telling the truth about this," she says. "They have saved us once before, and Corvus is correct in saying they put themselves in danger to deliver us this information. So, given this, what is our next step with the Titans? Govender?"

All eyes turn to Govender, who looks surprised, for a moment, to be directly called upon. As I recall, she's the councillor from Lan Iroh. The smallest of the islands on Nibiru, but home to some significant military facilities, which has likely never meant all too much until this moment. Govender has never held this much sway before, and judging by the calculating look in her eyes, she is eager to seize it. "Firstly, and most importantly, we must ensure that this information does not fall into Titan hands," she says. "It would give them everything they need to destroy us without setting foot on our planet, and give them an unbeatable advantage over us. That means that the information must not leak to our people. Nor can we surrender either the Kaisers or ex-president Leonis to Altair, since we can assume the knowledge would be handed over along with them."

Govender may be a steely woman, but she seems to be exactly what the council needs right now. They're listening.

"So," Govender says, "we cannot honor Altair's third demand. The first, I think we can all agree, is also out of the question. Given the Titans' history and culture, allowing them onto our planet when we know the risk of the Planetary Defense System would be unimaginably risky."

"It could also be our best chance at approaching this peacefully," Oshiro speaks up. "We could welcome them, as we did the Gaians."

Govender glances at them, her expression cool. "Forgive me, Oshiro, but now is not the time for foolish idealism. You saw the same message I did. Altair did not come here with peace in mind."

"The man is clearly here to make war," Heikki agrees. "We must try to keep him off the planet itself for as long as possible."

"Which brings us to his second demand," Govender says. "The matter of the Gaians."

A heavy silence settles over the room, broken only by Shey's sharp intake of breath; Scorpia protectively pulls her closer. I stare up at the council, at a loss for words. Surely, they can't be considering giving the Gaians up now.

"That is clearly off the table," Oshiro says, earning a few vehement nods from others around the dais.

"The idea grieves me," Govender says, "but I believe anything warrants at least a discussion at this point, with our entire planet at risk. We have not yet agreed to grant them a permanent stay. We would be breaking no promises by asking them to leave."

The council bursts into discussion at that, several of them speaking at once. President Khatri clears her throat and holds out one hand, palm up and fingers spread, requesting the attention of the room with remarkable politeness, given the situation. One by one, the councillors fall silent.

"I have always believed it is possible for our people to live in harmony, and this new threat does not change that," Khatri says. "This will be a test of our ability to work together, no doubt. But imagine how it would bring us together. Our people, side by side, standing against a common enemy. Do you really believe the Titans would stop with us, after the way they willingly destroyed one another on their own planet? And do you believe they would have a hope to overcome us if we stand together? Some of the

Titans may have survived, but we know from our drone reports that their losses were grave. This is not the full force of the Titan military we are facing down—in all likelihood, it is just some straggling survivors, come to bluff and bluster in the hope we will cave and let them take whatever they like from us. This is exactly what they want: to defeat us by dividing us. Let us show them we are stronger than they think, and our bond is not so easily broken."

There is a moment of consideration, as the councillors look around at one another; but, one by one, they nod.

"We will not abandon you in your time of need," Heikki says firmly. "As we had suggested previously—and recently confirmed among ourselves—we are prepared to offer the Gaians a home on our planet. That has not changed."

Shey lets out a small gasp, pressing one hand to her chest. Her face shines with relief. As for myself, I'm not entirely sure how to feel. A few months ago, I would be glad that the Gaians have a permanent home. But now…now, it may mean war for everyone here, Nibiran and Gaian alike. And it may mean the end of yet another planet in our system. Khatri's argument against the Titans smacks of typical Gaian hubris, and I fear what underestimating the Titans may mean…but I can't bring myself to argue for abandoning the Gaians, either.

"However," Govender continues, "I believe especially in light of this new information and the pending arrival of the Titans, it is important that our two people are truly unified. We can no longer be two peoples intermingling on one planet. We must become one."

"Meaning what?" the president asks.

"We believe it would be best to classify Gaia as a prefecture of Nibiru. A part of our planet, rather than an independent entity." Khatri's face darkens as the councillor continues. "As Nibirans, your people will be expected to adhere to all Nibiran laws. You will be granted a seat on the council and power equal to all of us."

"You're trying to subjugate us," Shey says before the president can speak. I glance sideways at her, surprised by the hostility in her voice. Color rises high in her cheeks, and her eyes are furious. She steps away from Scorpia's side and moves forward, looking up at the council. "To take away our ability to self-govern. Is that what you're saying? Now, of all times, you decide to propose this?"

The president doesn't even look Shey's way, but she doesn't reprimand her or speak up otherwise, either. She only looks to the council for their answer.

"This was our plan before we knew the danger coming, and we see no reason to deviate from it now. If anything, it is only more important. We are trying to unite our people," Heikki says, her voice growing frostier in response to Shey's heated tone. She looks down at her, lips pursed. "It would be unfair to grant the Gaians privileges or rights denied anyone else on the planet, do you not agree?"

"No," Shey says, her voice rising even more. "I do not agree. You would take away everything that makes us Gaian."

"Well, uh, much as I hate to interrupt..." I'm surprised to hear Scorpia speak up for the first time in several minutes, and turn to see her step forward, glancing around the room. "If the question of our loyalty is settled and you're not tossing out the Gaians, I think it's time for us to head out."

All eyes turn to Scorpia, but no one looks more surprised than Shey. "This is an important discussion. We can't just walk out without knowing what's going to happen."

"Is it important, though?" Scorpia asks, brow furrowing. "We've got a fleet of Titans bringing war to this planet any day now. We could all be dead in a couple weeks." She holds out a hand toward Shey. "We still have a chance to get out of here."

Shey falters. Her silence stretches out for one beat, and another. "The sovereignty of my people..."

Scorpia's face flushes. She lets the hand fall. "Sovereignty won't mean shit if they're all dead," she snarls, and heads for the doors. The guards hover in her way for a moment, but at a nod from Heikki, they step aside and let her go.

Shey looks at me in shock, her lips slightly parted. "Is she really going to leave?"

I stare at the doors she walked out of, feeling torn, and unable to answer. I should go after my sister. If she really intends to leave, of course I need to go with her. And yet, if there's a possibility I could prevent this from escalating to all-out war...

"She can't go," Oshiro says, before I have to make the decision myself. "We received the broadcast from Altair twelve hours ago, and traced its location. The Titans are likely already here, or will be within hours."

Relief and despair battle within me at the news. On the one hand, I don't have to decide between my family and the war. On the other—we're about to all be trapped in the middle of this conflict, as I always suspected we would be.

"I'll go after her," I say, turning to Shey. "You do what you need to do."

"Thank you," she says, softly.

But before I go, I have to try, at least once, to stop this. I turn to the council, bowing low, and wait until I have their full attention to speak.

"I feel that I must add something else," I say, slowly, trying to phrase this the best that I can. "All of you are discussing war as though it is something inevitable. However, especially now that we have the information about the Planetary Defense Systems, I do not believe that's the case. This information could be used to negotiate with the Titans."

Someone on the council lets out an incredulous sound, but when I glance around, it's impossible to tell which of them it came from.

"You saw the same message that we all did," Heikki says after a moment. "It's difficult to imagine how we can negotiate when they make such absurd demands."

"They also don't know what we know. It's true that my people are used to war, but I do not believe they would attack this planet if they knew it had the potential to render it completely uninhabitable. Surely, the Titans are seeking a home, not mindless destruction."

"Judging from the information you gave us, the Titans were perfectly willing to wreak mindless destruction on their own home. Though Leonis may have given them the weapon that destroyed their planet, they were the ones who chose to deploy it. Why should we expect them to choose differently now?"

"I—" I can feel my face coloring, and I hesitate, unable to find the words I need to argue against her.

"I agree with Corvus," Shey says. "I believe this could be an opportunity to open peace talks with Titan. The information about the Planetary Defense Systems could make them less eager to attack."

"It would also give them the knowledge that they don't even have to touch down on our surface to destroy us," Govender says. "We cannot ignore the history of the Titans, and this information is a weapon that can be used against us. The Titans would know they have the upper hand, and be able to threaten us into agreeing to anything they like. But if we do choose to share this information, perhaps we could use it as a bargaining chip with Deva to gain their support. Considering their current tension with Pax, I suspect they may also be eager for allies."

"That is an interesting point," Heikki says, "and one I believe should be discussed without an audience." She gives Shey and me a barely polite smile. "The council is grateful for your assistance, but that is all we wish to discuss with you for today. We will let you know if we need any additional information. And we expect that the two of you, and all else who know the information you've gathered about the Planetary Defense Systems, will keep it to yourselves. From this time onward, revealing it to anyone outside of this chamber will be considered treasonous." Her expression hardens as she looks between me and Shey, and then over the rest of the council. "It is time that we prepare for war, and wartime laws will be enforced. This is now a matter of planetary security."

Back at the dock, I find Scorpia arguing with a crowd of peacekeepers standing between her and the ship.

"Under emergency order of the council, no ships are allowed to leave or enter Nibiru," one of them is saying, with the stubborn air of someone who's already repeated this fact several times.

"For the last stars-damned time, we *work* for the council, I'm leaving on their orders," Scorpia says.

"No exceptions."

"You idiots—" Scorpia turns and sees me approaching, and relief chases away the beginnings of panic on her face. "Finally. Will you tell these assholes to let us go? I wanted to have the ship ready by the time you got here, but..."

I put an arm around her shoulders and pull her away from the group of peacekeepers, turning our backs to them. "Scorpia, we can't leave."

She stares at me, betrayal in her eyes. "Like hell we can't."

"The Titans are too close by now. We can't risk it."

"Says who? Your little friend on the council?" Scorpia scoffs. "I bet you a million credits they're lying to us. They just don't want us to leave knowing what we know. Did you see the way they looked at us in there? It's only a matter of time before they turn on us. Lock us up in Ca Sineh or worse. It's time to take a nice vacation on Deva and wait for all this to blow over."

"The council is on our side," I say. "You can't risk everyone by launching right now. It's not safe."

"It's not safe for us here—" Scorpia shouts, and a scream interrupts her.

I whirl around, my arm still wrapped protectively around Scorpia, and find the peacekeepers staring openmouthed at the sky. I follow their eyes, and my legs nearly give out beneath me.

Darkness spreads against the Nibiran sky—a fleet of massive ships, uncloaking one by one. Despair grips me as the full strength of the fleet slowly reveals itself—a terrifying wave bearing down on the planet.

CHAPTER TWENTY-TWO

Justice

Scorpia

A hundred Titan warships fill the sky. At the center of it all is a hulking monstrosity of a mothership, nearly as big as the gigantic alien vessel that brought the Gaians here, but this one all glossy, angular, human steel. The thing must be the size of a stars-damned city.

I don't care what Corvus says. There's never going to be peace. Not when the Titans brought a war fleet. And even with the Nibiran and Gaian forces combined, they don't have a chance against this. Nor do we have a chance.

I brace myself, ready for the first shot, which will trigger the planet's defense system and end it all when it's barely begun... but it doesn't come. The ships don't fire, don't move toward the planet. Still, the message is clear enough. War's coming.

And I brought us here. Trapped us here.

I stumble back, pressing a hand to my mouth to stifle the panicked noise that rises in my throat. "Fuck," I say, my fingers muffling the words. "Fuck this. I'm out of here. I'm done."

Corvus tears his eyes away from the fleet to look at me, and reaches out with one hand. "Let's get to the others—"

I don't hear the rest of what he says. I run, as fast as I can, away from those ships, and the family I've failed to protect, and everything else. Straight to the nearest bar, where people seem too drunk to have registered the danger above them just yet. I order two shots of their cheapest whiskey and keep going until I'm numb.

Hours pass that I'm barely aware of. Many hours, and many drinks, until it all starts to blur together. Once I start slipping, it's all too easy to just let myself fall. To give in to gravity's pull and keep tumbling downward. Especially when every time I glance at the sky and see the Titan fleet surrounding us, I'm reminded over and over again of the fact that I'm trapped. That I got us all trapped here in the middle of what will soon be a war zone.

Orion left me. Shey rejected me for her people once again. I can't blame them for it... but I also can't bring myself to face my family and the possibility that they'll turn on me, too. I can't stand the thought of the way that they'll look at me knowing I let them all down.

My memories fracture and everything fades. Just what I wanted. I throw up in a bar and get kicked out and—maybe spend a couple hours passed out on the sidewalk? I'm not really sure. I don't remember.

All I know is that by the time I get up again, woken by the menacing crackle of a storm brewing overhead, the bar is closed and the streets are empty. It must be very late at night, or very early in the morning. When I try to check, I realize I must've lost my comm at some point. Finally, shame and exhaustion and guilt over making my siblings worry drives me to the houseboat. The sky opens up when I'm nearly there, and I run the rest of the way, pelted by rain and wind.

Thank the stars they didn't lock down the house yet. Dripping wet and cold, I stumble through the door and head for the stairs. Corvus is waiting on the couch, but he only watches me pass and rises to lock the door behind me, saying nothing. Lyre is passed out next to the seat he left, curled up with a cushion clutched in her arms. Drom's room is empty, but I hear both twins' voices murmuring softly to one another inside Pol's. Corvus's door is open, and I'm surprised to see Izra sleeping in his bed. Guiltily, I realize that I forgot about her. I'm glad Corvus brought her here; like us, she has nowhere else to go.

My door is open, too…and in there, sitting on the bed with her hair up and a book in her hands, is Shey. I stop in the doorway, staring, and she sets the book aside and looks up at me.

My lower lip trembles. "You came back?"

"I'm not going to leave you now," she says, "no matter how hard you try to force me to." She holds out her arms.

I climb into bed, curl myself against her. I'm lulled to sleep by the distant rumble of thunder, and her hand stroking my wet hair.

I wake up feeling like shit. I almost forgot what this was like: my rioting stomach, the sledgehammer thumps on the inside of my skull, the raw and exposed feeling like all my emotions and sensations are dialed up to eleven after the time I spent numb. I'm desperate to grab another bottle of something to help me through this.

But instead I sit up and look over at Shey, sleeping with her wavy hair spread over the pillows and one hand extended toward the indent in the mattress where I was sleeping. I'm tempted to fall back into bed and stay there, but instead I drag myself to the shower. It's time to get my shit together.

Orion left me. That's something I'm going to have to learn to live with. But Shey…Shey stayed. She saw me at my worst and she stuck around. She showed me that maybe Momma wasn't right about us only being able to trust our blood after all. Now, I want to prove to Shey that she made the right choice. That I can do better. I *will* do better. I'll take care of her and my family. They all need me right now. I might be a grounded captain, but I'll have to figure out a way to be a captain nonetheless.

By the time I emerge, thoroughly scrubbed and feeling a little more human, everyone else is awake as well. Izra leans against a wall rather than joining everyone else at the table, downing mug after mug of black coffee. Corvus makes pancakes, with some of the last of our rehydrated fruit as a special treat, and Pol pours me a cup of coffee the moment I seat myself at the table. It's sweeter than I usually like it, but I thank him anyway. Even Drom refrains from making any insulting comments about my undoubtedly haggard appearance, and once Shey emerges from her own shower, I pull her onto my lap and bury my face in her hair, and everything feels like it's going to be all right.

But the drone of the television in the other room makes it impossible to forget the outside world for long. Even as we eat breakfast and I crack a few half-hearted jokes, the tension bleeds into the room. The newscasters speculate about the Titan fleet and their numbers, the announcement that Gaia has been officially declared a prefecture of Nibiru and their people are now classified as citizens rather than foreign visitors, and the council's reassurances that Nibiru is not considering itself at war with Titan. Yet.

I try to ignore it and keep the conversation and normality going as long as possible. But when the newscaster announces that the Nibiran Council is about to publicly make an official response to General Altair, we all wordlessly abandon our places at the table and crowd into the living room instead. The only exception is Izra, who immediately heads out onto the deck and sits with her legs dangling over the water.

The rest of us cram onto the couch. I reach over to squeeze Corvus's hand as the message begins. He squeezes back, hard enough that it almost hurts, but he doesn't glance at me. His expression is hard, mouth set into a grim line and eyes locked on the screen and the seven council members standing there to relay the message— along with President Khatri, sitting off to the side with her gloved hands folded in her lap and her eyes down.

"Well, how do you think this is gonna go?" I ask, in a weak attempt at filling the silence, but Corvus shakes his head.

"You know how it's going to go," he says, and sighs heavily. "Altair is a good man. Or at least, he once was. But it's too late to stop this now."

I force myself to bite my tongue as Councillor Govender steps forward to speak.

"This is a message for General Altair, and the other surviving citizens of Titan," she says, her voice ringing out with confidence though I can only imagine how frightening it must be to relay this message and know what it means. "We were overjoyed to learn that not the entirety of Titan was lost in the tragedy a few months ago, as we all thought. It is a miracle and a blessing that you remain alive. And Nibiru agrees that you must have justice for the wrongs done to you." She pauses, and swallows, and for a moment I get a small glimpse of the fear that must be churning wildly inside of her. But she continues on, her voice steady. "However, we cannot let innocent Gaians suffer for the crimes of their leader. And we cannot surrender Leonis until the Interplanetary Council holds her trial and determines her fate and what she knows about the events on both Gaia and Titan. With Titan already dangerous, and Gaia in rapid decline, it is more important than ever that we are patient and careful with our decisions rather than rushing toward the easiest answer. So we invite you: Please, join us on the Interplanetary Council and trust in the justice of law, rather than seeking revenge on innocents." She takes a deep breath.

"While we cannot invite you onto our already vastly over-crowded planet, we would like to offer you as much aid as we can afford. We are prepared to gift you enough food to sustain your people for the next six months, as soon as you provide us with your population numbers, in return for removing your fleet from the vicinity of our planet and returning to Titan. We wish nothing more than to assist in your peoples' recovery and resettling of your planet, and move forward peacefully."

The message ends, replaced by reporters discussing what this all could mean. Lyre turns it down, and the room is quiet.

"No apology from President Khatri," Corvus murmurs. "That's not a good sign."

"They probably think an apology would be an admission of guilt," Lyre says.

"But Titans will see the lack of one as an insult." Corvus shakes his head. "That whole message was insulting. They don't understand the Titans at all."

Lyre looks over at me. It feels like everyone is looking at me, waiting for me to say something, but I'm not sure how to comfort them.

"It's going to be all right," I say, finally, knowing even as I say it that it's an empty promise. "No matter what happens, I'm going to find a way for us to get out of here. We still have our ship."

It's maddening, really, that we finally have a ship, and now we're trapped anyway. I spent all this time thinking that getting a ship would solve our problems, but here we are, still grounded and helpless on Nibiru. Yet surely the Titans can't keep this planet barricaded forever. If a war comes, maybe it will distract them enough for us to slip past. Or maybe Nibiru will secure an alliance with Deva, and they'll grant us an opportunity to sneak through. But I have to hold on to the hope that we'll find a way out of here.

Before I can say more, the screen flashes, announcing a new

broadcast from the Titans. Corvus sits up very straight beside me, his fingers slipping free from my grip. I reach for Shey's hand instead, and she leans her head against my shoulder.

"They're responding so fast?" I ask. "And publicly?"

"It can't be good," Corvus murmurs.

From the first moment of the broadcast, it's obvious he's right. Altair's eyes are burning, intense. Even through the screen I can feel the rage radiating off of him, and my heart begins to thud in my chest. That's not the face of a man who is looking for peace, no matter what Corvus has said about him in the past.

"You speak of justice?" the general asks, his lip curling in contempt. "Is that what you call the outcome of the last Interplanetary Council? You were so eager to condemn us then—to call us barbarians, warmongers—and now you pretend to welcome us back with your insulting offer. You welcome the Gaians as citizens, but tell us to return to a planet still strewn with the bodies of those who died at their hands? We will not accept such treatment. This is a message for Nibiru, for Gaia, for the other planets listening out there: We will have none of your justice. We will create our own."

The message cuts off. As I stare into the blankness of the now-dark screen, it feels like a hole is gaping wide in my chest, and every piece of me is sinking in. That must have been the point of broadcasting such a declaration of war publicly: Altair wants the Nibirans to be afraid of what's coming. And they should be.

"Shit," I whisper. "It's really happening, then."

Corvus's eyes are shut so tightly he looks like he's in pain. "I knew it would," he says. "And yet . . . part of me still hoped—"

The rest of his words are cut off by the scream of a siren from outside. His eyes fly open, and I sit bolt upright, and a moment later both of us are on our feet and rushing to the window. I let out a gasp as I see the world outside, stumbling back a step and pressing a hand to my mouth.

The ships, which have been hanging threateningly in the sky for the last day, are descending toward the planet all at once, bearing down on Nibiru. Only the mothership remains above. I brace myself again for that first shot or an assault on Vil Hava—but neither comes. The ships are headed elsewhere, and holding their fire. But now, more than ever, it seems inevitable.

Corvus rushes toward the door. For a moment my feet stay glued in place with fear, but then I lurch after him. "Corvus, wait, it's not safe—" I say, but both my words and my feet come to a halt the moment I step outside. Corvus and Izra are both standing on the edge of the deck, their eyes locked on the approaching ships.

"Should we go somewhere?" I ask, turning to Corvus. He looks back at me, his expression flat.

"Where?"

"I don't know. Somewhere safe?"

His lips twist. "*Where?*"

"I don't…" I stop, one of my heels tapping anxiously against the deck. He's right. Nowhere is safe now that the planet is under attack, and given that it's only a matter of time until the defense system is triggered, it's going to get a lot worse. "What the hell are we supposed to do now?"

I expect Corvus to give me one of his world-weary looks and say something like *We have no choice, we have to fight*—but instead he only stares out at the ocean with an expression of infinite sadness, and doesn't say a word.

ACT TWO

CHAPTER TWENTY-THREE

The Inescapable Past

Corvus

We stopped it once, but war has come to the system despite our efforts. And this time, the perpetrator isn't a monster like Leonis, but General Altair. A man I know and trusted—a man who I served unquestioningly for three years. It still grieves me to imagine that he believes I'm a traitor now. And though I know I have to help the Nibirans against this invasion, I cannot imagine how I'm going to find the strength to fight against the Titans I once stood alongside.

I have to find the willpower. There's too much at stake. But how will I live with myself?

Scorpia shuts off the television, says a quick goodbye to Shey, who is heading off to check in with her Gaian contacts, and takes her seat at the head of the table with the rest of the family gathered around. I was afraid that this morning's events would send her into further backsliding, but instead they seem to have steeled her.

"All right," she says. "So, as we all know, we're stuck on this planet for now. I'm not gonna lie to you: Things are bad. They're probably going to get worse. But we've been through hell together already, and it didn't break us, and this won't, either. Plus, we're in better shape than ever right now. For one thing, we just got paid a shit ton by the council." Drom, at least, cracks a smile at that. "And we're also not alone. After everything we've done for them, the council will have our backs." She glances at me, but then away, her face betraying none of the doubt I know she must feel. "If it comes down to it, we can turn to them for shelter and protection, but for now I'm hoping we can stay on our houseboat and avoid the worst of the fighting. I can't promise that everything is going to be normal, or easy, but I can promise that I'll do everything I can to keep us safe, and that I'm going to get us off this planet as soon as I possibly can."

She looks around the table at us. We're all watching her, but nobody speaks, so she continues, "I'm thinking we stock up on supplies while we're here on Vil Hava. Nonperishable food, emergency first aid kits, anything else we might need. The markets on the smaller islands are likely overwhelmed right now. But we can't stay here; the Council Hall will make this island a target." I'm guessing she also intends to put some distance between ourselves and the council after the way they acted during our last meeting, but I'm glad she keeps that to herself. No reason to make our younger siblings panic more than they already are. "So where will be the safest place to dock? Do we go back to Kitaya? Lyre, what do you think?"

Lyre's head jerks up. She blinks at Scorpia for a moment before beginning to speak. "Oh. Well…there are no military bases on Kitaya, as far as I know. The only reason I can imagine the Titans may target it is if they want to take out the algae farms. About… seventy percent of the planet's algae comes from Kitaya, I believe." Her confidence grows as she goes on. "But that means the Nibirans will be eager to defend it, so it may be safer than other places. They may cede smaller islands with no strategic value if they must, but they can't lose Kitaya."

"Would the Titans target Kitaya for that reason?" Scorpia asks.

"Well, Kitaya is valuable in the long run, but if the Titans want to do more immediate damage to the Nibiran economy, there are easier ways to disrupt the supply chain. They could take out the supply boats that travel between islands. Or stock houses, processing plants, markets. Damage to Kitaya would be a loss, but the real impact wouldn't be felt for some time."

"Corvus?" Scorpia prompts. "Think the Titans are likely to go for a long-term strategy like that?"

"If they aim to fight a war that long, nothing we do will matter." I know I shouldn't say it, but the words tumble out of my mouth anyway. Scorpia gives me a pointed look, and I sigh, trying to come up with something less pessimistic. Our younger siblings still don't know about the Planetary Defense Systems, and letting them know how dire the situation is would likely only make them panic at this point. "We don't know how many Titans survived the bio-weapon, but we can assume they lost many. They'll certainly have a numbers disadvantage against the combined Nibiran and Gaian forces, but a technological advantage. I believe they'll want to hit hard and fast. And if they aim to resettle Nibiru rather than destroy it, it would be illogical to damage Kitaya."

"All right. That check out with you, Lyre?" After a moment, she nods, and Scorpia claps her hands together. "Well. That's the plan then. Stock up at the market today, and in the morning we'll head for Kitaya."

"I need to see Oshiro before we leave," I say. "I'll gather as much information as I can."

Scorpia nods. "Good. Lyre and Drom, I want you with me in the market. Izra and Pol, you inventory what we have here."

I pull Scorpia aside before I head out, waiting for the others to disperse before I speak. "We need to keep an eye on the twins

245

today. You heard what Drom was like back on the ship, and Pol will follow her if she tries to enlist."

"Yeah. I'll do my best to keep them separated until we leave Vil Hava." She hesitates, searching my face. "What about you? Do I have to worry about you running off to join the cause?"

"No," I say, without hesitation. "I'm not going to fight. I can't. Not again. Especially not against the Titans. It's all too…" I shake my head, unable to put my thoughts into words. "But I can't let the Nibirans be massacred by them, either. I have to give Oshiro as much information as I can to help them."

"We've done more than anyone could've asked for them already, Corvus. Don't feel like you have to give them anything more than what you want to give. It's not our fight."

I'm not sure I believe that, when we're stranded on this planet the same as everyone else, but I know Scorpia must know the reality of that more than anyone else. I squeeze her shoulder before heading out the door.

I stop at the sight of Izra sitting out on the deck. She's yet another problem on what is quickly becoming a long list. We barely got away with breaking her and Orion out of Ca Sineh, but with the council already mistrusting us, we can't afford to be caught with a fugitive hiding in our houseboat. I couldn't bring myself to throw her out on her own. Still, if the peacekeepers come looking…

"Izra," I say, walking over to her. Her shoulders and jaw are set in tense lines, and she watches me warily, as though expecting an attack. I crouch beside her and gesture for her to stay still as I draw my Primus knife. It surprises me when she complies.

She watches silently as I cut open the metal casing over her left arm. Once it crashes to the floor, she raises her weapon-infused limb, that strange intermingling of pale skin and black Primus material, and stretches out long-unused muscles.

"You could've done this the whole time," she says, lowering the arm and looking at me. I nod, and she scowls, her eye narrowing at me. For one moment, I'm certain she's going to punch me in the throat for my trouble, but instead, she only asks, "So why now?"

"Because I have enough people to feel responsible for," I say. And then, stepping back, I add, "And because you stayed."

Oshiro has already been moved to a secure military bunker along with the rest of the council, so I head there to meet them. Though war has not been officially declared yet, Vil Hava is already in turmoil. The crowd of protestors around the Gaian refugee camps has grown; one woman hoists up a freshly painted sign that reads NOT OUR WAR.

The docks, too, are busy. People are begging for rides—for a way to their family on the other islands, to the military base on Ziray where their sister is being deployed, to one of the smaller islands where they hope they won't be touched by the war. But while many people are looking to flee Vil Hava, even more are arriving. The horizon is dotted with ships. I pause to watch one overcrowded vessel unload a group of frightened-looking people carrying armfuls of belongings, and stay long enough to catch a few shreds of conversation on the wind—*Titans, occupation, Aluris*—before continuing onward.

But the most noticeable crowds are gathered around the recruitment centers. I never even noticed their presence here before. They must have been lost among the colorful market stalls before, but now the stalls are shut down and empty, stripped of their cheerful signs, and lines stream out the door and wind around the corners of the military buildings. So many young Nibirans eager to die. I'm sure Drom and Pol would be among them if they had the chance, but I have to hope Scorpia can find ways to keep them busy until I get back. Once we reach Kitaya, away from the war and the politics and the Nibiran crowds, I hope they will be less tempted.

Aside from the recruitment centers, most shops and other businesses have been shut down. Nibirans are nomadic even in peaceful times, living on houseboats and operating storefronts from collapsible stalls, so the entire island has transformed overnight. The buildings left behind look strange and lonely, especially with the storm shutters closed over their stained-glass windows. It's as though all the colors have been sapped, leaving the island dark and gray.

Even without an official war or news about what the Titans are doing, it's impossible to ignore the reality of the situation with that ship hovering in the sky like a constant threat, and all the smaller vessels traveling to and from it. It is a relief to step into the military center and have the sight of it cut off, even though the elevator descending into the earth brings me back to the underground facilities I frequented on Titan.

The building is busy, but Oshiro leads me to a small room where we can speak privately. A man steps in to serve us both mint tea and whisper something in Oshiro's ear, and then the click of the door behind him leaves us alone. We sit across a small, round table from each other, and Oshiro sets a comm on the surface in front of them.

"Thank you for coming to see me," the councillor says. "I understand how difficult this must be for you."

I dip my head in a nod, unable to speak. I resolved myself to coming here and sharing what I could with Oshiro, but that doesn't mean my heart isn't heavy over it. Part of me still feels like a traitor for being here, especially knowing my family was part of what drove the Titans to such desperate lengths. But in the end, Altair and the Titans are threatening the safety of an entire planet.

"What's the situation right now?" I ask, trying to keep myself businesslike.

"The Titans have occupied a large portion of Aluris," Oshiro says, pulling up a hologram map of the island. "Many of the civilians have been displaced. Others are still there, however, and most of the local officials and important personnel are being held in Titan custody. It makes it difficult for us to make any moves against them."

"But that means they're not killing them," I say, struggling to find a sliver of good in the news. "We're not past the point of no return yet."

"No. The Titans are holding back. Despite the occupation, there's still no official declaration of war on either side. But..." Oshiro leans back, shaking their head, a few strands of hair drifting loose from their ponytail. "The longer we let them stay on that island, the stronger their foothold will be. And if they're taking their first demand by force, we can only imagine they'll eventually come for the rest."

"You're talking about the Gaians."

"Yes." Oshiro sighs. "And...truth be told, I'm not sure we can stop them if they come at us head-on. We don't know how many of them there are. They've set up a perimeter around the area they seized, and with their ships and other tech, they're able to maintain complete air control. Any drones we send are shot down before they get close."

"So they're hiding their strength," I say. "Could be a bluff. Could not."

"Precisely. We have no way of knowing." Oshiro taps their fingers on the table, looking at me. "We do have a few photographs we were able to take from afar. Would you mind taking a look at them, seeing if anything jumps out?"

I hesitate, torn. I want to help Oshiro and the Nibirans. But the Titans haven't openly attacked them yet. They've taken an island, but according to Oshiro's information, no one is dead yet. Is it justified for me to give information that could potentially hurt the Titans? Then I truly will be a traitor—to Altair, to Daniil, to my home-planet.

"We're afraid, Corvus," Oshiro says gently, when I don't speak up. "We're well aware that the Titans have a technological and military advantage over us. We need to prove that we can put up enough of a fight to make them hesitate before attacking us.

There's no hope of negotiation if they believe they can crush us if they want to. Heikki and Govender already believe a war is inevitable, and the rest of us are barely holding them back from making a preemptive strike before the Titans do something drastic. Help me prove there can still be a peaceful solution to this."

A peaceful solution. That's all I want, in the end. But does the council truly want that, too, or is Oshiro only saying what I want to hear?

No. I can't think like that. Oshiro has been kind to me when they have no reason to be. The rest of the council may try to deceive and use my family, but Oshiro has become a friend. And I have to think beyond the council. I have to think about the millions of innocent lives that will be lost in this war. The soldiers who have no choice but to sacrifice themselves for their planet. The civilians who will be caught in the cross fire.

And Oshiro is right. No information I give the council will allow the Nibirans to crush the Titans. The most that they can hope for is a fighting chance. I may be able to help give them that—even if it makes me the traitor that Daniil accused me of being.

After a moment, I nod. "I can't fight them," I say. "I don't have it in me anymore. But I'll tell you as much as I can."

A bleak look flickers across Oshiro's face, but I force myself to maintain my resolve. I'm not ready to become part of another war, and especially not a war that feels like it's tearing my heart in two. The Titans, people of my birth-planet, whom I once fought beside and who now consider me a traitor. The Nibirans, who gave us a home when no one else would, so eager to condemn the Titans, who deserve some form of justice. The Gaians, people I was raised and educated among—once so proud, now adrift with no planet and an identity that the Nibirans are already moving to chip away with reforms. I can't bring myself to hate any of them. I can only mourn them all.

Oshiro flips through a series of images for me to assess: exosuits patrolling the perimeter on Aluris; a spider tank at rest; ships traveling to and from the mothership in the sky above Nibiru. I explain what I know about the various weapons and technology, stressing how formidable the exosuits are. When I fought in the war on Titan, I saw exosuits take down dozens of the more poorly equipped Isolationists, and I can't imagine the Nibirans will fare any better.

A shot of a group of soldiers gathered on the ramp of a ship gives me pause.

"Zoom in on that," I say, and lean closer as Oshiro does. "Her." I stab a finger at the familiar face on the image. "That's Helena Ives. She was a general on Titan." I trace the finger along the length of an ugly scar across her throat. It's the sort of scar that only results from someone very nearly managing to kill you. "But she's not wearing the uniform of a general now. And the scar is new."

"Interesting," Oshiro says. "So, recent changes in leadership, likely infighting. Would it be possible for us to negotiate with her if Altair proves implacable? Split their ranks?"

"Doubtful. Her reputation was reckless, power-hungry. Altair is certainly the more reasonable of the two."

Oshiro flicks through more images. The sight of war machines and weaponry fills me with cold apprehension for how terrible a clash this could be for the low-tech Nibirans... but they are not the worst. The ones that feel like a knife in my lungs are the rare photographs of soldiers at rest. Teams gathered around meals, staring in wonder out at Nibiru's ocean, holding one another in gestures of casual Titan affection. They provide me with nothing of practical use I can give Oshiro—only a deep-seated pain. I'm about to ask the councillor to stop the flood of images when another one catches my attention and halts my breath for a moment.

"I know him," I say. "Daniil Naran." He stands with one hand clasping another soldier's arm, that familiar, easy smile on his face. "He was on the ship we encountered on the way here. He used to serve beneath me. He was only a private when Titan fell. Now…" My forehead creases as I scrutinize his uniform. "A colonel? That can't be right."

"Is climbing the ranks like that unusual?"

"It's more than unusual. It's unheard of. Especially because he…" I cut myself off. I know from personal conversations with Daniil that he was considered disgraceful because of his Paxian father and his attempt to avoid mandatory military service in the first place. There was also the matter of him asking me to smuggle him off Titan on my family's ship. That information could be ample ammunition if the Nibirans wanted to seed instability in the Titan ranks…and could also be enough to get Daniil killed if it came to light. The Titans are not forgiving of treason.

"Because he what?" Oshiro asks.

"He never struck me as the ambitious type," I say, after a beat. No matter the situation, I can't betray a former friend like that.

I can tell Oshiro knows I'm holding back, but they don't press for more. They shut down the hologram device and lean back in their chair.

"Thank you. This has all been immensely helpful." They fold their hands in their lap, fingers fidgeting in a way that betrays discomfort. "There is one more question the others wanted me to ask you."

"I didn't know they were alive," I say, honestly. "I swear it."

The councillor relaxes a fraction. "Do you know how it's possible they survived?"

"Altair did mention to me once that he was building a fleet. He misled me about how far along his plans were." I pause, wrestling with my guilt, and then say, "Daniil…when I spoke to him during our encounter, he mentioned surviving because he was in Fort Sketa, one of our—one of the Interplanetists' main military bases. Sketa was one of the last places hit, so they must have had time to evacuate before the bio-weapon reached them."

"So perhaps just one military base survived," Oshiro murmurs. "That could be why they're so diligently hiding their numbers from us. There could be many fewer than we initially thought. How many soldiers would have been in Sketa?"

"I don't know." I find myself relieved that I can say that honestly. This is becoming too much; the guilt is weighing on me despite my initial resolve. "I was never cleared for that type of information." Before Oshiro can press for more, I stand and bow deeply to the councillor. "That's all I have for you at the moment. If I think of anything else, I'll contact you immediately."

Oshiro stands as well, returning my respectful gesture with an acknowledging dip of their upper body. "I understand. Thank you again, Corvus." They straighten up. "There is also the matter of your family's safety. The Titans know as well as we do that you hold valuable information, and the general made it clear on the broadcast that he intends to target your family. We would be happy to offer you placement in a secure facility, like other persons of interest such as myself."

The councillor says it conversationally enough, but my mouth still goes dry. "Is this an offer, or a demand?"

"An offer," Oshiro says. They hesitate for a moment, and then add, "Though if you are inclined to reject it, I may suggest moving to a location other than Vil Hava before the council can decide otherwise. I will always fight for you and your family, but of course, I am only one voice."

Delicately phrased or not, the message is clear. "Understood," I say. "Thank you, Iri, for everything. Please stay safe."

"You as well, my friend."

Yet even as we clasp hands in farewell, I can't ignore the warning that was laced into Oshiro's earlier words. We already knew the council didn't trust us fully. If this turns to war, I'm not sure how long we can expect to keep our freedom.

CHAPTER TWENTY-FOUR

The Former Hero

Scorpia

The market should be bustling on a sunny day like this, full of colorful stalls and merchants hawking their wares, children playing in the streets, music and good food. But now, nearly all of the booths are shut down, rumpled in a way that speaks of a hasty evacuation. The streets are empty. There's still a crowd, but instead of being spread out and relaxed, everyone crams around the few remaining stalls, trying to elbow their way through to the front of the line.

I hang back, eyeing the scene with a sinking stomach. "Shit. This is worse than I thought."

"I can make a path," Drom offers, cracking her knuckles.

"No. It's fine. We can wait. Just…shit, you know?"

Drom nods, her expression uncharacteristically troubled.

Lyre hovers close behind us, clearly intimidated by the crowd. "Maybe I'll stay here. I sent you a list, Scorpia."

I open my comm and flick through, eyebrows rising as I see an extensive log of food items and amounts, along with estimated prices. "That's some list. This will take a chunk out of our account."

"It's only going to get worse as time goes on."

She's right, but I still hate the thought of all those credits draining away. I remember what it was like to be hungry and stranded in my childhood. We have a nice little nest egg now that the council's paid us for our mission, and I have some Sanita left to sell, but there's no telling when or if Eri and Halon will make another trip here with more. Even if we manage to stay out of the war, we'll be jobless, and hunted, and trapped here, with our credits and food draining steadily away. If it gets bad enough and we have to sell the ship...

No. I can't think about that right now. We'll figure something out; we always do. I push my thoughts aside, nod to Lyre, and step forward to join the mob waiting to buy food. Drom stands at my side, a comforting presence among the wild-eyed Nibirans and their panic.

We slowly shift toward the front as people trickle off. Many of them argue with the merchants over the prices, shouting and swearing and calling them vultures... but most end up walking away with their arms full of goods anyway. Some of the angriest walk away empty-handed, and I realize after one glimpse at their faces that it's desperation that drove them to argue. My family is lucky to be able to pay these prices; others have no choice but to walk away with nothing.

It's one of those who first gets a good look at my face—the rest are too focused on making their way to the front—and stops. I try to turn away, realizing my mistake, but it's too late.

"Is that the hero of Nibiru?"

"Nope," I say, quickly. "Not her. I get that all the time, though, it's—"

They're not buying it. People start to turn, and then to crowd around me as they see my face. Drom tries to push them back, but there's too many of them for her to handle. Faces surround me—angry faces, hopeful faces. Hands tug at my clothes and my arms as I stumble back and try to free myself.

"You saved our planet. Will you do it again? Are you fighting for us?"

"I need you to tell the council—"

"Any news of the front?"

I can't make sense of all the questions being flung at me. I keep backing away as fast as I can—not fast enough. Drom is lost in the crowd already.

One woman clings to my arm as I try to pull away. "I'll give you five hundred thousand credits to take my family off the planet. Take us anywhere. Put us under if you have to—"

"I'm sorry," I say, yanking free. "I can't. I'm trapped here, too."

"If the Gaians weren't here, none of this would have happened!" another man shouts, pushing past the others to glare at me. "Your family did this!"

My boot slips, and I barely keep my footing. I look back and realize I've backed all the way to the edge of the water. *Fuck.*

"One million credits—"

"Your fault—"

"Save us!"

"I'm sorry," I say, helplessly, as it all blends into a blur of voices, angry and beseeching and desperate. "I'm sorry. I can't help. I can't do anything. I'm not a hero, I'm just…"

"You can't even take care of yourself," Momma says in my memory, adding to the weight of all the disappointment crushing me beneath it.

I'm frozen in place. A woman grabs my arm and yanks me forward—I'm not even sure if she's asking for something or accusing me, but either way, it feels right now as though I'm going to be pulled into the middle of the mob and torn to pieces by a million grasping hands.

Then one face falls away, and another, and Lyre shoves her way through, pale-faced and waving a stun-stick, with Drom close behind. As soon as they force a path to me, I sprint for home with them on my heels, and hope they won't notice the tears in my eyes.

I have to pull it together quickly once I get home. It's our last night on Vil Hava, which means my last night with Shey for a little while, since she has matters to attend to here. Corvus still isn't home, so while Drom and Lyre head back for a hopefully less eventful visit to the market, I enlist Pol's help with making dinner for everyone with our perishable food. I'm a stars-damned awful cook, but luckily we have some premade stir fry sauce I can throw the last of our fresh fish into.

"How're you holding up, kiddo?" I ask, leaning against the counter and scrutinizing Pol. Looking at him makes me guiltily realize I've barely checked in with him since we left Gaia. He doesn't look as bad as he did then, but he doesn't look good. He seems to have lost some of the weight he gained back while he was recovering here, and his skin has a sallow look to it.

"I'm fine," he says, but his hands tremble a little as he chops up the last of the vegetables. When he catches me looking, he grits his teeth, finishes the job quickly and haphazardly, and dumps them into the sauce. "Really. I'm fine. Just a little tired."

I almost forgot that part of our eagerness to get off-planet was to help him. We had high hopes that a doctor on Deva could tell us more about his ailment. Now he's trapped here, just like all of us, and I suspect the trip to Gaia took more out of him than he's willing to admit. "I'm sorry about how all of this ended up," I say, reaching over to rub his back. "I'm going to get us out of here as soon as I can."

He jerks away from my touch. "This is my home-planet. I'm exactly where I should be."

He storms off. I sigh and turn back to the food. No matter how hard Corvus and I try, I'm not sure we can keep the twins from enlisting forever. But that's not gonna stop me from doing my damnedest to keep us all together.

Corvus joins us just as I'm finishing the meal; he looks exhausted, but I suppose we all are after today. Shey is close behind him, so I throw on a smile and do my best to infuse the mood with a little bit of cheer.

It doesn't do much. Corvus barely speaks, Drom and Pol snipe at each other, and Lyre keeps looking under the table at her comm after I insist she keeps the news off for the night. Izra silently inhales her food and leaves. The others retire early as well, and Shey and I head down to my room. She sits with her back against the headboard, and I stretch out with my head in her lap.

"I wish you were coming with us," I murmur, looking up at her. It's hard to imagine waking to an empty bed tomorrow morning now that she's become a steady presence in it. We spent so long dancing around one another that it still feels like she could disappear from my life again at any moment. But Shey's been busy helping out at the refugee camps and working on organizing a protest of the Gaian subjugation, and I'm doing my best not to be annoyed about it.

"I'll come visit when I can." She runs her fingers through my hair in a way that makes me never wanna get out of bed again. "Don't look at me like that. These people need me. You don't."

"You crazy?" I snatch one of her hands and hold her fingers tight in mine.

She laughs. "You know it's true," she says. "You're doing a great job. Never doubt it."

After so many years of everyone expecting the worst of me, the praise makes me feel oddly self-conscious. It makes me think of those people at the market, all those hopes I could never rise to meet. It was easier, in a way, when people expected nothing of me. I clear my throat. "Well, trying to impress you is an excellent motivator," I say, trying to brush it off. "So it's all thanks to you, really."

"Somehow I don't think that's true." She leans over me, her hair tickling my face. "Are you *blushing*?" she asks, clearly delighted.

"Aw, shut up." I grab the back of her neck and pull her closer, pressing my lips against hers. She's still smiling, so I sit up and press her back against the headboard, kissing her harder, my hands snaking up to pin her wrists on either side of her. After a few moments I sit back, scrutinizing her face, and grin. "Now who's blushing?"

She looks up at me, biting her lower lip, and says, "I'm really going to miss you."

My grin fades away, and I loosen my hold on her wrists, tugging her forward onto my lap instead. "It'll be all right. We always find our way back together, right?"

"Always," she agrees, and pulls my face closer to kiss me again.

CHAPTER TWENTY-FIVE

Tarnished Gold

Corvus

At night, I sleep fitfully on the couch, waking at every little noise and listening for the telltale creak of feet on the stairs. The night passes, and I almost think I was wrong to be suspicious—but close to six in the morning, I startle awake to see both twins standing at the top of the stairs. Each has a bag slung over one shoulder and a matching expression of guilt at being caught.

I make my way to the front door and plant myself in front of it, folding my arms over my chest. Of course the twins want to fight for their home-planet. Of course they'd try to sneak out to enlist, knowing the rest of us would disapprove. "Let's wake the others and talk about this," I say.

"We've done enough talking," Drom says. "It hasn't done shit."

"We're not going to spend the war hiding out like cowards," Pol spits at me.

Coward. The word digs itself beneath my skin like it always does. Am I a coward for not fighting? Should I be joining the twins rather than trying to stop them? We spent so long trying to prevent war. Now that it's here, can we really turn our backs on it? I think of all the Nibirans who welcomed us and sheltered us, going up against an enemy with experience and technology the likes of which they've never seen before... but then I think of the look on Daniil's face when he said, *You were supposed to come back for me!"*

"We'll figure out a way to do something. But it won't involve throwing the two of you to the meat grinder."

Drom sets her jaw and pushes her braid over one shoulder. "You can't stop us."

Thinking back to our brief scuffle on *Memoria*, I suspect that she's right. I'm not the man I used to be, and I won't be able to handle the two of them at once if they really want to go. But even if that's the case, I have to do everything I can to keep them here, even if it hurts all of us. I plant my feet and roll my shoulders back with a deep sense of weariness. "Try me."

The twins exchange a glance. Drom hesitates. But Pol lets his bag fall from his shoulder to the ground and steps forward.

"It doesn't have to be like this," I say. My heart is heavy as I think about our fight on Titan, still so fresh in my mind, and his vulnerable expression during our conversation on *Memoria*. "You don't have to keep trying to be this person."

"Getting real tired of you being so fucking condescending," he says, and punches me in the face.

I stumble back a step, my head jerking to one side, but then plant myself and hold my ground. Anger rises in my chest, but sputters out just as quickly. I can't do this. Not with him. Not again.

Drom hangs back, gripping her bag tightly. "Pol—" she says, but stops, and makes no move to intervene.

Pol hits me again—harder this time, right in the nose. My back hits the door. Again I push down anger and the familiar urge to violence. That isn't who I am anymore.

"Is this really what you want?" I ask. I wipe my nose, drop the hand, and hold both arms wide open. "You think it's going to make you feel any better? Fine. Go on, then."

"Fuck you," he says, his face livid. His voice shakes like it can barely contain the anger packed into it. "Hit me."

I shake my head. "I'm not going to fight you."

He launches another flurry of punches and curse words at me, but each one is weaker than the last. I do my best to fend him off, and he soon exhausts himself and pulls back, his breathing labored.

Before I can say anything more, footsteps approach on the stairs. Pol keeps his eyes on me, panting for air, but Drom turns to watch Izra step into the room.

Izra yawns, pushing pale hair out of her face. "What are you emotionally stunted assholes doing now? You..." She trails off as she takes in the situation, eyeing the twins and their bags, my bloodied face. Her expression shifts and hardens. "Ah. I see you two are stupider than I thought."

"Who the hell are you to tell us about it?" Drom asks, sneering. She held back while Pol came up against me, but she seems eager for a target for her frustration now, rounding on Izra without a moment's hesitation. "Deserter. You think we can't handle it because you couldn't?"

I tense, expecting Izra to immediately launch herself into violent retaliation. But instead, the small woman's expression goes very cold, and she squares herself in Drom's direction. "You think that because you understand battles, you understand war," she says. "You're wrong. It won't go the way you think. It will be uglier than you can imagine."

"So we'll learn," Drom says.

"Or you'll die."

"Either way," Drom says, "we'll make a difference."

Izra laughs scathingly. "You think one more body will make a difference?"

Drom's face flares red. "If everyone thought that way, no one would fight."

"Yes, they would. Because the Nibirans and Gaians have no choice. Don't dishonor them all by throwing yours away. If you're going to choose war, so be it, but know what you're choosing: to take orders from people who will see you as a number. To place your life in the hands of comrades who have never seen a fight before. To die among strangers for a victory you'll never see."

Drom raises her chin. "I'm not afraid to die."

"Then you're a fucking idiot." She spits at Drom's feet.

Drom's eyes narrow. I see what's going to happen a moment before it plays out; the only thing I can do is grab Pol to prevent him from throwing himself into the middle of it. He struggles in my grip, spitting curses.

Drom swings. Izra steps smoothly to the side, and then close again before Drom can recover from the clumsy punch. She hits her with three quick jabs: the stomach, the solar plexus, the throat. Then she swings behind her and delivers a swift kick to the back of her knee. Drom goes down heavily, with a choked sound of pain.

Izra presses the barrel of her gun arm to the back of my sister's head. "Dead," she proclaims, and then lowers it again. "You're a good fighter. The Titans will be better."

Drom pushes to her feet. Her face is splotchy with embarrassment.

"The Nibirans know little about war and less about the Titans," Izra says. "I know a great deal about both. If you really want to make a difference, stay and let me teach you." She shrugs. "Or go, and die a stupid death for a planet that won't remember you. Your choice."

Drom rubs her throat with one hand, swallowing hard. "You can teach me that?"

"Yes," Izra says. She turns to look at Pol, still restrained by my grip. "And I can teach you even more. You need to relearn everything. Figure out how to fight when you no longer have a strength advantage. I can give you that."

I let go of Pol, and he stumbles away from me, giving me one last, resentful look before he turns his attention to Izra. His face is eager, but he waits, glancing at Drom.

Drom lowers her hand to her side. "Fine. I'll stay as long as it seems useful."

"Then you both had better go get some rest before we start. I don't work with half-assed students."

The twins retreat down the stairs, murmuring quietly to one another. I move out of the doorway and sink onto the couch, wiping the blood from my lips with the back of one hand before I look at Izra. "Thank you."

Her eye stays on the stairs the twins disappeared down. "It's a temporary fix. It's your job to keep them here in the long run."

"How?" I don't hesitate to ask it; now isn't the time for pride.

"That I don't know." She turns to me. "But I do know that you can't expect them not to repeat your mistakes if you don't tell them what you experienced."

I know what she means—she wants me to tell them about the war. To expose the piece of myself I've been trying so hard to keep separate from my family. Even the thought of it makes me feel ill. I wouldn't know where to begin. "It's not that easy," I say, haltingly. "They've all always seen me as this...this..." I grimace, but force myself to spit out the phrase I hate to hear from them so much. "Golden boy. This perfect older brother. That's who they need me to be. If I told them the truth, it would ruin everything they know about me."

Izra turns to me, her face twisted in its usual harsh scowl. "Idiot," she spits at me. "If they saw you leave as a golden boy and come back seeming still golden, then of course they won't take your warnings seriously." She jabs me in the chest with a finger, hard enough to hurt. "They don't understand it because they don't understand you. And that is your fault, not theirs."

CHAPTER TWENTY-SIX

Fleeing the Future

Scorpia

A thump wakes me. I rub my eyes and yawn, and before I can wake fully enough to wonder what the ruckus is, another, louder thump shakes the ceiling above me. At least the slightly concerning wake-up call is enough to distract me from the empty bed beside me.

I drag myself up the stairs to find that our living room has been transformed into a sparring ring. Somebody has pushed all the furniture against the walls to open up the floor in the center, where Izra and Pol are currently tussling. I would be concerned, except that Pol looks absolutely delighted about this, and Corvus and Drom are watching with no apparent distress from the couch.

Honestly, I'm just relieved that dawn has broken and the twins are still here. The only confusing part of the situation is that Corvus has bruises blooming all along the side of his face. I frown, hugging the wall as I make my way over to him so I don't interrupt whatever the hell is happening right now. "Did you guys start a fight club while I was sleeping?"

"Izra offered to give the twins some combat training," Corvus says.

"And you?"

"I don't fight for fun."

"So, what, Izra punched you in the face when you said that?"

Drom looks away from the sparring match to side-eye him, but he only says, "If Izra and I fought, we would both walk away with more than a couple of bruises."

I resist the urge to roll my eyes. He's certainly in a sour mood today, but I guess I can't fault him after everything that's been happening lately. So I leave him and the members of our budding fight club to make some coffee. The lack of caffeine or breakfast being prepared is honestly an even more concerning sign about Corvus's well-being. Just like Shey's absence, it's a sign that things are different now. I knew the problems wouldn't stay outside our walls forever, but I didn't think things would change this fast, or that I would miss normality so much after all the times I longed for adventure.

Everyone gathers on the deck to watch Vil Hava fade into the distance. The sea is dotted with ships, the vast majority of them heading in to the central island rather than fleeing it like we are. Some of them must be refugees fleeing Aluris; others hoping to find safety closer to the seat of the council; others still, I imagine, are eager to join the fight.

Vil Hava has never been our favorite island to dock on for long, but this time it feels harder to pull away. We're escaping the clutches of the council I trust less by the day, and getting away from the Gaians and the giant target the Titans have painted on their backs. But we're also leaving behind people we care about. Oshiro. Shey.

I know this is the right move, but I can't deny that it feels like we're running from our problems. It also feels like we can't outrun them forever, especially with that damn Titan ship always staring down at us. If this is really going to turn into a war—and at this point, I doubt we can avoid it for long, no matter what hopes Corvus is harboring—we're not going to be able to hide from it forever.

But maybe we can get just a little while longer of peace. Some time to lick our wounds. For Corvus to accept the one-two punch of the Titans returning and becoming his enemies, and for me to continue grappling with the tantalizing pull to drink away the stress of being trapped here. For the twins to find a way to help their home-planet without throwing themselves onto the front lines, and Lyre to find something to keep her brain busy enough to stop catastrophizing, and Izra to adjust to life with my family.

Once Vil Hava fades into the distance, and the flow of passing ships slows and then stops, it's just us out in the middle of the endless Nibiran sea.

"Well, there goes our service," Lyre says, lowering her comm with a defeated sigh. "We really are going to be cut off out here. Anything could be happening and we wouldn't even know it." She stares out at the ocean, chewing her lower lip. "I wish there was some way I could help."

Secretly I do, too, but I don't want Lyre dwelling on that and getting lost in her own head. "It's not like knowing about it is going to let us do anything," I say. "We'll probably have a couple days before it comes back, so... how 'bout you put that big brain of yours to use looking over our finances for me?"

Lyre shoots me a glare. "You're just trying to keep me busy."

"You really going to turn down managing our bank account?"

"Of course not. I just want to make sure we're all aware that I see right through your excuses."

"Noted."

She heads inside soon afterward, and the rest follow one by one. Pol is the last one left. He stares down at the water with a distant expression. Now that I take a closer look at him, I notice the sheen of sweat on his forehead, and the way he shivers in the light wind.

"You all right, bud?" I ask. He doesn't answer, so I reach over to touch his arm. His skin is hot beneath my fingers, and he jumps and blinks at me like he's surprised to see me here.

"I'm fine," he snaps, flushing.

"Okay," I say. "Just remember to talk to Corvus if you need any—"

But he's storming inside, so I let the sentence trail into silence. It's just me and the ocean now.

And that stars-damned Titan ship, which I swear gets bigger and uglier every time I look. I wave my middle finger at it before climbing to my feet and heading inside after the others.

I was eager to get away from the news and the crowds at first, but now that we're out in the open sea, the days pass with agonizing slowness. With all of us shoved into close quarters and alienated from the rest of the world, it could almost be like life on the ship, except for the constant brain-itch that always comes with being planet-side. Steering the houseboat isn't nearly as fun as piloting a spaceship, and anyway, there's no point when I can see nothing but open ocean and the auto-driver will pick a better route than me 100 percent of the time.

The others are getting antsy, too. We have two full days of nothing before we reach Kitaya. The twins spend most of their time training with Izra. Pol is tired enough to go straight to bed afterward—he's still not looking great, though he insists he's fine—but Drom prowls around restlessly whenever she's free, picking stupid fights with everyone. Izra avoids the rest of us as much as possible. Lyre goes over our inventory and the financial information I sent her about a dozen times, presenting me with a revised list of recommendations and complaints every time. When she's not busy with that, I catch her pestering Corvus with questions about Titan strategy and technology, and I have to tell her off for it more than once. Even without her prying, Corvus is so deep in his own thoughts that I can barely get a word out of him. Sometimes I catch him staring up at the Titan mothership with a look on his face that breaks my heart, but I don't know how to help him.

Everything will be better when we reach Kitaya. It has to be. No matter how terrible shit gets, life goes on. And it's not like we're strangers to living in a hostile world. I'm sure we'll find a way to get back to normal soon enough. And we've still got a ship, as I keep reminding myself. We just need to make it through this long enough for us to have a chance to escape all of this mess. I'll get us out of here. Shey, too. I'm not leaving her behind this time.

It's the middle of the night when we approach Kitaya, but I find myself tossing and turning in bed, checking my comm, wondering when our signal will be back and what news will be waiting for us. Eventually I give up and head upstairs, tiptoeing around the creaky bottom step so I don't wake anyone else. The houseboat's navigation, linked to my comm, says that we should be able to see Kitaya any minute now, which means it's about time to figure out what the world has been up to over the last couple days as well.

As I step out onto the deck, my gaze is first caught by that Titan ship in the sky, just as imposing as ever. Then I drag it downward, and my jaw drops.

Kitaya is in flames.

CHAPTER TWENTY-SEVEN

Fire

Corvus

I wake to Scorpia shouting. I stumble out of bed, grab my knife and a gun, and race up the stairs. The others trickle after me, bleary-eyed and confused. Izra is already on her feet, one hand holding on to the couch she was sleeping on, her gun arm aimed at the doorway.

"Everyone stay inside," I say, heading for the door. "Let me see what's going on."

Not a single one of them listens. They're right on my heels as I head out onto the deck, and come to a stop beside me at the sight over the edge of the houseboat.

Kitaya is burning. The flames stretch to the very edge of the island, and dark, acrid smoke covers the sky above, so thick it nearly chokes out the sun's ever-present light. I stand on the edge of the deck and stare, barely able to comprehend what I'm seeing, and think about how far the destruction must reach.

We're too far away to hear the screams—but it's easy to imagine them as I stare at the wall of flames. Ships are breaking away from the edge of the island, a good half of them already ablaze as well. Whatever happened here, it happened recently. And as I watch a Titan warship lift off from the island, I know exactly who's responsible.

The realization is like a knife in my chest. Kitaya was an island of algae farms and fisherfolk. Civilians. There are no military bases here, no strategic footholds to seize. Why come here? *Why* burn it? I thought the Titans came here because they wanted a home, but this... this is just mindless destruction. This is everything the Nibirans were afraid would happen. And I was the one who told them the Titans weren't as terrible as they believed.

"I don't understand," Lyre says from beside me, her voice very small. "We talked it through. An attack on Kitaya doesn't make any sense. The Titans have nothing to gain by destroying it. So why? Why would they do this?"

I say nothing, because she's right. There's no strategy I can see in this, only cruelty. It doesn't make sense unless everything I thought I knew about the Titans was wrong. But perhaps it's time to face that possibility.

"Those boats are going down," Scorpia shouts, over at the ship's manual controls. "We have to help them. I'm taking us in as close as I can. Corvus, get your boat to ferry people in. Lyre, Drom, prepare to help them up. Pol, find our med supplies for Corvus."

At least one of us is keeping her head. I try to shake off the shock and move to do as she says. The Titans, what this means for me, what it means for Nibiru if this attack was enough to trigger the Planetary Defense System—we have to push that aside for now. We have to focus on what we can do to help.

Scorpia draws us near-dangerously close to one of the burning boats. As I get into my fishing vessel, Lyre is already tossing out the life preservers, and Drom jumps into the water without hesitation, swimming toward the nearest form in the water.

This close, the air is heavy with smoke and screams. Flames dance across the surface of the water as though they threaten us even here. But I shut off my fear and steer close to the nearest burning boat and the struggling figures in the sea. Several swim close and cling to the side as I approach, rocking the hoverboat. My stomach sinks as I realize how many of them there are, and how little room I have.

"Weakest swimmers first," I say, reaching over the side to help up a clearly struggling young girl with a soot-covered face. "I'll be back for the rest. Stay calm. I won't leave you."

I make trip after trip, saving as many people as I can find, delivering them into the waiting hands of my siblings on the deck. As the smoke thickens further, I rip off a sleeve, dip it in the water, and wrap it around my mouth and nose to help breathe. Every time I ignore my growing exhaustion and turn to head out for another trip. I draw closer and closer to Kitaya's burning shoreline and find fewer and fewer survivors each time. The water near the island is choked with bodies. There are a surprising amount of uniformed Titans among them. Grimly, I think that it's likely they were victims of their own fire, as I doubt the Nibirans had much of a defense for a surprise attack on a civilian location like this.

After a return trip where I bring back only one badly injured man, Scorpia grabs my arm.

"I think we've done everything we can," she says, gently. "We should go before the Titans find us."

"No. We can stay longer. There must be more survivors, more…" I turn, and stop as I catch sight of the sea around us. There is no longer any movement in the waves, no longer anyone crying for help from the burning boats. The only bodies left in the waves are facedown and motionless, and there's no sound left but the brittle crackling of the fire.

Inside, our houseboat is full of tears and the smell of smoke, harsh coughing through raw throats, people looking for their missing loved ones. I push away my exhaustion and move among them, checking on the worst-looking ones, doling out our small supply of burn cream and pain relievers to those who need them most. For the rest, we can only manage cool water and a place to rest.

By the time I've settled everyone, my leg hurts so badly I can barely make my way down the stairs, and my eyes and throat are gritty from the smoke. We'll never get the smell of burning out of the house.

Scorpia is still at the wheel, and our younger siblings are all crowded into her room to sleep. I'm about to join them when it occurs to me that one face has been missing from the night.

I find Izra crouched in the corner of my room, her back against the wall, her gun arm aimed at the door. Her expression is feral and hunted.

I hold out a hand and crouch down in front of her. "We're not in danger," I say, and am surprised by how scratchy and raw my voice sounds. "Lower the weapon before you hurt someone."

She stares at me, her eye wide and unblinking, but after a moment she does as I say. I study her for a moment, unsure if I should reach out to her, but the look on her face makes me certain she would only bite my hand off if I did.

"They're going to take me," she says in a low, shaky voice.

I'm not sure if she's speaking of the Titans or the Nibirans, but my answer is the same. "I won't let them." I reach out, very slowly, and touch the tips of my finger to her arm. "You're with us now. Nobody is going to take you."

She stares at me for a few moments longer, her breathing gradually slowing. Her fingers wrap around my outstretched arm and dig in like it's the only thing keeping her afloat. Our arms press together—my branded wrist against the black box on her pale skin. For the first time, I know mine is the real mark of shame. A mark of guilt. Of compliancy.

If I was willing to become a weapon in Altair's hands, what Titan wouldn't? What wouldn't they do to win a war? I feel sick now, thinking of how I defended them. I want to cut this mark off my body and shed all my memories with it.

Everyone told me the Titans were monsters. I should have listened to them.

Once she calms down, I convince Izra to take my bed, and sit on the edge of the mattress until her breathing slows. Then I slip outside, shut the door softly behind me, and dial Oshiro's private number on my comm.

"I'll do whatever you need me to do," I say, the moment I hear the councillor's soft breathing on the other end. "They'll pay for this."

By the time we reach Vil Hava, a few important matters have developed. The first is that Nibiru has officially declared war on the Titans in response to their hostile invasion and the burning of Kitaya. The second is that General Altair has finally agreed to meet in person, a meeting that Oshiro has asked me to attend as a cultural liaison. The third is that, though I feel like I've been holding my breath the entire way back, the Planetary Defense System has yet to trigger on Nibiru.

Maybe it's luck. Maybe fire is close enough to a natural disaster that it didn't activate the alien technology. Maybe there's a delay, and we're all doomed regardless. It's impossible to know, and thinking about it only brings me to the verge of panic. I can't afford that—especially not when I have to focus on the upcoming meeting with Altair.

A few days ago, I would have taken this as a sign that peace would still be possible. Now, the fact that he's asked to meet days after the tragedy of Kitaya makes me sick to my stomach—and makes me wonder what he's planning.

I give Councillors Oshiro and Govender a quick rundown on Titan manners as we head to the meetup place: a ship on the outskirts of the burned husk of Kitaya. The choice leaves a bad taste in the back of my mouth, but I don't dare ask if it was chosen as an insult by the Titans or a dark reminder by the Nibirans; either way, it doesn't bode well for negotiations. Still, both sides have agreed to meet. That has to mean something. And despite my growing anger toward the Titans, I have to keep hoping this won't escalate more than it already has. The planet depends on it.

Oshiro is visibly nervous by the time we arrive, sweat beading on their pale forehead and robed arms clasped across their midriff.

"Altair wouldn't waste his own or anyone else's time," I say. "He wouldn't have agreed to this if he wasn't open to the idea of negotiating."

"I might have believed you before Kitaya burned," Oshiro says, and turns away.

Guilt twists my stomach. Kitaya was Oshiro's home and responsibility, and I know the councillor must feel the weight of it. I can't help but feel responsible as well, after I spent so long insisting that peace with the Titans was possible.

Govender watches the other councillor go before giving me a small nod of acknowledgment. "We appreciate the counsel," she says. "We're glad to have you on our side, Corvus."

I'm surprised by her words. I've never interacted directly with Govender much, but she didn't seem overly friendly to my family during the last council meeting. "Of course." I hesitate, looking after Oshiro's retreating form. "I've given you everything I can think of. Should I wait outside? Altair won't be pleased to see me."

"No," Govender says. "We want you with us."

Though I wonder at her reasoning, she strides off and leaves no room to discuss further. I follow her inside with the small array of peacekeepers, and remain in the back of the room while the councillors take their seats at the half-circle table in the center room. A similar one waits, empty, on the other side, with only a single chair.

Time trickles by. The Nibirans murmur among themselves, while I wait silently in the back of the room, my eyes never leaving the door on the opposite side. The room gradually descends into silence, and then rekindled, more nervous murmuring breaks out as the councillors check the time on their comms and look at one another.

Finally, there's the sound of a hoverboat arriving outside. I straighten up, a motion that ripples through the peacekeepers. The councillors at the table go still. A few moments later, heavy footsteps approach from outside.

The first person to walk through the door is Daniil. I tense, forcing a wave of emotion down as our eyes meet. His widen, but I don't let myself react. I can't let his presence mean anything to me. He is my enemy now, too, and I can't let myself forget it.

He looks smaller and leaner without the shell of armor he wore during our fight on *Memoria*. The colonel uniform hangs loosely on him. I wonder if he inherited it from someone who died on Titan.

Altair walks through the door next, and strides directly to the chair in the center of the room, with Daniil shadowing him. He takes a seat, and Daniil stays at attention to his right, hands clasped behind his back, feet planted, and eyes roaming the room restlessly but never meeting mine again.

Altair seems as weary and furious as he did on the broadcast. He didn't look at me when he walked in, but he glances over once he's seated. I hold his gaze, hoping he can feel the full weight of my judgment. He is not the man I thought he was. Maybe everything I knew about him was a lie the whole time. It's possible he built that fleet with the sole intention of starting a war like this.

Ex-general Ives comes through the door next. Even after being stripped of her former position, she must still hold a place of regard if she's here. The scar on her throat looks even more severe in person, and her face is more gaunt than I recall it being, with a sickly pallor. I file the information away for later; perhaps she's still recovering from the injury. She takes a position behind Altair just like Daniil did, assuming the same stance. Her eyes stay fixed on the seated councillors, and burn with hatred.

I bend down to murmur to Oshiro, "Altair is the highest ranked in the room. Don't acknowledge the other two."

The scrape of Altair's chair seems to echo around the room as he shifts forward in it, resting his elbows on the table and waiting for someone else to speak.

"Thank you for agreeing to meet with us," Govender says. "It has been...difficult to communicate without meeting face-to-face. We hope this can be a chance for both of us to rectify past wrongs and move forward without further violence."

Altair nods curtly, and says nothing. The two councillors exchange a glance, and Oshiro pulls out the bottle of liquor they brought along, showing it to Altair.

"We would be pleased to observe the customs of your people," Oshiro says carefully, "if that is acceptable to you."

Again, Altair only nods, his lips pressing together more tightly. Behind his back, Daniil and Ives both shift, very slightly.

Oshiro clears their throat. "Very well." They pull out three glasses. After Altair designates one, Ives crosses to retrieve it for him. He lets it sit in front of him, fingers tapping idly against the glass, and so the Nibirans do the same.

"You've chosen an interesting time to make a peace offer." When Altair finally speaks, the room feels more still than before, as though everyone is holding their breaths waiting for him to finish.

"We have always been interested in peace, General," Govender says. One of Oshiro's hands clenches on the table, and then relaxes with obvious effort.

Altair tracks the movement with unabashed interest. "You. Oshiro, is it? You were the councillor of Kitaya, were you not?"

Oshiro meets his gaze. "I am, yes."

Altair glares with such open loathing that I barely recognize him for a moment. "What a shame. You should have taken better care of your home."

Oshiro's pale face splotches with anger. A peacekeeper to my side lets out a low sound of outrage. I barely suppress a hot wash of fury myself. What could Altair possibly mean to do, rubbing salt into the council's open wound? Why such a look of hatred on his face?

Perhaps he has no intentions to negotiate at all, and is only here to bait their anger. But what could he hope to gain from that?

Before the councillors can offer any response, Altair smiles grimly and raises his glass to them. After a moment's hesitation, they raise theirs as well, Oshiro's hand shaking. But Altair only touches his to his lips, waiting for the two councillors to drain their glasses before he drinks his own. I wince—another blatant insult, another dent in my hope this ends with a peaceful solution—but wipe the expression off my face as Daniil glances over at me.

Since Oshiro is clearly still wrestling with their emotions, Govender speaks. "The council has drawn up a peace deal we hope you will find agreeable," she says. She places a written version on the table in front of her. Daniil retrieves it and places it in front of

Altair, but he folds his hands again, focusing on Govender instead of the pages as she explains the details aloud. Along with their previous offer of food and supplies, the council is offering to allow the Titans to stay on Aluris for three months, the same deal they made with the Gaians when they fled their planet. Altair leans back in his seat as she goes on, folding his arms over his chest now, his expression darkening with displeasure he doesn't bother to hide.

"And Leonis?" Altair asks, cutting the councillor off.

Govender stops, then swallows. My throat tightens in anticipation of her response. I know as well as she does that the Nibirans will never give up Leonis, not when she holds the information about the Planetary Defense Systems. She's far too valuable, and far too dangerous.

"We cannot, in good conscience, relinquish the ex-president to you," Govender says. "Her actions impacted the entire system. Therefore she must be held accountable for her crimes in front of the Interplanetary Council—"

"Good conscience," Altair repeats with a sneer. "Is that what it is? Because it seems to me that you have no conscience at all." He grabs the written peace agreement, rips it in half, and drops the pieces to scatter across the floor. "This isn't a peace offering. This is an insult. You're offering us what we've already taken, asking us to share space with the same people who tried to wipe us out, and you won't even give us the woman responsible for the attack?"

"The Interplanetary Council—"

"The Interplanetary Council was going to let her get away with it," Altair snaps. "All of you did *nothing* after my planet fell. I have no faith in any of you, and it is clear you have no respect for me. Especially when you parade this traitor around like a trained dog." As he gestures to me, it takes all of my willpower not to

280

flinch away from his contempt. He pushes his chair out with a harsh scrape and stands. "We have nothing left to talk about."

He heads for the door, flanked by Daniil and Ives, leaving a stunned silence in his wake. The councillors remain frozen in their seats.

For a moment I'm frozen as well. It's over. I just watched our last chance at peace slip away. I'll never be able to convince the Nibirans that it's possible to try to make amends with the Titans again after the way Altair just behaved. But *why*? Why would he even agree to this meeting if he never meant to attempt a reasonable negotiation?

Before I can stop myself, my feet propel me forward, toward the backs of the retreating Titans. Someone lets out a soft gasp behind me; someone else curses. "General Altair," I say. "Wait. I—"

I'm only a few feet away when Daniil whirls on me. In one smooth motion, he steps forward and delivers a sharp kick to my scarred leg. It crumples beneath me, sending me to one knee with a bony thud against the tile. I suck in a sharp gasp of pain and surprise, and look up at Daniil, who stands above me. Behind me, I hear the sound of the Nibiran peacekeepers drawing their stunsticks, and hold out a hand to signal them back.

"General?" Daniil questions without looking away from me. After a moment's pause, Altair slowly turns, gestures for Daniil to remain where he is, and walks over to me. His expression is icy.

"General Altair," I say. "You told me once that you were tired of war. Now you have a chance to put a stop to it. Please, don't walk away from this."

There's no hatred in his eyes, no acknowledgment of recognizing me—there's simply nothing at all. As though he's looking down on a complete stranger instead of a man who served him faithfully for years.

"That was before," he says. "When I had my eyes on a hopeful future." He steps forward, a muscle in his jaw twitching. "You, Kaiser...you're one of the only people in the system who knew how close we were to being free. Decades trapped on that planet, and we were finally so damn *close* to being ready to go find our new world. If I had more time, I would have taken everyone. The veterans, the civilians, the *children...*" His voice cracks. He looks out at the Nibirans, as if just remembering that they're still here, and draws back a step, recomposes himself. "But we didn't have the time or space. So I was only able to bring the soldiers." A humorless smile flits across his face. "And we brought the other planets the Titan they have always feared." He gestures toward the Nibirans. "Because you always feared us, didn't you? That is why none of you tried to lend us aid and stop our war. You must have been glad it kept us preoccupied. I bet the system breathed a sigh of relief when they thought we had been destroyed.

"For years, we reached out to you for help. We called ourselves the Interplanetists, we welcomed your trade. And the very first time another leader reached out, seemed to treat us as an equal, look where that got us." He shakes his head. "Never again."

Silence sits heavily in the room once he finishes. None of the Nibirans move.

"Your people deserve better than endless war," I say, desperate. "You still have a chance to give them a better life."

"This war?" Altair smiles again, just as cold as before. "This war will not be endless. In fact, I expect it will not be very long at all." He gestures, and Daniil steps away from me. "I hope you survive until the end, Kaiser. I want the pleasure of watching you die with my own eyes. You, and all the rest of your siblings." His eyes bore into me now, that hatred that was missing before now flickering to life. "You will die slowly. Screaming. Just like your mother did."

CHAPTER TWENTY-EIGHT

Uselessness

Scorpia

At Shey's instruction, I tie back my hair, slip my hands into gloves, and pull a mask over the lower half of my face. It feels like I'm prepping to enter a surgery room, not a refugee camp. "Is all of this really necessary?"

"Yes, Scorpia. It's hygienic." Shey reaches up to adjust my mask, and I scrunch my nose at her. "Plus, it will hide our identities. I'm afraid neither one of us is very popular among the Gaians right now."

"So remind me why we're doing this again?"

"You're under no obligation to accompany me."

I sigh as she turns away from me to gather her things. While I do have some serious misgivings about spending my time helping out people who have a long history of hating outsiders like me, I'm eager for a distraction. There are still fire and floating bodies waiting every time I close my eyes, and Corvus is off at that peace talk with the Titans that's all but certain to be a disaster. I tried to convince him not to go, but he was set on it.

Normally, a situation like this would call for a drink, or several drinks, but I'm still trying my hand at this whole sobriety thing. So, I get the much less fun option of getting dragged along by Shey to dole out food to Gaian refugees. Not my preferred activity of choice on any day, but I've always found it hard to say no to a face as pretty as Shey's, and I am eager to spend time with her after a few days away.

"I'm coming, I'm coming," I grumble, and hurry to catch up with her before she heads out the door.

I guess I shouldn't be surprised to find a crowd of protestors gathered around the main entrance to the refugee camps, but I am. Many are sporting the same old "go home" signs I saw on display at the inauguration ceremony, but now there are some new and possibly even more despicable slogans suggesting the Gaians should fight their own war. Seeing Shey's dismay only fuels my anger toward them, and I can't resist the urge to throw up two middle fingers as we pass by.

"If you're so damn patriotic, go enlist yourselves!" I shout at one of them, and pull down my face mask to spit at his feet.

Shey grabs my hand and yanks me away before he has a chance to retaliate. "You're not helping, Scorpia," she scolds, but her eyes still crinkle at the corners as she looks up at me.

Any hint of mirth dies as she leads me farther into the camps. Other areas on the island are crowded, especially with the extra load of the survivors of Kitaya and the civilians who fled Aluris. But many of them have been accepted into the homes of other Nibirans with room for them, or went into housing facilities usually reserved for providing shelter for the homeless.

This is different. The Gaian housing is little more than boxes stacked together to fit as many people as possible into the space. There clearly still isn't enough room, because crammed into the streets and other spaces between are hastily constructed shanties and tents. Many people are huddled with no shelter at all, hunching their shoulders against today's light drizzle of rain. I can't imagine what they do when the storms hit. The entire place reeks of too many unwashed bodies shoved together, and many of them look hungry and ill and tired.

I had thought—maybe even feared—I might feel some kind of sick satisfaction at seeing such a proud and often cruel people brought low, but instead, it's just…very sad, all around. The mood here is even more bleak than on other areas of Nibiru. Despite how crowded it is, it's eerily quiet.

As Shey and I head into the meal center we're volunteering at, I note how many more Nibiran peacekeepers there are here, guarding the food, than anywhere else in the camps. We start doling out small portions of rice and algae, and people shuffle in to get their food, accept it with small gestures of gratitude, and shuffle out without a word. It's like they don't even have the energy to speak. Or bathe themselves, judging from the smell.

"This is grim," I murmur to Shey, as we head out the back to take a break between shifts.

"What did you think it would be like?" Shey asks. "This is what most people don't understand. Some of the Nibirans think the Gaians are here to freeload, that we're living in some kind of luxury on Nibiran credits, but the truth is that we're barely surviving even with their aid." She shakes her head. "I thought it would get better when we were granted permanent citizenship on this planet. But now, with all the displaced Nibirans flooding in as well, it's only getting worse."

For once, I find myself without anything to say. Instead I only pull her against me, press a kiss to her forehead, and hold her there. But even as she relaxes her head against my shoulder, both of us end up staring at the sky—and I suspect she, like myself, can't tear her eyes away from the looming threat of the Titan warship, looking all the more like a promise that things can always get worse.

As soon as I step into the houseboat, I know something's wrong. It's too quiet. Lyre is the only one in the living room, and she's scribbling in a notebook with a half-manic energy. The television in front of her is muted, but the newscaster has a dour expression.

"What's going on?" I ask. "Is everything okay?"

Lyre doesn't look up from her notebook. "No," she says. "The peace meeting was a disaster. Now the Titans know that we're all here, and Corvus still isn't home, and they're probably coming for Vil Hava next, and..." Her voice trembles, and she impatiently wipes tears from her eyes.

"Okay, okay. Calm down." It concerns me to hear the news about the peace talk, but it's not like I wasn't bracing myself for it. Comforting Lyre is more important at the moment. She doesn't even look up as I approach the couch; she's busy working on a diagram of some kind. When I place a hand on her shoulder, she finally goes still. "Hey. Take a sec and breathe." Right now, I'm glad Corvus convinced me not to tell our younger siblings about the Planetary Defense Systems, because I can only imagine how freaked out she would be with that on her mind.

"I need to do something," she says, tears flowing freely down her face now. "The Nibirans have no chance in an all-out war, Scorpia. You know they don't. And we're trapped here."

I don't know how to argue with that. "Well, when Corvus gets home, we'll all sit down and talk about what to do next. But it's not like this is a problem you can fix. Don't drive yourself crazy thinking about all this."

"There has to be something I can do," she says. "I can't just sit around while people are dying out there. And I can't make sense of any of this. I don't understand how I was so wrong about Kitaya. I don't understand..."

"Lyre." I gently pry the notebook from her hands and set it aside. "I'm feeling it too. The helplessness. I know it sucks. But this is out of our hands for now."

She gulps back a sob, her eyes on the floor. "There's... there's something else."

"What?" I ask, but she only points at the kitchen before burying her face in her hands. I head in to find Izra sitting at the table, with a half-empty bottle of whiskey and a split lip.

"Told him it couldn't be me," she says, her words slurring together.

"What are you talking about?"

"Taught those assholes too well." She waves the bottle in my direction. "Whatever. Not my problem anymore. And I fucking told him, you know... I told him." She hiccups and rests her forehead on the table, still clutching the bottle.

She's so drunk I can barely understand what she's saying, but I have a sinking feeling I know what she means. I rush down the stairs. The twins' rooms, as I thought, are empty. My heart sinks—and then I turn and realize my own door is open.

"Drom? Pol?" I ask, heading inside. My closet door is half-way broken off its hinges, and my clothes are scattered across the room—along with some empty bottles and snacks I had hidden in here, Shey's books, and all of my other belongings.

Pol lies on my bed at the very center of the mess, staring at the ceiling. As I stop in the doorway, he props himself up on his elbows. "Please don't be mad."

Even if I wanted to, I don't think I could conjure up any anger. I simply don't have the energy left. I slump back against the door-way, sucking in a shuddery breath. "Oh, thank the stars, you're still here."

Drom isn't, and I know what it means. But at least Pol is still with us. I stay where I am for a few seconds. Then I let out a long sigh, pull a packet of Sanita out of my sleeve, and toss it onto the bed beside him. "That what you're looking for? I'm nearly out, so you better wean yourself off of this shit."

He looks down at it, and then back up at me, and his mouth pinches together in that way it always does when he's trying not to cry. "I'm sorry," he says, practically choking on the words as he forces them out. "We went to enlist. They said no to me. But she..."

I make my way over to the bed and sit on the edge of the mattress. Pol stares at me, his face still frozen in that verge-of-tears expression, until I beckon him. He immediately sits up and engulfs me in a hug, pressing his face into my shoulder. "Please don't be mad," he says again, and I rub his back with one hand.

"I'm not," I say. "It's okay. We all fuck up sometimes." I lean my head against his. If anything, I'm annoyed at myself. I should've seen this coming. But part of me knows that even if I had been here, it wouldn't have helped. If Drom set her mind to enlisting, she would've done it eventually. Right now, I need to do what I can: Help Pol deal with this. "But you need to take it easy. You're in no state to be fighting in a war."

"I'm in no state to do anything," he says, sniffling and turning away.

"C'mon. Even aside from all the shit you've been through, you're nineteen years old, you don't need to have it all figured out now. You know what I was like at nineteen?"

Pol wipes his nose and thinks. "Really drunk."

"Yeah. You remember." I laugh. "You would bring me breakfast when I was too hungover to get out of bed."

"And we would watch cartoons together."

"Right! I loved that stupid one with the fish." The memory makes me thoughtful. "You were a really sweet kid. Sensitive little thing. You know, I remember you hated fighting at first. I thought you were gonna be like me, not able to stomach shooting anyone."

Pol makes a face. "That was a long time ago."

He's deflecting, like he always does, but I circle around the issue rather than getting right at it and pushing him away. "I think the only reason you stuck with it was because Drom was a natural, and you wanted to be with her."

"I got good at it, too," he says, defensively.

"You sure did. Really good." I look over at him. "But did you like doing that? Did it make you happy?"

"Yeah," he says, immediately, and then again, "Yeah. I like protecting you all."

"But that wasn't all Momma made you do."

He pulls away from me, face screwing up like he's tasted something sour. "Don't make this about Momma."

Maybe I've pushed too hard—but I need to try to get through to him. "I remember the first time she asked you to shoot someone," I say, quietly. "I remember how much you cried afterward—"

"Look, I'm not stupid, okay? I know she was mean sometimes. Especially to you. But she could be nice, too." His voice wobbles. "She could be really nice to me. She would take care of me after fights."

As much as I want to snap at him, I repress the urge as I think back to what he's talking about. I do remember Momma treating his wounds after a fight, holding him like the kid he was. I don't know how it took me so long to realize what this is really about. As gently as I can, I say, "The only time I remember her saying anything nice to you was after you killed someone for her."

Pol's face reddens, mouth gaping for a moment before he says, "That's not true."

"Is that why you feel like it's so important to do that again? She made you feel like it was the only thing you were good for?"

"Stop."

"Because it's not. The rest of us can all see that. But Momma, she had this way of putting it into our heads that we were only good for one thing, whatever made us the most useful to her—"

"Shut up," Pol shouts, his eyes spilling over with tears. He wipes at them in frustration, choking back a sob. "You know what? Fine. Maybe you're right. Maybe that *is* all she ever praised me for, because it's the only thing I've ever been fucking good at. I don't have anything else. I'm not like you and Corvus."

I lean forward and wrap my arms around him. He tries to shove me off, but I cling tighter. After a few moments he gives in, pressing his face into my shoulder and heaving a sob. "We don't want you to be like us," I say. "Or like the person you used to be. We just want you to be okay. But even if you're not, we're gonna love you anyway."

Drom gets home shortly before Corvus, and we all gather around the kitchen table without a word. Shey is gone tonight, busy meeting with her Gaian sovereignty activist group, but everyone else is here. Izra kicks back in her chair with her boots up on the table. She's the only one who even pretends to be relaxed. The twins sit with their bodies angled away from each other, Pol slumped and red-eyed after our conversation, Drom's shoulders squared like she's ready for a fight, but no one's eager to pick one tonight. Lyre has her knees hugged against her chest and her eyes on Corvus. As badly as I want to break the silence, I instead chew my nails and wait for him to say something.

It takes him a long while, but nobody rushes him.

"This isn't going to end with peace," he says, finally. He looks directly at me, an apology on his face. "I have to fight."

I knew it was coming, but my heart still sinks. My mouth stays shut. I'm not going to support him in this—I can't, I just can't—but I know there's no point in fighting about it, either. All I can do is let him do what he feels he has to do, and be ready to pick up the pieces afterward. Stars know he's done it for me enough times in the past.

"Me too," Drom says. "I enlisted today." She sets her jaw in a stubborn expression I've seen far more often on her twin's face—that look that means there's a fifty-fifty chance of either tears or a punch being thrown if anyone pushes too hard. "It's my home-planet."

Corvus seems like he wants to argue—but I can see the moment his expression turns, with the stricken realization he can't tell her not to do it without making an enormous hypocrite of himself. He shuts his eyes, takes a deep breath, and opens them again. He doesn't say a word. Nobody does, though Pol bites his lip in an obvious effort to hold back fresh tears.

And beyond my worries for my siblings going to war—my pain for Corvus having to face this terrible thing again, my fear for Drom, who doesn't know what she's going into—my own selfish concerns bubble up and balloon into a deep sense of helplessness. I'm not made for war. I've got nothing to contribute to my family or the planet as long as I'm trapped here on the surface. So what the hell am I going to do?

CHAPTER TWENTY-NINE

Lockdown

Corvus

Afull squad of peacekeepers shows up at our door the day after the failed peace talks. They bring a signed order from the council to "accompany" us to a more secure location.

I tell my siblings it's for our own safety, since the Titans are now aware of our presence on this planet. Scorpia says it's more likely that the council is just trying to control us, make sure we're not going to flee off-planet at the first opportunity. I'm not sure which I believe.

Scorpia and the twins cause enough of a commotion to allow Izra to sneak away before the peacekeepers can find her, armed with the last of Scorpia's Sanita and as many credits as we could spare to help her. She disappears without so much as a goodbye. Scorpia sends a message to Shey letting her know we're moving, and then all that's left is to gather our sparse belongings.

The peacekeepers offer to help, but in the end, none of us has more to bring than we can carry ourselves. They shuffle us to an underground facility on Vil Hava, near the building where the Gaian presidential inauguration was held. As we travel down, crammed together in an elevator, the metal walls and fluorescent lights remind me of being on a ship...but once we emerge into the facility, the soldiers we pass in the halls make it impossible not to think of my days on Titan. These blue-and-gold uniforms, however, look nothing like the utilitarian garb of Titan soldiers. The blasters at their hips seem like toys compared to standard-issue Titan pulse rifles.

Poor bastards, I think as we pass by a fresh-faced cluster of Nibiran and Gaian troops. They're not real soldiers. Most of them are just fisherfolk and farmers and merchants shoved into uniforms. Even the ranking officers have never seen a day of real combat in their lives until this war, and probably never thought they would. They have no idea what they're up against.

The bunker is crowded, full of hallways lined with doors, and rooms crammed with beds. Since I don't have an official military title—the Nibirans seem to still be figuring out how to work around my status as a noncitizen—I'm allowed to stay in the same one as the rest of my family. Drom, however, is shuffled off to bunk with fellow recruits. She grumbles and shrugs off everyone's attempts at goodbyes, insisting there's no need when she'll be just on the other side of the same facility. But when she walks away, it feels somehow final.

Our room is small and bare, little other than four concrete walls and some bunk beds. The lack of a scuffle over bed choices is the first reminder that Drom's no longer with us, and nobody complains when Pol grabs the pillow from the extra bed and curls up with it. Everyone quietly retreats to their own bunks. Scorpia's half-hearted attempts at starting up a game of dice fall flat, and soon even she goes quiet. Pol sulks, cocooned in blankets and pillows, and Lyre is busy working on whatever project she's been consumed by ever since Kitaya. I'm glad she has something to keep her mind busy. But after a few hours of her silently working while I lay in bed and stare at the ceiling, she comes to sit beside me.

"Corvus," she asks, hesitant for some reason, "could you pass a message to Councillor Oshiro for me?" She pushes a folded piece of paper from her notebook into my hands. I automatically move to open it, but she grabs my hands and stops me. "It's private."

I frown at her, unsure what to make of that, and Scorpia swings her head over the side of the bed to look down at us. "You got a crush, Lyre? Making Corvus deliver a love note for you?"

"*No.*" Lyre glares at her. "Stop eavesdropping." She waits for Scorpia to flop back on her bunk, takes a deep breath, and looks at me again. "It's just that I . . . after Kitaya . . ."

Kitaya. Smoke thickening the air. Bodies floating around my boat.

I blink the flash of memory away, and before Lyre can continue, say, "I understand. Kitaya was important to you, too." It was painful enough for me, but I can only imagine what it was like for Lyre, who attended the university there. She likely has friends and teachers who are dead or still missing.

For a moment, Lyre looks like she wants to say more. But then she drops her eyes and softly says, "Thank you."

I toss and turn all night, feeling adrift in a building full of people who may die tomorrow, or else kill soldiers I once fought alongside. My heart aches for the Nibirans and Gaians who have never known war, and the Titans who have never known anything else. I still cannot bring myself to hate any of them. Guilt bites at my heart, fed by a sense of duty that compels me to do *something*. But I feel as though no matter what choice I make, I will regret it when all of this is over.

I push my reservations aside and arrange a meeting with Oshiro as soon as I can. The best thing I can do right now is find a way to make myself useful before I can second-guess my decision. And the Nibirans need me. I've seen the newsfeeds. The Titans didn't stop with Kitaya, and the Nibirans have no chance against them if the situation continues as it is. The Nibiran military is a mess, with little discipline and less experience. They need someone like me.

I expect Oshiro to lead me directly to a military base, give me a weapon and a uniform and a mission, but instead they take me to a nondescript building on the edge of Vil Hava. Oshiro is quiet on the way there; there's a haunted look on their face, shadows beneath their eyes, little hint of the energy and idealism that once made them such a popular political figure. The tragedy of Kitaya has changed them. It's also ruined anything we had resembling friendship, judging from the way they can't seem to meet my eyes. When I hand over Lyre's note, they pocket it without a word.

The building the councillor takes me to is small and unremarkable but for the heavy security around the single entrance. Inside, there are no soldiers or generals, but desks and screens and comms. Numbers and projections and coordinates. These are war-makers of a different type, and I have to bite back my discomfort. This is not what I wanted, but it's not my place to question the council, especially not now.

Oshiro takes me to a room in the back of the building, where a semi-familiar face waits.

"Corvus, you remember Councillor Govender?" they ask, their tone stiff.

"Of course." I scrutinize the woman who stands to meet me, remembering her logical but severe words on the Titans. Remembering, too, that she and Oshiro disagreed on some key points, which explains why Oshiro has suddenly become so tense and formal.

"I'm pleased to have an opportunity to become better

acquainted," Govender says. "Oshiro has done a wonderful job as a liaison thus far, but as the member of the council who generally oversees our military intelligence division, I wanted a chance to speak with you directly."

"So you're the one who can get me in the field," I say.

"I'm glad that you're eager, and we certainly have use for a man of your skills. All in due time."

"I wasn't under the impression we had much time to spare. If you're not putting me in the field, what am I here for?" I look at Oshiro, trying to understand, but again they remain silent while Govender speaks. It seems I'm being officially handed off. I can't deny that it stings, but I can't blame Oshiro for wanting to distance themself after Kitaya. I self-consciously touch the warbrand on my wrist and notice Govender's sharp eyes follow the motion, though her expression doesn't change.

"You're correct," she says. "We do not have time. But I'm afraid that there are some on the council who have reservations about placing their trust in you."

Her face reveals nothing about her personal feelings on the subject. She did mention military intelligence; I have the feeling she is used to keeping secrets. People who keep so much of themselves hidden often assume others do the same. I wouldn't be surprised if she didn't trust me. But I need her to, even though my first impression is that I should be careful of this woman.

"I'm not sure what else I can do to prove that I'm dedicated to Nibiru," I say. "So tell me what you want from me."

She smiles for the first time at that and pulls out a comm as if she's been waiting for those very words to come out of my mouth. She sits at the room's sole table, and gestures for me to take the chair opposite her. Oshiro remains standing behind me. "I've been over the notes about the Titans you gave to Oshiro. Helpful, but I find it difficult to believe that's all you can tell us."

Shame and guilt wash over me as I remember that meeting with Oshiro. I was conflicted then, holding back, and Govender knows it. She's right. I can't expect the council to trust me unless I'm willing to tell them everything I can. I need to give up my belief in the man I thought Altair was. Sever my ties with Daniil. Tell this woman everything I can about the Titans.

They will hate me for it. Many will die. The same people I fought alongside less than a year ago; the people I loved; the people I mourned.

But this is the choice I have to make. Altair claimed he was tired of war and painted a vision of a peaceful future on a new home. But now, he came here to kill the people who have welcomed us. He burned the island we had come to call home.

"I'll give you everything I know," I say.

Despite my resolve, as soon as I begin, I feel like I'm watching this scene unfold through another's eyes, watching the secrets spill from my own mouth. I listen to myself lay out the Titan rankings and army structures. The divisions of teams, the ways to tell who the leader of any given group is. I run through the weaponry, signs that a pulse rifle is starting to overheat, how a soldier's team will automatically pull together to shield off someone weaponless until they're ready to rejoin the fray. I tell her that lower-ranking soldiers will sacrifice themselves for their superiors without hesitation, and don't allow myself to think of the ones who died for me while I was on Titan. I explain how teams are close-knit enough to think of one another as family, and remember Daniil calling me a traitor.

When Govender pulls up a hologram of an exosuit, my mouth goes dry, and my words fail me again for a moment. It feels like forever since I've laid eyes on one of these, and like no time at all since I was in one myself, a paradoxical rush of feelings that steals my words for a moment or two.

Perhaps Govender mistakes my silence for hesitance, or perhaps it's only that the mask over her emotions has begun to slip, but her eyes feel accusatory now. "These suits have been slaughtering our people," she says. "We need a way to stop them. If we can't fight back, there will be another Kitaya."

I swallow hard, wishing I had better news to give her. "There's no easy solution. The exosuits are notoriously difficult to take down. But antiaircraft artillery can be effective, and they have a weak point here." I gesture to the back of the suit's neck, the small, vulnerable point where the helmet meets the rest of the suit, where a well-placed shot or carefully angled knife can puncture through metal to the vulnerable flesh beneath.

Before I can open my mouth again, a memory surges up of one of my own team members on the ground, held down by enemies, the sharp jab of a Primus knife taking her life. The spill of blonde hair, matted with frozen blood, when I pulled the helmet off. A shiver courses down my spine. I feel the chill, see her lifeless eyes staring up at me. What was her name? That soldier I lost? I grasp again and again at the dark spaces of my memory, and come up empty. The realization that I've forgotten it makes bile rise up in the back of my throat, and all of a sudden my stomach is threatening revolt.

But it's not the lost ones I should be worried about. Altair still lives. So does Daniil. What will happen if I come face-to-face with one of them in a fight? If I hesitate like I did against Daniil the first time, and one of my allies loses their life for it? Or if I stumble upon one of their bodies in the aftermath of a fight, knowing that I may have given the Nibirans and Gaians the information that killed them? I imagine Daniil in the exosuit with a knife plunging through his neck; Daniil's body sprawled out in the flowers of Vil Hava, eyes open and unseeing; Daniil standing silhouetted against the flames that consumed Kitaya, watching his soldiers slaughter Nibiran civilians.

I clear my throat, try to speak. Fail, and try again.

"Excuse me," I say, finally. "I need a minute."

I stand, nearly toppling my chair in my haste, and rush out of the room. Mind still reeling, I let my feet carry me through the hallway and out into fresh air. My lungs pull in gasps of oxygen like I've been starved for it as I channel all of my willpower into getting ahold of myself. I've almost managed to do so when another set of footsteps follows me out of the building and stops beside me.

"Corvus, I'm sorry," Councillor Oshiro says. Their voice is full of what sounds like genuine sympathy, but it only makes me feel worse. "This was a mistake. I can't imagine how difficult this must be for you."

"It shouldn't be difficult," I say through gritted teeth, blinking up at the sky once more before lowering my eyes to the councillor's face, letting them see the shame written all over my own expression. "They're the enemy now. They're the ones who..." I glance around, then lower my voice even though we seem to be alone here. "Have the power to wipe out this entire planet without even meaning to." I force more air into my tight chest. "They burned Kitaya. They rejected peace. There is no choice but to fight them."

Oshiro is quiet for a moment before saying, "I wish there was another way, as well."

"Do you?" I ask, my brow furrowing. "After Kitaya?"

Oshiro's face colors, and they drop their gaze and say nothing.

"I wouldn't blame you," I say quietly. "I don't understand why they would do such a thing, either. It's hard for even me to have much sympathy now, though I know that we're—" I pause and swallow. "That they're not the mindless killing machines everyone thinks they are."

Oshiro is silent for a long few moments before saying, "Regardless of what they've done, I don't believe anyone is as evil as their enemies make them out to be. Nor as good as they would like to believe they are." They shake their head. "But it does not matter at this point. As you've said—we know what's at stake. We have to do whatever it takes to end this, and save as many lives as we can."

I wish that made me feel better, but instead it only seems to worsen the sick feeling in my gut. Maybe I was hoping someone would be able to convince me that I was the wrong one here, help me start to think that what I'm doing is right. All I've ever wanted was to do something right for once, but that's never as easy as it seems. I let out a gusty breath, eyes fluttering shut. "You're right," I say. "They're not the evil, brainwashed soldiers everyone thinks. They're not the righteous warriors they believe they are, either. They're just...just people." Words tumble out—the words I wish I could've said in that room, instead of telling Govender all the best ways to kill the people I still love. "They believe in honor, and duty, and sacrificing themselves for the greater good. They believe love should never have rules and restrictions, but always be freely given, something to be shared rather than coveted. They believe in stretching the concept of family to include anyone who needs somewhere to belong."

Once I stop, a rush of embarrassment hits me, along with a burning sensation behind my eyes. I blink it away and look at Oshiro, feeling raw and vulnerable and afraid that nothing they could possibly say to me will feel right. There's a reason I haven't said this to anybody, not even my siblings. Right now, it feels like either too-sweet sympathy or the sting of dismissal will bring me crumbling down. And how could Oshiro understand, after what the Titans did to their home? How could anyone possibly understand the way I feel right now?

Oshiro quietly reaches out and takes my wrist, and I resist the urge to pull back. They press two long fingers to the war-brand on my skin. There's a strange expression on their face—something close to the agony I feel myself. I wonder if they're thinking of Kitaya.

"I wish I could have known them the way you do," Oshiro says.

A moment passes. Another. As I feared, there's a sensation of crumbling somewhere deep inside me, a sense of loss; and yet, as it passes, I feel stronger rather than weaker.

"I wish so, too," I say, my voice quiet. I let my hand remain under the councillor's fingers for a few moments before I pull back and nod, trying to channel as much gratitude as I can into my expression. "Let's resume the meeting."

CHAPTER THIRTY

The Deal

Scorpia

S trictly speaking, I'm not allowed out of the bunker without an escort. Practically speaking, bribes work as well here as anywhere else on Nibiru, and soon I'm standing in the streets of Vil Hava with sunlight on my face and fresh air in my lungs for the first time in days. I smile, turning my face to the sky, but it disappears as soon as I catch a glimpse of that damn Titan ship.

"Ugly bastard," I mutter, and set off down the street.

Over the last few days, it's become clear that everyone but me has something to contribute to the war effort. Corvus is off helping with military strategy, Drom is training with the other new recruits, Lyre is always sitting on her bed doing…I don't even know what the hell she's doing, scribbling away in that notebook of hers and tossing endless crumpled pages in the trash, but I'm sure it's important, because otherwise she wouldn't waste her time with it. She seems unhealthily obsessed, though, so I tried asking her to come out with me, but she only snapped that she was busy.

After a few days of moping in his bed, even Pol managed to harass the Nibirans into giving him a job hauling supplies around the facility on the days he's feeling well enough. I don't have the heart to tell him to stop, even though it usually exhausts him so much that he sleeps twelve hours afterward.

It's harder to think about the ones I care about who aren't here. Shey, who is always busy helping the Gaians, and refuses to come stay in the bunker with me, where it's safe, no matter how many times I ask. Izra, who's off doing stars-know-what, a wanted criminal lost in a world at war. Orion...it still hurts every time he crosses my mind. I asked Corvus if he had asked the Titans about him at the peace meeting, and his guilty silence was answer enough.

And me? I still don't know where I stand in this whole thing. What good is a grounded pilot? A captain with a scattered crew? I'm not sure, but I'm going to lose my mind if I keep sitting in the underground cage of the bunker doing nothing, so it's time to find out. I march right over to the Council Hall. The clerk is clearly startled to see me, and spends several minutes speaking in hushed whispers into his comm. Soon after, Councillor Heikki walks out, looking vastly displeased to see me.

"You do realize it is illegal for you to be wandering around Vil Hava alone," she says.

"Well, I needed to get your attention somehow." I lean against the front desk. "I'm here to offer my services as a pilot. There's gotta be something useful I can do. Give me a job."

She sighs. "Please keep this to yourself," she tells the clerk, before turning back to me. "Let's walk."

She heads out the door without waiting to see if I'll follow, but I grin as I go after her. "So you *do* have a job," I say.

Heikki walks slowly, hands clasped behind her back, and doesn't say a word for several minutes. I'm not about to complain, since this island is like heaven to my entertainment-deprived mind, even though the streets are nearly empty and the shops are mostly closed. I desperately want to try to find a pastry after days of military-issue slop, but Heikki leads me past it all, a small gaggle of bodyguards following several paces behind us.

She leads me to the edge of the island, toward the Gaian housing where I volunteered with Shey. Even more shabby tents and makeshift shelters have cropped up around it as new Nibiran refugees flee the spreading war.

"I do have something to ask of you," Heikki says. "The council hasn't approved it yet, but they will, and soon. We have no other choice."

Judging from the way she says it, she's not exactly pleased about that. I keep my mouth shut and wait for her to continue.

"This war is taking a toll," she continues. "And it is only going to get worse as time goes on. We have to consider not only the worst-case scenario, but what the future will look like if we win. We've asked the other planets for aid. Deva offered us a deal."

"Okay," I say. "An alliance with Deva makes sense to me. They've got money, they've got food. They're in the same boat as you as far as the whole..." I glance around and lower my voice. "Alien bullshit. So what are you giving them?"

"Talulah Leonis."

I blink, processing that. My mind jumps first to Shey. I know she hates what her mother did, but I doubt that means she'd approve of Nibiru using her as a bargaining chip. Especially to Deva, where criminals like her usually either disappear quietly, never to be heard of again, or are given a very public and sometimes very painful execution.

And as important as Shey is to me, this move will affect a lot more people than just her. I have to think bigger. Giving Leonis to the Devans will not only piss off the Titans even more, but probably the Paxians as well, since they've been at odds with the Devans. That's not even to mention the Gaians, who will be outraged. She's also more valuable than any of them know, with the information she holds about the Planetary Defense Systems. The Nibirans must really be getting desperate, if they're willing to go through with this.

Though I guess Leonis is subject to the will of the Interplanetary Council no matter who's holding her. She'll still be tried and judged by all of the planets. Even Titan gets a say in it, technically, even if they are at war with two of the others on the council.

"You'll risk the Devans finding out what she knows?" I ask.

"Better than the information going to the Titans," she says.

I mull that over. Part of me still wonders if all of this could have been avoided if the Nibirans had surrendered Leonis when Altair first asked. But I guess there's no point in thinking about that; it's far too late now. "So what does this have to do with me?"

"The Devans can't send ships to retrieve Leonis themselves without engaging the Titans, and they aren't willing to commit themselves to the war in any way before they have her safely on their planet. So we need to transport her there ourselves."

"Ah." I guess I should've expected this. Nibiru isn't exactly chock-full of skilled spaceship pilots, and this sort of mission will be far from easy with the Titan fleet surrounding the planet. At least some of the Titan ships have weapons systems; the news is always swirling with new theories about why they haven't fired on Nibiru yet. I'm not sure how I feel about the idea of transporting Leonis to safety while innocent people are left here to die...but if this helps end the war and gets my family to safety, I'm not going to be the one to raise moral issues with the council. In fact, I can already feel the hope building inside of me.

But I can't jump into this. I need more information if I'm going to risk my ship and my family for the council again. "And—even with me being a damn good pilot—how exactly do you expect me to get past an entire fleet?"

"You won't be alone. Nibiru does have some ships."

"Shitty ones."

"They are certainly outdated compared to your ship and those of the Titans, yes," she says, only a faint strain in her voice showing that my comment got to her. "And because we forbade any ships with weaponry or Primus technology from Gaia, the vessels the Gaians brought for their migration are not much better. None are as formidable as the one we gave to your family." I bite my tongue and choose to ignore the pointed reminder. "Even if they were able to make it past the fleet, the Titan ships would catch them long before they could reach Deva. And, admittedly, we do not have pilots with your level of expertise, after so many years of being largely cut off from the rest of the system." She pauses, her expression growing weary. "But they will be able to take some of the heat off of your ship. They will surround you, giving you the space you need to push through."

Surely Nibiran ships can't hope to fight Titan ones. It takes me a second to realize what she must mean. "They'll be sacrificed," I say. "For me. For Leonis."

"They will act as your shields. For all of us."

I'm not sure how I should feel about that—other than sick to my stomach, which is the immediate and visceral response. "Well," I say, after a few moments. "That's a pretty fucking heavy thing to lay on me."

Heikki turns to face me fully. "If there were any other choice, we would have taken it. Do you think we wish to sacrifice our own people? To lay all of our hopes with you?" Frustration breaks through her usually mild tone, and she takes a deep breath, her eyes fluttering shut for a moment as she struggles to compose herself. When she opens them again, she looks at me directly and openly. "I will be frank with you, Scorpia: I do not like this plan. I do not particularly like you, either. But, stars help me, I do trust you. You have saved our planet, and chosen to help us when you could have fled. I know that you will do the right thing once again." She inclines her upper body in a small bow—a respectful gesture, and not one that someone of her status has any obligation to give to someone like me. "If you agree, we will move forward within the week. You know how to reach me. Do not delay with your response. Every day without an alliance with Deva is another day of our people dying."

CHAPTER THIRTY-ONE

The Prototype

Corvus

After what feels like endless days speaking with various military personnel and answering an exhausting amount of questions about the Titans, I finally ask for a chance to return to the bunker to see my siblings. Govender offers to escort me to Vil Hava on her personal hovercraft. It feels generous, but I suspect it's mainly a way for her to continue to keep an eye on me. She has barely let me out of her sight for days. Meanwhile, Oshiro has been nowhere to be found. I'm surprised how much it hurts to realize the other councillor must be avoiding me. After our last private conversation about Kitaya and the Titans, I thought there was a chance to mend our friendship, but perhaps I was wrong. Or is this the council's decision? Do they not think Oshiro will watch me closely enough, given our more personal relationship? Do they still not trust me?

I shouldn't ask. But I have to know. "Councillor," I say, turning to Govender, who regards me with the same unreadable expression she always seems to wear. "Why am I working with you instead of Oshiro? Your choice, or theirs?"

"The council makes all decisions together," she says levelly.

"You're avoiding the question."

"I suppose I am." She studies my face. "Fine, then. The news will be public in a few days anyway. Iri Oshiro has resigned from their position on the council."

The news is so startling that I can't absorb it for a moment. Why would they do this? And so suddenly? Oshiro was a good councillor, and generally well-liked. I did have the sense that their influence was slipping in favor of councillors with greater wartime power, such as Heikki and Govender, but this still doesn't make sense to me. "Resigned? Why?" I ask, once I process my initial shock.

"They took the loss of Kitaya harder than anyone," Govender says. "I can only imagine they felt responsible for what happened."

I feel a burst of anger, remembering Altair's words to them during those so-called peace talks. Was that the final blow that broke Oshiro's idealistic nature? Made them give up their political ambitions? It hurts to consider.

"I know that you were close, but I want to reassure you that the rest of the Nibiran Council also holds you in high esteem," Govender continues, when I don't speak. "In fact, in light of your recent contributions to the war effort, we would like to offer you a more official title. Due to your status as an off-worlder, our laws don't allow us to give you a place in the military. Instead, we would like you to work directly for the council as a special operations agent."

So this is it, then. I knew it was coming, but I didn't expect it to be so soon, nor for it to come hand in hand with the information that the person I trust most on the council will no longer be here with me.

But I can't continue on as I am, half-committed to the Nibiran cause and still harboring uncertainty. I already have one sister out there fighting, and my other siblings are trapped on this planet. If the Titans win, we will die along with everyone else here. It doesn't matter what I want. I have a responsibility.

"I accept."

"I had hoped you would." She displays her rare smile. "As soon as you're done visiting with your family, I would like to officially put you in the field." Before I can process my feelings on that, she adds, "By the way, please pass along my thanks to your sister Lyre. Her thoughts on methods of defeating exosuits were very useful."

The topic change is so abrupt that it throws me off-balance. "What?"

She regards me with those clever eyes. "Councillor Oshiro passed Lyre's notes along to me, and I passed them along to my intelligence team. Soon they should have a prototype ready that implements her ideas. As well as the valuable information you gave us regarding the exosuits, of course."

I think back on the note I handed to Oshiro, the note Lyre let me believe was merely a personal letter expressing her condolences about Kitaya, and my world tilts sideways. "A prototype," I repeat.

"Yes. Your sister's ideas are quite advanced for her age. She was studying engineering at Kitaya's university, was she not? Perhaps we could offer her a more hands-on internship at—"

"Send me to test it," I say. Normally I would never dare to interrupt a councillor, but I fear if Govender continues with her thought, the idea of Lyre working alongside her intelligence people will make me lose my temper. My hands are clenched with barely restrained anger as it is; I force myself to relax them.

Govender is silent for a moment, studying me. "You're a valuable asset to risk in an experimental mission."

"I have experience with exosuits. The mission will have the greatest chance at success with me there."

"Hmm." Govender appears to consider it, though I have a

strong suspicion that she already knows what her answer will be. "You do have a point. But as I said, the prototype is nearly ready. We need to start preparations immediately, out on Lan Iroh. I was under the impression you wanted to spend time with your family on Vil Hava?"

It's true. The thought of not seeing them fills me with near-crushing disappointment. I desperately need a break from all of this, and yet...I can't ask the war to wait for me. And if my sister had a hand in this, I feel obligated to share the responsibility for it.

Seeing the look on my face, Govender says, "I can give you one hour here. That's it."

I suppose I should be grateful for anything. "Thank you, Councillor."

I'm not sure if I'm relieved or disappointed to find that Lyre is the only one waiting in our room in the bunker. I had hoped to have a chance to see everyone, but perhaps it's good that this conversation will remain private.

"Corvus," Lyre says, looking surprised to see me in the doorway. "You're back?"

I don't set my bag down. "Only for a short while. Where are the others?"

"Pol's in the kitchen. Scorpia is out." She looks like she wants to say more, but she hesitates as she reads something on my face. "What's it like out there? Is everything okay?"

I might sugarcoat my answer if it was anyone else, but I don't see the point with Lyre. "It's bad," I say, and sink onto my bunk with my bag in my lap. "The general plan seems to be to outlast the Titans since we can't outfight them. Use guerilla warfare and our advantage in water combat, avoiding direct conflict when we can. It may work, but we'll suffer heavy losses. We can only be grateful that they haven't been using the weaponry on their ships, perhaps because they don't want to risk damaging the planet too badly, since they mean to take it for themselves." I pause, looking at her. "Still, they have other technology. The exosuits are a problem. But I guess you know that already."

She blinks, stares at me for a moment, then says, "Oshiro wasn't supposed to tell you."

I shake my head. How the information went to Govender, and then to me, is beside the point. Even the fact that Lyre lied to me by omission is not important right now. "What were you thinking, Lyre?"

"What was I thinking?" she repeats, her face flushing. "I was thinking that you and Drom are going to be out on the front lines, and the rest of us will die just as surely if the Nibirans lose this war. I had to find some way to make a difference."

It hurts to hear my own thoughts from her mouth and realize that I've failed at keeping her away from this. This will make her a killer just as much as I am, and I'm not sure she's realized that yet. "Not like this." I shake my head. "Did you even think about what you were doing?"

"Of course I did," she says, folding her arms over her chest. "Extensively. The solution didn't exactly present itself overnight."

"I'm talking about what it means. That people will die because of something you helped design."

She blinks at me, and then straightens her spine before she responds. "People will die either way. This will make it less likely that you or Drom are among them."

I want to tell her that it's never that simple. But right now, maybe it has to be.

A week later, I'm treading water with a team of five, all too aware that the only thing between me and a burst of laser-fire is a thin layer of water-resistant fabric. These wetsuits are well-designed for utility in water, but I wish the Nibirans had come up with something less flimsy. Though I suppose it doesn't matter either way. Even with full body armor, our soldiers are pulverized by the dozens by exosuits, which is exactly what we're expecting to find today.

At the very least, the wetsuit has made treading water for three hours a simple thing, even with my bad leg. Webbing between the toes and fingers lends power to every stroke, and the fabric keeps me warm and dry. I've adjusted the buoyancy settings for not only my weight, but the weapon I carry.

"How much longer are we meant to sit here?" a voice crackles through the comm in my ear.

I resist the urge to snap at him. This man—a Gaian, I gathered immediately, before he even said a word—has been rubbing me the wrong way ever since we met. But I can't complain, since at least his broad shoulders and muscular build speak of some type of physical aptitude, while the three Nibirans look like they couldn't handle a flight of stairs without losing their breath. The moment I saw this team, I knew my superiors didn't have much faith in the prototype built from Lyre's designs. Then again, they're reluctant to throw anyone useful in the path of an exosuit. The statistical survival rate is so atrocious that they wouldn't even allow me to look at it. It took hours of argument for me to ensure I would be here to test the weapon myself.

"As long as it takes," I say. "Keep the comms clear. No chatter."

But even I can feel my frustration building as time ticks onward. There are battles raging elsewhere, and I know my team is itching to be there instead of here. I am, too. But intel says here, outside of an algae cleaning facility, is where we need to be. Lyre may have been wrong about Kitaya being safe, but she was right when she predicted that the Titans would try to disrupt the supply chain by targeting places like this. They've been sending small teams to scout and harass transport ships and processing build-ings, stealing or destroying food and other supplies and taking off before the Nibirans can amass a sizable-enough force to have any hope of fighting back. And the Nibirans don't have the soldiers to spare defending every fishery and algae farm on the islands, espe-cially not when numbers are one of their few advantages in more important fights.

Fortunately for us tonight, the Titans are eager to exploit that, and their eagerness makes them predictable.

"Something's coming," one of my soldiers says—a reedy young woman barely older than Lyre. A moment later I see the two dark shapes overhead, bulleting toward us.

"Down," I command, and we sink beneath the waves.

The world is silent down here, with the exception of someone gasping for air over the comms. The sound of their panic makes it hard to fight my own. There wasn't enough time for me to com-plete the full wetsuit training regimen, so breathing with several feet of water over my head still involves fighting basic instincts. Within these suits, we have enough oxygen to last an hour—but not if we're breathing like that. I'm about to tell them to calm down or at least mute themselves, but as the exosuits fly directly overhead, my nerves silence me.

When I fought alongside the Titans, it was easy to forget how terrifying the huge metal exosuits can be from an outsider's per-spective. Now that I see one up close again, it's impossible not to remember how easily they could rend flesh. My wetsuit would tear like paper if one of the Titans got ahold of me, and my bones would splinter like twigs.

But the exosuits pass overhead without noticing us. I wait a few minutes before surfacing, breaching just enough to get a look at where they've gone. One suited soldier disappears into the algae plant. The other lands on the edge of the water, keeping watch over the waves. I duck down as their gaze passes over the area where my team hides.

"Branson, prepare to take a shot. Lead them out above the water," I command, my voice a low murmur though I know there's no way the Titan can hear me.

Despite his earlier abrasiveness, at least the Gaian is good at following orders. I'm not sure any of the others would have the guts to do this, but he moves away from the team without complaint, surfaces, and takes aim.

"Everyone else, stay down until my command." I pause, ready myself. This is it. Whatever happens from here on out is my responsibility. "Fire."

Beneath the water, it's difficult to see much of what's happening. But I can picture the shot clanging uselessly against the Titan's suit, and I don't have to imagine the dark blur of it heading toward us in response.

"Hold," I say, watching the Titan draw closer to my Gaian soldier, who maintains his position valiantly though I can hear his breath quicken over the comms. I wait, and finally, as the exosuit raises its pulse rifle, I say, "Dive."

Branson plummets down to join us beneath the waves. The exosuit hovers overhead, turning in a slow circle to search for us. I had hoped they might pull back farther, have more fear of the water, but we'll have to work with this. It's only a matter of time before they call in their friend for backup.

"Everyone up. Harass and dodge counterfire like we discussed."

My team surges upward, the nervous Nibiran woman a little later than the rest. I wait for a few seconds, prepping the weapon and praying it works. I surface in time to see one of the Nibirans move too slow and take a face full of laser-fire. I curse, and heave the weapon up so the barrel points out of the water, taking aim at the exosuit. As they swing their pulse rifle in my direction, I fire.

Their laser-fire goes wild as a net launches at them and closes around the suit, magnetized clasps securing it shut, weights dragging them downward. They struggle against it, engines heaving to keep them aloft. They fall one foot, two—and stabilize. It's not enough to bring them down.

I dive under again, adjusting the buoyancy settings on my suit and narrowly avoiding a burst of fire. The exosuit is still struggling to break free. I work to reload my weapon—but it takes time, and a cut-off scream over the comms tells me another one of my teammates pays the price for it. I surge upward as soon as I can, activating my suit's buoyancy assistance to lend me speed, though it will make it harder to dive under again in time. I line up a second shot as the exosuit sets its sights on me, and fire.

This time, the net cinches tightly around the suit and drags it down into the water. It thrashes to stay afloat, but loses the fight quickly, and sinks like a stone, all the way down to the bottom. The suit is far too heavy, and not designed to function in water. As Lyre must have surmised, there was no need for it when Titan had no liquid water on its surface.

Branson whoops over the comms. I take stock of him and the last remaining Nibiran, a leathery-faced older woman.

"Good work. Spread out and wait. When the soldier evacuates, we'll catch them on the way up, and recover the suit afterward."

Those who remain of my team spread out to comply. We wait, eyes on the suit resting on the bottom of the ocean floor, just close enough for us to see it. A minute ticks by. Another. I know from experience that those exosuits don't have much oxygen. The soldier has to eject soon if they want to live.

Unless they don't.

I've been foolish. I know Titan military training: death before capture. This soldier isn't going to eject if they know we're here. They'll choose to die instead.

"They're really going to stay there and drown," Branson says, reaching the same conclusion after enough time has passed. He chuckles. "These Titans are crazy fuckers."

I turn to him, anger flaring up in my chest. But before I can speak, a blurred shape approaches from the corner of my eye, above the water. I dive instinctively. My brain catches up a moment later to remember the second exosuit. My mouth is slower still. *"Down!"*

It takes two seconds. Two seconds too long. As I continue to dive, the water above me goes murky with blood. The dark shape of the exosuit rises up above the water with another wriggling form grasped in its hand: the last member of my team. Her screams over the comms nearly deafen me, but I leave them on, and force myself to watch as the exosuit tosses her at a terrifying speed toward the nearby shore.

The comm cuts off. I stay where I am. So does the exosuit, a dark shape silhouetted against the sky, barely visible through the red-stained water. Then it, too, turns and disappears, leaving me under the water in silence and solitude.

Councillor Govender doesn't even give me time to shower before asking for a debriefing. I'm forced to walk into a room of military personnel with my hair still damp and my wetsuit clinging to my skin, and admit that we failed.

A room full of unsurprised faces stares back at me.

"I'm the only one who made it out," I say, my voice hoarse and my chest hot with shame. I barely had time to acquaint myself with my squad, but I still feel the weight of guilt. Their lives depended on me, and I let them down. Once, I had become used to this feeling—as much as any person can. Now, the pain feels fresh. "The first shot wasn't enough to take the suit down. We miscalculated. The second took it under, and as we thought, it wasn't able to surface again. But by that time…" I trail off as the room erupts in startled murmurs, and look at Govender for an explanation.

"So you did manage to destroy an exosuit," she says, leaning forward eagerly. "*And* you survived."

"Yes," I say. "But only one of the two suits, and it couldn't be recovered. We lost four soldiers for a pile of metal."

The room is suddenly much more interested in what I'm saying.

"Specialist Kaiser," Govender says, "with all due respect for the dead, this is wonderful news." Several heads around the room bob in agreement. I stare, uncomprehending. "The numbers for combat against exosuits are…devastating, to put it lightly. The few we've managed to destroy have taken dozens of lives with them." She smiles. "Run us through every detail. We need to start utilizing this technique on a mass scale as soon as possible."

CHAPTER THIRTY-TWO

Fate

Scorpia

Finally, I've got a chance to get off this planet and back in a ship, yet I can't seem to decide how I feel about it. As Heikki emphasized, Nibiru is losing lives by the day—but I need to think about this. Delivering Leonis to the Devans isn't the same as killing her myself, but I know I'll still feel the weight of my part in it. And, even indirectly, doing this for the council will mean making myself a part of the war.

At least slipping out of the facility is easy after I do it the first time. On the rare occasion that a guard turns down a bribe, I just have to wait out the six hours until the next shift shows up. And since Corvus was gone yet *again* by the time I returned from my meeting with Heikki, off on whatever task the council has given him now, I have nothing better to do than sneak out whenever I can. I spend my time wandering the streets of Vil Hava, looking out at the ocean and considering what Councillor Heikki asked of me.

But today I have an even better reason to sneak out: Shey finally has time to see me. It's been difficult over the last couple weeks, since I've been trapped in a locked-down facility, and she's been busy with her usual political bullshit. I wish I could focus fully on how excited I am to see her again, but instead, my stomach is coiled with dread over breaking the news about her mother. I have no idea how she'll react to her mom being used as a bargaining chip, let alone me being the one to deliver her.

Shey picks a café near the heart of Vil Hava to meet. I arrive ten minutes early, order an espresso for myself and one of those fancy-ass teas she loves, and wait, jittery, in a corner booth.

She's five minutes late, which is unlike her, but that doesn't stop me from breaking into a huge grin and jumping up to greet her before she can even reach the booth. She smells like Gaian food and sweat—neither pleasant on their own, together a uniquely terrible aroma—but I sweep her into a hug anyway, and kiss her long enough that she's grinning and a little out of breath by the time I finish.

"I missed you," I say, kissing her forehead, and her temples, and her nose, until she laughingly breaks away and nudges me into the booth.

"I missed you, too," she says, smiling across the table at me. "I'm surprised they allowed you to leave the facility. Isn't it risky?"

"Well, *allowed* is a strong word," I say. She sighs at me, and I grab her hand and kiss her knuckles, unable to keep my hands off her. "But I really wanted to see you."

"Normally I would never approve of such sneaking around, of course, but I suppose I can make an exception this time." She studies my face. "How has it been? How are Corvus and Drom?"

"They're fine. I think. Haven't seen much of them. And I, um..." I pause, trying to find a way to tell her about my conversation with Councillor Heikki, but my tongue tangles. I clear my throat. "You go first. What have you been so busy with that you're neglecting your poor, attention-starved girlfriend?"

Shey blinks at me, and slowly smiles. "I don't think I've ever heard you use that term before."

"Oh, well, I..." I stammer, turning red, but she squeezes my hand.

"I like it," she says. But a moment later, as my embarrassment fades, so does her smile. Her demeanor turns serious. "I've been mostly helping out in the refugee camps. So has Izra, actually."

"What? Really?" I've reached out to Izra a couple times, but she hardly ever responds to my messages.

"Yes. She initially came to hide in the crowd, but after we ran into each other, I asked her to help with some...security issues." She glances around to make sure no one is close enough to over-hear, but everyone in the restaurant seems involved in their own conversations. "The peacekeepers are stretched quite thin, as you can imagine, and the Gaian refugee areas don't seem to be of par-ticular priority for them."

"So you asked *Izra*?"

"I was very clear that killing anyone would only make the situ-ation worse, and she's only meant to act as defensive security," she says quickly. "She has been a little...overenthusiastic at times, but otherwise I'm glad to have her around, especially since I haven't been able to be present as often as I like lately."

"Why's that?"

"There's something else I've been working on, too."

"Of course. Because clearly helping all those refugees isn't enough to have on your plate."

She hesitates, and then says, "It's an alternative plan to the Nibiran Council's idea of subjugating Gaia." My smile fades, but she pushes onward. "I'd like to instead propose an alliance where we would be equals on this planet. If we can do that—prove that two peoples can truly coexist, I believe it could encourage better relations with the other planets, as well. It would—" She looks up at me, and stops, frowning, and pulls her hand away from mine. "You disapprove?"

"Oh, uh." I wasn't aware it was showing that clearly on my face. I'm not sure how to tell her that I meant what I said in front of the Nibiran Council when this came up before—I think we have plenty of bigger issues—without sounding like a complete asshole. "No, I'm just surprised, I guess. But go on. Do you have Khatri's support?"

Shey groans, but at least I've successfully distracted her from my feelings on the matter. "No. That's one of the hurdles. At this point she's already given up most of her power, so it doesn't matter much as it is, but people still respect her. Unfortunately, she'll echo anything the council says. And the council most certainly does not approve. I've been trying to plan a public demonstration for weeks now, but they refuse to give us the proper permits."

"I mean, if you care that much, then fuck the permits."

Shey nods. "I reached the same conclusion. We're going ahead with it anyway."

"Aw, my little rebel." I smile, but it falters. Shit. I don't want this to go badly, but I'm not sure if I can leave here with a clear conscience if I don't say what's on my mind. "But..." I lean back in my seat, my leg jumping as I try to gather my thoughts. "Honestly, I...I gotta say, the council may have a point?"

The look Shey gives me is shocked, and bordering on offended, but her voice is level as she asks, "How so?"

"It's gonna incite an uproar. Among the Nibirans, the Titans, everyone. Gaia has made a lot of mistakes, Shey." I hold up a hand before she can interrupt. "I know they didn't know what your mother was doing, but they voted her into office. They supported what she stood for, and frankly, everything she did was just a natural extension of that. She wasn't exactly subtle about how she felt toward the other planets. You can't hand power to a xenophobe and then act shocked when she does something terrible with it."

Shey's expression starts defensive, but as she considers what I say, it slips gradually toward dismay. "I...I know that you're right," she says. "But I have to believe that my people still have good in them. That our culture has things worth saving. Do you suggest that we have to give up everything that makes us who we are because of our mistakes?"

"I don't know," I say, honestly. "But if you want to keep it, you need to earn it. Prove that you've learned from those mistakes rather than trying to bury them. I mean, shit, Khatri hasn't even apologized to the Titans."

"It must be the council's decision. It's hard enough for them to keep morale up among our peoples as it is."

"Yeah." I tentatively reach for her hand again, and squeeze when she lets me take it. "The issue is complicated as hell. I didn't mean to try to ruin everything you've been working on."

"No, no. Thank you for being honest with me." She smiles at me. "It's refreshing, really. Sometimes it feels like you're the only one willing to tell me the truth."

I take a deep breath. That went better than expected, so I guess it's time to lay everything on the table. "Well then, in the spirit of honesty, I'm afraid I'm going to have to throw one more thing at you."

I slip into her side of the booth, both to make sure we aren't overheard and for an excuse to put an arm around her. But she pulls away from me as I explain the request from Councillor Heikki, her frown deepening.

"I already told them I'd do it," I say. "But I wanted to see what you thought, too. I mean...she may be a terrible monster and all, but she's still your mother." And I have plenty of experience with how complicated that can be. "You're not gonna hate me for shipping her over to the Devans as a peace offering, are you?"

Shey lets out a small laugh. "No, Scorpia. It's not like you're killing her. Whether it's here or on Deva, she'll be tried and judged by the Interplanetary Council, and I'm not going to stand in the way of that. I think you're doing a good thing."

"Well, okay." I'm relieved to hear she reached the same conclusion as me despite her personal ties. It makes me more confident that this isn't such a terrible idea. "And...I know you've got shit to do here, but this might be your only chance to jump ship before this place really goes to hell." I cut myself off there, hoping she knows me well enough to know what I really want to say.

She's silent for a long moment, but finally says, "I'll come with you."

I'm so overwhelmed with relief that words fail me. Instead, I pull her into a tight hug, resting my chin on top of her head. "Thank the stars," I murmur. "We're leaving in three days."

She stiffens in my grip, and slowly pulls away. "So soon?"

"Yeah, I mean, it's..." I stop when I see the look on her face, my stomach twisting uneasily. "What?"

"That's the day of the demonstration I'm planning." She shakes her head, expression clouding. "I didn't think you would be leaving so soon. With the Nibirans, and their planning, I thought..."

"Maybe I can get the council to postpone," I say, half-heartedly, but we both know that's never going to happen. The Nibirans are rushing to get this done as quickly as possible. It'll take a week to get to Deva as it is, another week for any aid to get back here, and every day without securing an alliance is a day that more people die in this war. And another day they risk triggering the defense system and losing their entire world. "Or you could do your demonstration earlier, or...or they can find a different pilot, for all I care."

Shey's expression is already resigned. "I'm sorry, Scorpia. You know none of that is possible." She takes both of my hands. "It seems fate is getting between us again. Perhaps this is where I can do the most good, anyway."

"No." I yank my hands away from her. "Fuck that. This isn't fucking fate. This is you choosing your people over me, *again*, because this is how it always is with you stars-damned Gaians, and this is how it's always going to be. Isn't it?"

Shey's face crumples. "Scorpia—"

"You said you would stay with me. That doesn't mean you get to stick around only when it's convenient!"

"It doesn't mean giving up everything I care about for you, either," she says, her voice sharp, but a moment later she softens again. "Let's not say goodbye like this. Please."

I want so badly to keep raging at her, to pour out all my anger and hurt and drive a wedge between us so I can convince myself it was my choice to walk away...but after a moment, my shoulders slump and the fight drains out of me. Doing that isn't going to make me feel any better. And I'm not sure I can handle any more regrets.

Deep down I know she's right, anyway. I can't ask her to give up her people any more than she can ask me to give up my family. We both have to do what's right for us, even if it means drifting apart. And even if it means me letting her go when it feels like I need her most. I need to find the strength to do this on my own.

After a moment, Shey gently takes my hands again and pulls me toward her, wrapping an arm around my waist and putting her head on my shoulder.

"Just my luck to fall for a Gaian," I mutter.

She pulls back. "What did you say?"

"Nothing. Nothing." I yank her in close again before she can see my blush, and hold her tight, wishing it was enough to keep her at my side.

CHAPTER THIRTY-THREE

Responsibility

Corvus

Once again, Councillor Govender personally escorts me back to Vil Hava by armored hovercraft. I spend the ride in silence. They yanked me off the front lines after my first "success" at taking down an exosuit, which still feels far from the victory they're eager to claim it as. But explaining my strategy to military officials has been even more exhausting, in its own way. At least in the middle of a fight there's not much room for thinking. Now, thinking is all I can do. Every time I have to explain that mission again, I picture the four bodies of my team floating in the water, and the exosuit lying on the ocean floor with the Titan soldier suffocating to death within—and I think of that rippling endlessly outward, my words creating a thousand other similar situations that I'll never see but will share the responsibility for.

We've almost arrived at our destination when Govender finally speaks.

"You've done some incredible work for us, Specialist Kaiser."

She hesitates, and after a moment, reaches out and places a hand on my shoulder. "Work that will save a lot of lives. Thank you."

Even with the bone-deep ache in my body, I feel a spark of pride. That's what I have to remember: the lives I've saved, not the ones I've taken. All of this is to spare lives, not end them.

I nod at her, and she pulls back and continues, "We had hoped to keep you off the front lines for a while, but a situation has come up."

"I'm happy to serve however I can." The words come automatically. For a moment there's a flicker of uncertainty—didn't I say these words on Titan, as well?—but she goes on before I can question it further.

"We've located what seems to be a Titan base, a few miles off the coast of Kitaya. There have been a large number of their soldiers coming and going from this location. They're the only reason we were able to locate it, in fact, as the base is completely invisible to our radars."

"Cloaking? Or Primus technology?"

"We're not sure, but we have to expect the worst. Which, given what we know from Gaia, is quite bad, indeed." She pauses to let that sink in. "We've been trying to investigate the facility, but the Titans have it under heavy guard. However, our underwater teams have been able to record a strange sound coming from the facility." She pulls out her comm and plays a clip for me. I frown at the noise—an odd, warbling keen that sounds almost like a trio of people singing slightly out of tune. It makes the hair rise on the back of my neck.

Govender pauses the clip and doesn't bother to hide a shiver of her own. "We have no idea what could produce such a sound," she says, "and it's been too dangerous for us to get close. And as you know, we do not currently possess the means to go head-to-head with the Titan army. We cannot launch a full-scale assault on the base without sustaining heavy casualties, and it seems inadvisable to do so without having some idea what may be waiting within, and if it is worth so much loss of life."

"So you're arranging a stealth mission."

"Precisely. And due to your unique understanding of the Titan military, we would like you to be the one to lead it. You will be guiding a small team of four into the base, where you will be expected to learn as much as you can about its operations and purpose. Subtlety is the priority here."

"I understand," I say with a nod. "How soon do we leave?"

"The day after tomorrow," she says. "We'll pick you up in the morning to get you acquainted with your team."

Tomorrow morning. My heart sinks. Only one night with my siblings before it's back to the war. But I'm in no position to decline. The council is counting on me.

When I arrive back at our room, I'm surprised that Scorpia is there. She glances over at the door as it opens, and does a double take when she sees that it's me. I hadn't thought about how long it's been since we last saw each other until now, and I feel a sudden rush of uncertainty. Will she be angry at me for being gone so long? Upset that I've been neglecting the family? I remain in the doorway, letting my pack fall to the floor, while she climbs to her feet and takes a few steps toward me.

"Oh, hey, look who decided to grace us with his presence," she says, and then launches herself forward and engulfs me in a hug. I wrap an arm around her, smiling despite my exhaustion. "Seriously, though," she says, pulling back and scrutinizing my face. "These councillors running you all over the planet, or what? Where have you been?"

"They're keeping me busy. Though, as I recall, last time I stopped by you were away as well."

"I had my own meeting with a councillor. We Very Important Terrorists have moved up in the world," she teases—but the amusement drops after a moment. She sits on her bunk, gesturing for me to take the opposite one. "I need to talk to you about that, actually." Once I take a seat, she continues, "The council's sending me off on another job."

She pauses, chewing her bottom lip, and I try to hide the despair that rolls through me at her words. Not Scorpia, too. Not another one of my siblings dragged into the war. Drom is on the front lines, Lyre is designing weapons...I thought Scorpia was the one I didn't have to worry about. She's made mistakes in the past, but she has never been a killer, and I thought she would be the one to teach our younger siblings that they don't have to be, either.

Finally, she says, "They're asking me to transport Leonis to Deva as a prisoner, in order to secure an alliance with them."

I take a moment to process that. I'm not sure whether or not to be relieved. It may not put her on the front lines, but it will likely be even more dangerous. "Is that possible, with the Titan fleet surrounding Nibiru?" It makes sense that the council would want to get Leonis off their hands given the volatile situation here, especially if it means an alliance with Deva. Leonis being here means a greater risk of the Titans forcibly taking her for themselves, and learning everything she knows about the Planetary Defense Systems.

Scorpia looks a bit put out by my response, clearly expecting more enthusiasm. "The council seems to think so. There's this plan to use their own ships as shields for me." She swallows hard. "They wouldn't risk something happening to someone as important as Leonis unless they were pretty damn confident it was going to work."

"And an alliance with Deva could change everything for us."

Scorpia's eyes flicker at my use of *us*, but I ignore it and continue, "This war has already been going on for too long. Every day longer runs the risk of triggering the defense system."

"That's what I thought, too," she says. "So I told the council I'd do it. We leave in two days. I'm going to need your help convincing Drom to come, though."

Two days. That gives me pause. I hadn't expected it to be so fast...and hadn't realized Scorpia would assume I could go. But that was foolish of me—of course she would expect me to put the family first. And I should. So why am I so hesitant? "Drom will never agree to come," I say, after a few moments. "And...I have obligations here as well. I'm supposed to go on another mission in a couple of days, and I don't know how soon I can be back."

"What?" Scorpia's eyebrows draw together. "I got us a way off-planet. This is what we've been waiting for. Isn't it?"

"I'm involved now. The council needs me. I can't turn my back on all of this."

Scorpia stares at me for a moment, and then abruptly stands up and begins to pace the room. I stay where I am, hands on my knees, watching her move back and forth and bracing myself for an inevitable explosion.

Instead she says, very calmly, "These political fuckers are up to some political fuckery."

"...What?"

"They planned this," she says. "There's no way it's a coincidence that they're sending us on two separate missions at the same time."

"We're both valuable resources with very useful skill sets. Of course they're putting us to use. That doesn't mean there's some grand conspiracy."

"They want to force us apart. They've been doing it for weeks now. It's the same shit Momma used to do to us. They're manipulating us into doing what they want." She laughs under her breath. "Stars, I'm stupid. No wonder Heikki was so willing to let me off-planet. They'll have you here as a hostage. They know I'll come back." She shakes her head. "And Shey's demonstration being planned for the day I leave...of course. They hoped she'd just leave with me. Fucking of *course* they planned this."

As much as I want to deny the accusation outright, her words give me pause. I think of how difficult it has been for me to return to my family, and how Scorpia happened to not be around the last time I was here. Plus, there's the issue of Oshiro stepping down, which I still don't understand. I've tried to contact the ex-councillor, but the number I have saved has been disconnected, and Govender seemed unwilling to give me another way to contact them.

Perhaps Scorpia has a point. Something is happening here, something we don't know enough to fully comprehend. But it doesn't change anything.

"The council is doing everything they can to win this war. They're not forcing us to do anything that we haven't agreed to."

Scorpia sinks onto her bunk again. "I don't get it. Why are you so eager to condemn people like us—like Eri and Halon, or Orion, or Izra—but you put people like the council on a pedestal? They're the ones who are all the same."

"That's not true."

"It is. You're buying into their bullshit, just like you always do. Trying to be the golden boy again."

I fight back a flash of anger. "I'm trying to be a good person. And you think you know better? Just because you have no sense of loyalty?"

"Loyalty?" She stares at me. "Loyalty to who, Corvus? The Nibirans aren't your people. Neither are the Gaians. You've spent all these months talking about the Titans as though they're your people, but now you're fighting against them. Is that what you call loyalty?"

"The situation is far more complicated than that," I say, though her words fill me with cold shame.

"Complicated or not, you're just doing what you've always done," Scorpia says, her voice rising now, face splotching with color. "You're so desperate to throw the past away and fit in wherever you go. So eager for someone to give you a gold star that you latch on to the first authority figure you can find and build your whole identity around them. You did it with Momma, with that general of yours—"

"Don't act like you know anything about what I went through on Titan."

"You're right. I don't. But I can see that it's still hurting you." Scorpia leans forward, her expression softening into something almost pleading. "Don't let them do this to you again. Don't let them make you into someone you don't want to be."

"As if you didn't do the same to me? Trying to force me to be a criminal again even after I told you over and over that it wasn't the life I wanted? You're only angry about this because I'm not what *you* want me to be."

Scorpia stares at me. "I didn't think…" she says, and then stops, swallowing. "I'm sorry."

Maybe they shouldn't be, but those words are enough to crush my anger down to sputtering embers. "It's too late for me," I say, lowering my voice. "I am who I am already. I'm a soldier. The only thing I can do now is find a way to use it for something good. I'm not fighting for the council. I'm fighting for the only home I have left, and for the Nibirans and the Gaians who don't have a choice. And for Drom, and Pol, and Lyre, because I don't want them growing up in a world torn by war. I don't want the twins to watch their home-planet become what mine was. I don't want them to have to grow up to be like me." I shake my head, dropping my eyes to the floor. "Look, I'll be wary of the council. I'll try not to let them manipulate me. But I can't walk away from this. I have an obligation to see it through to the end."

Scorpia looks at me, her jaw working silently for a few seconds, before proclaiming, "Fuck. All right." She presses a hand to her forehead, one leg jumping nervously. "But I can't stay here. I need to do this Leonis thing. It's the only way I can help, and at least I can get Pol and Lyre out of here. Maybe Izra, too. I know Drom won't come."

"Go," I tell her. "Do what you need to do."

"But...I...You're staying here, and so is Shey, and..." She shrugs helplessly. "I don't have such a great record of making decisions on my own. What if I screw this up?"

"You won't," I tell her, without a moment's hesitation. "You're not who you used to be. You don't need us."

Slowly, her face shifts from misery to determination. She swallows, and nods. "Okay," she says. "Just promise me you'll still be here when I get back."

"You know I can't promise that."

Scorpia sighs. "You know, it wouldn't hurt you to lie sometimes."

I'm not sure how Scorpia manages it, given how difficult it's been to get everyone together over the last few weeks, but she gathers everyone together in our room in under an hour. Pol shows up with a bunch of premade meals I suspect he stole from the kitchen, and Lyre manages to scrounge up a bag of dice. Drom shows up with nothing, but her presence alone is all we could've asked for. She looks tired, and doesn't talk much, but she sits shoulder-to-shoulder with Pol, and he occasionally manages to make her smile. Lyre avoids me for the first half of the night.

Finally, when the others are distracted by an argument about Scorpia cheating, I pull her into a hug.

"I'm sorry," she whispers, leaning into me.

"It's all right, Lyre." I ruffle her hair. "I forgive you. As long as you go with Scorpia and get out of here."

"But…" She stops herself there, pulls back, and nods at me. "Okay."

We don't talk about what's to come. Nobody tries to convince anyone else to go, or stay. Everyone is just glad to be able to spend some time together. We pass hours throwing dice and shooting the shit and pretending that everything is the same as always, and that everything is going to be okay.

At the end of the night, after Drom has returned to her unit and Pol has cried himself to sleep and Lyre has dozed off with her comm still clutched in her hands, Scorpia and I sit alone, saying nothing, just being together. We both stay awake until the early morning, when a knock at the door comes, announcing it's time for me to go.

Scorpia stands with me, and hugs me tightly.

"Good luck," she says.

"You too."

CHAPTER THIRTY-FOUR

Old Friends and Old Enemies

Scorpia

After Corvus leaves, my last days on Nibiru pass so quickly I can hardly believe it, and all of a sudden I find myself standing in the familiar Ca Sineh elevator. The Nibirans don't have many forces to spare, so they thought it would be easier to escort both Leonis and me to the waiting ship together. This place makes me queasy as I remember coming down here dozens of times to visit Orion. I've been trying not to think about him over the last few weeks; trying not to imagine all the things the Titans probably did to him after he went over to their side.

I remember how desperate I was to get him out of this place, how hard I tried to cheer him up when his imprisonment was sucking the life out of him. All of that, and he abandoned me in the end. It still hurts to think about. Now I have to move forward not only without him, but without Shey, or Drom, or Corvus.

Even Izra turned down my invitation to come, leaving me with only three of the original eight we had on *Memoria*.

Once, this would've been unthinkable. I would've given up, or found a way to bribe or force them to come with me. I could probably convince Corvus if I really wanted to—poke at those weak points I know he has—but in the end, that would only make him hate me. He's right—I've already dragged him unwillingly along too many times. And Drom is going to do whatever she wants to do, she's made that clear enough. I can't take Corvus away knowing it would leave her all alone here.

So it's up to me, then. I'm pushing forward, but it doesn't mean I feel anything close to confident about how this is going to go. I still don't even know how I feel about transporting Leonis off-planet, no matter how necessary it might be. I thought getting Shey's and Corvus's approval would make me feel better, but my doubt lingers.

"Just a quick in and out," the guard says, while I shift from foot to foot beside him. "The Titans don't know Leonis's location, so we don't anticipate any problems, but we don't want to risk being spotted."

I frown, dragging my thoughts back to the present. It takes a few seconds for me to realize why my instincts are crying out with alarm. Leonis's location. Orion. The Titans.

"Shit," I say. The guard stares at me, a wrinkle forming between his brows. I open my mouth to say something, but think better of it. There's no use in causing a panic. If the Titans haven't hit this location yet, it's not like me saying it now will make things any better. "Let's just hurry up," I say. "I wanna get this done with."

"I assure you we're on the same page, ma'am," he says, and leads me down the hall. The prison is swimming with guards, even more so than I remember. I'm guessing I'm not the only one concerned about this location being a potential military target. All of them seem restless, their shifting eyes and alert postures at odds with the absolute silence that blankets the prison. My already wound-up nerves tighten even more as we make our way to Leonis's room at the very end of the hall. The guard stops outside.

"After Leonis changes into less conspicuous clothing, we'll escort you out of the prison to a waiting hoverboat, and then to your ship," he says. "An outfit of guards will be riding on board with you, in case we encounter any trouble along the way. However, close combat is a last resort."

"A whole outfit of guards, just for me?" I ask, feigning amazement. "Wow. I'm touched."

The man stares at me, that wrinkle forming between his brows again. "They're not for you, ma'am. They're for the prisoner."

"That's..." I blow out a breath, deflating. "It's a joke."

"I would prefer not to joke about matters of planetary security, ma'am."

"Stars above, this is gonna be a long trip," I mutter—and the prison shakes around us. Somewhere above us, there is the muffled but unmistakable sound of an explosion.

I yelp and press myself against the wall. It places me right next to a window with an ample view of the ocean depths outside, and I brace myself, expecting water to come pouring down on our heads and drown us down here. It doesn't, but I still know we're far from safe if the prison is under attack.

Especially since this place's whole purpose is to trap people inside.

My heart pounds even louder than the alarm that begins to wail. Guards from elsewhere in the prison all rush to their stations, with only the one at my side remaining unmoving.

"The Titans are here? Now?" I ask, my voice strained. I really have the worst fucking luck. I'm guessing the "only one way in or out" design didn't account for full-scale military attacks against the prison. "There has to be an emergency exit for the guards, right?"

"There's only one way to evacuate this place," he says, and turns to the keypad, typing in a code. The door to Leonis's cell slides open, with a hiss from the air lock. "Get in."

"What?" I ask dumbly as the second door opens as well, revealing the tiny interior of the cell, with an alarmed-looking Talulah Leonis sitting on her cot. "Get in? With her?"

Down the hall, laser-fire echoes off the prison walls. The Titans must have forced their way down the elevator shaft already. But I hesitate, unwilling to trap myself in a tiny place with Leonis, of all people. If I'm gonna die here, I want to die with a blaster in my hand, not drown with *that* woman.

"Just let me—"

The guard shoves me hard, sending me stumbling into the cell. "Safest place to be right now," he says, and hits the button to lock the cell again. All sound, including the ear-shattering scream of the alarm, is sucked out of the room.

"No, wait!" I scramble to my feet and lurch forward, but both doors have slammed shut, sealing us in. "Shit. *Shit.*" I bang a fist against the metal door and suck in a shaky breath. It feels like the room is closing in on me, the weight of the ocean overhead crushing me beneath it. I rest my forehead against the door, fighting back panic.

After a stretch of silence, Leonis says, "Trust me, I'm not entirely pleased with the situation, either."

I grit my teeth and turn. Dressed in a prison-green shirt and slacks, with her hair tied back in a simple bun, Leonis looks hardly anything like the severe president I remember. She looks old. The lines in her face run deeper, and the bags beneath her eyes are heavier. Everything about her seems a little... smaller, somehow. I don't feel a single ounce of pity for the woman, but it's hard to remember why I was so intimidated by her, once.

We stare at each other for a few moments. I wonder what she sees when she looks at me. I was just a smuggler last time we met. Now, I'm doing official work for the Nibiran government, and dressed to fit the part. It gives me a small surge of pride, even given the circumstances.

"I was wondering when I'd see you again," she says.

I force a smile at her. "If I had known how pathetic you look, I would've come to visit a lot earlier."

"I'm sure you'll get your due soon as well, smuggler scum."

Once, her words might've cut me, but now I only roll my eyes and turn back to the door. I press an ear against it, trying to gauge what's going on outside, but I can't hear a single thing through the air lock.

"Ugh," I say, straightening up again. My heart is still pounding, but I'm not going to let Leonis have the satisfaction of seeing me scared. "This prison is a lot better designed than the ones you Gaian morons had."

"Ours were more temporary. We knew how to properly dispose of criminals."

"Still proud of that, even though you're the criminal now?" I raise my eyebrows at her. "Your hypocrisy really knows no bounds, huh?"

"I'm not ashamed of what I did to get here, and I will gladly take whatever punishment I receive for it." She's still smiling, and I would very much like to punch the expression off her face, but I know I throw terrible punches. "I saved my people. Nothing anyone can do to me will ever make me regret that."

"No, *you* very nearly led your people into a war that would've gotten them, and the whole system, killed." As hard as I'm willing myself not to let her get to me, my voice is growing heated now. "Even if you had taken Nibiru by force, you would've had no chance against the Titans now without the help of the Nibirans.

339

So, really, me and my family are the ones who saved your people." I give an exaggerated bow. "You're welcome," I say, and, unable to help myself, add, "bitch."

Leonis regards me with the same cool, clinical gaze, but at least she keeps her mouth shut now. I pace the tiny cell, glancing around the room to see if anything could be useful if the Titans break in here. But of course, the cell is stripped bare to contain the dangerous prisoners it's meant to hold. There's barely enough room for me to walk three steps before I have to turn around.

"I have to admit," Leonis says after a minute of silence, "when they told me I was being transported, I assumed that was a polite way to mean 'execution.' But I suppose they would have sent your mad dog of a brother for that."

I grit my teeth but don't allow my pacing to falter. Can't let her see a reaction. "Trust me, if it were up to me, you would be getting an execution."

"But I'm not. I suppose that means the Nibirans have use for me yet."

"You're meant to be put on trial by the Interplanetary Council, remember? Due process, and all that. And the Nibirans have standards, unlike you."

Leonis lets out a small laugh. "So you're a Nibiran lapdog now, are you? I suppose I shouldn't be surprised. I've seen how easy it is to buy your loyalty."

I open my mouth to fire back, and instead let out a startled squeak as the room lurches around me. I grab on to the nearest piece of furniture—the edge of Leonis's cot—and look around in bewilderment. "What the hell was that?"

Leonis says nothing, but hunkers down in her bed, a hint of fear on her usually stoic face enough to make me start to panic. Outside, I hear the hiss of the air lock.

"What are you—" I ask, and yelp as the floor rushes up to

meet my face. I'm plastered across the floor of the cell, screaming, before I know what's happening, unable to even raise my head as the entire cell shoots upward through the water. It takes me a few seconds to realize what's happening through my panic. We're heading up to the surface. The prison is being evacuated, just like it was when we broke Orion and Izra out of here. But unlike that time, the people waiting on the other side aren't going to be freeing us. They're going to drag us straight to the chopping block.

As we break the surface, I struggle to my feet with a gasp. The cell is bobbing on the waves now, and the floor rocks and rolls beneath my feet. I grab on to a wall to stay upright, and make my way over to the door, banging a fist against it. There's no point, of course. It's still impossible to get free or tell what's going on outside. We won't know what's coming for us until they're here.

"Shit," I say, turning away from the door. "Shit, shit, shit."

"Not a pleasant experience, is it?" Leonis asks, still in bed, looking extremely ill.

"It's about to get a lot less so. Damn it, we're sitting ducks in here."

"I suppose you should be pleased with yourself," she says. "Dying trapped in a place like this next to scum like you is one of the worst fates I can possibly imagine."

"It's not exactly on my preferred list of ways to go down, either. Now shut up and let me figure a way out of this." I lean back against the sealed door—resisting the urge to bang my head against it in frustration—and squeeze my eyes shut. The feeling of being trapped here is half-familiar, an echo of times I've been locked up on Gaia. But rather than making me freeze, the thought is soothing. I got out those times. I can do it again now. "You have anything that could pass for a weapon?" I ask, opening my eyes again.

There's a long pause. "I've been locked in prison," Leonis says. "How would I possibly get my hands on a weapon?"

I let out a small groan. "You're a terrible criminal." I survey the cell, hoping there's something Leonis has missed, but she appears to be right. There's nothing even close to useful. Everything's bolted to the floor except for her thin blanket and lumpy pillow.

As a grating sound comes from the other side of the door, I lurch away from the metal and let out another string of curses. Time's up; they're already here, cutting through fast by the sound of it, which means they're definitely not prison guards here to rescue us. And I still have absolutely nothing to work with.

Except, of course, my own bullshit.

"Your clothes," I say, already starting to wrestle my own shirt off. "Swap me. Now."

"What? Why should I—"

"You wanna die in here?" I snap at her.

She stares a moment longer, and then grudgingly begins to undress. I wriggle out of my own clothes and throw on her prison uniform, which is thankfully loose and shapeless enough that it fits me decently, aside from the too-short pants.

"Get under the bed," I tell her. "Now. I don't have time to explain."

She scowls but lowers herself to the floor without complaint.

"Faster, old woman," I say. "Unless you wanna wait for the Titans to cut their way in."

She shoots me a dour look, and crawls beneath the bed just moments before there's a sudden screech of metal, and the door rips free from its hinges. I whirl around to face the new, gaping hole in the wall, stumbling backward a few steps. At first there's nothing but a tinted visor, but then a uniformed Titan steps into my line of sight. They stare at me wordlessly for a moment before yanking their helmet away to reveal a plain-faced young woman with a thick scar across her nose.

"Who the hell are you?" she asks. Past her, I hear snatches of shouting and laser-fire carried by the wind, signs of a struggle over the prison—but I try to ignore it. I need to concentrate on the trouble right in front of me first.

Fear radiates through every cell of my body, but I force on a scowl instead of showing it. "Who the hell am I?" I ask loudly. "You're the one cutting into *my* cell!" I take a step forward and fold my arms across my chest, desperately hoping that I'm a big enough distraction and Leonis did a good enough job of hiding herself under the bed for this woman not to look too closely. "This a jailbreak or something?"

The woman's eyes narrow. She turns to shout over her shoulder, "Leonis isn't here!"

"What?" answers a voice—a voice so familiar that I'm glad the Titan is distracted enough to miss my gasp. "This was her cell, I know it was—"

Orion steps into view. His face mirrors my own shock. We both stare at each other, while I try to conjure up anger at seeing him again, but can only manage to find relief that he's still alive, and a wrenching sadness when I notice the war-brand tattooed on his wrist.

"You two know one another?" the Titan woman asks, her eyes narrowing in suspicion. She gives me another, harder once-over. "You do look familiar..."

There's no time to think too hard about this. "Yes, we know each other," I say, my voice coming out a croak. I clear my throat and try again. "We were crewmates on the *Red Baron*," I say, giving Orion a pointed look. "We were locked up together here. Can't believe you left us behind, old friend."

He pauses. The Titan woman glances back and forth between us. My heartbeat is loud in my ears. This is it. Orion knows what I'm trying to do. Now he either goes along with lying to the Titans—in a way that might come back to bite him later—or turns me in. He's already betrayed me once; what's stopping him from doing it again?

Orion gives me a long, steady look. "Hey, you would've made the same choice in my shoes," he says. "But it wasn't personal. I hope you know that."

It's all I can do to stop my shoulders from sagging with relief... both because he's decided to go along with what I'm saying, and because it's impossible to miss the double meaning in his words. I swallow a lump in my throat and manage a semi-watery smile and nod. "Well. Now I do."

Orion clears his throat, glancing at the Titan woman and back at me. "So...what are you doing in Leonis's cell?"

"Is *that* why they moved me in here?" I ask. "The guards swapped me over a few days ago."

"So Leonis is where, exactly?" the Titan woman asks, bristly with impatience.

"I don't know." I shrug. "Heard they might be moving her to Lan Iroh."

"There's a military bunker there," Orion says, nodding. "It makes sense. They knew she was a target."

My heart warms a little, even as it aches at the same time; just the two of us, sharing a lie on opposite sides again. Maybe this is where we're always meant to be.

"Shit," the Titan woman says. "Stars damn it, we don't have time for this." She jumps off the cell, speaking rapidly into her comm. Orion and I remain where we are, staring at each other.

"I'm going to Deva," I say, quickly and quietly. "Come with me."

He glances over his shoulder at the Titan soldier, hesitates, and shakes his head. "I can't," he says. "If I go with you, they'll just follow us." He points at the war-brand on his wrist and half smiles. "Don't think they're ever going to let me back there now, anyway."

I bite the inside of my cheek, wishing there was a way to make this work, and keep him with me. But the Titan is shouting at him to go. "All right," I say, after a moment. "Be safe."

"Maybe we can have a drink when this is all over," he says, wistfully.

"Maybe," I agree, though I know neither of us really believes it.

As the Titans retreat, Leonis crawls out from her hiding space and stands up, brushing herself off with as much dignity as she can manage. Now that it's all over she looks rather shell-shocked.

I straighten up as well and lean against the wall. My heart is still pounding, making me unable to completely relax, but I'm grinning anyway. Leonis frowns up at me.

"You saved my life," she says.

My smile vanishes. "No," I say. "I saved *my* life, and stopped a valuable pawn"—I gesture at her—"from falling into Titan hands. So if you're thinking about thanking me, you can fuck right off."

"Still," she says, scrutinizing me. "You could've killed me yourself. That's what you want, isn't it? It's certainly what your mongrel of a brother would've done."

I step forward, my hands clenching at my sides. "Call my brother that again, and I just might," I say. "But I'm not here to kill you. I'm here to transport you. Like I said, you're not even a person to me anymore—you're a pawn. A product that needs to be smuggled elsewhere. So that's what I'm going to do." I consider her, pursing my lips in thought. "But I'm *definitely* going to need to gag you for the trip."

CHAPTER THIRTY-FIVE

Infiltration

Corvus

A mile out from the burnt husk of Kitaya, my team and I slip off the boat and beneath the surface, each of us making only the tiniest splash as we hit the water. My wetsuit absorbs most of the shock of the cold, but I'm still uncomfortably aware of the water all around me, and how very alone we are out here in the great ocean as the hoverboat speeds back toward land. Just like the last time I wore a wetsuit, I can't help but be aware of how easily laser-fire would shred me... and my team, as it did the first time.

But I have to shake that off. This is a stealth mission, not a combat one, and there's no reason I should lose anyone today if I do this right. I regulate my breathing, and once I'm sure I can stay calm, I signal the others and kick off in the direction of the Titan base, following the directions on the electronic map built into my suit's arm.

We swim another mile away from the nearest landmass before I signal everyone to stop. They spread out wordlessly around me, keeping their movements still and controlled. This team is better trained than my last one, but it's hard for me to have much confidence when I wasn't even granted enough time to learn their names. But maybe that will make it easier than last time.

I hear the muffled thumps of the approaching hoverboat's motor before my suit's radar notes it, and signal everyone to prepare. We gather and wait as the Titan vessel draws closer, until its silhouette blots out the sun. Still, I hold my fist up to signal *wait*. When the boat is directly overhead, I drop my fist. We all surge upward at once. A few feet below the boat, I press the button on the inside of my gloves, and needle-thin hooks emerge from each fingertip. I surface, and reach out to the vessel hovering about a foot above the water. When I press my fingers to it, the hooks snag in the bottom of the ship. For a moment it feels like the vessel's speed is going to rip my arms from their sockets—but then my feet hit and attach as well, and I press myself flat against the bottom of the boat to reduce drag as much as possible. Slowly, my body adjusts to the movement and my stomach stops roiling. Once I'm certain I'm steady, I check to make sure my team made it as well. Three dots blink on the hull around me, and I breathe a sigh of relief that echoes in my helmet.

I can tell we're getting close when I hear the sound: that familiar warbling from Govender's recording, recognizable and even more disturbing in person. My helmet should distort the sound, but it doesn't seem to. However, the comm in my ear crackles with static as we get closer, making it impossible to communicate with my team and confirming my fears: This is Primus technology we're dealing with.

As the hoverboat eases to a stop, I stay still despite my stiff and aching muscles screaming for release. The boat lowers into the water, and I detach and let myself sink. The rest of my team follows suit, even without my verbal order. We wait below. With the comms system down, I worry how we're supposed to know when the Nibirans cause the distraction meant to allow us to infiltrate the base.

But I have nothing to worry over. The explosion is loud enough for us to hear it clearly beneath the waves, shaking the boat above us and the facility beyond. The Titan hoverboat peels off in the direction it came from. After another few minutes of waiting, I kick up to the surface and haul myself over the edge of the dock.

The facility is smaller than I expected. It's just another ship, a scouting vessel from the look of it, simply designed and not built to hold more than a few teams of soldiers. But this one is mostly empty—the majority of its occupants must have gone to investigate the Nibirans' distraction. My team quickly dispatches the remaining few, and I leave them behind to keep an eye out while I push deeper into the facility. The presence of whatever technology this facility holds will cut off the enemy's communications as well as our own. It will be harder for them to find out what's happening, but also harder for me to find out if things go wrong for us.

But there's no time to consider that. The best thing I can do is finish this, quickly, and get out again. I don't want to lose anyone this time. So I rush forward, following that strange, building sound. I'm lucky not to encounter anyone else along the way. But my worry mounts as I find nothing but empty hallways and nearly bare rooms, personal quarters and supplies, nothing indicating what makes this location so important to the Titans.

Until I step into the ship's cargo bay.

As the door slides open, the cold strikes me first. Once, it was familiar to watch small clouds form in front of me with each breath; now, it shocks me to realize exactly how far the temperature has dropped in one step, slicing right through my wetsuit. I pause before continuing onward.

The second thing to strike me is the noise. Here, it echoes off the metal walls. The first time I heard it, I thought it sounded like three voices singing together. This close, I feel as though I can discern the three threads of sound even more, hear them wavering together and apart, together and apart, over and over again, overlapping for barely a moment before separating out again. Dread washes over me in similar waves, always reaching its peak right as the sounds begin to overlap, only to retreat with slight relief again. As though my body knows something that my mind doesn't understand yet. As though it fears something I haven't even begun to comprehend.

I want, more than anything, to turn and walk away. To escape whatever this is. But I force my feet to keep moving toward the railing, and look over, down into the main hold of the cargo bay.

I'm not sure how I would describe it even if I tried. Something...something almost like flesh—a hideous, quivering mass of it, which expands and contracts as I watch, one moment a dense orb and the next spreading across the floor in a seeping puddle, then back to an orb, making the transitions in flickering, impossible motions. It looks as though it's struggling to break free from something, though it has no walls around it that I can perceive.

I slowly move down the stairs toward it, trying to memorize as many details as I can, even though merely looking at it makes my mind reel. It's pale, off-white, but with a multicolored sheen where the light hits it. I've seen that shifting color before—in the vials that my family transported, the ones holding a bio-weapon that ended most life on Titan.

Did they bring a Primus weapon here, after one was used to destroy their planet? After they saw how quickly the use of one could spiral out of control? No. They couldn't have...Altair never would have agreed. He always claimed to loathe Primus technology.

But he never authorized the slaughter of innocent civilians when I fought under his command, either. Yet Kitaya still stands a graveyard, and a testament that perhaps I never really knew the general at all. In the end it seems I was another victim of Titan propaganda, just as brainwashed as Izra accused me of being. I cannot assume that anything I think I know about Altair is correct now.

But I need further proof before I report to the council. I need to make sure that I'm right. I pass across the room to a computer, a high-tech hologram device. No amount of tapping the screen or fiddling with the controls produces any effect. It's locked. The Nibirans gave me a Gaian-made device that may be able to force its way through the security, but it will take time. And it won't take long for the Titans to discover that the explosion was a diversion.

Before I can further scrutinize the computer, a nearby door opens. The man who walks through is tall and pale in the way of most Titans, dressed in military gear but unarmed. I raise my gun to his head, and he freezes, hands held aloft.

"You work here?" I ask. He looks at the brand on my wrist, his expression perplexed. I step closer and jam the gun against his skull. "Answer me."

"Y-yes," he says, his eyes finally meeting mine. "I'm a scientist. Not a soldier. Please, don't shoot."

"Do as I say, and I won't." I grab him by the shoulder and shove him over to the computer. "Unlock it."

"I don't—"

"I can do it with or without you, but only one way ends with you still breathing."

The man looks at me, quaking slightly beneath my gun, perhaps trying to assess the truth in my statement. After a moment's pause, his fingers find the keyboard and unlock it with his fingerprints. I shove him down to his knees and take control of the device, flipping through a few files before reaching into my pack for a comm and plugging it into the computer.

I watch the files flicker across the screen as they load onto the device. Most of it doesn't make any sense to me—numbers, charts, spreadsheets—but hopefully will mean something to the Nibirans who sift through it. Some phrases, however, catch my eye: Detonation. Blast radius. Fallout zone.

It's a bomb. A Primus bomb.

After all of Altair's talk of justice, he intends to do the very same thing Leonis did to his planet? Even not knowing about the Planetary Defense Systems, he has to understand what a threat Primus technology is after he saw its devastating use on his own planet. He knows exactly the kind of destruction a weapon like this could wreak. How could he do this? Especially if he plans to take the planet for his own people? I can't comprehend it. Something in the back of my mind insists that this can't be right, that this isn't the man Altair is...but I can't deny the evidence that's staring me in the face. And I've been wrong before. I can't be blinded by loyalty again.

As I try to process it, an alarm begins to blare, dousing the room in green light and drowning out the odd song of the thing in this room. I tear my eyes away from the computer and find the Titan scientist has moved while my attention was caught; his fingers are pressed to a panel hidden on the side of the computer. He meets my eyes with a steely gaze.

"For Titan," he says, any sign of his former quaking gone.

I could shoot him. Perhaps I should. But I can't bring myself to fire on an unarmed man; not this time. I rip the cord out of the computer, praying it downloaded enough proof for the Nibirans, and shove it into my bag before running for the door.

I race out of the facility, joining up with the rest of my team as I move. We've almost made it to the exit when a Titan soldier comes in from the outside, weapon drawn. Not an exosuited soldier—just a boy in body armor.

My soldiers open fire, but the boy retreats behind the door for cover, raising one armored arm to defend his face. He opens his mouth to shout an alarm, and I lunge forward, pulling my knife and slashing it across his throat in one smooth motion. He lets out a choked gurgle, falling to his knees, warm blood spurting out against me. His hand gives a final twitch before he goes still; the war-brand stares up at me from his wrist like an accusation. The same mark that mine bears.

The soldier in the exosuit chose to die by their own volition; this is the first Titan I've killed with my own two hands. Before now, it was easy not to think about the consequences of my actions, the people dying because of them. Too easy, I think now, looking down at the body. This soldier is so young. He didn't understand what he was dying for, only what he was told to do.

"Sir?" one of my own soldiers calls to me, pulling me back to the present. I nod at him and force myself to move ahead. The rest of the Titans are coming this way fast, their boat racing toward our location. I'm relieved not to have to fight anymore. We slip into the water and begin the long swim toward our rendezvous point. That boy's face lingers in my mind—but soon enough, it's replaced by the memory of that pulsing, terrible thing we found in the base.

Long after we leave the threshold of the effects of the alien technology, the comms stay silent. My team knows better than to ask questions I won't have any answers to. And while I can't explain what I just saw, I know that all of us understand, on a deep and primal level, that what we found is something worse than we could've imagined.

What we saw is a way to end this world.

CHAPTER THIRTY-SIX

To the Stars

Scorpia

I t takes at least an hour for the Nibiran military to chase the Titans away from Ca Sineh, but finally peacekeepers pick up Leonis and me from the cell, shuffle us inside an armored hovercraft, and take us toward the waiting ship. Outside, I can still hear the fight raging between the Nibiran and Titan forces, but being in an armored vehicle feels leagues safer than floating out in that cell. I sit in the back of the vehicle, while Leonis has a peacekeeper on either side, keeping her firmly restrained. Even amid all this chaos, it still gives me some petty satisfaction to see her treated as a criminal while I'm free.

We make it to *Memoria* without trouble, but the peacekeepers rush us inside, and when I spare a glance at the horizon I see that more Titans are on their way. They must have caught on to our plan. I hope Orion won't be held responsible. No matter what transpired between us, our encounter reassured me that we're still friends, in the end.

I'm surprised how good it feels to step onto *Memoria*. We only made one trip in this ship, and I still stand by the fact that she's fairly hideous, but she's grown on me. And regardless of how our last trip ended, I still have some good memories starting to replace the old, bloody ones: of dinner in the mess hall, laughing with Orion in the kitchen, spending nights with Shey in the captain's quarters.

The big ship feels empty now, with only Lyre and Pol waiting for me in the cargo bay. Everyone else is staying, pursuing their own paths.

I force on a smile for my little siblings, pulling them both in for a hug. Pol looks like he's been crying, and Lyre's face is scrunched up like she's trying very hard not to.

"Hey, hey, wipe those looks off your faces," I say, ruffling Pol's hair. "This isn't forever. And it's gonna be fun. It's our first time having a bona fide ex-president-turned-felon on board!" I glance over at the peacekeepers taking Leonis into the spare room we're using as a brig, and lean close to my siblings to whisper, "We can totally throw food at her for fun."

"Captain Kaiser?" one of the peacekeepers says, returning from dropping Leonis off. "The prisoner is secure. We need to go immediately—"

The rest of his sentence is drowned out by an explosion outside. It's close enough to rock the ship, and I stumble, barely keeping my feet. The peacekeepers race out onto the dock and begin to exchange fire with an enemy I can't see. The Titans must be here, already, faster than we expected.

I step forward, ready to join the fight, but one of the peacekeepers shakes her head at me.

"You need to go," she says. "Proceed with the plan. We'll hold them off here."

"What? But—" I stop with a gasp as the peacekeeper takes a stomach full of laser-fire, and lurches forward to fall, facedown, on the dock. I stumble backward, hesitate for a moment—but there's no point in trying to figure out a better plan. People are dying every second that I wait, and I can't let their sacrifices be in vain. I slap the button to close the ramp, then head toward the cockpit. Looks like it's just the three of us. I'm not sure if it's possible to run a ship with a crew this small, but we'll have to do our best. "You heard them," I say. "Pol, go strap in for launch. Lyre, with me."

We race to the cockpit and take our respective chairs. I can't even savor the joy of being behind a wheel again, because I can see the Titan force just outside of my viewing panel, and it's clear at a glance that there are far too many of them for the Nibirans to handle. The peacekeeper was right. We have no choice but to go, even though it means leaving them behind to be slaughtered.

Luckily for us, the Titans don't have anything capable of damaging a ship. As the ship begins to rise, they turn their fire on us, but the shots ping uselessly against our hull, and we launch skyward. All around, additional ships rise to join us: our doomed escort. There are disk-like Nibiran ships, more angular Gaian ones, a mismatched variety of spacecrafts all acting as our living shield.

As we break atmosphere, my instincts scream at me to push forward and race for freedom. But I hold the ship back instead, keeping pace with the slower ships. They surround *Memoria* in a tight formation as we launch toward open space. I brace myself as I see the Titan ships beginning to circle toward us on the radar. They're not even bothering to cloak themselves. Maybe they want us to see them coming.

Yet somehow it still comes as a shock when they take down the first Nibiran ship. I gasp as I see the disk-shaped vessel dive in front of us to take a shot. It breaks apart, torn clean in half by the Titan weaponry. The fleet around us quickly shifts to cover the gap, but soon another ship goes down. And another. There is a flurry of motion all around us as the other ships intercept each shot the Titans try to lock on to *Memoria*. I try not to think of how many people are on board; autopilot could never move with a reaction time like that, especially not on ships that old. Those are living, breathing pilots sacrificing their lives for this mission.

"Is this supposed to happen?" Lyre asks in a small voice. I had almost forgotten she was here beside me, no doubt internally panicking about having to copilot for me.

I shake off my horror and try to sound reassuring. "Yes. This is what they're here for. We're still okay." Not that it makes me feel any better. More lives lost for me. For Leonis. I swallow hard, trying to calm the riot of emotions in my chest.

"That ship on the left," Lyre says. "They're getting too close—"

"They'll correct their course. It's fine."

"And the wind is shifting, we need to—"

"I've already got it. Lyre. Relax." I take a deep breath. I'm already tightly wound enough without my sister's freaking out making it worse. "Hey, Shey's leading some kind of demonstration today," I say without looking up from my controls. "Could you see if you can find a broadcast?"

"Of course I can, but—"

"Play it."

"I really don't think now is the time. Don't you need to concentrate?"

"What I really need right now is to not think about what's happening out there." I tear my eyes away from the viewing panel, just for a second, so she can read the plea on my face. "Play it."

The ship shudders as another craft explodes, a piece of shrapnel scraping against our side. I grit my teeth and fight to keep us steady. I don't have time to glance at Lyre again, but she must do something, because a couple minutes later an image flickers to life on one of our screens. I only get one glance at it—Shey standing in a field of red flowers, surrounded by a crowd of other Gaians—before I have to focus again, but it's enough to ease some of the tightness in my chest. While I focus on the wheel, her voice begins to play over the speakers.

"It would be easy to say we are not responsible for what happened to Titan," Shey begins, and the sound of her voice brings an ache to my chest as I think of how far away she is now, and getting farther still. I'm leaving her. Or she left me. It doesn't matter now, I guess; in the end, we've been pulled apart, like we always seem to be. "It is true that none but a small circle of my mother's cabinet members knew what she had planned, and fewer still had a direct hand in it."

A failing Gaian vessel slams into a Titan warship, and they both go down. More ships fall around us in bursts of brilliant fire. A piece of one slams into our side, but I keep us steady and focus on Shey's voice.

"But that does not mean we are free from blame. I and many others turned a blind eye to my mother's hatred. We voted her into power. We did not question her beliefs or push back against her policies. We stayed quiet, and that means we cannot be truly considered blameless.

"So today I am no longer staying quiet. Today I choose to speak up, and to confront our past mistakes. Because if we bury them, if we forget them, then we are setting ourselves up to repeat them."

The ship shudders around us as a shot breaks through, and *Memoria* takes her first direct hit. "Shit," I mutter.

"One of our landing mechanisms was damaged," Lyre says.

"That's fine. That's a problem for later. We're almost there."

"We cannot change the past," Shey continues, and again I cling to her voice like an anchor, even as the broadcast crackles faintly, losing its quality as we draw farther from Nibiru. "We cannot fix our mistakes. But we can look at them, honestly and openly, and promise that we will not forget them, nor allow them to happen again. To General Altair, and to all Titans, I would like to say: I am sorry. I am sorry for what you have suffered, and for my silence that allowed it."

I glance over at the screen again and—blinking away tears—see Shey holding out her hands, palms up, in a gesture of apology. All around her, the movement ripples through the crowd, as the camera moves back to reveal hundreds, thousands of Gaians mirroring the gesture. Thousands of the proudest people in the system, offering their apologies and condolences to the Titan survivors.

She listened. She really listened. Maybe it's far too late for it to make any difference, but it feels like it matters. Like she's proving people can listen to one another, and change, and do better, even in the middle of a war like this.

And there, ahead of us: open space. There's nothing between us and Deva. I crank up our speed and let loose, our ship surging ahead of both the last struggling Nibirans and the Titan ships closing in on us, and I let out a whoop of excitement as we fly toward open space. Toward Deva, and the promise of freedom, and safety.

And away from the war. From Shey. And Corvus, Drom, Orion, Izra…so many people I care about still trapped down there, still fighting, whether it's on the front lines like my siblings or with words of peace like Shey. Or those like Orion and Izra, just doing their best to survive in a world where they have no place.

The rush of seeing stars ahead of me fades quickly, and I sink down in my chair as we pull farther and farther away. As much as I've been trying to convince myself that this will be worth it, and we can come back for everyone, it hurts to think about how we've left half of our family—and more than half of our crew, the people so close to my heart—behind.

CHAPTER THIRTY-SEVEN

Last Resort

Corvus

Standing in the middle of a silent Council Hall, I describe the alien horror we found in the Titans' possession. Words could never do it justice—couldn't properly convey the icy terror that pulses through my veins even speaking of it—but, judging from the somber expressions on the councillors, I convey the gravity of the situation effectively enough.

"We can only assume the worst: that it's a weapon, and a weapon capable of enough damage to trigger the planet's defense system, if not to wipe us out by itself," I finish.

The room is quiet. The councillors bow their heads and avoid looking at one another, or at me. President Khatri sits in the seat that Oshiro once occupied, her hands bare. She keeps hiding them in her lap, clearly uncomfortable with having them exposed.

"Well," says Govender. "We have only one option. We must end this now."

"And how would you suggest we do that?" Heikki asks. "If it were that simple, we would have done it already."

"No, we would not have, because we know the cost of it. We did our best to avoid it. We thought a long war would work in our benefit, so we have been content to let it drag out, surrendering time and land to preserve lives. But we can no longer rely on starving them out, not with a threat this immediate and severe. Now, it is the time for us to push back. We throw everything we have at them."

"The only fights we've won are those we choose when and where to fight," Heikki argues. "We exercise caution and use our advantages: our knowledge of our world, our superiority in water combat and skirmishes rather than all-out battles. If we attack them on their own grounds, on their own terms, we give up all of that. We will lose."

"We do have one other advantage: our numbers. We will overwhelm them through the sheer mass of our forces." Govender looks around the room. "We already suspect that we vastly overestimated the Titans' numbers initially due to their mobility. If they're as thinly spread among the ships as we now believe, they have no chance of withstanding an all-out attack."

"Yet we also know how many lives it takes to destroy a single exosuit, if we aren't fighting them over water. We know that many of our forces are still untrained, unorganized. They break rank in the face of Titan intimidation, and we don't even have enough supplies to properly equip them. If what you're suggesting is possible, it would be a hard-earned victory. We would lose many."

"Yes," Govender agrees. "Many. But not all. And not our planet itself. That is the reality that we face if we do not find a way to stop the Titans from using this weapon."

The entire room descends into stunned silence. I feel rooted in place as I realize what Govender is arguing for. I've seen the statistics for how many soldiers we lose for every one of theirs we take down. In a head-on battle, our forces would suffer unimaginable losses.

But no one proposes an alternate idea. The silence stretches on, and one by one, the faces of the councillors shift to resignation. It isn't my place to speak. I should consider myself lucky that they haven't asked me to leave already. But surely someone has to speak up. Someone has to push back against this rather than silently accepting it.

Instead, Acharya only breaks the silence to ask, "How soon can we make our preparations?"

"The Titans know we saw the weapon," Govender says. "We will have to proceed immediately."

"Surely this cannot be the only way," I say, before this can go any further. "There is still time to try for peace."

"Peace?" Govender repeats scathingly, and I'm surprised how much her tone burns me. We've spent much of the last couple weeks working together, but now she looks at me coldly. "The Titans threaten us with an alien weapon of mass destruction, and you suggest peace? Altair threw our suggested peace proposal at our feet, and you expect us to grovel before him once again?"

"I expect you to do whatever is possible to save your people," I snap back, unable to contain my anger, though I know it won't help me. This feels like a betrayal, though it shouldn't. "Give them a home on this planet. Give them Leonis. Give them whatever it takes to stop this before it's too late to turn back."

"It is already too late," Govender says. "We tried to offer them a home, and you saw with your own eyes how that went. If we offer Leonis to their barbaric idea of justice, they will know the truth about the Planetary Defense Systems, and Deva and Pax will turn on us. We don't have time to waste trying to make peace with these people when they have proven, over and over, that they have no intent of accepting it. The Titans are monstrous."

361

"The Titans could not even manage to make peace among themselves, when the rest of them still lived," Heikki says. "How can we expect them to do any better with us? Especially with the Gaians involved? We have a duty to our allies, and to our own people, to protect them."

Around the room, the other councillors nod and murmur their assent. Govender is winning them over, one by one. And how can I hope to convince them? How is it possible when they've lost their people and their homes—and when it's so much easier to believe the enemy is a monster?

"Thank you, Specialist Kaiser, for your briefing and your input," Govender says, finally. "That will be all for today. I trust you know to keep this matter private until we reach a final decision."

It's clear from their faces that they already have, but all I can do is bow my head and accept it.

Govender walks me out of the council room. I can barely look at her. Anger and grief battle within me, but I stay silent. I've done what I can. Now there's nothing I can do but await orders, as I always do. Scorpia was right—I've fallen back into my old habits without even realizing it. And now I'm in too deep to dig myself out. I need to see this through to the end.

But I also need to find out the truth, if I can.

"We need to know as much as possible about this weapon before the attack happens," I say. "Do you have any captives I can interrogate?"

"Live soldiers have proved enormously difficult for us to capture," she says, which isn't a no. I wait, and she folds her hands in front of her. "I would have to ask for assurance that your...interrogation...would not end with a body on our hands."

My stomach rolls with revulsion as I realize what she's saying.

She thinks I want to torture a captive—and, again, she's not saying no. That speaks volumes not only about her, but of what she thinks of me. *The Titans are monstrous*—and, clearly, she still thinks of me as one of them. Still a vicious animal, just a trained one. A useful one. Whatever faith I had left in her disappears in an instant, but I keep my face neutral. "You have my assurance."

"Then I will arrange it. I doubt you'll get anything useful. We've tried everything we can, you understand, but they've given us nothing." Some hint of what I feel must show on my face, because she adds, "We had to do everything we could to find out the Titans' plans. I would never allow this otherwise, but...if you could find something out, it would prevent an unimaginable amount of violence and death."

"One life versus millions."

"Precisely."

I tell myself that she's right. That torturing a Titan soldier would be justified, if it gets us the information we need. That lives can be measured and weighed against one another like any other number. But somehow all I can think of is the look in Izra's eye when she told me how the Titans used her own anger against her to turn her into a weapon. How I knew she was telling the truth when she told me I hated her for being strong enough to walk away, when I never was. When I did every terrible thing the Titans told me to do and convinced myself I couldn't be held responsible for it.

Now, I think back to Scorpia's words, and wonder if she was right. If I've walked into the same situation once again. Part of me wants to leave now, wash my hands of this. But if I do, they will ask someone else. Someone with no reason to sympathize with the Titans. Someone who will say yes without thinking twice about it.

So it has to be me.

*   *   *

Govender escorts me by hovercraft to a nearby military facility, and bids me farewell as the elevator carries me down into the bowels of the building. It's sterile and cold down here, all featureless metal walls and no windows, eerily reminiscent of similar buildings on Titan.

The room they take me to is small—no windows, one door, no furniture but two chairs in the middle of the room. The Titan prisoner waits in one of them.

I can't even bring myself to call the soldier strapped to the chair a man. He's barely more than a boy, with only the faintest hint of fuzz on his pale face. The boyishness is only exacerbated by how thin he is, his cheeks hollow and his collarbone jutting out beneath his green prison garb. Fair, greasy hair hangs across one of his eyes, and the other—a striking blue—tracks me as I enter the room. When I stop in front of him, his eyes drop from my face to the brand on my wrist, and recognition flits across his face, followed quickly by disgust. He spits on the floor, narrowly missing my shoe.

I try to conjure up a similar hatred for him, but I can't. I only feel pity. "Is that any way to greet a fellow Titan?"

"You're no Titan." He leans back in his chair, flipping his hair out of his face to give me the full strength of his glare. "I know who you are, traitor."

I pull up a chair and flip through his file on my comm. The whole time I can feel his eyes on me, pure venom in his glare.

According to his file, he's been a prisoner for just short of one week...nothing close enough to justify him becoming this thin. It's not a product of being a prisoner, then. He was going hungry long before this.

Despite that, according to the file, he's been rejecting food ever since he arrived. Resisting to the point that Nibirans had to hold him down and force-feed him just to keep him alive. Even then, he tried to force himself to throw it up. He wants to die. According to their notes, the Nibirans find it a tragic side effect of Titan military training. That he believes his life is worthless now that he is a prisoner, and that he wants to die out of some sense of nobility. But I see something else. I see a boy who is desperately trying to end his life, and quickly, before he loses his willpower.

I see a boy who knows something, and is trying to die before it can be forced out of him.

I lower the file. "Arkadi Vogel?"

"That's *Sergeant* Vogel," he snarls at me. I almost laugh, but his expression is deadly serious. I look from his face to the file again.

"Sergeant? How old are you?" I ask, incredulous. He keeps his mouth shut. Still, it's hard to believe he's any older than twenty. And a sergeant? It's not unheard of, but it's strange.

The soldier we killed on *Memoria* was young, too—I remember being shocked by it when I dragged her body to the cryosleep chamber. So was the soldier from the exosuit we reclaimed. The one in the Titan facility. All of them have been so damn young.

My mind flickers back to my fight with Daniil, the guilt in his voice when he said, *"He sent everyone. Everyone but me."* I sink heavily into the chair, leaning back, file still in my hands. Altair said at the peace talks that he only had time to save soldiers. Soldiers from Fort Sketa, where I saw him last...where they hold basic training.

I lean forward in my chair, reach out, and lay a hand on Arkadi's shoulder. He blinks rapidly, and then flinches away from my touch, lips pulling into a snarl—but not before I catch a brief glimpse of that look I saw so many times on the faces of fresh recruits, that longing for contact that they always had after basic. My mind flickers briefly to Councillor Govender doing the same to me, and I fight back a wave of disgust. That's not important right now.

"Arkadi," I say, softly, "how long did you fight in the war on Titan?"

"Two years," he says, too fast, a knee-jerk reaction.

"Where was your first fight?"

"I—" His expression flickers.

I lean back in my chair again, and shut off the comm and the file. I know all I need to know. "You're a fresh recruit," I say. "You all are. Altair's fighting a war with a bunch of fucking kids. Starving ones, from the looks of it." Something occurs to me then—something I'm not sure I want to face, as uncomfortable realization begins to creep up on me, but I must. "But of course you would be starving. There was hardly any food on Titan to begin with, and you've been out on those ships for months without access to more. But... then, why burn Kitaya?"

"Why?" he scoffs—but as he looks at me, his expression shifts. "Oh." A lopsided approximation of a smile crawls across his face. "You *don't* know?"

"Know what?"

"Right," he says, softly. "We saw the news reports. How they framed it. We burned it because we are nothing but crazy soldiers, right? Monstrous warmongers. Slaughtering civilians for no reason at all."

"I used to live on Kitaya," I say. "There was nothing there but algae farmers. What reason could you have?"

"Yes. The farmers and their underwater fields. That's why we went. Troops gotta eat, right? So we get there, and our orders are to harvest it and take it back to base. But some people, they don't listen. They're too hungry. They start tearing into the algae the second we pull it out of the water." His eyes flicker away from me, lost in thought. "I didn't. I wanted to, but I just became a sergeant, you know. When the last one died. I had to prove I could control my soldiers. So I held them back. They fucking hated me for it. But about thirty minutes later they were ready to kiss my boots, because half of the people who had eaten were on the ground puking up blood, and the other half were already dead." He leans back in his chair, his eyes finding mine again. "I know it doesn't make it right, what we did. But they're the ones who started it. We never hurt nobody before they poisoned us."

It takes a moment for it to sink in. Even when it does, I can't believe it. As the news stressed when the Titans burned it, Kitaya provided a large percentage of this planet's algae supply. "The Nibirans never would have poisoned Kitaya. Their own people will suffer because of the loss of that island. And with the burden of the refugees as well . . . people will starve."

"Not as fast as we will," Arkadi says. And I think back to the last time I spoke to the council. Words I barely processed at the time now echo in my ears: *We can no longer rely on starving them out—*"

Lyre said that it wouldn't make sense for the Titans to target Kitaya. She never understood how she was wrong about that.

I think back to Altair's scathing words to Oshiro at the peace talks. His anger over the timing. Oshiro stepping down afterward. The council cutting a deal with Deva, which is known for food exports.

They did this. They *planned* this. They created the tragedy that won me over to their side. Maybe they thought it would be enough of a blow against the Titans that it would prevent an all-out war . . . but that doesn't excuse it. The Nibiran Council sacrificed their own people, and they've been manipulating me this entire time.

"I don't blame them," Arkadi says, when I remain silent. "It was a smart move. I'm sure we would have done the same. But don't go convincing yourself you've got any kind of moral high ground here. We're at war." There's a darkness in his eyes that seems decades older than his body. "Nobody stays good in a war."

I ponder the young sergeant's words as I leave the facility. Maybe he's right. But I have to try to save as many people as I can, and I realize now that it can't just be the Nibirans and Gaians. The Titans are still my people.

And I know what makes them tick. Much as this boy tried to hide it, I found the truth anyway: They're all fresh recruits, half-trained soldiers. No wonder Daniil skyrocketed up the chain of command, when he's one of the few left with extensive combat experience. And if we can take out the leaders, that chain will collapse, leaving the rest of the young army vulnerable—and perhaps possible to save. Scorpia was right, after all: In the end, it's the ones at the top who are all the same. There's no reason those at the bottom should suffer for it.

I suspect Altair will be too far from this fight for me to get to, but there will be others. Sergeants, lieutenants, colonels. Ives. Daniil. If I cut off the heads of the Titan army, perhaps the rest can be convinced to surrender.

If I had any faith left in the Nibiran Council, I would explain this all to them. But after what I learned, I can't trust them. They were willing to sabotage their own island, risk their own civilians, for the sake of winning the war. I can't bring myself to believe they would show any mercy to the Titans.

Part of me wants to think that all of this was orchestrated by Govender. Looking back now, it's easy to see that she's been manipulating me this entire time. She was the one who wanted me at the meeting with Altair to show him that I had turned against him. She convinced me to give up everything I knew about the Titans when my anger was still fresh toward them after Kitaya.

She let slip that Lyre had helped design the prototype and made me feel grateful that she allowed me to risk myself testing it. And now she's revealed her true colors by pushing for this suicidal final battle. I have no doubt that the sabotage of Kitaya was her doing.

But as I just saw in the council hall, she's not acting alone. The plans might be hers, but the council only acts if the majority supports it. Even Oshiro, who I have no doubt voted to save their island, concealed the truth about Kitaya. Right before they handed me over to Govender to be used as a weapon and then abandoned me.

So I have no allies on the council now. If I want to save the Titans, I will have to do it without their approval. But I'll need people at my side who I can trust. Drom, for one. And…I'm surprised who's next to come to mind. One of the few people who understood what a lie planetary loyalty is all along.

I take out my comm and carefully compose a message, erasing and rewriting it a half dozen times before I can bring myself to hit the button. I don't want to do this. But I have to.

I hate to ask this of you, but it's important. One last battle. We need everyone who can help. If I can promise a pardon, will you fight on Nibiru's side?

Izra's response comes almost instantly: *No.*

I lower my comm. That's the end of it, then. No matter how disappointed I might be, I won't push her to do this, not after what she's already been through.

A moment later, my comm chimes again. Another message shines up at me:

But I'll fight on yours.

CHAPTER THIRTY-EIGHT

A Change of Plans

Scorpia

About an hour out from Nibiru, the Titan mothership looms on our radar, and then out the viewing panel. I can't help but tense as we approach it, even though it's clear the vessel has no weaponry and we could easily outmaneuver it. In fact, the closer we get, the easier it is to tell that the ugly thing is just a huge generation ship, similar to—though much smaller than—the ships in the pictures I've seen of the ones that left Earth long ago.

"The Titans must have built this for their journey out of the system," Lyre says, staring out at it in wonder.

"Altair wasn't lying when he said they were looking for a peaceful future," I murmur. "They must be using it as a base of operations now." With all of the smaller Titan ships keeping Nibiru surrounded, this weaponless hulk isn't under threat. It must be where the general himself is staying, far from any danger.

Titans, and Nibirans, and Gaians. All of them fighting and dying while the people up high stay safe. Even if I go through with this plan, turn over Leonis and secure a deal with Deva, where does that lead? It'll take another two weeks to get there and back. Another two weeks' worth of losses in this stupid war. And then—what? The Devans arrive and slaughter the Titans? Wipe them out once and for all? Everyone is so eager to paint the Titans as the villains, but I see them as a people far from home, lost and scared. Is this the end they deserve? A brutal massacre after a lifetime of war?

"Scorpia, we have an incoming message from Nibiru," Lyre says.

"Ugh. What do those assholes want now? Change of plans already?" But as she pulls up the message, the face that fills the screen isn't one of the council members.

"Scorpia." Corvus says my name like an apology. "By the time you get this, you'll already be gone. I made sure of it." He takes a deep breath. "You were right. The council has been lying—to us, and to everyone. Maybe telling the truth would have only made things worse, but..." He looks down, shaking his head. "It doesn't matter. The Titans have a Primus weapon. A bomb of some kind, we think. Something capable of destroying Nibiru if we don't stop it. There's too much at stake. I have to fight. I'll probably already be in the thick of it by the time this reaches you. But I want you to know it's not because of the council's orders. It's because of what will happen if I don't. I wish there was another way, but I have to do this." He looks into the camera again, steadying himself. "If we win this, we'll still need that alliance with Deva to help us recover from the war. If we don't...well, I guess it's your choice how to use Leonis, then." There's a long pause, while he seems to figure out what else to say. Finally, he adds, "I'd tell you to look after the others, but I know I can rely on you to do that, regardless. Just... trust yourself, Scorpia. You're stronger than you think."

The message ends. Even though he didn't say it, I know it was meant to be a goodbye. I stare at the screen long after the image dissolves into static, trying to keep myself calm for Lyre's sake. It's hard not to think of everything that led up to this point and dwell on all the things that went wrong, all of the things we could've fixed. If I had insisted on Corvus and Drom coming with us… if we had defied the council's orders and told the Titans about the Planetary Defense Systems right away…would any of it have made a difference? Led us on a better path?

I don't know. I can't know. But there's no point in thinking about this anyway. I need to look toward the future, and decide what we can do now. Down there on Nibiru, our siblings are making a last stand. I'm not going to flee to Deva for a possibly pointless alliance knowing that. We need to find our own way to fight. But how?

I tap my fingers against the wheel as an idea begins to form in my mind.

"Change of plans," I say to Lyre, who looks entirely unsurprised by the news. "Sorry in advance. You're not going to like this. But you're going to have to trust me." I turn toward her, giving her my full attention. "There's something important I need to tell you. Something I should have told you a while ago. And I need you right now, more than ever."

After my explanation to Lyre, I call Pol to the cockpit and show them both the major controls: which indicators going green means a life-threatening problem and which they can ignore, which screens Pol should focus on while Lyre is steering—and most importantly, how to activate autopilot.

"Really, autopilot should be able to land on its own, when you get to that part. It's not like you're trying to pull anything tricky," I say, standing with a hand on the back of each chair. "The landing gear is a little bit damaged, so it definitely won't be comfy, but she's a tough ship. She'll handle it. And so will the both of you, as long as you're securely strapped in." I flash a smile. "It'll be easy."

Both of my siblings stare up at me with wide, worried eyes, Lyre in my chair and Pol in the copilot's position.

"Literally nothing about this is easy," Lyre says.

"This plan is dumb, even for you," Pol contributes.

I sigh. "I know this is hard, but we've all got our parts to play. And someone's got to take our prisoner over to the Titans."

"So let me do it," Pol says without hesitation. "It's not like I'm—"

"No," I say, firmly, and lay a hand on his shoulder when his expression falls. "Sorry, buddy, this is my moment of glory. You'll get yours someday, don't worry." I crouch between their two chairs. "Lyre, you're in charge until I get back. Remember what I told you. If things go bad, you get to Deva, and take care of Pol. Pol, you listen to her, and make sure she doesn't think too hard. Like when she's making the face she's making right now, you gotta tell her to cheer up, all right?"

"Cheer up," Pol says, nudging Lyre's leg with one knee. "If we survived this long with Scorpia at the wheel, there's no way being a pilot is that hard."

They both break into nervous laughter. I grin a bit myself, rolling my eyes.

"Yeah, okay, you little asshole. Maybe wait until I'm gone for jokes like that." I straighten up. "You two are gonna be just fine."

And I have to believe that. I have to make myself believe it, or I'm never going to be able to walk away and do what I need to do. But deep down, I know that it's true. We Kaisers are always stronger than anybody gives us credit for. We've been strong together, and now it's time to prove we can be strong on our own, too.

But of course, the moment I back toward the door, both of my little siblings rise from their seats again.

I stop, folding my arms over my chest. "C'mon, you two, don't make this harder than it has to be."

"I just want to reiterate once again how foolish this idea is," Lyre says.

"Yeah," I say. "Doing foolish things is kind of my specialty. But it's worked out so far, hasn't it?"

Her lower lip wobbles. "I hate this," she says. "First Corvus, then Drom, now—"

"Hush. You know I always come back."

"I also know you make a lot of promises you can't keep."

"You're right," I admit. "I can't promise that this is going to work, or that I'll be able to get back to you even if it does. I don't know what's going to happen. But I can hope. That's all you can do, sometimes, and you just gotta let that be enough."

Lyre sucks in air through her teeth and, after a moment, manages a small nod. She sets her lips into a thin line and raises her head. "I'll look after Pol and the ship until you're back, then."

"Wouldn't trust them with anyone else," I say.

Quiet seeps in, and we stand here looking at each other, neither one of us sure how to proceed now. Part of me wants to drag her into a hug goodbye—but she looks so brittle right now I think that kind of affection might just make her shatter. And anyway, that's never been us.

Pol, on the other hand, hugs me so tightly I feel like my ribs might crack.

"Wow," I say, straining for breath. "You're getting stronger, huh?" I pat him on the back, and he releases me after a few seconds, wiping his eyes. "Okay, you two. Take care of each other."

With that done, I fetch our prisoner. Leonis is handcuffed and strapped into her launch chair, and tracks me with cold eyes as I cross the room and begin to free her from the chair. She's silent up until the point where I start pushing her toward the door.

"Where exactly do you think you're taking me?" she asks, stiffening up and trying unsuccessfully to dig her heels into the floor. "I deserve the dignity of my own room."

"You don't deserve any dignity at all," I tell her, sliding her forcibly across the floor. "You should be glad I'm not tossing you out the air lock."

She relaxes a little at that, and I suppress a laugh. But she starts resisting real fast again as soon as she notices I'm taking her to an escape pod.

"Lady, I am trying to be as civilized as possible here, but please know that I am not above beating an old woman if necessary," I tell her, very gravely. "In fact, if that old woman is you, I will take great pleasure from it."

Still, she refuses to move. I send her through the doors with a literal kick in the ass. The sight of her stumbling into the escape pod and falling on her knees, looking very indignant all the while, is enough to cheer me up considerably even given the circumstances. I step inside and shut the doors, which means it's just the two of us in this very cramped and tiny escape pod. It's a simple vessel, egg-shaped, not much bigger than a Ca Sineh cell. There's little more than a couple of crammed-together seats and a highly simplistic control panel.

"How fun. Never been in one of these." Distantly, I'm aware that I'm hitting the level of anxiety where I desperately try to pretend nothing is wrong, but that's better than a full breakdown, so I'll roll with it. Making stupid jokes is much better than admitting to myself that even if this plan works out perfectly, it's going to make everyone hate me. The Nibirans I'm defying, the Devans I'm breaking a trade with, the Paxians who want Leonis for themselves...and the Gaians, who I don't really care about, except for Shey. Shey is *definitely* going to hate me.

But I'm not doing this for love. I never much liked being called a hero, anyway.

I strap myself into the chair in the front, skimming my fingers over the controls, which seem fairly intuitive. "Strap in."

"Where do you intend to take me?"

"Regardless of the answer to that, I can promise you it's going to be a lot more comfortable if you're in a chair."

She glares at me, but makes her way over to one of the seats regardless. The moment she's strapped in, I hit the release button, and the escape pod slides out of *Memoria* and into open space. I turn to watch the ship as we drift away from her, feeling a little wistful as I see her name written in my own hand across the side.

"They were right," I mutter. "It *is* crooked." I blow the ship a kiss goodbye before turning my attention to the gigantic Titan vessel we're heading toward.

Behind me, Leonis gasps as she does the same. "Stars above. Tell me that's not where you're taking us."

"Afraid so," I say, cheerfully.

"Listen to me," she says, her face going very pale. "Whatever you believe you're doing here, it's not going to work. We can make a deal—"

"Shut up," I say, and crank up the speed enough that we're both slammed back in our chairs. Barely able to lift my head away from the seat, I let out a delighted laugh.

"You're going to get us both killed!" Leonis shouts—her voice terrified enough that I regret I can't turn around and get a good look at her face. "The Titans will execute us!"

She might be right. But I have to try.

CHAPTER THIRTY-NINE

The Last Stand

Corvus

As I gear up on the dropship, I try not to think about anything other than the body armor I'm strapping on and the weapon at my hip. This—this is simple. It's familiar. Combat and war are what I'm used to. I'm a soldier. A role that's been almost disappointingly easy to slip back into.

Beyond that, everything gets more complicated. During the war on Titan, I couldn't afford to think about issues of morality... or perhaps that's just something I learned to tell myself. I didn't know the enemy, never spoke to them face-to-face, never learned all the small things that come with really understanding someone. I never fought side by side with them, trusted them to watch my back, slept under the same roof, ate meals crowded together for warmth. I never loved any of them.

This... this is different. Both sides of this war are my own people in their own right, and neither is clearly right or wrong. The poisoning of Kitaya and the island burning, the Gaians' past sins and the Nibirans' secrets and the Titans' thirst for vengeance...

It's all mixed up in my head now. I still can't bring myself to feel anything for either side other than a deep sense of grief.

But it doesn't matter now. It can't matter. Because if we lose here, the Titans will deploy their bomb and unknowingly destroy everyone, themselves included. The only hope for any of us is if we take victory here and now. So that's all I can try to do. I'll leave the thinking—and the mourning—for afterward. Right now, I have to fight.

On my left side, Izra gears up with practiced fingers, her face as hardened as always. On my right is a stranger, a Nibiran who trembles as he adjusts the straps of his armor. I tried to convince Drom to stay with me. I have enough sway with the council that I could've secured her spot on my team with ease. But she refused. "If I die, you'll get distracted," she said. "And same for you. We can't afford it. We gotta make sure we can fight till the end." In true Drom fashion, she refused to budge on the matter once she decided. She wouldn't even tell me where she's fighting. I could've looked it up, of course—but part of me fears she might be right. If I hear she's fallen in battle, I'm not sure I'll be able to go on. The best I could do was force her to take my Primus knife.

Izra, on the other hand, told me she doesn't trust "any of these Nibiran and Gaian fuckers" to watch her back, and insisted on being right at my side.

Once I'm fully geared, I turn to survey the rest of my squadron—all fifty of them. I've never led this many people before. Many of them are young, scared. Others are older, scarred...and still afraid. But even with the brand on my wrist bared, even though I'm not one of them and they all know it, they all look at me with hopeful, expectant faces. Not a single one of them shows a hint of disapproval or hostility. Not even the Gaians all huddled together in one corner, watching Shey's peace demonstration on one of their comms. They're all trusting me.

I look down at my war-brand, take a deep breath, and clear my throat. My team snaps to attention.

"I know that many of you are afraid," I say. "There's no shame in it. I'm afraid, too. It's good to be afraid, because it reminds you of how much you have to lose. It reminds you of how much you have to *protect*. It reminds you what you're fighting for.

"Because none of us are fighting just for our lives today. We are fighting for our neighbors, our friends and family"—I pause, looking down at the tattoo beneath my brand, the mark I chose, the mark of my blood—"and for our planet. We fight for everything that makes our lives worth living. I'm not going to lie to you and tell you that you will all survive today. Most of us won't. But I can promise you that when we win, it will be worth it. Each of us that falls will be one more stone on the path to a better future.

"We don't fight because we hate our enemy, nor out of a desire to live. Not for revenge or for justice. We fight out of love: for the planet that is our home, and for the people we leave behind. If we die today, we die for them. So that one day, they will look out the window at the endless ocean, and know that the world is at peace."

The ship is silent as I finish. But as I look out over the faces of the people whose lives are now in my hands, I watch their expressions shift from fear and doubt to grim determination. I watch them become soldiers, and prepare to fight for the future of their world.

The first man dies before we touch down on the shore of Aluris. A pulse rifle spray riddles him with holes as we're descending from our dropship, spattering those around him with fine red mist. The rest of us hit the ground and roll, and a moment later I've already forgotten his face, because I'm too focused on the enemy in front of me.

Muscle memory clicks in as my emotions shut off. It is easy to remember being a soldier. I push forward, firing shot after shot,

Izra screaming war cries at my side. The others rally around us like a beacon; they fight hard enough to make any Titan proud.

I know within the first ten minutes that it won't be enough. For every soldier we take, we lose three—if we're lucky. More for exosuits, much more, though fortunately they're thinly spread among the Titan troops. And this even with me and Izra leading the charge here, and her Primus weapon cleaving through enemies with brutal efficiency. I can only imagine how we're faring elsewhere, how Drom is faring—but I can't think of it. I can only move and shoot. The only way through is forward.

The Nibirans told us that the Titans are weak and starving and grossly outnumbered. That may be true, but they also fight like they have nothing to lose. I watch a woman with her guts spilling out gun down three of my soldiers before she finally falls—watch a man with his legs blown off go back into the fray with nothing but hands and teeth—watch a failing exosuit dive into a group of my soldiers like a battering ram and smash their own helmet in as they hit the ground.

It takes no time at all for the battlefield to become a mess of blood and mud, people dead and dying and screaming their victories. Two heavily armored Titan spider tanks crawl through the chaos, raining down fire. I lose Izra somewhere—fallen or just elsewhere, I'm not sure. No time to check when there's a steady stream of enemies coming at me. I wish I had Sanita to dull the thudding terror in the back of my mind. I wish Drom were here—

My focus wavers, and I regain it only to find a huge metal fist swinging toward my head. I barely duck the blow—which would've taken my head clear off my shoulders—and feel the rush of air in its wake. My boots slip on something wet and sticky as I lurch back, and I crash down to the ground as my bad leg gives out. I rise again with a grunt of effort as the exosuit looms up above me.

My knee throbs with sharp pain; something's slipped out of place or broken. This is it, then. I shut off my comm so no one has to hear me die, and rush the suit rather than trying to run, launching myself at them. I'm barely a foot away from their chest and midair when they catch me between their metal hands, instantly stopping me and holding me in place. The breath leaves my lungs. But I'm close—close enough to strain forward, whip my gun around the back of the suit's head, and fire directly into the pressure pads where it's weakest.

The helmet jerks. The exosuit freezes for a moment—and then it begins to squeeze.

I fire again and again as the pressure builds. No use. My body armor begins to crack from the weight—and then splinters. Something inside me gives way as well, with a blinding rush of white-hot pain. I scream, and blood bubbles out of my mouth along with the sound. My vision begins to go white.

The suit jerks. I wrench myself back to consciousness to see a familiar black Primus spear jutting out of its shoulder. I can hear Izra shouting—but it's distant. She's far, too far. Using the last of my strength, I drop my gun and grab the spear, the serrated edges tearing into my palms as I rip it free, and stab it as hard as I can into the side of the suit's helmet.

The suit jerks again, and goes still. The pressure around my torso doesn't increase…nor does it disappear. I take a gurgling breath, fighting for air, and panic hits me as I realize that the suit must have frozen in place as the flesh inside died. I still can't move, can't breathe—the whiteness is still closing in, eating at the edges of my vision. Fuck, not like this, not after everything that's led here—

And Izra is at my side, breathing hard. I try to say something but can't find the air. She scrutinizes the metal hands locked around me, carefully aims her Primus gun, and fires. The spear takes off a few fingers of both metal and flesh, and nicks my side. I'm grateful just to have enough air for a small, inadvertent gasp of pain. I try to squeeze free from the space she's created, and the pain very nearly makes me black out.

"Stay still," she says—but even as I do my best, it becomes apparent there's no angle for her to get a good shot. She lets out a low growl, jabs her gun arm into the crevice between me and the hand, and *shoves*. Her teeth grit and her veins stand out with the effort. It seems impossible, but slowly she pushes the hand back a half inch—and with a grunt of effort, another—and, finally, with a scream of pain as skin and muscle tears around the Primus material implanted into her body, I tumble free. She half manages to catch me, and we both go down, bloody and panting, my head on her lap.

She looks down at me, her hair matted with blood and mud, her gun arm dangling limp and gory at her side, and says, "Should've stayed at my side, you fucking idiot."

I might laugh, if I wasn't afraid it might break something already half-broken inside my chest. But the moment of mirth fades as my consciousness fully returns, and with it, the sound of the battle raging on around us. It feels too good to rest here. I need to get up while I still can.

I sit up halfway, my body screaming in pain.

"You need a medevac," Izra says. "Turn your comm back on and call one in."

"There are no medevacs," I say, and am distantly surprised at the hoarse rasp my voice comes out as, the small rattle in the back of my throat. "That was a lie from command. Nobody's leaving here until it's over."

"Should've known," Izra says. She pushes me up with her good arm, grimacing with effort, and I lean down to help her up as well. Her arm looks even worse than I thought it would, still hanging uselessly.

On my feet, I cough up a mouthful of blood, wipe my lips, and hobble around to the back of the exosuit. I remove the badly damaged helmet, rip out the portable comm, and stick it on my own ear, but there's only faint static on the other side. I keep it anyway, just in case it's useful, and search for the emergency release button inside the suit. Once I press it, the metal peels open, and the body inside tumbles out into the mud. I size her up, and then the suit. The fit should be close enough, once I shed my broken body armor.

"Help me with this," I say, fumbling with the straps.

Izra only stares at me. "Don't tell me you're thinking about getting into that thing."

"We're the only two who can fly it, and you're too short."

"Do not tell me I ruined my fucking arm for you to go out there and kill yourself!"

I pull myself free of one of my armor's sleeves, spit out more blood, and look her in the eye. "We're losing this fight," I tell her, honestly. "If I don't do something to change it, we're all going to die."

She only keeps staring, so I grit my teeth and pull off one shattered piece of my chest plate. It comes away sticky with blood and hurts like hell. If she refuses, I'm not sure I can pull this off on my own. "We don't have time," I say. "Help me."

"Is that an order, sir?" she asks, her voice frosty.

I want to tell her I know how she feels right now, how she must be afraid of ending up the sole survivor once again. I want to explain that going back into that fight will be the hardest thing I've ever done, but I have to do it anyway. Because I meant what I said: If I don't do this, we'll all die. And we don't have time.

Even so, I can't bring myself to do it.

"It's not a command," I say. "But I am asking you. Please."

Izra stares at me. She sets her jaw, averts her eye, and steps forward to help me with the rest of the armor. She's silent as she helps peel it away, piece by broken piece, revealing wounds I wasn't aware I had because my body is one pulsing source of pain. She doesn't flinch when I cry out in pain, nor when she has to slowly pull out one jagged fragment that's buried a few inches deep in my side. Once it's all gone, she offers me her good arm to steady myself as I climb into the exosuit.

It's far from a perfect fit. The hips are too wide, the shoulders narrow enough to squeeze painfully, the arms so short that my fingers are crammed up inside. It'll hurt, but I can take it. The suit gradually closes in around me, a familiar metal embrace. I bend down to pull the serrated Primus spear from the broken helmet, straighten up with it in hand, and look down at Izra. She suddenly seems very small.

"Thank you," I say, even though it's not nearly enough, and what I'm about to do is going to make her hate me. I clear my throat, turn my comm back on, and say, "Requesting medical evacuation for special ops agent Izra Jenviir at my current location."

Izra's eye goes wide. "You *fucker*—"

I launch upward, and back into the fray.

Wearing an exosuit reminds me how it feels to be a Titan. I forget the clunky controls of a machine not built for me, the pain radiating through my body, the growing signs that this battle is verging on unwinnable for us. I forget everything but the feeling of pure power. This suit's other weapons are depleted, leaving only its fists. Fists are more than enough. Inches of steel make every blow a battering ram. I cut down enemy after enemy, fighting my way through to the thick of the battle and searching for whoever is leading the enemy forces here. When I get surrounded I launch up, surveying the field, and see a handful of my soldiers grappling with another exosuit.

I dive straight forward. The closest soldiers see me coming and scatter, but the Titan must think I'm an ally. They don't move until it's too late, and I slam them into the ground and smash at their helmet repeatedly with my fists until they stop moving.

The Nibirans hang back, uncertain how to handle an exosuit suddenly turning on its own. But as I straighten up and raise my head, a ragged cheer goes through the ranks.

"To me," I shout, and push forward, punching into the Titan ranks.

All around us, our allies are still dying, our numbers advantage waning quickly. We are losing the battle. But my forces fight with renewed vigor, and we are a spear piercing the Titan defense, heading straight for the heart. Soon I can see their commander, an exosuit with a black slash across its chest, just like the one I once wore.

I know the Titans. I know their dependence on hierarchy. If we take down their leader, we can end this.

When we reach the commander, they turn to see me approaching. I see the way they briefly go still in recognition, and know exactly who I'm about to face. Not Altair, who wouldn't risk himself on the front lines like this. Not Ives, who would have rushed me already with her boundless fury.

There's a soft *click* as someone enters the same channel as me on the Titan comm; I had almost forgotten I was wearing it.

"You look like shit," Daniil's voice says in my ear. "You've gone soft, Corvus."

"I'll give you one chance, Naran. Stand down and end this."

Daniil's only response is a burst of surprised laughter—a sound both infuriating and achingly familiar. I grit my teeth and rip the comm out of my ear, tossing it into the mud. I don't need the distraction.

"Spread out and form a perimeter," I say to my own soldiers. These are my people. Not Daniil. Not anymore. "Make sure we're not interrupted."

I lift off the ground and launch toward him.

CHAPTER FORTY

Bargaining

Scorpia

The Titan ship looms bigger than I could have imagined as we approach. I press myself close to the viewing panel and gawk, awed despite the fact I'm probably headed to my death right now. In the seat behind me, Leonis is murmuring under her breath. Maybe she's talking to herself, maybe she's praying to those creepy aliens she loves so much—at this point, I don't give a shit.

As I hoped, the Titan ship pulls us in once we're close enough, a long mechanical arm extending to put our little escape pod in a headlock and pull her into the docking bay. As the door seals behind us, and a group of Titan soldiers swarms our vessel, I unstrap myself from my chair. Showtime.

I walk out with my hands above my head, palms out, and try my best not to shit myself as five Titan soldiers turn their guns on me.

"Hi," I say, and clear my throat. "My name is Scorpia Kaiser. I'm here to talk to General Altair." I glance back at the escape pod before looking at them again. "Tell him I brought a present from the Nibiran Council."

The Titans say nothing as they march me through the quiet and empty hallways of the ship. I chew the inside of my cheek. The urge to break this silence is almost unbearable, but I'm pretty sure these soldiers are just waiting for a good excuse to shoot me, and I'm not going to hand one to them. Instead I keep my mind busy admiring this gigantic spacecraft. It's all glimmering metal and shiny, transparent doors. A brand-new ship, clearly built for comfort and function rather than military security. I've never seen anything like this. Many hallways are closed off and seem to be still under construction, but we pass signs designating a sick bay, a greenhouse, a nursery. This ship was never built for war, which gives me a pang of sadness.

The soldiers lead me into the heart of the ship, to a large, sealed door that requires two of them to scan their eyeballs to enter. As it opens, those two march inside with me and take their posts on either side of the door, while the others shut it from the outside.

This room is circular, high-ceilinged, and clearly unfinished. It might've been meant to be a courtroom, or a church. General Altair sits at the front of the room, behind a huge desk on a raised platform. Two images play side by side on a holoscreen projected above the desk. On one side, the familiar words of Shey's apology speech play. The other, I realize with a flicker of horror, is a bird's-eye view of a battlefield, a gigantic clash between two forces. Is that happening right now? Are Corvus and Drom there?

Altair flicks the image to the side, making it disappear, and turns his attention to me. I stand a little taller, hands clasped behind my back. This is it, then. I thought I'd be more afraid. Maybe I'm less of a coward than I thought after all... or maybe I've already accepted that it's too late for fear.

I remember the poise and charisma that Altair radiated when I first met him, as well as the unfiltered anger transforming his face in the broadcast he sent to Nibiru. In comparison to those two versions of him, the man in front of me looks tired. His body slumps like it's getting hard to hold up his own weight. His hair is a disheveled mess pushed to the side of his gaunt face, the bags beneath his eyes making him seem decades older than he looked the first time we met. It's hard to believe less than a year has passed since that moment when he sat across the table from my mother and bought a weapon that would kill his planet and start all of this.

"Scorpia Kaiser." Even his voice seems ground down. There's no fire left in him now, just a weary sort of resignation that almost makes me want to pity him, regardless of the situation. I remember the way Corvus spoke of him—the look on his face when he called him *a good man*—and am grateful he doesn't have to see him now. "I must give credit where it's due: You've surprised me. I expected you and your family would be cowering in whatever safety the Nibirans provided for you."

"Then you don't know us very well at all."

He leans back in his chair, and regards me with the same weariness he seems to look at everything else. "And I hear you brought me a present. Surprises upon surprises. Or perhaps not, if this is meant to be a misguided attempt to buy freedom for yourself and your siblings. Playing over to the winner's side the moment it's clear who it's going to be." He scrutinizes me. "Is that what this is? A suicide jump from a burning ship? Do you think this ends with you walking out of here alive?"

"You mistake me," I say. "This is a gift from the Nibiran Council. I'm only the delivery girl."

"Is that so?" he asks. "A gift that they sent with absolutely no warning, even knowing it meant I would shoot their ships out of the sky?"

"Maybe the council wasn't exactly unanimous about sending this gift," I say; the words come easily, since I already thought this lie up on the way here. "Maybe some of them wanted it sent elsewhere, but I'm siding with the ones who think you deserve a little bit of justice." I smile, hoping he won't see the mess of nerves behind it.

He surveys me for a moment longer before his gaze shifts behind me. He gestures to one of the soldiers waiting by the door. "Bring her in, then."

The door opens again, and I move to the side to watch as the soldiers march Leonis in just like they did with me. She burns with hatred, turning her glare first on me and then on Altair, where it remains locked. For a moment I can see the fear in her, and wonder if this will finally be the moment she decides to bow down and beg for forgiveness. But after a moment, she lifts her chin and squares her shoulders, staring down Altair without a hint of remorse.

Altair looks at Leonis for a long moment, his mouth set in a grim line and his eyes like two windows into the dark emptiness of the space between the stars. With slow and careful precision, he unclips the laser pistol from his belt, clicks the safety off, and fires a single shot through the center of Leonis's forehead.

The sound of my gasp is swallowed by the thump of her body on the floor. I stare for a moment, openmouthed, but snap it shut again when Altair looks from her to me.

"Oh," I say. "Well, that was . . . efficient."

He only continues to look, the gun still in his hands—and quite frankly, I'm surprised I haven't already met the same fate as the ex-president leaking a red puddle out onto the metal floor.

"So that's handled." The adrenaline is hitting me now, as if realization has finally caught up with my body, and my mouth refuses to shut. "Justice is served. Hurray. The Nibirans will be so, so . . . pleased." An uncomfortable laugh bursts out of me. I clap a hand over my mouth, clear my throat, and lower it, looking again at the body.

Shit. Shey is really going to hate me for this.

"I thought you'd beg for your life," Altair says, reminding me

I have more pressing problems, no matter how much that one hurts. "But perhaps you're not quite as stupid as I thought."

"Oh, no, I knew when I walked in here that there was a strong likelihood this was gonna be the end. But the fact that you haven't decided to shoot me yet is, uh, encouraging?"

Altair leans back in his chair, tapping the barrel of his gun against the side of his leg and studying me like I'm a puzzle he can't quite figure out. "You really walked in here with no plan whatsoever?" he asks, sounding frustrated by the thought. "Your mother would be ashamed." He levels the gun at me.

"Wait, wait, wait," I say, frantically. "There is one more thing I have to offer you."

Altair smiles coldly, but he doesn't fire. "There it is. Of course you have some kind of trick."

"Not a trick," I say. "Just the truth." I take a deep breath. If they didn't already, the council will label me a traitor for this. But it doesn't matter. This isn't just a ploy to save my own skin; this is for a whole planet. For the whole system. If I don't tell someone now, I may never get another chance. "Before your fleet arrived here, my family and I went to Gaia. We were investigating what happened there. And we found something. Something buried beneath the surface since the Primus were alive. What's happening on Gaia right now—what's happened on your planet already—it's all because of—"

"The statues," Altair says, and I cut off abruptly, my mouth still open. "You found out about the statues. And the storms."

"You...you already knew?"

"If you figured out all of that, I'm sure you figured out that the statues on Titan were activated many years ago," he says. "You think we never managed to piece it together ourselves?" He shakes his head. "Few of us were privy to that truth, and the decision was made long ago that knowing wouldn't make the situation any more bearable for our people. Most were resigned to it. But I began to build my fleet the day after I found out."

Despair spreads over me like cold water. I thought this was a valuable bargaining chip, but it turns out it's worth nothing at all. "Then why? Why attack Nibiru? You said you intended to take this place for your own people, but if you knew all along that an attack would trigger the defense system, then..." I trail off, shaking my head. "Then all you really cared about is revenge. You're just the madman they think you are after all." I'm surprised at the bitter sting of disappointment. I spent all this time arguing that we're all people. I thought even the political fuckers had *something* resembling a heart. Is it possible I was wrong all along? I was fighting for nothing? I gave up my life for nothing?

Altair lets out a single, dry laugh. "You don't know anything about me."

"I know that by doing this you put not only an entire planet in danger, but also your own people. You're forcing them to fight for no reason, stringing them along with this false hope that they'll have a home at the end..." I shake my head. "You're no better than Leonis."

"It's truly astounding how quick people are to believe the absolute worst about their enemies," he says softly, lips curling at one corner in an expression that could be either a smile or a grimace. "Once you realize that, it's all too easy to use it against them. You know only what the Nibiran Council knows, which is precisely what I want them to know."

I stare at him as the truth slowly sinks in. "You let them find that bomb," I say. "If it's even a bomb at all. You knew it would trigger the defense system. So you never intended to use it."

"And I never intended to lose a slow war to starvation, either," he says. "I didn't expect the Nibirans would be cold enough to sabotage Kitaya, but once they did so, it was easy enough to see their plan. And easier still to lead them astray about mine. Force them into a battle they have no hope of winning. Hatred is a weapon that cuts both ways, if you know how to use it. And we Titans are well acquainted."

He's right. The Nibirans likely didn't doubt for a moment that the Titans intended to use that bomb, not given their history, and the assumption the Titans didn't know about the defense system. The Nibirans knew a straightforward confrontation would be absolutely devastating for them, but what choice did they think they had? I think of my siblings out there on the front lines right now, and despair clutches me again. Did Corvus fall for it? Does he believe what everyone else does about the Titans? Or, if he's figured out the truth, will he be strong enough to go against what the council says?

"You don't need to do this," I say, my voice dropping to a low and desperate whisper. I don't care if I sound weak right now. I'll beg if I have to. "You can end this, right now, before it gets any worse. I gave you what you wanted. Leonis is dead. History will remember her as a failure and a monster. You have your justice— now take the peace your people deserve. Give them something other than the war they've always known."

"I will," he says. "When all of this is over, my people will have peace, and a home that isn't trying to rid itself of them like they're a parasite. They will have everything they've earned." He stands and steps off the platform. I hold my ground and my breath as he approaches. "But they will not share it with the Gaians who despise them, nor the Nibirans whose best offer of peace was to send us back to a dying world. Even if I wished for that future, they would never follow me. I barely convinced them to come this far." He presses his gun to the bottom of my chin. "If it's any solace to you, I take no pleasure in this. But it's too late. We've suffered too many insults, lost too much. The only peace my people will accept is one that we earn in blood."

CHAPTER FORTY-ONE

Traitors and Soldiers

Corvus

Daniil and I collide midair with a metal-on-metal screech, grappling with each other and fighting gravity's pull.

He swings an armored fist at my face and forces me back. One strike to the head and I'm done for; he could crush my skull like a rotten fruit. But my Primus spear evens the odds. The next time he swings at me, I counter it rather than dodging, driving the serrated blade straight through one of his palms. He jerks and recoils. The black blade rips free, slick with blood.

I force him onto the defensive now with quick jabs and thrusts, circling around him and searching for an opening. He doesn't give me one, dodging and weaving through the air. I feel clunky and slow in comparison to him. Whether my exosuit is failing, or my body, I'm not sure. But I have to find a way to end this soon.

I force him back, and back, away from the thick of the fighting and toward the shore. He dodges my attacks with ease, but doesn't seem to notice or care when I push him out over the water. Finally, when I make a particularly clumsy stab at his chest, he grabs my wrist and twists the exosuit's arm to the side with a squeal of metal. The tip of the spear scrapes across his armor, carving a shallow cut across his chest. He holds me there, but I grab his other arm tight with mine, crushing it against his body. We fumble, awkward—but gradually, I begin to twist, forcing him down. Too late, he realizes what I'm trying to do, and begins to struggle in earnest—but I ram forward at full speed, taking us both under the waves.

We sink. Without my helmet, water instantly floods my suit, along with my nose and ears and eyes. It's too murky to see. Panic grips me, but I force myself to hold on to Daniil as we continue plummeting downward. I wait until he stops thrashing, long past the point where either of our exosuits could get free, and eject myself from the suit.

It was easy to forget how much my body is hurting with the suit protecting me. The moment I'm free, it rushes back: the pain in my chest, the weakness of my leg. My entire body feels as though it's failing. But I force myself to take the Primus spear from my suit and kick upward toward the surface. My lungs scream for air, and I fight the urge to open my mouth, gulp water, and be done with it.

Finally, I reach the surface. I tread water, sucking in great gasps of air even though each one sends jabbing pain through my chest. It's tempting to stay here and catch my breath, but the cold is already making my legs go numb. I force myself to kick toward land.

By the time I make it to the shore—near enough to the fighting for me to distantly make out the sounds of laser-fire, cries of triumph and pain—my adrenaline has fully drained away. My body is exhausted. I barely drag myself onto land before collapsing. I press my forehead to the cool mud and struggle for air, spear still clutched in my numb hands. No one comes to my aid. Either my beacon broke in the water and they assume me dead, or we have no soldiers to spare.

I click on the comm on my ear with one shaking hand and am surprised to find it still works. Soon I almost wish it had broken, because none of the news flooding in is good. The channel is full of announcements of the dead and dying, and unanswered calls for help. I can't bring myself to add my own voice to the stream of despair.

I get only a few minutes' reprieve before Daniil hauls himself out of the water behind me. I still can't find the strength to lift myself up, so I can only turn and watch as he retches and snorts out water, on his hands and knees on the shore. I'm dully surprised that I beat him here even with my injuries, until I remember—of course—most Titans can't swim. He's lucky he made it here at all.

Especially given how weak he looks. Out of the exosuit, his wet uniform clings to a body far too thin for it. His cheeks are hollowed out, his bones prominent. I remember misattributing his changed appearance to a poorly fitted uniform during the peace talks, but there's no mistaking it now. He's shed weight rapidly in the weeks since I've seen him. Perhaps I still have a chance to beat him, even with my wounds—but there's no joy in the realization.

Yet I force myself to my feet, the Primus spear in my hand. I have to end this. I'll kill him, and give the rest of the Titans a chance to live, even if I don't survive to see it. It's too late for people like Daniil, who have already become a part of the machine... though I know I'm partially responsible for that myself. Maybe it will be fitting if we go down together.

Daniil looks up at me as I rise. Water streaming from his hair and uniform, he staggers to his feet as well, one foot slipping in the mud before he steadies himself. "Maybe not so soft after all," he rasps. He fumbles in his pocket, pulls out a knife, and waits for me.

I tackle him. We fight on the ground—desperate, already exhausted. There's no honor in this. Nothing noble about two soldiers grappling in the mud. Soon we're both cut up, filthy with grime and blood, wheezing for air. I stab through the muscle of the arm he holds his knife with; he slams his other fist into my wounded ribs, nearly making me pass out, but I push through. I'm close. Close to the end. I can tell that he knows it, too. There's no fear in his expression—only something close to relief.

I rip the spear free from his arm, aim at his heart, and thrust downward. It pierces the skin, draws a cry of pain out of Daniil—and I stop, unable to push it in farther and deal the killing blow. My hands tremble on the spear. I will myself to do it—to end it, once and for all—but I can't.

Killing him here would win us this battle. Maybe even turn the tide of the war. But then what? Will this happen again, and again, until we wipe ourselves out like the Primus did? Or will I live to see the end of it, carrying fresh nightmares and guilt, knowing that I paid for my survival with the death of someone I once loved? Someone who, with just a few revisions of history, I would still be fighting alongside now?

The thought from before plagues me again: I'm one of the people who did this to him. I was his sergeant. I ordered him to kill people. To torture them. And then I left him behind. He's not a part of the war machine I'm fighting against, he's another victim of it. Or maybe he's both. Maybe everyone is both.

Regardless, I can't do this. I won't. I'm tired of this, the endless fighting, the necessary cruelties, the wars fought at the behest of those in power. I'm tired of cutting off pieces of who I am and convincing myself it's worth it.

Back on that battlefield, people are dying. Titans, Nibirans, Gaians—all my own people in some way. People who are not good or evil, but somewhere in between, the same as me. The same as Daniil. I lift my spear, toss it aside, and stand. Looking down, I hold a hand out to him.

"You know I'm not the traitor they say I am," I say, "and I know you're not the mindless soldier you're pretending to be."

He lays there, still breathing hard, hair plastered to his forehead with sweat and blood. He looks from my hand, to the spear on the ground. After a moment, he reaches out and takes my hand.

We stand together, our hands still clasped, his expression wary.

"No one else needs to die today," I tell him. "I wasn't responsible for Titan. No one here was. My mother was responsible, and she died for it. Leonis was responsible, and she will never walk free again. The Gaians have apologized for their part. Everyone here today is innocent." I let go of his hand, but hold his gaze. "It can be over. We can decide that it's over, here and now."

The hope on Daniil's face is dim, hesitant, but it's there. Yet he shakes his head.

"Altair will never agree," he says. "And the council—"

"Fuck them," I say. "Fuck all of them, and fuck their orders. They're not here. They're not the ones fighting this war. And they're not the ones these people here—all of them"—I sweep my hands out over the battlefields around us—"will listen to. They will follow us. We can break the cycle if we just show them that it's possible. We can fight for peace rather than fighting each other."

"Easy for you to say when you're losing a war."

"Everyone is going to lose this war. You know it as well as I do. Even if we don't wipe each other out beyond recovery here, someone will come to clean up the remnants." I shake my head. "Come on, Daniil. I know this army of Altair's is little more than a bunch of half-trained kids. It's not too late to give them a better future. Stop this, and the Nibirans will negotiate. You have my word."

Daniil scrutinizes me for a long, long moment. "Here I always thought you were such a good soldier," he says, and sighs. "Altair will have my head for this." And then, raising a hand to the comm attached to his ear, he says, "Stand down, all. Situation has changed. Waiting on updated orders from the general."

To my own people, I say, "Cease fire. Hold where you are."

A chorus of confusion answers me, but I only repeat the order until it dies down. Around us, the fighting slows to a trickle, and then stops. A fragile hush settles over the battlefield. I suspect one stray shot could break it and, orders be damned, the fighting would resume. But no shots come. The delicate peace lasts, for now, as an entire battlefield holds their breath.

CHAPTER FORTY-TWO

One Last Trick

Scorpia

F uck, okay, wait," I say, the second the barrel of Altair's gun touches my chin. Adrenaline pulses through my body, but I force myself to stay as still as possible. "Honestly, I was really hoping I could pull this off through the sheer power of love and truth and all that, but you were right. There is a trick. And trust me, you're gonna want to hear this before you pull that trigger."

"Everyone seems to remember some vital bit of information the moment they have a gun to their head," Altair says. He doesn't lower the pistol, but he's not blowing my brains out, so that's a plus. "Why should I trust anything you have to say right now?"

"That's the best part, really. You don't have to. You just have to wait a few minutes, at which point you should receive a delightful message from the Nibiran Council promising all sorts of wonderful things as soon as you release me alive." I clear my throat. "Was hoping it would arrive *before* I had a blaster pointed at me, but you know how Nibirans love to deliberate over every little thing."

"You believe your life is worth so much?"

"Well, I'm definitely worth nothing dead, so you don't have a whole lot to lose by waiting to find out."

Altair frowns. After a long, tense moment, he lowers the gun. "I'll admit my curiosity has been piqued. I suppose there's no harm in waiting to end this."

My shoulders slump in a rush of relief that's enough to make my knees go weak. Especially so when I glance over at Leonis's body, which is still facedown on the floor.

"You don't think you should maybe have someone move that while we wait?" I ask, nose wrinkling. Altair completely ignores me as he returns to his chair, keeping his gun in hand and aimed at me.

Just when I'm really starting to sweat, wondering if something has gone horribly wrong with my admittedly poorly thought-out plan, the door opens. I step to the side as a soldier rushes to Altair, bending to whisper urgently in his ear before handing him a comm. He salutes before rushing out again, casting a glance both at the body and at me, and looking considerably more surprised by the latter.

I watch Altair's face shift as he reads through the message. And reads it again. And again. Every time his eyes return to the top, his eyebrows move a little higher and a little closer together, slowly morphing into an expression that might be comical if my life wasn't on the line.

"This is…" he begins, haltingly, and lowers the comm to his lap as he looks up at me. "They wouldn't make this offer even for the life of a councillor. Let alone…" He gestures at me, as if my inadequacy is so great that it defies mere words.

"The power of blackmail is a wonderful thing," I say, feeling quite pleased with myself.

"You blackmailed the council into a peace offer."

"Honestly, at this point, they really shouldn't have been surprised."

His expression makes an abrupt shift from confusion to slow-growing anger.

"Stop smiling," he says, his voice dropping to a growl. "I still haven't decided whether or not to kill you yet."

I oblige.

"Now explain."

"The council is very strongly invested in the rest of the system not finding out about the Planetary Defense Systems," I say quickly, my former confidence withering beneath Altair's glare.

"As am I. It would cause absolute chaos."

"Well, then, you should also be invested in me staying alive, because if I don't check in with my sister in five hours, she's going to blast that information to every single news agency in the system."

Altair stares at me in complete disbelief. "Not even you would dare."

"I really, really would."

"It's madness."

I shrug. "It's a mad world."

Altair continues to stare at me. I watch the emotions war on his face, imagining him playing through a dozen different scenarios as he tries to find a way through this that ends with me dead. His shoulders slump, and he sits back, his mouth setting into a grim line. Much as I try to fight it, I can't help but smile a little. I've won, and he knows it.

"I must admit that I admire your tenacity," Altair says. "Though the absolute recklessness of this 'plan' is infuriating in a way I can't put into words."

I pause, unsure how to respond to that. "Thank you," I settle on, after a few seconds.

His face twists. "You are a fool," he says, anger rising in his tone now. "And you are a coward, playing games with me while good people die for what they believe in down on that planet. This will not be the clean victory you think it is. My people will be furious. Ives will never stand for it, and she still has pull, even after I shut down her first attempt at a coup. Blood will be spilled over this decision. And even if we reach a peace agreement now, do you truly think it will hold when we're all forced to coexist in a shrinking system? When people here begin to starve from the loss of Kitaya?"

My smile is gone now, but I'm not going to let him make me believe this was a mistake. "Yes," I say. "I think it can hold. I think people can change, if you give them a chance to."

"So eager to sermonize, when your family is responsible for setting all of this into motion," Altair says. "I suppose you have to believe that, in order to be able to live with yourself. But I see you, and I know you, and I do not forgive you for what you've done."

"Guess it's a good thing it's not up to you, then," I say, unable to help myself.

"But that doesn't mean I have to let you walk away free," he says. "You cannot keep gambling with other peoples' lives and remaining unscathed. Someone should have taught you that lesson a long time ago."

I take a step back, fear surging up and cracking my confidence. "You saw the Nibiran peace offer. They need me alive."

"Yes. And live you will. I'll make sure of it." His eyes bore into me. "But you must be punished." He pauses, considering me, and says, "I believe your brother mentioned you were a pilot..."

He calls to the soldiers at the door. Before I can even consider running, they grab ahold of me and drag me up to Altair.

I wish I was the type of person who could face their punishment with their head held high, but the truth is that I scream my ass off from the moment Altair grabs his knife to the moment that it's done, and then I collapse into sobs right afterward. It isn't so much the hot flash of pain that gets me, though that's nearly enough to make me black out right then and there. It isn't the sickening gouts of blood, either, even though I know I'll never forget that coppery smell thickening the air, or the sensation of my life spattering out. It isn't even the dull thump of my severed hand hitting the floor or the sight of it lying there, lifeless, while I stare in mute horror.

It's all bad, every bit of it, but the absolute worst thing is the sense of loss. It's looking down at the new stump of my wrist and almost being able to feel the hand still there, but seeing nothing. Absolutely nothing. It's trying to curl my fingers and nothing happening. It's the realization that this isn't some mindless cruelty inflicted on me by Altair, who looks on grimly as the soldiers drag me from the room. He knows exactly what he's doing. He knows exactly what he's taking away from me.

I'll never be able to fly again.

As that thought sinks in, overwhelming all the pain and the other horror, I finally, blissfully, lose consciousness.

CHAPTER FORTY-THREE

Cease-fire

The cease-fire order spreads across the planet like a ripple, and then a wave, building as it moves through Nibirans, and Gaians, and Titans alike. A few soldiers pull back, and lay down their arms—and then many do, and then most, until it is only a scarce few still clinging to their weapon like it's the last lifeboat in a tumultuous sea. Some find themselves feeling naked without a gun in hand. Others are so glad to get rid of them that they weep openly as they surrender them to the ground, and hope they never have to pick them up again.

Few people in the system would believe how many of the latter are Titans. None but the Titans themselves understand what this moment really means for them. It is the first time in any of their lives that they have not been at war.

But this is not a moment of triumph. There is no celebration. It is much too late for that. Too many lives have been lost—on Titan, on Kitaya, and on the battlefields today. Too many lie dead or dying, still. Instead, the moment comes as a sigh of relief. Not with joy, but with a weary sense that finally, *finally*, it is over.

Most of those on the battlefields spend their first few minutes of peace in silence and stillness, clasping their siblings-in-arms, or holding their hands up to the sky, or kneeling with their heads bowed. But slowly, as if in a dream, both sides shift into movement. Soldiers reclaim their wounded and their dead, or retreat back to their own people, eager to turn their backs on the carnage of the last few hours, but already knowing they will never forget it. Titans, Nibirans, Gaians—all of them have been left with scars today. The war will be a scar on the history of the system itself, a reminder of all the wrongs that led here, and all the pain that resulted.

But here—for now—the fighting is over. A hush falls over an entire world.

A Nibiran girl lets an alien knife tumble into the mud and cries, because she has never been so glad to see the end of a fight.

A Gaian woman clasps her hands to her chest and thanks the stars for this new peace—for her people, and for all people—even as her heart aches for the death of a monster she couldn't help but love, and a hero she doesn't think she can ever forgive.

A daughter of the stars looks down at her scarred wrist, and bitterly hopes that the future will be worth it, if not for her then for everyone she holds dear.

And in the midst of it all, in the center of what will come to be known as the bloodiest battle of this short and brutal war, two soldiers from enemy sides stare at each other. They are both bleeding, both mourning, both tired in a way that few other people— even here—can understand. They have faced each other before as comrades, as friends, as enemies. Now, they look at one another and aren't sure what they see. For the first time, it is their choice, and no one else's. Now they can decide who they want to become.

CHAPTER FORTY-FOUR

Nobody's People

Corvus

We don't receive an invitation to the peace talks.

We wouldn't go even if we did. Regardless of the fact that our actions helped lead to peace in the end, it's still an ongoing debate whether my choices in the final battle constituted treason or not, and Scorpia's explicit disregard of the council's orders most certainly did. As of now, the council is too wrapped up in peace negotiations and recovering from the war to pay us much heed, but we're not going to wait for them to decide what to do with us.

There is still the question of whether or not we'll be able to make it through customs without trouble, but fortunately, I have a couple of last favors to call in.

When we arrive at the customs office, loaded up with our paltry belongings and enough supplies to last us for a long, long journey, a thin shadow peels away from the building to join us. I halt, shifting my bag to one shoulder.

"I didn't think you would come in person," I say.

"I wanted to ensure you wouldn't have any problems," Iri Oshiro says. It's strange seeing them in plain civilian's clothes rather than the blue council robe they've always worn before. "It's the least I can do."

We stand back as the former councillor steps inside to speak to the customs agent. It's not a quick conversation, but just as I begin to think about which of our weapons are most easily accessible if we have to fight our way through to the ship, Oshiro reappears and waves us through. My family trickles by, one by one, stealing glances at both the ex-councillor and the customs agent, who looks far from pleased but makes no move to stop us. But nobody makes a comment to either one, not even Scorpia, who has been quieter than usual ever since she faced Altair.

"The others you asked about will be cleared as well, if they come," Oshiro says as I pass by. I nod, and intend to continue without comment, but they say, "I'm sorry I dragged you into all of this. Truly, I am."

I stop, turning to them. I suppose I should have known this conversation would be necessary. "It would have happened eventually," I say. "I'm not the one whose forgiveness you really need."

I'm not the one they failed. All those people on Kitaya...but the councillor doesn't need me to remind them of that. I can see the guilt of it written all over their face.

"I fought it," they say, softly.

"I know you did." Again, unspoken: It wasn't enough. They never should have accepted it, even if the other members of the council overruled them.

Oshiro's shoulders sag. The silence lasts long enough that I almost think the conversation is over, but finally they ask, "How does one make amends for something like this?" Their head lifts, eyes meeting mine again. "How do I move forward?"

I glance at the backs of my family and Izra heading toward the ship, considering the question. Most of us are guilty of something terrible at one point or another, myself included. Have we made up for it? Is it enough to be forgiven? I'm not sure. "All you can do is try to be better. And never stop trying." I turn back to Oshiro. "You still have a voice here. Use it for good. Help the Titans, the Gaians, the refugees. If you're not sure where to start, speak with Shey Leonis."

Oshiro nods, and says, "I will." They turn to go, but pause. "Ah, right. One last thing. I heard you asked the council for this, so..." They pull out a piece of paper and hand it to me.

I unfold it, scan it quickly, and put it into my own pocket. "Thank you."

Rather than say goodbye, they bow to me—deep, respectful, apologetic—and I leave to be with my family.

The others are already busy packing up *Memoria* by the time I arrive at the ramp. The ship was damaged after Lyre and Pol half-crashed it down on Nibiru, but some quick repairs were enough to get her back in working order.

Nobody complained about leaving Nibiru this time. We're all in agreement that it's time for us to go. And Scorpia was right all along: This was never truly where we belonged. Our only real home is a ship, and each other. We're not sure where we're going yet, but nobody really cares, so long as it's away from here.

Still, as I head down from my room to help the others, I pause to glance at the broadcast of the peace talks on my comm, and fight back a surge of bitterness. It doesn't escape my attention that all the people sitting at that table have very little to do with the peace they're finalizing. None of them fought and bled and sacrificed for it. They let their people do that for them. Or—in the case of me and my family—they let outsiders take all of the risk, and all of the punishment.

Pol pauses halfway up the ramp, catching his breath. His arms are stuffed with Lyre's belongings as well as his own. He's been recovering lately, slowly gaining back his strength, but he looks shaky today.

"Don't overexert yourself," I tell him as I pocket my comm and head down to help share the load.

"Yeah, I know, I know," he grumbles, but hands over half of the boxes he's carrying without complaint.

Drom brushes past us without a word. She hasn't said much at all over the last couple of days, ever since she came back to us with a fresh scar cutting across her right eye. From the looks of it, she was lucky not to lose it. Pol watches her go but doesn't rush to follow her. I've told the others to give her the time and space she needs. It hurts to look at her. All I ever wanted, through all of this, was to spare my siblings what I went through. With her, I failed, and that scar will always serve as a reminder.

By the time I make it back from Pol's room, everyone seems to have finished loading the ship. Lyre and Scorpia must be up in the cockpit, preparing for launch, and everyone else in their own rooms. Only Izra remains, sitting out on the edge of the dock, her silhouette alone against the ocean and red Nova Vita beyond.

She doesn't look up as I lower myself to a seat next to her. Her arm hangs in a sling at her side. The doctors did what they could, and for the most part managed to save her mangled arm, but the gun implanted in it is dead and useless now.

"Didn't want to watch the peace talks?" I ask, looking out at the ocean alongside her.

"Bunch of assholes talking about how hard they worked for peace behind their little desks, while the rest of us fought?" Her lips twist. "No, thanks."

"Yeah." I rest my hands behind me and lean back. "I'm just glad that it's over."

"For now."

409

"For now," I agree. "That's the best we can hope for."

She says nothing. After the silence ticks on for a few seconds, I reach into my pocket and pull out the piece of paper Oshiro gave me. "I have something for you."

I unfold and hand over the document. Izra scrutinizes it, her expression first uncomprehending and then shifting into something I can't read. "It's an official pardon," I say, once the silence stretches out too long and I wonder if I've offended her somehow. "Signed by the council. It will protect you from the Titans, as well. You don't have to hide from anyone anymore. You'll always have a home on Nibiru."

"For honor and sacrifice on the field of battle," she reads. Her lips twist into one of her little half smirks, though it looks forced.

"You've earned it."

She reads the document again, carefully folds it, and slips it into her pocket. "I see. So I'll be staying here on Nibiru, then."

I frown, taken aback at the bitterness in her tone and how quickly she jumped to that conclusion. "If that's what you want, then yes, you're welcome to do whatever you like."

Her eye shifts up to me, and she frowns. "If that's what I want?" We both stare at each other now, equally confused. "Isn't that what this is about? You're saying you want me out?"

"What?" It finally clicks into place why she's been looking at me like this, and I sigh. "No, Izra, that's not what this is about. I'm just making sure that if you stay with us, it's because you want to, not because you have nowhere else to go."

She blinks at that. Her mouth works, forming words she doesn't actually speak. But an instant later, the moment of vulnerability vanishes, as her eye narrows and her lips purse. "And what do you want?"

"I don't..." I suppress the urge to sigh again. Why does she have to make this so difficult? "As I said, I want you to do whatever you want. It's your choice now."

"Yes, I'm well fucking aware of that at this point," she snaps. "Now tell me what *you* want."

The back of my neck heats up. I hadn't anticipated this turn in the conversation—hadn't really considered how this conversation ended at all, frankly, since I had no idea what to expect. I'm not sure what point she's trying to make with this, but I don't see any purpose in being dishonest. "I suppose I would prefer if you stayed."

She stares up at me. I brace myself for an inevitable rejection or some joke at my expense, but instead she nods, and says, "Well, then I *suppose* I have nowhere better to be."

My shoulders relax. After a moment, I smile, and she smiles back.

But it vanishes as she looks away, her eye widening in shock. I follow her gaze to see two figures heading up the dock toward us, each with an oversized bag slung over one shoulder. Relief surges up inside me as I climb to my feet. I wasn't sure if either of them would accept my invitation.

"Let me get Scorpia," I say, and squeeze Izra's shoulder before continuing up the ramp.

CHAPTER FORTY-FIVE

Traitors, One and All

Scorpia

As I run Lyre through the launch procedures again—at her insistence—I toy with my prosthetic hand, unable to get used to the plastic feeling of my fake fingers, or the brief delay in their every action. This hand will slow me down. It's not a great prosthetic, just a hastily fitted, clunky Nibiran one. I can still grip things and perform all basic functions, but it'll affect my piloting. I could get a better model on Deva or Pax if I have the credits, someday, but somehow I doubt it will ever be the same as my real flesh and blood. I could still be a decent pilot, but I don't think it'll ever feel like me again. And it's always going to hurt, sitting at the wheel and knowing that.

Still, I'm the best option we have. And Lyre is still our best option for copilot, though I'm not particularly looking forward to that. She thinks way too much for this, and I'm pretty sure we're going to drive each other insane by the time we get to wher-ever we're going. But at least we'll get there. And I just have to keep reminding myself that the loss of my hand bought peace for everyone on Nibiru, and freedom for my family. I have to believe it will be worth it. The system better not fuck this up again.

"Scorpia?"

I turn to see Corvus waiting in the doorway, looking nervous enough that I instantly begin to worry that something's gone horribly wrong.

"What? What is it? Peacekeepers?"

"I didn't want to mention it because I wasn't sure whether or not they'd come, but...I believe we have a couple of last-minute additions to the crew." He clears his throat. "If you'll have them, that is. Captain."

My first thought is of Shey—but I quash that real fast. Even aside from the fact that she completely hates my guts, she's busy today delivering food to the Titan troops with other volunteers, a fact that the news has been discussing at every opportunity. She's been a media darling ever since she led the now-famous Gaian Apology, which means it's impossible for me to go anywhere without seeing her face. Yet another one on the long list of reasons I'm eager to get off this planet.

Regardless—she definitely won't be here today, not when she won't even answer my calls, so I have no idea who he could be talking about.

"New additions?" I ask, frowning at him, but he only gestures for me to follow. We head out, down the stairs and through the cargo bay, and I stop on the ramp at the sight of Izra facing down our two new arrivals on the dock outside. One of them is a man I don't recognize, marked by brand as a Titan, though his skin and hair are unusually dark for one.

The other is Orion.

He looks up and makes eye contact with me. We both freeze. His lips curve into a tentative smile a moment before Izra steps forward and punches him in the stomach. The Titan man steps away, as Corvus and I rush forward, but before we can reach them Izra has wrapped her arms around him in a painful-looking hug instead. She buries her face in his shoulder.

Orion bends over, gasping for air, and pats her on the back with one hand. "I missed you, too," he says, wincing.

Once it's clear she's not about to murder him, I glance at Corvus, unable to hide my shock. "You invited him back?" I ask. "After everything?" I never even told him about my encounter with Orion during the war, the way he saved me. I thought it might be easier for everyone to simply forget.

"You told me everyone deserves a second chance," Corvus says. Then he frowns. "I suppose this is a third chance for him, really, but..."

"Old friends get third chances, too," I say, grinning. I step forward as Izra finally releases Orion; she doesn't turn away quite quickly enough for me to miss her wiping tears from her eye. But I turn my attention to Orion, who is standing back, looking at me. There's a lot I want to say to him: apologies, and thanks, and all sorts of things. But instead I jut out my good hand and say, "Welcome back."

He shakes my hand, breaking into a relieved grin. "Thanks for having me, Captain."

I turn to the man beside him, who's standing with the quiet attention of a trained soldier. I'm not sure what to make of him. He looks tired, and malnourished, and both his chest and hand are wrapped in bandages. But beneath all that, there's something about his face that I like. Despite all the marks of war and pain, the lines around his mouth speak of an easy smile, which is something I haven't seen much of among Titans. "And you are?"

"Daniil Naran," he introduces himself, and automatically moves his hand toward his chest in a Titan salute. He catches himself at the last moment, flushes, and lets his hand drop to his side. "I'm...your brother's..." He glances at Corvus, trailing off uncertainly.

"Old friend," Corvus says.

Judging from the look they share, the story is a lot more complicated than that, but I'm not about to pry. Not right away, at least, but I do make a mental note to get that juicy story out of Corvus someday when the dust has settled. "Well, my brother's judgment is good enough for me," I say, and hold out my hand to him, too. "Welcome aboard. I'm Captain Scorpia Kaiser."

He reaches for my hand, but then pauses. "For the sake of transparency, I should probably tell you that I've committed treason against the Titans. I suspect there will be a warrant out for my arrest very soon, if there isn't one already."

I grin, and close the distance between us to clasp his hand with both of mine. "Even better," I say. "I think we're all traitors of one kind or another at this point. Welcome to *Memoria*, Daniil."

There's that smile of his. "Thank you, Captain."

I leave the three Titans on the dock and head inside with Orion. He keeps glancing down at my prosthetic hand, so eventually I stop and hold it up for him to get a better look.

"You like my new accessory?"

"I—" He winces. "I'm sorry."

"Oh, it's not so bad," I say with a shrug, though it still hurts me even to look at it. "I want to say it was worth it, but I guess we don't really know that for sure yet." I clear my throat and lower the hand, which still doesn't feel like it belongs to me, and likely never will. "It'll work well enough for most things, but...I don't think I'll ever be the pilot I was. So I'm really glad to have you back."

He blinks at me, taken aback. "What? No, I...I never expected...I mean, after what happened..."

"Please," I say. "As your captain, I'm asking you to be my pilot.

And I wouldn't do that unless I trusted you, fully and completely. Wouldn't really be a fresh start if I held the past against you, would it?"

He stares at me for a moment longer, swallows, and nods. "Of course, Captain. If those are your wishes."

"They are." I smile. "I'll be your copilot, but only until I can train someone else up to take my place."

"You're giving it all up?" he asks, his brow furrowing. "But... you love piloting. You're a great pilot."

I smile wistfully. "I do. And I was." I will myself not to get choked up. It's definitely hard for me to give up piloting. It was my first role on a ship, and it'll always be part of me. But really, I suspect I would've had to give it up at some point.

"So what about you?" Orion asks. "What will you do?"

"You kidding me?" I grin. "I'm the fucking captain. I'll have enough on my hands, with you assholes."

We walk into the cockpit, where a screen is showing yet another replay of Shey's apology speech. I sigh; the media sure does love that shit. As Lyre hears me enter, she quickly turns it off, but it doesn't matter. That image of Shey in the field of flowers is already burned into my brain, and just imagining it is enough to make my stomach twist with pain again.

I tried to reach out, after what happened. I tried to explain, to beg for one last goodbye. She ignored it all. The message was clear enough. I guess I can't blame her; I know from experience that having a monster of a parent doesn't make their passing any easier. Leonis was still her mom, and I killed her, and that's not the kind of issue we can fix. Not when our relationship was already rocky from the start.

So I've watched that clip of her, probably a hundred times now. I've memorized it all at this point: the red flowers, the thousands of Gaians gesturing their apology, the speech inspired by the last conversation we ever had. An apology doesn't mean anything if they don't follow up on it…but it's more than anyone would've expected from the Gaians, I think. And it's a start. A small step toward real peace, and real unity.

Shey may hate me now, may never forgive me, but she still believes in what I said to her. My words inspired this, and hers inspired me to do what I did and make this peace possible. No matter where we end up now, nothing will take away the impact we've had on one another. Maybe that's the best outcome you can hope for, with this sort of thing: walking away from each other as better people than you were when you met. Anyway, I suspect I'll have plenty to keep me distracted from the heartbreak of leaving her behind.

"Where are we off to now, Captain?" Orion asks, taking a seat in the pilot's chair.

"Well…" I take my place as copilot and flip through the ship's cameras, waiting for everyone to get strapped in and ready. My family and the strays we've collected. It already feels right, having everyone here. "Let's start by getting the hell away from here."

After that, I'm not so sure yet, but I'm sure I'll figure something out. I've got a damn good ship, and an even better crew, and the future doesn't scare me anymore.

CHAPTER FORTY-SIX

No Safe Harbor

Corvus

After the others drift inside, and the moving is finished, Pol comes out to sit on the ramp. I take a seat beside him, looking out over the open Nibiran sea and the red sun.

"I guess we're probably never gonna come back here, huh?" he asks, his eyes on the waves.

"Probably not." We've committed various crimes on various planets before, but given the particular nature of those crimes and our public-facing roles here, I doubt we'll be able to escape these ones so easily. "But you never know. The system is changing rapidly."

"So no Nibiru, no Titan…" He glances over at me. "You and I are kind of homeless like Scorpia now, huh?"

"I guess we are." I suppose, in a way, I already was after what happened to Titan, but it was hard to truly feel it when Nibiru opened its arms to us. But now, Titan, Gaia, Nibiru…none of the places I've considered home throughout my life will accept me. They all consider me a traitor.

Once, that would have broken me. And I do feel a sense of grief about it. Yet it's hard to regret my decisions when the system is at peace again. The Titans may hate me, but because of me they have a future other than endless war. The Nibirans, too, are now safe on their planet, and the Gaians have a chance to figure out how to forge a future better than their past.

And I will be all right without their acceptance. I still have *Memoria*, and my siblings, and our new crew members. Most of us are in the same situation that Scorpia has always lived with: We have no legal place in the system, other than this ship.

I climb to my feet and offer a hand to Pol. After a moment's hesitation, he lets me help him to his feet. We step onto *Memoria*, leaving behind a world at peace and setting off for an uncertain future. We are deserters and traitors and criminals, and the entire system may never accept us, but we will find a way to move forward, together. We always do.

The story continues in . . .

The Nova Vita Protocol:
Book Three

Acknowledgments

Many thanks to:

My agent, Emmanuelle Morgen, for loving my messy characters and tirelessly working to help me tell their stories right.

Ari, for diving deep into the first draft of this book and providing fantastic notes.

My editor, Bradley Englert, for always pushing me to dig deeper and work harder, as well as Hillary Sames, for helping bring the characters and story to life with her thoughtful feedback.

Lisa Marie Pompilio for another dazzling cover, and Ellen Wright, Bryn A. McDonald, my copy editor, and everyone else part of the brilliant team over at Orbit, for all their hard work and support.

My family: Mama, Papa, Todd, Lucas, Gramma, Chris, and all the rest, for always loving me and lifting me up. I couldn't do any of this without you.

Aidan, for listening to my anxious rambling and making me laugh even on my worst days. I love you.

My friends, especially the D&D party I dedicated this book to, for all the adventures together that make my life worth living.

And, last but not least, a big thank-you to my readers. I am so grateful for your messages, reviews, and enthusiasm.

extras

orbit

meet the author

Photo Credit: SunStreet Photo

KRISTYN MERBETH is obsessed with SFF, food, video games, and her dog. She resides in Tucson, Arizona.

Find out more about Kristyn Merbeth and other Orbit authors by registering for the free monthly newsletter at orbitbooks.net.

if you enjoyed
MEMORIA

look out for

NOPHEK GLOSS
Book One of The Graven

by

Essa Hansen

When a young man's planet is destroyed, he sets out on a single-minded quest for revenge across the galaxy in Nophek Gloss, *the first book in this epic space opera trilogy by debut author Essa Hansen, for fans of* Revenger *and* Children of Time.

Caiden's planet is destroyed. His family gone. And his only hope for survival is a crew of misfit aliens and a mysterious ship that seems to have a soul and a universe of its own. Together they will show him that the universe is much bigger, much more advanced, and much more mysterious than Caiden had ever imagined. But the universe hides dangers as well, and soon Caiden has his own plans.

He vows to do anything it takes to get revenge on the slavers who murdered his people and took away his home. To destroy their regime, he must infiltrate and dismantle them from the inside, or die trying.

CHAPTER 1

Tended and Driven

The overseers had taken all the carcasses, at least. The lingering stench of thousands of dead bovines wafted on breezes, prowling the air. Caiden crawled from an aerator's cramped top access port and comforting scents of iron and chemical. Outside, he inhaled, and the death aroma hit him. He gagged and shielded his nose in an oily sleeve.

"Back in there, kid," his father shouted from the ground.

Caiden crept to the machine's rust-eaten rim, twelve meters above where his father's wiry figure stood bristling with tools.

"I need a break!" Caiden wiped his eyes, smearing them with black grease he noticed too late. Vertebrae crackled into place when he stretched, cramped for hours in ducts and chemical housing as he assessed why the aerators had stopped working so suddenly. From the aerator's top, pipes soared a hundred meters to the vast pasture compound's ceiling, piercing through to spew clouds of vapor. Now merely a wheeze freckling the air.

"Well, I'm ready to test the backup power unit. There are six more aerators to fix today."

"We haven't even fixed the one!"

His father swiveled to the compound's entrance, a kilometer and a half wide, where distant aerators spewed weakened plumes into the vapor-filled sky. Openings in the compound's ceiling steeped the empty fields in twilight while the grass rippled rich, vibrating green. The air was viciously silent—no more grunts, no thud of hooves, no rip and crunch of grazing. A lonely breeze combed over the emptiness and tickled Caiden's nose with another whiff of death.

Humans were immune to the disease that had killed every bovine across the world, but the contaminated soil would take years to purge before new animals were viable. Pasture lots stood vacant for as far as anyone could see, leaving an entire population doing nothing but waiting for the overseers' orders.

The carcasses had been disposed of the same way as the fat bovines at harvest: corralled at the Flat Docks, two-kilometer-square metal plate, which descended, and the livestock were moved—somewhere, down below—then the plate rose empty.

"What'll happen if it dissolves completely?" The vapor paled and shredded dangerously by the hour—now the same grayish blond as Caiden's hair—and still he couldn't see through it. His curiosity bobbed on the sea of fear poured into him during his years in the Stricture: the gray was all that protected them from harm.

"Trouble will happen. Don't you mind it." His father always deflected or gave Caiden an answer for a child. Fourteen now, Caiden had been chosen for a mechanic determination because his intelligence outclassed him for everything else. He was smart enough to handle real answers.

"But what's up there?" he argued. "Why else spend so much effort keeping up the barrier?"

There could be a ceiling, with massive lights that filtered through to grow the fields, or the ceiling might be the floor of another level, with more people raising strange animals. Perhaps those people grew light itself, and poured it to the pastures, sieved by the clouds.

Caiden scrubbed sweat off his forehead, forgetting his grimy hand again. "The overseers must live up there. Why else do we rarely see them?"

He'd encountered two during his Appraisal at ten years old, when they'd confirmed his worth and assignment, and given him his brand—the mark of merit. He'd had a lot fewer questions, then. They'd worn sharp, hard metal clothes over their figures and faces, molded weirdly or layered in plates, and Caiden couldn't tell if there were bodies beneath those shapes or just parts, like a machine. One overseer had a humanlike shape but was well over two meters tall, the other reshaped itself like jelly. And there had been a third they'd talked to, whom Caiden couldn't see at all.

His father's sigh came out a growl. "They don't come from the sky, and the answers aren't gonna change if you keep asking the same questions."

Caiden recalled the overseers' parting words at Appraisal: *As a mechanic determination, it will become your job to maintain this world, so finely tuned it functions perfectly without us.*

"But why—"

"A mechanic doesn't need curiosity to fix broken things." His father disappeared back into the machine.

Caiden exhaled forcibly, bottled up his frustrations, and crawled back into the maintenance port. The tube was more cramped at fourteen than it had been at ten, but his growth spurt was pending and he still fit in spaces his father could not. The port was lined with cables, chemical wires, and faceplates stenciled in at least eight different languages Caiden hadn't been taught in the Stricture. His father told him to ignore them. And to ignore the blue vials filled with a liquid that vanished when directly observed. And the porous metal of the deepest ducts that seemed to breathe inward and out. *A mechanic doesn't need curiosity.*

Caiden searched for the bolts he thought he'd left in a neat pile.

"The more I understand and answer, the more I can fix." Frustration amplified his words, bouncing them through the metal of the machine.

"Caiden," his father's voice boomed from a chamber below. Reverberations settled in a long pause. "Sometimes knowing doesn't fix things."

Another nonanswer, fit for a child. Caiden gripped a wrench and stared at old wall dents where his frustration had escaped him before. Over time, fatigue dulled that anger. Maybe that was what had robbed his father of questions and answers.

But his friend Leta often said the same thing: "You can't fix everything, Caiden."

I can try.

He found his missing bolts at the back of the port, scattered and rolled into corners. He gathered them up and slapped faceplates into position, wrenching them down tighter than needed.

The adults always said, "This is the way things have always been—nothing's broken."

But it stayed that way because no one tried anything different.

Leta had confided in a nervous whisper, "*Different* is why I'll fail Appraisal." If she could fail and be rejected simply because her mind worked differently, the whole system was broken.

The aerator's oscillating unit was defaced with Caiden's labels and drawings where he'd transformed the bulbous foreign script into imagery or figures. Recent, neatly printed labels stood out beside his younger marks. He hesitated at a pasted-up photo he'd nicked from the Stricture: a foreign landscape with straight trees and intertwined branches. White rocks punctured bluish sand, with pools of water clearer than the ocean he'd once seen. It was beautiful—the place his parents would be retired to when he replaced them. Part of the way things had always been.

"Yes, stop everything." His mother was speaking to his father, and her voice echoed from below, muffled and rounded by the tube. She never visited during work. "Stop, they said. No more repairs."

His father responded, unintelligible through layers of metal.

"I don't know," she replied. "The overseers ordered everyone to gather at the Flat Docks. Caiden!"

He wriggled out of the port. His mother stood below with her arms crossed, swaying nervous as a willow. She was never nervous.

"Down here, hon." She squinted up at him. "And don't— *Caiden!*"

He slid halfway down the aerator's side and grabbed a seam to catch his fall. The edge under his fingers was shiny from years of the same maneuver. Dangling, smiling, he swung to perch on the front ledge, then frowned at his mother's flinty expression. Her eyes weren't on him anymore. Her lips moved in a whisper of quick, whipping words that meant trouble.

Caiden jumped the last couple meters to the ground.

"We have to go." She gripped a handful of his jacket and laid her other hand gently on his shoulder, marshaling him forward with these two conflicting holds. His father followed, wiping soot and worry from his brow.

"Are they sending help?" Caiden squirmed free. His mother tangled her fingers in his as they crossed a causeway between green pastures to a small door in the compound's side. "New animals?"

"Have to neutralize the disease first," his father said.

"A vaccine?" His mother squeezed his hand.

Outside the compound, field vehicles lay abandoned, others jammed around one of the Flat Docks a kilometer away. Crowds streamed to it from other compounds along the road grid, looking like fuel lines in an engine diagram. Movement at farther Docks suggested the order had reached everywhere.

"Stay close." His mother tugged him against her side as they amalgamated into a throng of thousands. Caiden had never seen so many people all together. They dressed in color and style according to their determinations, but otherwise the mob was a mix of shapes, sizes, and colors of people with only the brands on the backs of their necks alike. It was clear from the murmurs that no one knew what was going on. This was not "the way things have always been." Worst fears and greatest hopes floated by in whispers like windy grass as Caiden squeezed to the edge of the Flat Docks' huge metal plate.

It lay empty, the guardrails up, the crowds bordered around. Only seven aerators in their sector still trickled. Others much farther away had stopped entirely. There should have been hundreds feeding the gray overhead, which now looked the palest ever.

Caiden said, "We'll be out of time to get the aerators running before the vapor's gone."

"I know..." His father's expression furrowed. The grime on his face couldn't hide suspicion, and his mother's smile couldn't hide her fear. She always had a solution, a stalwart mood, and an answer for Caiden even if it was "Carry on." Now: only wariness.

If everyone's here, then—"Leta."

"She'll be with her own parental unit," his father said.

"Yeah, but—" They weren't kind.

"Caiden!"

He dashed off, ducking the elbows and shoulders of the mob. The children were smothered among the taller bodies, impossible to distinguish. His quick mind sorted through the work rotations, the direction they came from—everyone would have walked straight from their dropped tasks, at predictable speed. He veered and slowed, gaze saccading across familiar faces in the community.

A flicker of bright bluish-purple.

Chicory flowers.

Caiden barked apologies as he shouldered toward the color, lost among tan clothes and oak-dark jerkins. Then he spotted Leta's fawn waves, and swung his arms out to make room in the crowd, as if parting tall grass around a flower. "Hey, there you are."

Leta peered up with dewy hazel eyes. "Cai." She breathed relief. Her knuckles were white around a cluster of chicory, her right arm spasming, a sign of her losing the battle against overstimulation.

Leta's parental unit wasn't in sight, neglectful as ever, and she was winded, rushed from some job or forgotten altogether. Oversized non-determination garments hung off one shoulder, covered her palms, tripped her heels. She crushed herself against Caiden's arm and hugged it fiercely. "It's what the older kids say. The ones who don't pass Appraisal're sent away, like the bovine yearlings."

"Don't be silly, they would have called just the children then, not everyone. And you haven't been appraised yet, anyway."

But she was ten, it was soon. The empathy, sensitivity, and logic that could qualify her as a sublime clinician also crippled her everyday life as the callous people around her set her up to fail. Caiden hugged her, careful of the bruises peeking over her shoulder and forearm, the sight of them igniting a well-worn urge to protect.

"I've got you," he said, and pulled out twigs and leaves stuck in her hair. Her whole right side convulsed softly. The crowds, noise, and light washed a blankness into her face, meaning something in her was shutting down. "You're safe."

Caiden took her hand—firmly, grounding—and back-tracked through the crowd to the Flat Docks' edge.

The anxious look on his mother's face was layered with disapproval, but his father smiled in relief. Leta clutched Caiden's right hand in both of hers. His mother took his left.

"The overseers just said gather and wait?" he asked his father.

"Someday you'll learn patience."

Shuffles and gasps rippled through the assembly.

Caiden followed their gazes up. Clouds thinned in a gigantic circle. The air everywhere brightened across the crowds more intensely than the compounds' lights had ever lit the bovines.

A hole burned open overhead and shot a column of blinding white onto the Flat Docks. Shouts and sobs erupted. Caiden stared through the blur of his eyelashes as the light column widened until the entire plate burned white. In distant sectors, the same beams emerged through the gray.

He smashed his mother's hand in a vise grip. She squeezed back.

A massive square descended, black as a ceiling, flickering out the light. The angular mass stretched fifty meters wide on all sides, made of the same irregular panels as the aerators. With a roar, it moved slowly, impossibly, nothing connecting it to the ground.

"I've never..." His mother's whisper died and her mouth hung open.

Someone said, "It's like the threshers, but…"

Massive. Caiden imagined thresher blades peeling out of the hull, descending to mow the crowds.

The thing landed on the Flat Docks' plate with a rumble that juddered up Caiden's soles through his bones.

A fresh bloom of brightness gnawed at the gray above, and beyond that widening hole hung the colors and shapes of unmoving fire. Caiden stood speechless, blinded by after-image. Leta gaped at the black mass that had landed, and made her voice work enough to whisper, "What is it?"

Caiden forced his face to soften, to smile. "More livestock maybe? Isn't this exciting?" *Stupid thing to say.* He shut up before his voice quavered.

"This isn't adventure, Caiden," Leta muttered. "Not like sneaking to the ocean—this is *different*."

"Different how?"

"The adults. This isn't how it's done."

Caiden attempted to turn his shaking into a chuckle. "The bovine all dead is a new problem. Everything's new now."

The crowd's babble quieted to a hiss of fear, the tension strummed. A grinding roar pummeled the air as the front side of the angular mass slid upward from the base, and two tall figures emerged from the horizontal opening.

"Overseers!" someone shouted. The word repeated, carried with relief and joy through the crowd.

Caiden's eyes widened. Both overseers were human-shaped, one tall and bulky, the other short and slim, and as he remembered from his Appraisal, they were suited from head to toe with plates of metal and straps and a variety of things he couldn't make out: spikes and ribbons, tools, wires, and blocks of white writing like inside the aerators. They wore blue metal plates over their faces, with long slits for eyes and nostrils, holes peppering the place where their mouths would be. Besides their build, they resembled each other exactly, and could be anything beneath their clothes.

"See, it's fine." Caiden forced himself to exhale. "Right, Ma?"

His mother nodded slow, confused.

"People," the shorter overseer said in a muffled yet amplified voice.

The crowd hushed, rapt, with stressed breaths filling the quiet. Caiden's heart hammered, pulse noosing his neck.

"You will be transported to a clean place," the other overseer said in a husky voice amplified the same way. The crowd rippled his words to the back ranks.

"With new *livestock*," the first added with a funny lilt on the final word.

"Come aboard. Slow, orderly." The overseers each moved to a side of the open door, framing the void. "Leave your belongings. Everyone will be provided for."

Caiden glanced at Leta. "See? New animals."

She didn't seem to hear, shut down by the sights and sounds. He let her cling to him as his father herded them both forward.

Caiden asked, "Where could we go that doesn't have infected soil? Up, past the gray?"

"Stay close." His father's voice was tight. "Maybe they discovered clean land past the ocean."

They approached the hollow interior—metallic, dank, and lightless—with a quiet throng pouring in, shoulder to shoulder like the bovines had when squeezed from one pasture to another. Caiden observed the closest overseer. Scratches and holes scarred their mismatched metal clothes, decorated in strange scripts. Their hand rested on a long tool at their hip, resembling the livestock prods but double-railed.

Caiden's father guided him inside and against a wall, where his mother wrapped him and Leta in her strong arms and the mob crammed tight, drowning them in heat and odor.

"Try to keep still." The overseer's words resonated inside.

A roar thrummed to life, and the door descended, squeezing out the orange light. The two overseers remained outside.

Thunder cracked underfoot. Metal bellowed like a thousand animals crying at once. Human wails cut through and the floor shuddered in lurches, forcing Caiden to widen his stance to stay upright. His mother's arms clamped around him.

Children sobbed. Consoling parents hissed in the darkness. Leta remained deathly silent in Caiden's firm grasp, but tremors crashed in her body, nervous system rebelling. He drew her closer.

"Be still, hon." His mother's voice quavered.

She covered his ears with clammy hands and muffled the deafening roar to a thick howl. The rumble infiltrated his bones, deeper-toned than he'd thought any machine could sound.

Are we going up into that fire-sky, or into the ground, where the livestock went?

The inside of machines usually comforted him. There was safety in their hard shell, and no question to their functioning, but this one stank of tangy fear, had no direction, and his mother's shaking leached into his back as he curled around Leta's trembling in front. He buried his nose in a greasy sleeve and inhaled, tasting the fumes of the gray. His mother's hands over his ears thankfully deadened the sobs.

"Soon," she cooed. "I'm sure we'll be there soon."

if you enjoyed
MEMORIA

look out for

THE GIRL WHO COULD MOVE SH*T WITH HER MIND

Book One of the Frost Files

by

Jackson Ford

Full of imagination, wit, and random sh*t flying through the air, this insane adventure from an irreverent new voice will blow your tiny mind.

For Teagan Frost, sh*t just got real.

Teagan Frost is having a hard time keeping it together. Sure, she's got telekinetic powers—a skill the government is all too happy to make use of, sending her on secret break-in missions that no ordinary human could carry out. But all she really wants to do is kick back, have a beer, and pretend she's normal for once.

But then a body turns up at the site of her last job—murdered in a way that only someone like Teagan could have pulled off. She's got twenty-four hours to clear her name—and it's not just her life at stake. If she can't unravel the conspiracy in time, her hometown of Los Angeles will be in the crosshairs of an underground battle that's on the brink of exploding....

ONE

Teagan

On second thoughts, throwing myself out the window of a skyscraper may not have been the best idea.

Not because I'm going to die or anything. I've totally got that under control.

It wasn't smart because I had to bring Annie Cruz with me. And Annie, it turns out, is a screamer. Her fists hammer on my back, her voice piercing my eardrums, even over the rushing air.

I don't know what she's worried about. Pro tip: if you're going to take a high dive off the 82nd floor, make sure you do it with a psychokinetic holding your hand. Being able to move objects with your mind is useful in all sorts of situations.

I'll admit, this one is a little tricky. Plummeting at close to terminal velocity, surrounded by a hurricane of glass from the window we smashed through, the lights of Los Angeles whirling around us and Annie screaming and the rushing air blowing the stupid clip-on tie from my security guard disguise into my face: not ideal. Doesn't matter though—I've got this.

I can't actually apply any force to either Annie's body or mine. Organic matter like human tissue doesn't respond to me, which is something I don't really have time to get into right now. But I can manipulate anything inorganic. Bricks, glass, metal, the fridge door, a sixpack, the TV remote, the zipper on your pants.

And belt buckles.

I've had some practice at this whole moving-shit-with-your-mind thing. I've already reached out, grabbed hold of the big metal buckles on our belts. We're probably going to have some bruises tomorrow, but it's a hell of a lot better than getting gunned down in a penthouse or splatting all over Figueroa Street.

I solidify my mental grip around the two buckles, then force them upwards, using my energy to counteract our downward motion. We start to slow, my belt tightening, hips starting to ache as the buckles take the weight—

—and immediately snap.

OK, yeah. Definitely not the best idea.

TWO

Teagan

Rewind. Twenty minutes ago.

We're in the sub-basement of the giant Edmonds Building, our footsteps muffled by thick carpet. The lighting in the corridor is surprisingly low down here, almost cosy, which doesn't matter much because Annie is seriously fucking with my groove.

I like to listen to music on our ops, OK? It calms me down, helps me focus. A little late-90s rap—some Blackstar, some Jurassic 5, some Outkast. Nothing too aggressive or even all that loud. I'm just reaching the good part of "So Fresh, So Clean" when Annie taps me on the shoulder. "Yo, take that shit out. We working."

Ugh. I was sure I'd hidden my earbud, threading the cord up underneath the starchy blue rent-a-cop shirt and tucking it under my hair.

I hunt for the volume switch on my phone, still not looking at Annie. She responds by reaching back and jerking the earbud out.

"Hey!"

"I said, fucking quit it."

"What, not an Outkast fan? Or do you only like their early stuff?" I hold up an earbud. "I don't mind sharing. You want the left or the right?"

"Cute. Put it away."

We turn the corner, heading for a big set of double doors at the far end. My collar's too tight. I pull at it, wincing, but it barely moves. Annie and I are dressed identically: blue shirts, black clip-on ties, black pants and puffer jackets in a very cheap shade of navy. Huge belts, leather, with thick metal buckles.

Paul picked up the uniforms for us. I tried to tell him that while Annie might be able to pass as a security guard, nobody was going to believe that the Edmonds Building would employ a short, not-very-fit woman with spiky black hair and a face that *still* gets her ID'd at the liquor store. Even though I've been able to buy my own drinks like a big girl for a whole year now.

I couldn't be more different to Annie. You know how some club bouncers have huge muscles and a shit-ton of tattoos and piercings? You know how people still fuck with them, starting fights and smashing bottles? Annie is like that one bouncer with zero tattoos, standing in the corner with her arms folded and a scowl that could sour milk. The bouncer no one fucks with because the last person who did ended up scattered over a six-mile radius. We might not see eye to eye on music—or on anything, because she's taller than me—but I'm still very glad she's on my side.

My earpiece chirps—my *other* one, the black number in my right ear. "Annie, Teagan," says Paul. "Come in. Over."

"We're almost at the server room," Annie says. She sends another disgusted look at my dangling earbud.

Silence. No response.

"You there?" Annie says.

"Sorry, was waiting for you to say *over*. Thought you hadn't finished. Over."

"Seriously?" I say. "We're still using your radio slang?"

"It's not slang. It's protocol. Just wanted to give you a heads-up—Reggie's activated the alarm on the second floor. Basement should be clear of personnel." A pause. "Over."

"Yeah, copy." Annie says. She's a lot more patient with Paul than I am, which I genuinely don't understand.

The double doors are like the fire doors you see in apartment buildings. The one on the right has a big sign on it, white lettering on a black background: AUTHORISED PERSONNEL ONLY. And on the wall next to it, a biometric lock.

Annie looks over at me. "You're up."

My tax form says that I work for a company called China Shop Movers. That's the name on the paperwork, anyway. What we actually do is work for the government—specifically, for a high-level spook named Tanner.

For some jobs, you need a black-ops team and a fleet of Apache choppers with heat-seeking missiles. For others, you need a psychokinetic with a music-hating support team who can make a lot less noise and get things done in a fraction of the time. You need a completely deniable group of civilians who can do stuff that even a special forces soldier would struggle with. That's us. We are fast, quiet, effective and deadly.

Go ahead: make the fart joke. Tanner didn't laugh when I made it either.

The people we take down are threats to national security. Drug lords, terrorist cells, human traffickers. We don't bust in with guns blazing. We don't need to—not with my ability. I've planted a tracking device on a limo at LAX, waving hello to the thick-necked goon standing alongside the car while I zipped the tiny black box up behind his back and onto the chassis. I've kept the bad guys' safeties on at a hostage exchange—good thing too, because they tried to start shooting the second they had the money and got one hell of a surprise when their guns didn't work. And I've been on plenty of break-ins. Windows? Cars? Big old metal safes? Not a problem. When you can move things with your mind, there's not a lot the world can do to keep you out.

Take the lock on AUTHORISED PERSONNEL ONLY, for instance.

You're supposed to put your finger on the little reader, let it scan your fingerprint, and you're in. If you're breaking in, you either need to hack off a finger (messy), take someone hostage (messy, annoying), hack it locally (time-consuming and boring), or blow it off (fun, but kind of noisy).

My psychokinesia—PK—means I can feel every object around me: its texture, its weight, its relation to other objects. It's a constant flood of stimuli. When I was little, Mom and Dad made me run through exercises, getting me to really focus in on a single object at a time—a glass, a toy car, a pencil. They made me move them around, describe them in excruciating detail. It took a long time, but I managed to deal with it. Now I can sense the objects around me in the same way you sense the clothes you're wearing. You know they're there, you're aware of them, but you don't *think* about them.

If I focus on an object, like the lock—the wires, the latch assembly, the emergency battery, the individual screws on the latch and strike panels—it's as if I send out a part of myself to wrap around it, like you'd wrap your hand around a glass. And then, if I'm locked on, I can move it. I don't have to jerk my head or hold out my hand or screw up my face like in the movies, either. I tried it once, for fun, and felt like an idiot.

It takes me about three seconds to find the latch and slide it back. The mechanism won't move unless it receives the correct signal from the fingerprint reader—or unless someone reaches inside and moves it with her mind. It's actually a pretty solid security system. I've definitely seen worse. But whoever built it obviously didn't take into account the existence of a psychokinetic, so I guess he's totally fired now.

"And we're good." I hop to my feet, using my PK to pull the handle down. I haven't even touched the door.

"Hm." Annie tilts her head. "Nice work."

"Was that a compliment? Annie, are you dying? Has the cancer spread to your brain?"

"Let's just get this over with."

We're on this operation because of a clothing tycoon named Steven Chase. He runs a chain of high-end sportswear stores called Ultra, which just means they're Foot Locker stores without the referee jerseys. If that was all he was doing, he'd never have appeared on China Shop's radar, but it appears Mr. Chase has been a very naughty boy.

Tanner got a tip that he was embezzling money from his company. Again, not something we'd normally give a shit about, but he's not exactly using it to buy a third Ferrari. He's funnelling it to some very shady people in the Ukraine and Saudi Arabia, which is when government types like Tanner start to get mighty twitchy.

Now, the U.S. government *could* get a wiretap to confirm the tip. But even if you go through a secret court, there'll be some kind of paper trail. Better a discreet call gets made to the offices of a certain moving company in Los Angeles, who can look into the matter without anything being written down.

And before you start telling me I'm on the wrong side, that I'm doing the work of the government, who are the real bad guys here, and violating a dozen laws and generally being a pawn of the state, just know that I've seen evidence of what people like Chase do. I have no problem messing with their shit.

We're not actually going anywhere near Steven Chase's office. Reggie could hack his computer directly, but it would require a brute-force attack or getting him to click on a link in an email. People don't do that any more, unless you promise fulfilment of their *very* specific sexual fantasies. The research on that is more trouble than it's worth, and you'll have nightmares for months.

Chase is in town tonight. He flew in for a dinner or an awards show or whatever rich people do for fun, and it's his habit to come back to the office afterwards. He should be there now, up on the 30th floor. He'll work until two or three, catch a couple hours of sleep, then grab a red-eye back to New York. Which works just fine for us.

If you can access the fibre network itself—which you can do in the server room, obviously—you can clamp a special coupler right on to the cable and just siphon off the data as it passes by. Of course, actually doing this is messy and complicated and requires a lot of elements to line up just right . . . unless you have me.

The cables from every floor in the building run down to this room. The plan is to identify Chase's cable, attach a coupler to it, then read all the traffic while sipping mai tais on our back porch. Or in my case scarfing Thai food and drinking many, many beers in my tiny apartment, but whatever.

Chase might encrypt his email, of course, but encryption targets the body of the email, not the sender or subject line. If he emails anyone in the Ukraine or Saudi, we'll know about it. It'll be enough for Tanner to send in the big guns.

The server room is even more dimly lit than the corridor. The server banks stand like monoliths in an old tomb, giving off a subsonic hum that rumbles under the frigid air conditioning. Annie tilts her chin up even further, as if sniffing the air. She points to one side of the door. "Wait there."

"Yes, sir, O mighty boss lady."

She ignores me, eyes scanning the server stacks. I don't really know how she's going to find the correct one—that was the part of the planning session where they lost me. All I know is that when she does, she's going to trace it back to where it vanishes into the floor or wall. We'll open up a panel, and I'll use my PK to float the coupler inside, attaching it to the cable. It can siphon data, away from the eyes of the building's technicians, who would almost certainly recognise it on sight.

As Annie steps behind one of the servers, I slip my earbud back in. May as well listen to some music while—

"Shit," Annie says.

It's a quiet curse, but I catch it just fine. I make my way over to find her staring at a clusterfuck of tangled cables spilling out of one of the servers. The floor is a scattered mess of tools and loose connections. A half-eaten sandwich, dribbling a slice of tomato, sits propped on a closed laptop.

"Is it supposed to look like that?" I ask.

Annie ignores me. "Paul, we've got a problem. Over."

"What is it? Over."

"Techs have been in. It wasn't like this this morning; Jerian would have told me."

Jerian—one of Annie's Army. Her anonymous network of janitors, cleaners, cashiers, security guards, drug dealers, nail artists, Uber drivers, cooks, receptionists and IT guys. Annie Cruz may not appreciate good hip-hop, but she has a very deep network of connects stretching all the way across LA.

"Copy, Annie. Can you still attach the coupler? Over."

Annie frowns at the mess of cables. "Yeah. But it'll take a while. Over."

Joy.

"Understood," Paul says. "But we can only run interference for so long on our end. You'd better move. Over."

Annie scowls, crouching down to look at the cables. She takes one between thumb and forefinger, like it's something nasty she has to dispose of. Then she stands up, marching back towards the server-room doors.

"Um. Hi? Annie?" I jog after her, earbud bouncing against my shoulder. "Cables are back there."

"Change of plan." She keys her earpiece. "Paul? Tell Reggie to switch over the cameras on the 30th floor. Over."

"Say again? Over."

"We're going up."

I don't catch Paul's response. Instead, I sprint to catch up with Annie, getting to her just she pushes through the doors. "Are you gonna tell me why we've suddenly abandoned the plan, or—"

"We can't hide the coupler if they got people poking around the cables." She reaches the elevator, thumbing the up button. "We need to go to the source."

"I thought the whole point was *not* to go near this guy. Aren't we supposed to be super-secret and stealthy and shit?"

"We're not going to his office, genius. We're going to the fibre hub on his floor."

"The what now?"

"The fibre hub. Every floor has one. It's where the cables from each office go. We'll be able to find the right one a lot faster from there."

The interior of the elevator is clean and new, with a touch-screen interface to select your floor. A taped sign next to it says that floors 50–80 are currently off limits while refurbishment and additional construction is completed, thank you for your patience, management. I remember seeing that when we rolled up: a big chunk of the building covered in scaffolding, with temporary elevators attached to the outside, and a giant crane in a vacant lot across the street.

When the elevator opens on the 30th floor, there's someone standing in front of it. There's a horrible moment where I think it's Steven Chase himself. But I've seen pictures of Chase, who looks like an actor in an ad for haemorrhoid cream—running on the beach, tanned and glowing, stoked that his rectum is finally itch-free. This guy is...not that. He has lawyer written all over him: two-tone shirt, two-tone hair, one-tone orange skin. Tie knot as big as my fist. Probably a few haemorrhoid issues of his own.

He eyes us. "Going down?"

"We're stepping off here, sir," Annie says, doing just that.

He moves into the elevator, mouth twisted in a disapproving frown as his eyes pass over me. Probably not used to seeing someone my age working security in a building like this. I have to resist the urge to wink at him.

I haven't seen inside any of the offices yet, but whoever built this place obviously didn't have any budget left over for the hallways. There's a foot-high strip of what looks like marble-textured plastic running along at chest height. There are buzzing fluorescent lights in the ceiling, and the floor is covered with that weird, flat, fuzzy carpet which always has little lint balls dotted over it.

"Jesus, who picked out the paint?" The wall above the plastic marble is a shade of purple that's probably called something like Executive Mojo.

"Who cares?" Annie says. "Damn building shouldn't even be here."

I sigh. This again.

She taps the fake marble. "You know they displaced a bunch of historical buildings for this? They just moved in and forced a purchase."

I sigh. Annie's always had a real hard-on for the city's history. "Yeah, I know. You told me before."

"And you saw that notice in the elevator. They just built this place. They already having to fix it up again. And the spots they bought out—mom-and-pop places. Historical buildings. City didn't give a fuck."

"Mm-hmm."

"I'm just saying. It's messed up, man."

"Can we get this done before the heat death of the universe? Please?"

It doesn't take us long to find the right office. Paul helps, using the blueprints he's pulled up to guide us along, occasionally telling Annie that this isn't a good idea and that she needs to hurry. I pop the lock, just like before—it's even easier this time—and we step inside.

There's no Executive Mojo here. It's a basic space, with a desk and terminal for a technician and a big, clearly marked access panel on the wall. By the desk, someone has left a toolbox full of computer paraphernalia, overflowing with wires and connectors. Maybe the same dickhead who left the half-eaten sandwich in the server room. I should leave a note telling him to clean up his shit.

The access panel is off to one side, slightly raised from the surface of the wall. Annie pops it, revealing a nest of thin cables. She attaches the coupler, which looks like a bulldog clip from the future, then checks her phone, reading the data that comes off it. With a grunt, she moves the coupler to the second cable. We have to get the correct one, and the only way to do that is to identify Chase from his traffic.

There are floor-to-ceiling windows on my left, and the view over the glittering city takes my breath away. We're only on the 30th floor, not even close to the top of the building, but I can still see a hell of long way. A police helicopter hovers in the distance, too far for us to hear, its blinking tail lights just visible.

The view looks north, out towards Burbank and Glendale, and on the horizon, there's the telltale orange glow of wildfires.

The sight pulls up some bad memories. Of all the cities Tanner had to put me, it had to be the one where things burn.

It's bad this year. Usually, it's some kid with fireworks or a tourist dropping a cigarette that starts it up, but this time the grass was so dry that it caught on its own. Every TV in the last couple of days has had big breaking news alerts flashing on them. The ones tuned to Fox News—you get a few, even in California—have given it a nickname. HELLSTORM. Because of course they have.

This year's fire has been creeping towards Burbank and Glendale, chewing through Wildwood Canyon and the Verdugo Hills. The flames have made LA even smoggier than usual. A fire chief on one of the TVs—a guy who managed to look both calm and mightily pissed off at the same time—said that they didn't think the fires would reach the city.

"Teagan."

"Huh?"

"You got your voodoo, right?" She nods to the coupler. "Float it up into the wall."

"Oh. Yeah. Good idea."

The panel is wide enough for me to lean in, craning my head back. The space is dusty, a small shower of fine grit nearly making me sneeze. Annie shines a torch, but I don't need it. She's got the correct cable pinched between thumb and forefinger. It's the work of a few seconds for me to find it with my *voodoo* and pull it slightly outwards from its buddies, float the coupler across and clamp it on. Annie flicks the torch off, and the coupler is swallowed by the shadows.

What can I say? I'm handy.

"Aight," Annie says, snapping the panel shut. "Paul? We're good. Over."

Follow us:

f **/orbitbooksUS**

🐦 **/orbitbooks**

▶ **/orbitbooks**

Join our mailing list
to receive alerts on our
latest releases and deals.

orbitbooks.net

Enter our monthly
giveaway for the chance
to win some epic prizes.

orbitloot.com

"Copy that. We're getting traffic already. Skedaddle on out of there. Over."

Skedaddle? I mouth the word at Annie, who ignores me. She replaces the panel, slotting it back into place, then turns to go.

As we step out of the tech's office, a voice reaches us from the other end of the hallway: "Hey."

Two security guards. No, three. Real ones. Walking in close formation, heading right for us. The one in the centre is a big white guy with a huge chest-length beard, peak pulled down over his eyes. He's scary, but it's the other two I'm worried about. They're young, with wide eyes and hands already on their holsters, fingers twitching.

Ah, shit.